Flash Rip

Also by Keira Andrews

Gay Amish Romance Series
A Forbidden Rumspringa
A Clean Break
A Way Home
A Very English Christmas

Contemporary
Santa Daddy
Honeymoon for One
Valor on the Move
Test of Valor
The Winning Edge
In Case of Emergency
Eight Nights in December
Road to the Sun
The Next Competitor
Arctic Fire
Reading the Signs
Beyond the Sea
If Only in My Dreams
Where the Lovelight Gleams
The Chimera Affair
Love Match
Synchronicity

Historical
Kidnapped by the Pirate
The Station
Semper Fi
Voyageurs (free read!)

Paranormal
Kick at the Darkness
Fight the Tide
A Taste of Midnight (free read!)

Fairy Tales (with Leta Blake)
Levity
Rise
Flight

Flash Rip

BY KEIRA ANDREWS

Flash Rip
Written and published by Keira Andrews
Cover by Dar Albert
Formatting by BB eBooks

Copyright © 2019 by Keira Andrews

ISBN: 978-1-988260-42-6

Acknowledgements

Thanks so much to Anara, DJ, Elaine, Mary, Leta, and Sharna for their invaluable assistance, be it beta reading, vetting my Aussie-isms, editing, or proofing. And special thanks to Elaine for her extra help with Malaysian cultural sensitivity. <3

Author's Note

Anyone familiar with Sydney's Bondi Beach will recognize the similarities to Barking Beach, which I set south of Perth. While Bondi was absolutely an inspiration, Barking and its lifeguards are completely fictional.

Chapter One

THE HEMSWORTHS APPARENTLY had another brother, and he was a lifeguard at Barking Beach.

The guy's name actually happened to be Liam, but Cody Grant thought he resembled Chris—thirties, six-three and muscular, with short, tousled, sandy-blond hair. His beard was a bit more than scruff but not too thick, and his eyes were deep blue. Very Thor, minus the long locks and magic hammer.

As Liam Fox peeled off his blue uniform shirt, he certainly looked like a superhero, revealing a six-pack—or, holy shit, was that an *eight*-pack?—with hair sprinkled perfectly over his pecs.

A woman jogging across the sand openly stared and then stumbled, red-faced. *Same, girl,* Cody thought, watching Liam race into the surf with a rescue board. *Same.*

Cody and his fellow trainee, Mia, were at the north end of Barking Beach for orientation, which had been interrupted by a middle-aged man flailing in the water, having gotten in over his head, literally, when he'd stepped off a sandbank. Cody, Mia, and head lifeguard Teddy stood watching Liam haul the gasping man onto his board.

By them a sign read:
DANGEROUS CURRENTS: NO SWIMMING
There was even a picture of a stick figure swimming with a

giant red X over it. Cody squinted out at the dozen people in the water directly in front of the sign. "People just don't read, I guess?"

Teddy laughed. "Nope. Welcome to Barkers. I like to start with a little talk here by the water, and now Foxy's giving us a rescue demo. Couldn't have planned it better if I tried. As you can see, people can get into trouble in a blink. Especially tourists. And they will, because the one thing you can count on is bloody tourists not paying attention to the warnings." He grinned, the white sunblock on his lips giving him a ghoulish look.

Liam—*Foxy*, which was a fitting nickname if Cody had ever heard one—had paddled the middle-aged man the ten meters or so back to shore and was pointing down the beach toward the safe swimming area marked by red and yellow flags.

Teddy said, "Even when the surf is gentle like this, people can get themselves in trouble by panicking. And you've both been clubbies for a few years, so you know how rough it can get in the impact zone when the swells are up and those waves really hit."

Mia said, "I joined Nippers when I was five, and I got my SRC when I was thirteen. So I was a clubbie for more than a few years." She gave Teddy a nervous smile. "Um, for the record."

There was a hint of a smirk on Teddy's sun-worn face. He was around forty, wrinkles in the corners of his eyes and pale hair buzzed short. "I know, Ms. Jee. That's one of the reasons you're here."

Cody hadn't earned his Surf Rescue Certificate until he was sixteen, but to be fair, he'd only moved to Western Australia from Canada and joined the local Surf Life Saving Club at thirteen. His swimming experience had been in pools and lakes until then. He didn't share any of this since it was irrelevant—he'd damn well earned this opportunity.

Teddy said, "We had dozens of people try out this season for the two trainee spots. Both of you are qualified and don't need to prove anything. Except out there."

Cody inhaled the briny air and dug his toes into the wet sand, gazing out at the crystal-clear blue water of the Indian Ocean. Gulls cried, bickering over some scraps. People swam, most splashing safely in the shallows. Others relaxed on the beach, dozing or reading. It wasn't insanely crowded yet since it was still spring, but Cody knew thirty thousand people could cram onto the single kilometer of sand and sea.

Liam jogged back to them, holding the handle of the long rescue board. He was soaking wet, glistening drops of water caught in his chest hair, his navy uniform board shorts clinging to his meaty, sculpted thighs. He slid the board back into its metal holder on the sand by the danger sign, bending to fiddle with something. Across his incredibly fine ass, the shorts read: LIFE-GUARD in white block letters.

"Good work, Foxy!" another lifeguard called as he drove up in one of the ATVs and hopped out. "Showin' off for the newbies, hey?" He pushed up his Ray-Ban sunnies and grinned with a slightly horsey mouth full of teeth. His ginger curls were damp, and he gave Cody and Mia an enthusiastic handshake.

"Hiya! I'm Brandon, but everyone calls me Ronnie."

Cody tried to puzzle out the nickname. "Ronnie?"

"The hair," Ronnie said. "Ronald McDonald."

"Oh! Gotcha." Cody could see it, actually, with the toothy grin and gangly frame. Ronnie seemed about twenty, Cody's age.

Ronnie said, "You giving them the same inspirational speech you gave me a couple years ago, Cyclone?"

Teddy shrugged. "Pretty much." His name was Edward Tracy, and apparently there was some famous cyclone from back in the day that was called Tracy—hence the "Cyclone" nickname. Teddy seemed pretty laid-back to Cody, and the nickname might have been ironic. There could be many layers to Aussie nicknames, although some were just whacking an "o" or "y" on the end.

Teddy cleared his throat. "Here goes. You're both starting at the bottom. Over the next seven months, if you swim to the top, I might have jobs for you next season, or even over the winter since we patrol the beach all year. The first step is passing your traineeship and qualifying. So work hard and be willing to learn. Et cetera, et cetera." He was holding two official turquoise, long-sleeved uniform shirts, which he handed over. "Try not to stuff up too badly."

Ronnie hopped back in the ATV. "As rousing as ever, mate! That's why they pay you the big bucks!" He drove off with a wave.

Teddy grinned. "Also, taking the piss out of each other is always encouraged."

The lightweight shirts provided sun protection and were emblazoned front and back with *LIFEGUARD*. Mia pulled hers on over a navy bathing suit, freeing her long, dark ponytail from the collar. She was of Malaysian descent, and after the final trainee competition, Cody had heard an old guy hanging around the beach call her a "wee stunner," even though she was five-ten and actually two inches taller than Cody.

Cody wore navy boardies like all the other guys. Liam's still clung to his thighs distractingly, and Cody really wished he would put his shirt back on. He was trying to be a professional here. Liam's face was distracting enough—those *cheekbones*—let alone his bare chest dripping wet. With those red nipples looking so...bite-worthy.

Is that a word? Wait, don't answer that. Focus!

Liam solemnly handed over their navy *LIFEGUARD* baseball caps. Cody curved the stiff brim so it would fit better. He'd just had his brown hair trimmed short, and he smoothed the cap on his head. They'd already received their lifeguard-branded jackets, sweatshirts, and other gear, but it was nice to have a little ceremony of sorts.

"Looking good." Teddy gave Cody and Mia the shaka sign

surfers used—thumb and pinky finger extended and three middle fingers curled in. "Now you've got to live up to the title. It doesn't say 'trainee' on your shirts. With members of the public, you're full-fledged lifeguards. Ready for your first day? Whaddya reckon, Foxy?"

"Too right they are," he answered in a sexy rumble of a voice, giving a serious nod.

It was still surreal to Cody that he'd achieved his goal. He'd been coming down to Barking Beach—really Barkininy Beach or just "Barkers" to the locals—since he'd moved to Perth. He'd absolutely idolized the lifeguards in blue. Also lusted after them, but what gay teenage boy wouldn't?

"Foxy's the senior lifeguard on duty today, so he'll keep an eye on you two while I'm doing paperwork in the office," Teddy said, jerking a thumb over his shoulder toward the squat council building in the distance beyond the grassed area and parking lot. "Don't be too hard on 'em, Foxy. Wait 'til their second day for scrubbing the shower block."

A hint of amusement tugged Liam's lips. "We'll see how this arvo goes." He scratched his throat, the scrape of his beard audible, and yep, that was another tug of lust in Cody's belly. The afternoon—"arvo" to many Aussies—would be a disaster if Cody didn't focus.

He vowed right there to only think of Liam Fox by his real name, because "Foxy" was way, *way* too on the nose. Lusting over another lifeguard was not in the job description. Forget Liam's broad shoulders and gorgeous blue eyes. Also his red nipples and wet abs. And he probably had a great smile. Cody hadn't seen him truly smile yet, but he imagined it would light up his handsome face, and—

Hello, that's not how you stop lusting over a colleague!

He and Mia followed Liam across the sand to the lifeguard tower, and Liam asked, "You know what 'Barkininy' means?"

Mia eagerly answered, "It means 'bite' or 'biting' in the indigenous Noongar language."

"Very good," Liam said. He seemed much more serious and *official* than Teddy did, even though Teddy was the boss.

Cody had known the meaning too and tried not to resent Mia for answering before him. He said, "It's an apt name for the beach. The rips can be brutal, huh? I heard there's been a big spike in drownings and near-drownings along with the influx of tourists after Barking was named Australia's top beach a few years back." He cringed at himself. *Like this is news to Liam? He works here!*

Liam dutifully said, "You two have done your homework. So you know there are three openers on at five. First light is around five-ten this time of year, and it'll get earlier as we head into summer. There are usually six people on shift through the day—more during the silly season or if it's a scorcher. As trainees, you'll be shadowing us, and also patrolling on your own if need be."

"The silly season" was the Christmas school holidays, when beach attendance would explode as the temperature rose. It was mid-October now, and the beach was busy already.

Liam finally pulled his shirt on over his head, most of the water that had hung on his skin now evaporated in the sunshine. Not that Cody was looking too closely or anything. There was a reddish, oval AFL football tattooed on Liam's right arm, so he must have been a big fan of the sport.

Mia twisted her fingers together as they crossed the sand, and Cody wanted to tell her to breathe. He was nervous as hell, but he could imagine it was ten times worse for her. There had been the odd female lifeguard in the past, but at the moment the service on Barking Beach was entirely male.

A young family watched their lifeguard procession curiously from under their bright umbrella, and Cody waved to the toddler, the girl clapping in delight and waving back, nearly stomping her little sandcastle in her excitement as her parents laughed. Cody laughed too, the knot of tension loosening a few degrees.

I've got this. I'm not going to stuff it up.

The wide-windowed lifeguard tower sat in the center of the one-kilometer stretch of beach, one story high, with a concrete ramp in the back that zigzagged up from a narrow access road along the park. The ground floor of the tower was a garage and storage area where the buggies and boards and other equipment were locked up nightly.

Liam led the way up the flight of wooden stairs from the sand to a landing and the main door on the side of the tower. A sign read:

ONLY KNOCK IN CASE OF EMERGENCY OR SERIOUS INQUIRY

Cody smiled to himself. He could tell the council had created that formal, wordy sign. Being ushered inside that door by Chris Hemsworth's lifeguard doppelganger was possibly the most epic moment of Cody's life thus far, and he took a moment to savor it.

Up a few steps to the right was the semicircle main area, the front windows curving to give a clear view to the south end of the beach and north to a rocky headland. Coogee and Fremantle were up the coast. There was always a steady stream of cargo ships waiting for entry to Freo's commercial port, and one steamed by in the distance.

"Hiya," a young man said, sitting in an office chair at the long, low counter—what the Aussies called a "bench," although Cody still thought of a bench as something to sit on. The counter extended all the way across under the windows. There were a couple of landline phones, notepads and pens, and a computer monitor showing the CCTV feeds from tower cameras.

The blond man wheeled around with a grin. "I'm Damo. Welcome to Barking Central." He nodded to the guy beside him in another office chair, who was peering out at the northern end of the beach through binoculars. "This is Hazza on the binos."

"G'day." Hazza only looked away from the water for a moment to smile before peering back out. He was in his late twenties, with dark skin, his almost-black hair shaved around the sides and curly on top.

Cody supposed Damo's name was actually Damian, and Hazza was likely Harry or Henry. At school, Cody'd somehow been called "Sneezy" for a few months because he—wait for it—sneezed a few times on the first day. "Codes" he could deal with, but he hoped to avoid anything ridiculous.

Damo tucked his long, shaggy hair behind an ear and said, "Welcome to the best job in the world. Sun, surf, and heaps of topless chicks." He gave Cody an exaggerated wink and said, "Don't let 'em distract you too much."

Here it was already, Cody's golden opportunity to announce that he was gay. He opened his mouth and... No. He aborted, instead laughing and keeping his smile in place as Hazza told a story about meeting his now ex-girlfriend on the beach back when he was a trainee and how jealous she'd been whenever he rescued anyone young and pretty.

Cody still had a chance to clarify that he was gay, but his gut told him to hold off. He sure as hell wasn't going back in the closet, but he'd let himself get through the first day—maybe the first week or two—before he declared himself. It wasn't his style to lay low, and it made him antsy. But strategically, it made sense to let the guys get to know him first.

Damo said, "This one time, there was a chick who—" He broke off, looking at Mia and chuckling awkwardly. "Actually, since we're co-ed this season, I should be more politically correct. Didn't mean any offense."

Cody glanced at Mia, whose brow furrowed as she said, "None taken."

"Cool." Damo whirled back around, catching himself on the drawer-less counter before he picked up binoculars and looked to the south.

Liam said, "You should be more professional on duty no matter who's working."

"I know." Damo winked over his shoulder. "It's a good thing I'm so charming, hey?"

Hazza dryly said, "Good thing." After a beat he added, "And strangely single."

They laughed, and Liam said to Mia and Cody, "Look, we're all mates here, and we have fun, but we know when to be serious too."

Damo shot Liam a raised eyebrow. "Some of us more than others. Just saying." He turned back to the window.

Liam chuckled, but it was awkward, his big body hunching. He scratched the back of his neck and stared at his bare feet. Considering he looked like a freaking movie star, he seemed suddenly uneasy in his own skin. It was curious, and Cody almost squeezed his arm, wanting to reassure him. Fortunately, he kept his hands to himself.

The radio by Hazza crackled. "North end to Barking Central. Got a couple of heads out the back. Croc's waking up. Might have to go for a paddle."

Looking through the binoculars, Hazza muttered, "Yep. They're floundering. Just off the sandbank. Looks like two teenage girls." He spoke into the walkie. "Copy that, Ronnie. I've got eyes on them."

Damo wheeled over next to him and peered through his own binoculars, both of them staring intently, all joking vanished. Cody squinted into the distance, but the tower was too far away to really see anything without assistance. Hazza said into the radio, "Yeah, you'd better get wet. Doesn't look like they can swim a bloody stroke."

The tinny voice said, "Yep, Central, I'm in."

As Damo went back to surveying the rest of the beach, Cody and Mia crowded in behind Hazza eagerly. Hazza spoke through the radio. "Nicky, Ronnie needs a hand out the back of the Croc."

"Double rescues can be tricky," Liam said, grabbing a spare pair of binoculars. "If someone's free, always best to get backup." He stared out for a few moments, then passed the binoculars to Cody, leaning close, a big hand on Cody's shoulder as he pointed. His breath tickled Cody's cheek, his voice low. "See them? You know how to focus the binos?"

It was warm in the tower with the midday sun, despite the AC unit chugging in the corner and fans mounted on the ceiling. Sweat gathered under the brim of Cody's cap, his skin prickling. "Uh... Yep, got them. Thanks." Liam moved over to Mia, and Cody breathed deeply, adrenaline pumping as he watched the rescue unfold.

Barking's regular rip current was nicknamed "the Croc," and the name said it all. As the tide got lower, the current pulled water out at a few meters per second in a merciless funnel. The best way to get out of a rip was not to swim to shore against it, but sideways out of the corridor. Of course, most tourists didn't know this. Some locals didn't either, especially if they panicked.

The two girls flapped their arms, trying to fight the current and wearing themselves out. Their heads were close to going under, hair over their faces, waves washing over them. Ronnie kneeled on a long blue rescue board, powering forward with both arms. He had to get through the impact zone where waves broke, paddling against the merciless thrust of the ocean, then angling over and using the rip to get him out quickly.

The exhausted girls clung to Ronnie's board as he reassured them. Liam said, "It's tough to balance two patients on the board to take in, so Nicky will come out and collect one of them. You guys know this from being clubbies, but we're going to go through everything."

"Absolutely," Mia said as Cody nodded.

Liam said, "Most of us grew up in the volunteer system too,

and you might do the odd rescue, but it's nothing compared to being a professional lifeguard. The volunteers do a great job up at Coogee and other beaches, but it's full-on here and getting busier every season."

"There we go." Hazza turned away, apparently satisfied as Ronnie and Nicky paddled the patients back into the beach, catching waves to help them along.

Damo asked Cody, "Where were you a clubbie?"

"Mullaloo, in the northern beaches. It can get big, but there aren't nearly as many people. Mostly locals who usually know better."

"North of the river! Had a mate move up to Scarborough and never saw him again," Damo joked, everyone chuckling. "Although I hear the kite surfing's wicked up there." He glanced at Cody over his shoulder, giving his blond hair a toss. "What's that accent?"

"Oh, right. Canadian." Over the years, he'd picked up a lot of the lingo, but his accent had stayed stubbornly Canuck. After a disastrous attempt to force an Aussie accent to fit in, he'd let it be. "I moved here when I was thirteen."

"Big move," Damo said.

"Why'd your family come here?" Mia asked.

"My dad's from Perth, but he got a scholarship to do his undergrad in Vancouver. Met my mom there. Eventually came back for a post-doc research grant. He's a scientist."

"Cool," Mia said. "Are your folks still up in Mullaloo?"

"Nah, my mom missed skiing too much, and my older sisters went back to Canada for uni, so they're all in Vancouver again." No one wanted his life story, so he shut up before launching into how his parents had fully expected him to go with them and attend university back home.

Liam said, "You must miss them."

"Oh yeah! Doesn't mean I don't love them and everything."

Cody was admittedly a little defensive about his choice to stay in Australia. Some people couldn't imagine living so far away from their family, and sometimes he felt like he was deficient since he was so independent.

"Of course not," Liam agreed, and Cody couldn't tell if he meant it. He cursed himself for overthinking. Liam probably didn't give a crap one way or the other.

"There's ocean in Vancouver, isn't there?" Mia asked.

"Oh yeah, but the Pacific Northwest's not like *this*. It rains a ton. It's a lot colder. It's paradise here. I love it."

"'Course you do." Hazza shot him a grin. "This is the greatest spot on Earth, mate. Now we'll see if you can keep up with the Aussies, eh?"

Damo shook his head. "With those chicken arms? I dunno. Rescue board alone is what? Ten, twelve kilos? Let alone with a patient on top."

Cody bit back an indignant response about how much he could bench press and that being short didn't mean he was weak, and *he did not have chicken arms!* Plus, he *was* an Aussie now, thank you very much. But if he let teasing get to him the very first day, he'd never make it. He shrugged carelessly. "Pound for pound, chickens are stronger than lions."

Damo and Hazza glanced at each other, brows creased. "Is that true?" Hazza asked. "Nah, a chook can't be as strong as a lion. Could it?"

Liam said, "I sincerely doubt it. All right, let's get you two out there." He nodded to Mia, who had stood by silently while the guys ribbed Cody. "Ready?"

"Absolutely," she replied seriously, spine ramrod straight like a soldier at attention.

It was time to actually be a Barking *lifeguard*. Mia and Cody were issued their walkie-talkies and bum bags holding basic first aid supplies. Damo nodded to the zippered pouch and asked Cody with too much innocence, "What do you call that?"

Cody attached the pouch around his waist. "I know you want me to say 'fanny pack,' but trust me, I learned that one the hard way."

Damo laughed. "Come on, it's your vagi—" He broke off, looking guiltily at Mia.

Mia calmly said, "You can say 'vagina' in my presence. Or 'fanny.'"

"Just messing with the Canadian." Damo said. "They've got some funny words over there."

"'Flip-flops!'" Hazza laughed. "That's my fave."

"All right, back to work before we get into a thong discussion," Liam grumbled, beckoning Mia and Cody to follow him out of the tower and into one of the ATV buggies, this one with orange painted on the roll bar. After dropping off Mia to shadow a lifeguard at the south end of the beach, Liam left Cody with Ronnie farther north and went off on patrol.

Ronnie sat in a parked buggy, his gaze roving over the water. Cody took the other seat, reminding himself to breathe as he surveyed the water and settled in. This was it. He was lifeguarding. Sure, he'd done it as a clubbie, but this was for *real*. At the lifesaving club, there were always a bunch of volunteers on each shift. There was little pressure. Now he was being paid to be responsible for people's lives.

"Nervous?"

Cody admitted, "A little."

Ronnie laughed easily. "I get it. I was a trainee not too long ago. Got hired on since someone left. Hopefully the same'll happen for you and Mia. First day's nerve-racking, but it shouldn't be too hectic this arvo. Don't sweat it."

"Is the second day easier?" Cody adjusted his sunnies, squinting as the sun glittered off the water.

"Nope." Ronnie grinned. "I still get nervous. Still want to

impress. Some of the guys have been doing this for years and years, back when it was just weekends, before all the tourists started coming. One of the senior blokes, Rich—Chalkers, we call him—he's over fifty and grew up on this beach. Knows it like the back of his hand."

"So, no pressure."

Ronnie laughed. "Not a bit. But listen, the fellas are a good bunch. They can be tough on ya, but they just want you to learn and be your best. Try not to take it personally if you get some stick."

"Cool. Teddy seems pretty mellow?"

"Yeah, he's good. But he's always watching. He doesn't go off too often, but if you deserve it, he will. Not that he yells or anything, but you don't want to disappoint him. That's the worst feeling."

A couple of teenage girls walked by, giggling and whispering. Ronnie gave them a wave, his gaze barely flickering from the water. "Foxy can be a real stickler. He's wound pretty tight. He's a good bloke, don't get me wrong. Just not as chill. With most of the boys, you know from the tone of their voice on the radio how serious a situation is." He laughed. "Harder to tell with Foxy."

After twenty minutes of watching and waiting, Liam returned in the orange buggy. He walked over to them and said, "Not much happening."

As if the universe hissed, "*Just watch*," Ronnie's spine stiffened, his attention zeroed in on something in the water. Cody's stomach swooped as he scanned the waves and the people swimming there despite the warnings. He didn't see anyone—

Wait. *There.* A man floundered off the sandbank, head bobbing under, the rip pulling him out.

"Reckon you'll be in, mate," Ronnie said to Cody. "He's not going to be able to get back."

Standing at Ronnie's side, Liam added, "But if you want to

watch this one, I can—"

"I've got him!" Cody was already tossing his sunnies and cap into the back of the ATV. His radio was clipped to his bum bag, and he unhooked the bag and tossed the lot into the back as well. He was *in*! He nearly landed on his ass, spinning to grab the long blue rescue board from the carrier on the side of the ATV before bolting for the water.

"Shirt off!" Ronnie yelled after him.

Shit! The fewer clothes on, the faster and lighter he'd be, and drowning patients had less to grab and pull under in their panic. Cody jolted to a stop and yanked off his blue uniform shirt, dropping it to the sand before grabbing the board and racing into the surf, splashing through the shallows and stretching out on his belly on the board, paddling, his arms doing a front crawl, legs kicking in the air. Like most people, keeping them still while he swam hard with his arms was like patting his head and rubbing his belly.

As he reached the shore break, he pushed to his knees and powered with both arms in unison, ducking his head into the frothing, salty wave. The board soared up on the cresting water, the nose lifting, and for a horrible moment he thought he might be pushed back and tumble over as the wave broke.

But then he was over the top, and he paddled against the incoming surf, eyes locked on the bobbing head and hand flailing for help. He realized he was holding his breath and forced an inhalation.

A surfer appeared in his peripheral vision as he caught the rip, and when he reached the man, she was holding him up on her board. Cody almost overshot them, and he sat up straight, straddling the long board. He reached for the man's arm and hauled him over. To the woman, he said, "Thanks!"

She nodded and paddled away, heading back out to the lineup where surfers waited their turn for the next set. He knew surfers often helped lifeguards, although Cody wondered if he could have been faster to get out. Hazza in the tower was watching him, and probably all the others too. Liam definitely was. Was Cody doing everything he should? He ran through the checklist in his mind.

"You right?" he asked the man, who coughed and sputtered. "You're okay. Catch your breath."

The husky, dark-haired, older man didn't seem to understand him, or if he did, he was possibly in shock. He gasped and clung to the board, draped over it, his legs still in the water. Cody squeezed his shoulder, gauging the incoming swells and the best way to get the patient back to shore.

He'd practiced it many times as a clubbie and in the lifeguarding course he'd taken, but doing it with a volunteer wasn't the same at all as having an actual shivering, scared person's life in his hands.

"You're okay. I've got you. Get on your stomach and put your head at the front of the board." He gave the man's shoulder a gentle push, and then a firmer one, glancing back at the approaching waves. When he turned, the man's head was practically in Cody's lap.

"No, head up front," Cody repeated, pointing. "That way." He reached down and tugged one of the man's thick legs toward him.

The man seemed to get the idea, and he stretched out on his belly with his head facing forward. Cody did the same, his face practically in the man's butt as he paddled, keeping the patient's weight toward the back so they didn't nosedive when the next swell hit. Now he just needed to get the patient to shore without being hammered by a wave.

Easy.

Glancing back, he paddled hard, hard, *hard*, and then the surge lifted them with that sensation of flying as they caught the wave, riding the crest of it toward the shore. The patient laughed in delight, and Cody almost did too. They hit the impact zone and didn't nosedive, instead riding almost all the way, the patient rolling off at the end. Cody helped him up, and Ronnie met them on the sand, Liam watching from the buggies.

After a minute assessing the patient, the man insisted he was fine now and returned to his family on the beach, clearly embarrassed. Ronnie clapped Cody's wet shoulder. "Nailed it! That was textbook."

Then Cody saw the smile creasing Liam Fox's ridiculously beautiful face. It was all white teeth and charming crinkles, and that smile was directed at *him*. It was beyond stupid to feel a fresh bolt of adrenaline, but he couldn't resist basking in the attention for a moment.

Grinning, he picked up his shirt by the ATV and shook off the sand, his pulse still racing. His first rescue was in the books, and he'd *nailed it*.

Hazza's voice came through the radio. "Chook's first rescue!"

"Oh God, is that going to be my nickname?" Cody groaned.

Damo's voice came on. "Go the chook! You legend."

Ronnie howled with laughter. "Sounds like you've got your nickname, Chookie!"

Cody turned to Liam, but he was already back to business, watching the water, his smile gone without a ripple of it remaining on the surface. And no matter how much his logical brain argued against it, Cody's stubborn soul vowed to make Liam smile again.

Chapter Two

"IT *IS* HIM!"

If the woman had meant to whisper, she did a shit job of it. Liam shoved the metal pole of the dangerous currents sign deeper into the sand, straightening it after the wind blew it crooked. Pretending he hadn't noticed anyone, he toyed with the string from his uniform hoodie, one of the navy ties sticking out from the neck of his jacket. He kept his gaze on the gray, choppy water.

Please don't. Please stop. Just…please.

From the corner of his eye beneath the mirrored aviators he usually wore rain or shine, he could see the middle-aged man and woman pointing at him and edging closer. He considered retreating to the buggy twenty meters away where he'd left Cody, but it was good for Cody to have some time patrolling alone in his first week.

Best to just get it over with, so Liam looked at them and said loudly, "G'day."

They straightened up, caught out with embarrassed laughs. The woman said, "Hi! Sorry to bother you, but you look familiar."

You know exactly who I am, so spit it out already. He could have simply told them and confirmed their suspicions, and probably should have. It happened at least a few times a week that someone would recognize him and go on and on about his glory days. Sometimes it was a few encounters a day when the beach was packed.

As much as he wanted to get the interaction over with, he found himself being contrary in the next breath and not making it easy for the couple in front of him. He should appreciate it more—and he knew they meant well—but after so many years, Liam wished people would forget him once and for all.

"Did you used to play footy?" the man asked. He was actually wearing a blue and gold Eagles T-shirt that stretched over his beer belly.

"I did before I got injured. Liam Fox." He stuck out his hand, back to wanting to get it done.

"Oh my goodness!" the woman exclaimed. "I knew it was you! I was a big, big fan. We both were!"

Liam nodded and tried to smile as they praised him and all the glorious things he used to be, every word pressing salt into the wound that was never left alone long enough to heal. At moments like this—when strangers treated him as if playing a game put him on the same level as the Anzac heroes, as if he'd fought for his country and not been grossly overpaid to drop punt a ball—he swore his knee ached, the old injury flaring up like a ghost rattling its chains.

It was all in his head, but he shifted to his right foot, bare in the cool sand, taking pressure off his left leg. He imagined that if he looked down, that traitor knee would be red and swollen and horribly out of joint.

After reciting a litany of Liam's ancient accomplishments, the man exclaimed, "You could have been the best. The very best!"

He'd heard those words too many times to count over the years, and it was still a kick in the balls. He hadn't lasted long enough in the game to be anything but a footnote of lost potential. A bloody waste.

The bloke's smile faltered, and perhaps he'd realized the trip down memory lane had heaps of potholes in it for Liam. The man said, "Anyway. It's a real pleasure to meet you. A real thrill."

Liam managed to smile for real. "Thank you. Pleasure's mine." When they made no move, just staring at him as though he were something magical, like a unicorn that had just trotted onto the beach, he asked politely, "Where are you from? Locals, or…" If only the beach were busier to give him an excuse to escape.

The woman answered, "Yeah. Well, Mundaring, so inland." She peered up, squinting as the shark patrol helicopter droned by overhead. "Many sharks spotted this year?"

"A few. Spring's a good time for it." The chopper patrols went through autumn, later each year with the changes in weather patterns.

After a few beats of silence, the man seemed eager to make more conversation and asked, "Are there nets out there?"

Liam nodded, keeping his eye on the handful of swimmers nearby. The clouds were thick and the air cool, so the beach wasn't busy, especially since it was a Wednesday and rain was due. "Hard to say how effective nets and drum lines really are. Some studies say not at all. They're only deterrents. Sharks get inside nets all the time." He shrugged. "It is what it is. I've been on the service here ten years, and I've never seen a man-eater up close. They are out there, but odds are a lot better of being killed by bees or lightning. Or a dog."

"Right." The man laughed. "Or in your bathtub, I heard." He shook his head. "You've worked here a *decade*? That's mental! Doesn't seem like it can be that long since you played. Remember your first qualifying final? You scored that goal with only seconds left. It was epic, mate. Epic!"

Yes, Liam remembered the roar of the crowd that had reverberated in his chest for what felt like days, the crushing hugs from his teammates, being hoisted on their shoulders and carted around the field like a king. Aussie rules football was a religion to many, and he'd been a god. He nodded.

"I can't believe you're really here. Just...being a lifeguard!" the woman exclaimed. "Like a normal person!" She blushed. "I mean—not that—I only mean—"

"I understand," Liam said. *You mean that I used to be remarkable, and now I'm nothing.* If only he *was* "normal." Whatever "normal" meant, it sure as hell wasn't him.

"Uh, you must have a wife and kids by now?" the woman asked, clearly trying to fill the awkward silence.

He groaned to himself. Bad enough from his parents, let alone strangers. "No." He cleared his throat. "Well, it was great to meet you both. Have a fun day. Swim between the flags before the rain comes."

"Could we grab a pic?" The woman smiled hopefully.

Since Liam's arms were longest, he took her phone and snapped the selfie of the three of them, giving a practiced grin. Once they were finally gone, practically skipping away, he sighed, his radio coming to life. Damo said, "Making the fans happy, eh, Foxy?"

Liam glanced at the tower and wished he could give it the finger. In the radio, he muttered, "Yeah, the people love me."

He ached to just say stuff it all and tell everyone how he really felt. He'd accepted the end of his footy career—hadn't had a bloody choice, had he? It'd been over before it really began, barely four years with the Eagles, out of the game at twenty-two.

He felt like a failure and a complete dickhead for not appreciating the lingering attention, the irritation battling with guilt. Every selfie and autograph hollowed him bit by bit, like the curling barrel of a wave. Eventually, the wave would collapse in on itself and the water would be washed back out to sea. He was thirty-four, and the best years of his life were long gone.

Maybe he should finally tell everyone the truth about *every-*

thing and see if they wanted his autograph then. Stop hiding. Stop following his rules. Everyone thought they knew him, from his family to the boys on the service to perfect strangers. But if he actually told them why he didn't have a wife…

"No fucking son of mine is going to turn out a faggot."

He tasted bile, and as always, the fear won. No matter how often he toyed with the idea of coming out, in the end he retreated back into the darkness, pulling the virtual blankets over his head.

There would undoubtedly be media attention with headlines throughout Australia, talking heads on TV going on about him fancying blokes, millions of strangers debating and dissecting it. Dissecting *him.* The idea of exposing this secret, private part of himself that he'd hidden for almost as long as he could remember was unbearable. He felt naked just thinking about it, his heart racing.

But worse would be the reaction of his family. His father's voice echoed in his mind again, words that Stuart Fox surely wouldn't even remember. He'd said heaps of bigoted things over the years, but this particular sentence had been branded in Liam's brain.

"No fucking son of mine is going to turn out a faggot."

Then another voice joined in, Lorenzo's Italian accent thick, the long-ago words dripping with disgust, his lip curled as he stared down at Liam on his knees.

"I thought you were a real man, no? It should not be like this."

Liam shifted, queasy with remembered shame. Now his skin prickled with the sensation of being watched, and he braced for more attention, banishing the voices and the mess of memory and humiliating emotion.

Yet as he turned his head, it wasn't more fans, but Cody looking at him. A strange little shiver rippled down Liam's spine at the intensity in Cody's gaze. His eyes were a rich chocolate brown, although Liam couldn't see the color from so far. He didn't know why he'd even thought about it.

Cody jerked his head back to the water and the handful of teenagers there ignoring the warning signs. Even though it was a crap day with few swimmers, he should have been keeping his focus solely on the ocean. Liam was about to go over and tell him that, but let it go. Cody'd been doing a good job since he'd started several days earlier.

Standing by the buggy, Cody had his jacket hood up against the wind. The boys had started calling him Chook, but Liam didn't think it fit. He was more like a bulldog, maybe? Except not stocky. He was small, but he had a tight, lean body, wiry and strong. There was something about him—something different from the other lifeguards that Liam couldn't put his finger on.

Maybe it was because Cody was originally Canadian and hadn't grown up surfing Barkers like most of the guys. While everyone on the service could certainly turn it on when need be, and any competition between them from a foot race to eating corn chips would be hotly contested, overall they were a laid-back bunch.

Cody had a different kind of intensity to him. Like the way he'd raced in for that rescue his first day, showing no hesitation, not intimidated in the slightest. Liam had been nervous as hell doing his first rescue, and he'd been proud of Cody even though they'd barely met. Although Mia had proven herself intense and on the ball too during their first week as trainees.

Then Liam realized *he* was the one watching Cody now when Cody glanced toward him. Liam quickly fiddled with his bum bag. God, he hated the dreary, gray days when he was stuck in his damn head. He'd be glad when he could escape to the gym, stick in his earbuds, and get lost in sweat and the strain of his muscles.

"HOW ARE THEY doing?" Teddy asked as he came up to the tower's main area a few days later.

"Haven't killed anyone yet," Damo replied.

Liam, Bickie, and Teddy chuckled on cue, and Liam watched Mia as she paddled a man who couldn't swim a stroke back into shore. Even between the flags, they had to be vigilant.

Liam turned his binos to the north end. Cody was taking a turn on the orange buggy's bullhorn, shouting at swimmers to go between the flags, pointing down the sand. No one paid him any mind. They wouldn't until the swells dug out another channel and the sandbank dropped away in a heartbeat. Then the people who couldn't swim but were determined to experience Barking Beach got a gutful of saltwater and more than they bargained for.

Through a bite of ginger biscuit—his love of which had resulted in his nickname and a slightly soft belly—Bickie mumbled, "Mia's done a good job with that bloke. He's a big boy, but she only tipped once getting him on the board."

"I tell ya, I wouldn't mind her doing—"

"*Damo,*" Teddy warned. "Don't finish that sentence."

He sighed dramatically. "I know, I know. Sorry, Cyclone."

"Besides being a trainee, she's barely eighteen," Liam noted.

"I'm only twenty-one!" Damo protested, whirling around in his chair with an affronted expression. He wrinkled his nose. "But now that you say it, I feel even more like a dick." He turned back to the windows. "So even though we're all thinking it, I will officially refrain from discussing Mia's hotness."

Liam patted his back a little harder than strictly necessary. "Excellent plan." Damo was a good bloke and had grown into an expert waterman since he'd been a teenage trainee himself. But sometimes his mouth got away from him.

Teddy said, "Yes, you officially will refrain." Then he mussed Damo's hair, the scolding over.

"She's real serious, hey?" Bickie said, brushing back his floppy brown hair. "Good though. Knows her stuff. Same with Chook."

Picking up the binos again, Liam scanned the sand, looking for signs of trouble. Bag thieves, drunk backpackers, whatever. Always something going on at Barking. After a minute, he focused on Cody again.

Cody stood on the back of the buggy now, one of the lifeguards' favorite spots to get a better view of the water while still being close to it. Arse in the air, he bent over the roll bar, presumably to talk to Ronnie, who was sitting inside.

Swinging around, Liam scanned the south end of the beach instead. In the background, Teddy puttered, opening the fridge at the bottom of the three stairs down from the main area and grumbling about the stench. Damo watched the water in front of the tower, rolling a pen between his fingers. Half-sitting on the bench, Bickie finished his lunch. Sometimes the days could stretch out like this, lazy and uneventful with a few run-of-the-mill rescues and not much else.

"So how do you guys do it?" Damo asked.

Liam didn't lower his binos, watching a few swimmers at the south end wrangle an inflatable strawberry. "Do what?"

"Kick back and ignore the fact that the hottest chicks in WA—maybe in all of Australia—are on this beach wearin' togs that are little more than dental floss."

Bickie laughed hard. "Years of experience, mate. Besides, Cyclone and I are married men."

From the back, Teddy piped up. "Yep, that helps. Heaps. Jill would have my bollocks for brekkie if I was perving on women at work."

Liam chuckled, still scanning with the binos. "That's for sure."

"And Foxy here's always been a heartbreaker," Bickie said. "He never gives much away. Still playing hard to get, eh, Foxy?"

"Yep," Liam agreed.

If they only bloody knew. He could picture Teddy, Bickie,

and Damo swiveling toward him, the water forgotten as they stared in utter confusion, especially Teddy, who'd been a brother to Liam as long as he could remember. Then realization. Horror. Disgust.

No, it was better for everyone that he kept himself to himself.

While he'd played in the AFL, he'd dated a string of women, sleeping with some of them, but never seeing the same girl more than a couple of times. His intention had been to not get attached, nor the girls get attached to him—to keep everything casual since his focus had to be on the game anyway. To go through the motions so no one dug deeper.

Of course, he'd ended up with a reputation. A "ladies' man," his father had boasted to his mates. There had been lots of nudges and winks and good-on-yas. Although now his dad and most people were puzzled and frustrated that he hadn't settled down.

Damo sighed heavily. "I really shouldn't have said that about Mia before. It's just, sometimes I swear my balls are so blue they're going to fall off."

"You're trying too hard," Bickie said, sipping from a juice box. "Hit the bars and let the birds come to you. They will. I mean, it's a shame about the face, but you've got nice hair."

They all laughed, and Damo shuddered. "Shaz wanted me to cut it. She kept on about it. One of the reasons we broke up, I tell ya."

"Ronnie to Central. We've got a bloke with an allergic reaction—he thinks to something he ate. It's not too bad at the moment, but might need the epi, so we're bringing him up to the tower. Should probably call an ambo just in case. Twenty-five years of age, no other health conditions."

"Copy that," Liam said into the radio.

Beside him, Damo was already dialing the phone. "Ambulance, please." After a pause, he said, "This is the Barkininy lifeguards calling…"

Liam went back to monitoring the water. It was sunny and getting warm, more and more people coming down as the day went on. As he scanned, his mind returned to Damo's question.

It wasn't hard at all for Liam to ignore the topless women at Barking, but he didn't let himself think about the blokes either. He hadn't made the AFL at eighteen without discipline.

While his mates had been out late partying in year twelve, he'd had early nights and earlier mornings of training. He'd played for the North Mandurah JFC for years, and while he was still finishing the last few months of school, he moved up to the East Perth's Colts team, then quickly to the Reserves and the League. Dad would have been happy for him to leave school, but Mum put her foot down for the first time Liam could remember. And the last.

He'd thrived with discipline and rules. Still did. Looking at the beach now, it was chockers with gorgeous, shirtless men. He worked shoulder to shoulder with fit men day in and day out. But his rule against never lusting over teammates in his footy days had transferred seamlessly to the lifeguard service.

He'd established this rule in year eleven after being tackled at practice by Colin Biggins, aka Biggs or Biggsy. As Liam had sprawled on the field, his cheek mashed into the grass, Biggs on top of him, he'd first realized with a shocking jolt that he wanted to be fucked by a bloke. In the heartbeat after hitting the ground, that amazing weight holding him down, he'd gotten rock hard, his prick trapped painfully in his jock.

He still wasn't sure why it was that tackle and not the million before that had done it. He'd known he fancied other boys, which was frightening enough. He'd tightly locked away those feelings and dated a neighborhood girl who thought he was a gentleman for not wanting to do much more than hold her hand. But *this*? The rush of lust was all new and *grown-up* and truly terrifying in its wrongness.

He'd taken his time getting to his feet, Biggs reaching down a hand with a grin on his pimply face, clueless of the earthquake inside him. Liam had jerked off furiously that night, imagining the grass against his cheek, letting Biggs fuck him as hard as he wanted.

That had led to a series of automatic erections when he so much as glanced at Colin Biggins on the coach to away games, let alone in the locker room. Liam knuckled down and trained himself to shut off, and by the time he was drafted by the Eagles, he was an expert in denying that part of himself until he was alone and safe in the dark. Then he'd had his hand, and that was enough. It'd had to be.

He could never breathe a word of it to anyone—not that he was gay, and sure as hell not that he wanted *that*. He could never let himself think of other players the way he had Biggs that day on the pitch.

As a lifeguard, the rule had remained strictly intact, his colleagues taking the place of teammates. He didn't lust over other lifeguards, or blokes on the beach. He didn't shit where he ate. It was as simple as that. In fact, the rule had been folded into a bigger one: Never hook up in Australia or with an Australian. Period.

Even in Sydney or Melbourne he was still recognized, and forget about locally. There were only about two million people in the whole Greater Perth Area. He sometimes lurked on the sex apps and saw the same blokes around Barking and Freo. They were like small towns, and no matter how careful he was, word would spread. He couldn't trust anyone not to gossip. Or worse.

The idea of pictures or video of him online had acid churning his stomach. God, if people *knew*... No, he couldn't trust anyone. He took his chances overseas once or twice a year with strangers who didn't know the AFL from a hole in the ground, and that would have to do. And maybe next time he'd work up the nerve to ask for what he really wanted...

Lorenzo's laughter echoed through his mind, and he cringed. Even after ten years, the humiliation was as fresh as if it had been yesterday.

"How's south end looking?" Teddy asked, standing behind Liam and giving his shoulder a friendly pat.

"All good," Liam said, flinching guiltily and refocusing.

As Teddy and Bickie discussed a potential bag thief, Ronnie and Cody arrived with the patient suffering an allergic reaction. Liam watched the water, picking up the binos every so often, half-listening to the first aid going on in the small medical area at the back of the tower. The patient was on the first aid bed, like the kind in doctors' exam rooms. Seemed okay for the moment, so Liam left Cody and Ronnie to it.

"You training in the morning?" Damo asked him.

"Of course." Work, train, eat, sleep. Repeat in various orders. He usually lifted at Barking's outdoor gym by south end if the weather was good and ran along the bike path connecting Barking to Coogee and Freo up north. If it was too wet or chilly, he hit a twenty-four-hour gym nearby with rows of machines under fluorescent lights.

"If I can get out of bed, I'll join you."

Liam shrugged. "You can. Whether you will or not is another story."

"You make it sound so easy, Foxy! Have you ever slept in?" Damo asked.

Teddy said, "He did once when he was twelve. Had the flu and his mum hauled him back to bed kicking and screaming."

Everyone chuckled, and Liam didn't answer, peering at two men a few meters from shore. He got on the radio. "Central to Mia. Keep an eye on the two fully dressed blokes off second gate. They haven't gone in too deep yet, but could happen any second."

"Copy that, Central," she replied.

"Are they wearing *jeans?*" Cody asked from behind Liam, suddenly standing close. The ambos had arrived up the tower's ramp and were assessing the patient.

"Yeah." Liam shifted in his chair. "You'll see it sometimes with tourists. It can be a religious thing—staying covered up and all that, but obviously it's dangerous unless it's one of those full-length bathers some Muslim women wear. With cotton or denim or whatever, it weighs you down so quickly. If you see someone wearing their clothes in the water, chances are they can't swim either, so keep vigilant."

When he glanced back at Cody, Cody was watching him with those deep brown eyes. Freckles sprinkled the tops of his cheeks, and his eyelashes were so thick it almost looked like he was wearing eyeliner. Liam couldn't seem to look away.

There was something about the intensity in Cody's gaze that reminded Liam of fans, but Cody was too young to have watched him play. He probably hadn't even been living in the country. Was it possible he was...

No. Liam shut down the train of thought before it could derail and smash through his rules.

Cody said, "Got it." He smiled, dimples appearing. "Thanks."

"Uh, sure." Liam found himself smiling back. As he did, Cody's grin deepened, and Liam shifted uneasily. "What?" Was there a joke? The boys were often pranking each other.

But Cody shook his head. "Nothing."

"Chook, are you working in the morning?" Damo asked. "If not, you should come train with us."

"*Us?*" Liam snorted, going back to the familiarity of scanning the waves.

Laughing, Cody said, "Thanks. That would be cool, but most mornings I run down to South Beach with my landlord's dog to swim. She broke her hip last year and isn't as mobile as she was. Mrs. Delfino, I mean. Not the dog. But maybe I'll bring her down one morning. The dog. Not Mrs. Delfino."

"Codes, we're back on patrol," Ronnie said from the tower's side door, and Cody hurried after him. The patient left with the ambos, and quiet settled back in. Damo twisted his hair around a pen as he scanned, Bickie finished his lunch and went to do a sweep of the beach, and Teddy returned to his office. A fly buzzed around the glass, and the air con rattled distantly.

Damo sighed. "I wish—" His spine stiffened. "Got three heads out the back."

"The Croc?" Liam wheeled over.

"Nah. Practically in front of us." Damo peered through the binos. "They just went. Shit, two more. I'm in." He pushed back his chair and bolted from the tower.

Liam grabbed the radio. "Central to all lifeguards on the beach. We've got a flash rip at the north side of the flags, between second and third gate. Damo's in. He'll need backup. Ronnie and Cody get down there. Bickie stay north."

Liam watched the flailing swimmers, the current dragging them out with no warning. Usually the lifeguards knew where the currents would start pulling and when, but the ocean surprised them with flash rips too. As Damo paddled hard, Ronnie and Cody joined him. Liam checked the south corner, leery of calling Mia up to the flash rip and leaving too much of the beach unattended.

In the end, the five swimmers were rescued, and they shifted the flags. They could plan and prepare for the Croc, knowing each day when the tide turned that the currents would pull. It was logical and steady. Flash rips had them scrambling and on edge. Liam scanned uneasily, waiting for the bottom to fall out without warning.

Later, as Liam watched Cody paddle in a patient who'd gotten out of their depth, the beach seemingly back to normal, Damo asked him, "Foxy, do you think that girl—"

"No."

"But how do you—"

"Discipline, mate." In the distance, Cody ran a towel over his lean, tan chest, then his head. Even through the binos, Liam could see the way Cody's brown hair curled at the ends when it was wet.

He turned away and repeated, "Discipline."

Chapter Three

"**S**HOULD I CLEAN the windows?" Mia asked.

Liam waved her off. "Nah, head home. Good job to-day."

"But—" she broke off, glancing around, frowning. "There must be something I can do. I'm happy to stay and help."

"Honestly, it's all good. See you tomorrow. Enjoy your night."

"Don't have to ask us twice!" Hazza said as he and Nicky headed out. Liam gave them a wave as they left, the tower door shutting behind them. Mia sighed and followed, dragging her feet.

One of the trainees the year before had been more interested in catching waves and picking up chicks than doing the actual job. This season, Teddy seemed to have chosen far better. Over a fortnight, Mia and Cody had both proven themselves eager and determined.

The sun was going down, and they'd made it another day without losing anyone. The last one in the tower, Liam sat by the windows, gazing out at the water and the few swimmers left. The lifeguards were officially off-duty as of six-thirty p.m. this time of year, and the beach was almost empty now.

He loved this peaceful time of day when the crowds faded, the evenings refreshingly cool. The cafe up by the bike path would be closed, and aside from the odd sunset-watchers and dog-walkers, most people would be gone.

On crazy days at the height of summer when the sun didn't go down until after seven or eight, the crowds and heat would linger and they'd work later. For now, the lifeguards could get home at a decent time. Not that Liam had anything to do at home except eat cereal for dinner, have a few beers, and watch *Ambulance Australia*.

About ten surfers still tried their luck on the four-foot swells. The after-work guys usually kept going until it was truly too dark to see. Liam watched one catch a good ride before bending his head to finish his supervisor shift report.

They'd moved the flags down the beach that arvo, and he'd jotted down the time and new placement. Now he went back to fill in the reason for the move, which was that a few people were dumped by increasing swells as the wind came up.

"Don't they know dusk is prime time for shark attacks?"

Liam thumped his bad knee on the bottom of the long bench that curved across the front of the tower, familiar dull pain pulsing. "Christ!" He spun the chair to find Cody standing at the top of the steps with wide eyes. "I thought I was the last one," Liam said.

"Sorry!" Cody smiled, those dimples appearing. "I volunteered to stock up the first aid kits."

"Ah. That's why Mia was so keen to stay late as well." Liam followed Cody's gaze down and realized he was rubbing his scarred knee rhythmically. This pain had been brief, barely a whisper of the agony he'd felt years ago.

He turned back and picked up his pen. "Thanks for doing that. I'll pull down the shutters and lock up, so you can leave anytime."

"Okay," Cody said. "Cool. Sorry if I scared you."

"Nah, no worries." Liam flipped over the paperwork. As he went through the routine, checking off boxes when necessary, he could hear the odd sound from the medical area of bags being unzipped and boxes being opened. When he peeked at one point, he met Cody's gaze over the top step.

It was Cody's turn to jump. He whipped his head down, fumbling a package of gauze. Liam didn't say anything, but he shifted in his chair uncomfortably. What was Cody staring at? *Did* he know who Liam was? Maybe his old man was a fan or something. But instead of making him frustrated and resentful and guilty, the attention from Cody sent a ripple of excitement through Liam.

No. Never going to happen.

Liam resolutely bent back to his report, and minutes ticked by in silence but for the sound of Cody finishing the restock, which wouldn't take long. Then, from the corner of his eye, Liam spotted a figure in a wetsuit racing across the sand. Heading straight for the tower.

He grabbed the binos and scanned. When he reached the north end, Liam's heart skipped. The surfers in the lineup out on the water were waving madly.

"*Shit.*"

"What's wrong?" Cody asked, appearing beside him.

"Someone's hurt. Get the backboard, collar, and defib. This might be a resus." With only two of them left, he had to abandon the protocol of always having one guard in the tower, and it was technically after hours anyhow. He raced out and down the stairs, jamming the key in the lock and yanking up the garage door.

He slotted in a rescue board on the side rack and stopped the buggy at the bottom of the stairs. The end of the backboard thump-thump-thumped down the steps, the red defib bag over Cody's shoulder and neck collar in his hand. He shoved it all in the back and hopped onto the other seat, kneeling on it, one foot on the sideboard as Liam took off.

They went flat-stick across the sand, avoiding a few couples watching the sunset, slowing as they neared the surfer running toward them. Breathing hard, dark hair streaming behind him, the man shouted, "Bloke got hit right on the back. Can't feel his legs."

Shit. "He conscious?" Liam asked. "Breathing?"

"Yeah, last I saw."

Liam nodded. "You have a mobile to call an ambo? Thanks, mate." He recognized the surfer as a local, and the locals could be relied on to know their location and bring the paramedics down to the right place.

In the vibrant orange splash of light, the sun below the horizon now, Liam could make out the clump of surfers out on the water when he parked at the north end. He pulled off his shirt, grabbed the neck collar and rescue board, and said to Cody, "Be ready with the backboard. I'll get the collar on him out there. Have the defib ready to go just in case." He hesitated. This was a lot for a trainee to handle. "You right?"

Cody didn't pause as he lifted the backboard. "I've got this."

Liam raced into the surf, tossing down the board and hop-pushing a few times before he got on, paddling as hard as he could with the neck collar gripped in one hand. The surfer had said the patient was breathing, but with a spinal injury that could change at any moment. Adrenaline surged, his heart banging like a drum.

The patient was partly on his back on a board, several surfers around holding his legs up and trying to keep him still as the swells rolled through. The man was about fifty and bald with brown skin, one of the locals who worked an office job and raced down to Barking when they got home from work.

One of the surfers said, "He was duck-diving under the wave, and the other bloke didn't realize and went for it. Newbie slammed the nose of his board into his back."

"I'm so sorry!" a young man blurted. "I tried to stop!" He clutched two boards, one of them likely the patient's.

"It's all right, buddy," Liam said, taking charge. "We know it was an accident." Straddling the rescue board, he leaned close to the patient, a swell lifting them all. "What's your name?"

"Steve."

"Right, Steve-o, I'm Liam. Ambo's on the way. I'm going to get this collar on you. Just a precaution. How are you feeling?"

"Hurts," Steve hissed, clenching his jaw.

"I know. Where? In your back?" He unhooked the collar and fitted it as gently as he could, nodding to the surfers to help hold the board steady, which wasn't easy in deep water. They'd moved Steve out of the impact zone, but water still swirled and swelled. "Just say yes or no—don't nod or shake your head."

"Yes. Middle back."

"Out of ten, if ten is the worst pain you've ever had, where's it at?"

"Seven, I guess?"

"Any numbness or tingling in your feet or hands?"

"Can't feel my feet. Fingers are tingling," Steve gritted out.

"All right, mate. You're doing great." He didn't want to lie and say everything would be all right. Not with a spinal. But he'd seen it happen before that numbness subsided and feeling returned once swelling went down. He prayed that would be the case for Steve, but worst-case scenario was obviously that he wouldn't walk again.

"Any pain in your neck? Remember, say yes or no—don't move your head."

"No," Steven answered.

Slowly, as steadily as possible, Liam and the surfers got Steve to shore, Cody splashing in to meet them. As soon as they could stand, they walked the board in, carrying Steve on it like a stretcher, careful of every step and movement, trying to keep him as still as they could.

The defib and backboard waited on the beach by the buggy. They eased the board under Steve, tipping him on his side and then back down on the count of three. Cody followed Liam's instructions with confidence, which wasn't easy with spinals. Liam was always very aware that a patient's future was literally in his hands and that a stuff-up could paralyze them.

As sirens wailed in the distance, he sent Cody in the buggy to bring down the ambos while he administered pain relief to Steve, getting him to suck on gas that would take away the pain with any luck. It was dark now, the red and blue lights eerie by the tower. Gulls cried.

A few surfers remained, encouraging Steve. The tall, thin bloke who'd hit him paced the sand, jiggling his hands and breathing hard, coming too close and apologizing again. "Stay back," Liam told him impatiently. At least it wasn't during the day, when a ring of death would form, bystanders crowding around the injured patient.

To Steve, he said, "You're doing really well." The briny air was chilly now, and Liam carefully tucked a silver emergency blanket around him.

Cody arrived with the ambos, and Liam briefed them, helping when asked. The surfer who'd hit Steve stood by the glow of the buggy headlights where the ambos worked, his hands in his short hair. He looked like he was going to spew, making plaintive noises when he wasn't even the one who'd gotten a board slammed into his back. Liam felt sorry for him but was about to tell the guy to get his shit together since he wasn't helping. Then Cody approached him.

"Hey, buddy." Cody gave his shoulder a friendly pat. "What's your name?"

"Huh? Me? Jeff."

Cody spoke in a low, reassuring voice. "Hey, Jeff. I'm Cody. Pretty scary what happened, eh?"

Jeff nodded tightly, now looking like he might burst into tears.

"I'd be freaking out if I were you. You're doing great."

It was a lie, but Liam could see the tension ebb in Jeff as the guy looked to Cody hopefully. "Yeah?"

"Oh yeah, I'd be off my head."

Jeff's cheeks puffed as he blew out, his arms dropping to his sides. "I should have been watching more carefully, but I wanted the wave. I just learned to surf at the end of last summer."

"I learned late too. I'm from Canada originally. What about you?"

"I grew up in Alice."

Cody said, "Alice Springs? You're a long way from home."

"Yeah." Jeff took a deep breath. "Yeah," he repeated. "I really didn't mean to hurt him."

"Of course not." Cody rubbed his back, then patted his shoulder. "I once fin chopped a girl with my board. Her calf was split open, but I was more upset than she was. Those Aussie girls are tough."

Jeff smiled shakily. "They are."

As they watched the ambos work on Steve, Cody stayed by a much calmer Jeff, his hand on his shoulder. Liam stood a few feet away, shifting uncomfortably, feeling like he was intruding, which didn't make any sense. They all breathed a little easier when Steve reported that he could feel his toes again and wiggled them on command.

Cody murmured to Jeff, "The ambos and doctors will take good care of him."

"I just wish..." Jeff scrubbed at his face. "It happened so fast."

"You tried to pull off the wave when you realized he was there," Cody said firmly. "You did the right thing. Collisions happen sometimes."

Shivering in his wetsuit, Jeff nodded. "Thanks, man. Thank God you guys were still here."

Cody *still* had his hand on Jeff's shoulder. "Yeah, good thing. But you would have handled it. You brought in Steve's board, right? We'll keep it under the tower for him, safe and sound. Hey, could you do me a favor? Want to bring it up there for us? Leave it

39

by the garage door. It'd be a big help."

Jeff nodded eagerly. "Can I do anything else?"

"Just go home and get a good night's sleep. That's what I'm gonna do."

"Okay." Jeff nodded again, exhaling loudly. "Yeah, that's a good idea." He looked to Steve and the ambos crouched by him. "Tell him I really am sorry."

"I will. If you want to stop by tomorrow, we'll let you know if we've heard anything. Get some rest. And thanks for your help with the board."

"Right. Anytime." Jeff smiled at Cody before scooping up his board under one arm and Steve's in the other, practically running to the tower to do as Cody asked.

Liam watched him go, not quite sure how Cody had managed Jeff so well. He was supposed to be the trainee, yet he'd handled Jeff's panic much better than Liam had.

It was time to transport Steve to the waiting ambulance. Cody drove at a slow pace, Liam and the ambos keeping hold of Steve on the backboard across the rear of the buggy. "Little slower," Liam called out, and Cody adjusted immediately, easing off the gas and keeping them at an even walk.

Behind the tower, they waved off Steve, and Liam hoped the hospital would ring the next day to update them. Sometimes they did, or the coppers did if they were involved, depending on the injury. The pavement of the access lane was cool under their bare feet, and Liam and Cody watched the red and blue lights fade in the darkness, the steady hum of the incoming tide replacing the siren. There were sweet-smelling flowers blooming in one of the park's gardens, and the scent caught the breeze.

Liam exhaled, rubbing his bare arms, gooseflesh rising on his damp skin. He'd have to fetch his uniform shirt from the buggy. "Good job. That was hectic."

Cody smiled up at him with those dimples. "Thanks. You

seemed so calm."

Liam half-laughed. "Don't let me fool ya. My heart was in my guts. Spinals are intense." He inhaled the cool, salty-sweet night air. He had to close up the tower and amend his report, but for the moment, he just wanted to stand next to Cody and breathe. "You were calm yourself. I'm impressed with how you handled that bloke. Jeff."

"Poor guy. I'd be about to have a nervous breakdown too if I hurt someone like that."

"I don't think you would." Liam said it before he thought, and winced. "I don't mean that you wouldn't care."

Cody laughed, his raised eyebrows visible in the glow of the light at the top of the tower stairs above them. "I hope not."

Liam smiled. "I meant that you'd stay in control. Although you said you panicked when you cut that girl's leg."

"Oh, I made that up. Just wanted to distract him and make him feel better."

"Well, you were great with him. Calmed him and made him feel useful." Cody had been commanding, but kind. Liam wasn't sure why he was so impressed. He supposed because Cody was still young and only a trainee.

"Thanks. Guess I followed my instincts."

"Good on ya." Liam lifted his hand up for a casual handshake, and Cody did too, slapping his palm and clasping for a moment. He smiled up at Liam, and Liam smiled back, and they were still holding hands—

Not *holding hands.* He pulled away with a lame little laugh. Cody looked up at Liam, silent for a moment. "Hey, wanna grab a beer? My shout."

Liam was shocked to find he wanted very much to say yes, but he recovered and shook his head. "Still have the paperwork to finish up. Go on and have fun with your mates. I'll put the buggy away and lock up."

"Right." Cody nodded, turning away. "Right," he repeated. "I finished the first aid kits, so I'll grab my stuff. Have a good one."

Back upstairs after storing the buggy and Steve's board in the garage and changing into jeans and a sweatshirt, Liam added the late rescue to the report. He hadn't pulled down the shutters yet, but all he could see was his reflection and the empty tower behind him.

The other lifeguards would likely all be home, either having dinner with their families or girlfriends or relaxing. Or maybe out at the pub, like Cody probably was. He could imagine Cody laughing with other blokes, those dimples in his freckled cheeks.

For a second, Liam could hardly breathe, the surge of loneliness so powerful it would have knocked him over if he'd been standing. He rubbed his left knee, that phantom pain throbbing. With his other hand, he took out his phone and scrolled through the news aimlessly.

He answered a text from his sister-in-law, Cora, about the weekend barbecue for his nephew's fifth birthday. He'd skipped out on the party after his niece's christening earlier that spring, chucking a sickie when the thought of the small-talk and nosy questions from extended family had been too much to take. It had been a shitty thing to do, and he cringed with guilt as he sent an assurance he wouldn't miss Jamie's party, along with a few smiley-face emojis.

Liam returned to the news, then thought about checking his email...

But instead, he found himself opening a different app he kept hidden in several subfolders, watching his thumbs tapping his phone as if they belonged to someone else. The app told him it had been thirty-three days since he'd logged on.

His profile picture greeted him—a mirror shot of his bare chest, his body turned enough that the footy tattoo on his arm wasn't visible. Brown hair led down under his belly, the pic cut off just above his cock. The irony that he'd taken the pic in the closet mirror wasn't lost on him.

The little green light was on, showing him—username Matt123—as online. "Matt" was the fake name he gave overseas, although he'd used his own name that first disastrous time when he'd met Lorenzo. He cringed, shoving away the memories of that mocking laughter.

When Liam had registered for the app a few years ago, he'd kept it simple. His location was a general "Perth," although he really lived south of there in Barkininy.

It only took a minute for a message to appear:

Hey sexy. What are you into?

Liam's pulse skipped like a stone over a glassy, almost-flat swell, the kind they got on Barking at dawn when the wind was still. He hesitated before tapping his phone.

I'm versatile.

It was the answer he gave when he was feeling brave, or perhaps reckless. Needy. Lonely. *Brave* was a joke considering this was just a pathetic game he played. It wasn't real and never would be. He had rules for a reason. He had to, because if a hookup recognized him and spread gossip—or worse, had a hidden camera...

Three dots appeared in the text box to show that user Hot-Gay69 was typing a response. His profile pic appealed: a little older, maybe forty or so. Broad, hairless chest, a gleaming smile and handsome face.

With those muscles? And you're six-three? Come on, you've got to be a top.

Disappointment flared, bright and searing, before fading into resigned acceptance. This was the typical response Liam got at the mere notion that he might want to bottom. That he was too big, too muscular, too so-called manly to want that. HotGay69 wrote:

Want you to fuck me til I can't walk straight.

A moment later the man added: *I'm out in Beaconsfield. Can come to you. And go down on you. Bet your cock's massive. Cut?*

Why did Liam even open the app and chat with guys he was never going to meet? He wouldn't be hooking up with HotGay69 or anyone else in Australia. Instead he'd be jerking off alone in his little house a few blocks away. So why did he torture himself?

For some fucked-up reason, Cody's dimples flashed through his mind. Which really was bloody stupid for so many reasons. Liam usually fantasized about guys as big as, or even bigger than, him—although it wasn't a requirement for a hookup.

It had been several months since his last trip, a week in Thailand. He'd been able to screen out the Aussies and Kiwis on the apps and had holed up in his hotel room, inviting up Swedish and Chinese tourists who seemingly had no clue who he was. Or who he'd been. It was still a risk—it certainly wasn't impossible someone foreign might know the AFL—but it had been so long since he played, and he needed *something*.

It wasn't that Liam hated topping. Sure, he could get off in a tight hole. And he could admit he'd had opportunities to push further and insist that he was serious about wanting to bottom, if he'd dared broach the topic. Usually he didn't have the guts to even hint, just giving the men what they all seemed to want from him.

He could imagine HotGay69 now scoffing at the idea if Liam suggested it, and it was all too humiliating on so many levels. Especially considering what had happened when he *had* tried bottoming once. When he'd begged for it.

The memory surged like a shark with open jaws, shame taking another chunk from him, Lorenzo's laughter ringing out. Liam stared at himself in the dark windows, the empty tower bright behind him. His yellow-tinted reflection looked back—the face so many people knew.

With a shout, he hurled the water bottle. The hard green

plastic bounced off the glass, crashing back down to the desk and rolling onto the floor.

"Fuck!" Panting, Liam stared at himself, bloody lucky the window was reinforced. "*Fuck,*" he repeated. His voice was too loud in the silence. "I'm off my head."

Turning away from his reflection, he scooped up the bottle. A smiling sea turtle gave him two flippers up. The bottle had been a birthday gift from his nephew, who'd bought it with his own money at the aquarium up at Hillarys—a fact little Jamie had been extremely proud of.

Holding the bottle, Liam stared at the grinning turtle rather than back up at himself in the glass. Would he even get to see Jamie and his new niece if the truth came out? If *he* came out? Even if their parents disowned him, surely Liam's big brother wouldn't. But he and Greg had drifted apart over the years, and Greg didn't even really know him, did he? No one did.

Avoiding his reflection, Liam swiped up, quitting the app and leaving HotGay69 hanging. He slid the paperwork neatly in its slot and locked the tower behind him, walking home alone through the dark, sleepy streets of Barking.

Chapter Four

CODY BLINKED UP at the high ceiling of his studio, which arched in an inverted V, like a little church. The wood tended to creak and pop with temperature changes, and it had woken him earlier than planned. The light around the edges of the navy-blue curtains was weak, the sun not up over the houses to the east yet.

Stretching out naked, the thin blanket tangled around his legs as his brain powered on. Its first order of business was to remind him that he'd asked out Liam Fox the night before, and he cringed. Well, not *asked him out*, asked him out, but still. The last thing Liam probably wanted to do was hang with a trainee after hours.

"Go on and have fun with your mates."

Cody had been buzzing on the high of the rescue and working together so well. It had been thrilling, to really feel like a full-fledged lifeguard and not a trainee. And Liam couldn't have known that his offhand comment had stung. There were plenty of people Cody was *friendly* with, but no one who was actually a close friend these days.

Liam surely had plenty of friends and no need for another. Especially not one who lusted after him despite his best efforts to shut that shit down. Granted, it was tough to stop wanting to climb Liam like a tree considering he was a walking wet dream, but there was something more there too.

Something mysterious about him—a loose thread that Cody wanted to tease out and unravel. He got a strangely lonely vibe from Liam, which didn't make much sense given the aforementioned walking-wet-dream thing. Cody really would love to have a beer with him.

Liam didn't wear a wedding ring, and Cody had the impression he was single. He could admit he was dying to see Liam's profile on the dating apps. Not that he was going to waste time searching hetero apps just to see if he was on there. Although maybe he'd see if Liam had a SnapChat or Insta...

"So I can slide into his DMs?" he asked aloud, shaking his head with a laugh. "Or I could do something productive." If he kept obsessing about Liam, he'd end up wanking and wasting his morning off.

Instead, he hopped up and grabbed his to-do list from the fridge door on his way into the bathroom across from the bed. The studio was a rectangle with glass doors at each end, one leading to his patio and the other to the gate on the laneway that gave access to the garages for the houses on Manning and South Terrace. The studio was squeezed in beside Mrs. Delfino's garage, and the laneway gave Cody his own entrance.

His place was separate from her house up on Manning Street, which perched atop a steep yard that started just beyond his covered patio. Thick passion fruit vines ensured privacy for them both.

While Cody pissed, he scanned the list, groaning at the first item—which he'd been putting off for two weeks. When he was done in the bathroom, he tugged on a faded Captain America T-shirt and plaid boxers, opened his laptop at the long dining table in the middle of the studio, and hoped the conversation would be better than he expected.

"Hey, Dad." Cody waved when his father's goateed face appeared in the Skype window. "How ya goin'?"

Robert grimaced. He wore a tie and dress shirt, and his short dark hair was neatly parted. He pushed his silver-framed glasses up his nose. "I wish you didn't insist on speaking like..." He took a sip of red wine from a crystal glass. "*That.*"

Cody barely resisted rolling his eyes, although he had to admit he had said it on purpose. "Yeah, well. This is how the people I know talk." His dad was the snobbiest Aussie ever. He'd worked hard at losing his broad drawl and now spoke with what sounded more like an upper-crust English accent. "Is Mom home yet?"

"Michelle?" Robert called. "It's Cody."

She appeared in the frame, wiping her hands on a tea towel and bending over Robert's shoulder. "Hi, sweetheart! So good to see your face."

"You too." Cody gave her a smile. Her blond hair was pulled up in a knot. Over a turtleneck, she wore a sedate, cream-colored apron that was probably from Williams Sonoma. In black script, it quoted Shaw: "*There is no sincerer love than the love of food.*" Undoubtedly a gift from his dad. "Is this a bad time?"

"No, just getting dinner ready," Michelle answered. "Administered about fifty flu shots today. The morning *flew* by." She was a pharmacist who also loved puns. She grinned. "See what I did there?"

Cody grinned back. "Good one, Mom."

"How are you doing? Oh, we miss you, sweetheart."

"Miss you too. And good. Great! Work's going really well. I pulled a couple backpackers out of the rip yesterday. There was a southerly and it was tricky, but I got them both back to shore without help."

His mom made delighted noises while his dad sipped his wine. He was at the dining table, probably grading papers. He said, "And what are you planning once the summer's over?"

Cody's jaw clenched, and he forced a smile. "The season goes to May, but they still have a skeleton crew on all through the winter. Hopefully there's going to be a full-time position, and it'll go to me or Mia, the other trainee. I'm doing everything I can to get that job. And if not the full-time yearly spot, then full-time seasonal for next year. Then it's really only three or four months I need to find something else. I can go back to bartending in the winter."

"Yes, but then what?" his dad asked.

Michelle put her hand on his shoulder, laughing half-heartedly. "Sweetheart, you know this is what Cody's always wanted to do."

"Plenty of kids want to be beach bums. It doesn't mean they should be." When Michelle thwacked his arm, Robert insisted, "I'm just saying what everyone else thinks. That lifeguarding is fine for the summer, but it's time Cody got a real job if he's truly not going to university."

"*He* doesn't want to be an academic," Cody said, fisting his hands under the table. "School was fine, but you know I've never loved it like the rest of you." His sisters were firmly on track for post-grad degrees like their parents.

Robert scoffed. "Please. You don't have to be an *academic* to get your degree. Isn't that boyfriend of yours going to Murdoch? That hoon's not exactly a Mensa candidate."

Cody choked down the urge to defend Tommy just to argue with his dad. "Ex-boyfriend. For, like, way over a year now. And you know we only really dated because we were the two out guys at school." They'd had some good times, usually involving too much beer, but Cody didn't particularly miss him. Tommy's passions were muscle cars and illegal drag racing, which they often called "hooning" in Australia.

His father pursed his lips. "Yes, well, I don't know that you'll find a more suitable candidate mucking around on the beach."

Gee, I'm so glad I called. "Lifeguarding is a real job, Dad. It's a profession. I'm not chilling at the Burnaby Y telling kids to stop peeing in the pool. I'm helping people! Saving lives! Lifeguarding is serious here."

Robert sighed. "You forget I grew up there, Cody."

"You grew up in the Swan Valley, and you've never liked the ocean. You hardly ever went when we lived in Mullaloo, and you have no idea what it's like at Barking. And no, I'm really not going to uni. We all can't be biomedical researchers who listen to Mozart and hate sports."

"You know I'm an avid skier like your mother."

"Yeah, because skiing is expensive enough that it qualifies as an acceptable activity." Cody flattened his palms on his bare thighs. "I'm never going to be an academic, Dad. But I'm learning to be a damn good lifeguard. I love it. I love the water. I love the beach. That doesn't make me a 'beach bum.' This is a real job that requires real skill."

"Of course it is, sweetheart," Michelle soothed, ever the peacemaker. "We're so proud of you."

Before his dad could say anything else, Cody unloaded the rest of his frustration. "All through school, I volunteered hundreds and hundreds of hours as a clubbie. I worked part time at the mini golf to make money for surf lessons and every water safety training course I could do. Since year twelve, I've got my advanced resus certificate, my senior first aid, my watercraft license. More surf school. I did my TAFE classes in sport and recreation, all while working nights at the pub. I've put on twenty pounds of muscle at the gym. I don't know how much harder I can work. Just because uni's not for me doesn't mean I'm a slacker." He sat back and exhaled, crossing his arms.

After a few moments of silence, Robert sighed, taking off his glasses and rubbing his eyes. "You're right. You've always been a hard worker, and you've always known your own mind. I just wish you'd apply that tenaciousness to getting a degree." He lifted a hand before Cody could object, Michelle visibly tightening her grasp on his shoulder. "Hear me out. I understand that you don't think you'll need a degree. But it's a minimum requirement for so many jobs. Right now you're young, and you want to be active and outdoors. But you won't be young forever. You might be able to get by on the council salary, but what happens when you're older and want more? I don't want you to close the door on a world of opportunities. It's so much easier to get your BA while you're young. While we'll happily pay for it. You can still surf and lifeguard—they have casual positions, don't they?"

"Yes. But Dad, you're talking about office jobs. I don't want to be trapped behind a desk. It's not me."

Michelle tilted her head. "To be fair, you're still young. You don't really know who you are yet." She raised a hand as Cody opened his mouth to argue. "Although you've proven mature beyond your years, staying in Perth and going after your goals. This is just something to consider, all right? When I was your age, I was sure I was going to be a doctor. But it wasn't for me. It took me a year in medical school to figure that out before I switched to pharmacology. Besides, having an undergrad degree in your back pocket can't hurt."

"I hear what you're saying. But if I can't be a lifeguard, I'll be a personal trainer, or a tradie."

Robert actually wrinkled his nose. "Such as what? A carpenter? A plumber?"

Cody rolled his eyes. "You won't be sneering the next time your toilet gets clogged and you need someone to clear out the shit."

"Don't be crude, sweetheart," Michelle said, wincing.

"It's true and you know it!" he protested. "Look, I should get going. I've got stuff to do this morning before my shift at the beach." He yawned.

"Late night?" Michelle asked. "Meet anyone special lately?"

"Mom, can we not?" Cody heard the whine in his voice and added in a measured tone, "Like I told you, I've been way too busy for anything serious. I don't think you and dad want to hear about my hookups." Not that there had been heaps to report on. He'd been laser-focused on training and making it onto the service at Barking since he and Tommy had finally put their so-called relationship out of its misery, far past its expiration date.

"Indeed not," Robert said dryly.

As his older sister wandered into frame and waved, Cody said, "Hey, Gwen!"

"Hey!" Water splattered her glasses, and she took them off, blotting the lenses with the bottom of her blouse. "How's it going in paradise? Has it rained in weeks?"

He grinned. "Twice. One time was at night, so it doesn't really count."

She groaned. "I love Vancouver, but this constant rain gets real old after a while. *Ugh.* Speaking of *ugh*, are these two giving you a hard time?"

Robert sipped his wine. "It's our job, dear. And we do it well."

They all laughed at that, and the tension that had been driving Cody's shoulders up to his ears eased. Even though he and his dad had little in common but DNA, Cody knew he wanted the best for him. He loved his parents, and they loved him, even if they were a pain in the ass.

Once they ended the call, Cody could breathe again. He took his pen and scratched *Skype Mom and Dad* off his list with more force than was necessary. The other stuff was boring AF—laundry, groceries, cleaning. He'd had *scrub out the fridge drawer* on his weekly to-do list for an embarrassingly long time.

But maybe first he'd just do a quick Google search on a certain senior lifeguard...

"Holy shit!" Cody blinked at the laptop screen, the results

displaying a row of pictures at the top of the page with a ton of sites, including a Wiki page.

Leaning in, Cody stared at Liam wearing the distinctive sleeveless jersey and short-shorts of the AFL. He'd played for West Coast, the uniform a familiar blue and gold. When Cody and his family had moved to Perth, he'd studied Aussie rules footy to fit in at school. He'd happily hopped on the West Coast Eagles bandwagon and still had a hoodie in his closet.

But apparently Liam had played before Cody's time. He read the Wiki entry, his heart sinking at the description of Liam's knee injury. That explained the scars he'd noticed, and also the football tattoo on Liam's arm. God, it was brutal how young he'd been when his career had ended.

Liam had been *famous*. That explained the weird interaction on the beach Cody's first week when a couple had wanted a picture with Liam. Cody had assumed they were tourists, but now he realized they'd likely been fans.

He scrolled through the pics, almost drooling on the keyboard. Liam had been tall and powerful even as a teenager, all lean muscle and teeth gritted in determination. The short-shorts clung to his meaty ass, and *oh God, imagine fucking him.*

And maybe Cody should just get it done—jerk off thinking about Liam and get it out of his system. His boxers were already tented, and he almost tripped kicking them free during the several feet to the bed, not bothering to take off his shirt.

The lube was waiting in the bedside table, and he slicked his cock with a groan of relief, easing down his foreskin. The windows were all still shut in the studio, although he didn't care who heard as he moaned loudly, stroking himself hard and fast as he imagined a tumble of fantasies.

Kissing Liam and rubbing against that beard—sucking an undeniable mark on his throat—riding his cock and coming all over him—getting him on his hands and knees and pounding that incredible ass—making big, strong Liam scream and shake—taking Liam apart with his mouth and dick, sucking and fucking every way there was—

Legs splayed, Cody came all over his Captain America tee, gasping and shuddering, imagining Liam was there with him, that his undoubtedly massive cock was spurting too.

"Fuck me," he muttered. There. He'd gotten it out of his system and could scratch if off his virtual to-do list. No more fascination with Liam Fox. It was done.

From outside, Charlene barked, probably at the tall gate that separated Cody's patio from Mrs. Delfino's steep yard. Charlene would be eager for their usual run down to the beach.

Cody sprawled half-naked, a sticky mess, the fantasy images of Liam still filling his mind even though they should be gone. Vanished! Poof! Out of his system. Clearly he needed to add hooking up to his to-do list, because it had been too long.

As he stood, he grimaced down at his shirt. "Definitely need to do laundry." Charlene barked outside as if in agreement, and Cody pushed any lingering thoughts of Liam Fox firmly out of his head.

Chapter Five

"SWIMMERS, COME STRAIGHT back to shore!" Through the handheld megaphone, Cody did his best to sound authoritative. Standing by the water's edge, he cleared his throat and pressed the talk button. "We need you to move south and swim between the red and yellow flags."

"Doing great!" Baz called from where he sat in the buggy, a bare foot propped on the dash, cap pulled low over his sunnies. "You're not askin', you're tellin' them. Be forceful."

A big, bald man in his forties of Tongan descent, Baz seemed so laid-back that Cody couldn't imagine him getting very worked up. He'd been a big-wave surf champion, though, so he had to have some competitive fire.

The megaphone attached to the buggy's T-bar was currently broken, so Cody had to use a spare. Taking a deep breath, Cody shouted, "Come back to shore! Move down the beach and swim between the flags! The tide's going out, and there is a dangerous rip here."

The thirty or so people in the water splashed and laughed on the sandbank and ignored him utterly. He gritted his teeth. Having orders ignored was beyond frustrating.

"Come in to shore!" He took a deep breath and lowered his voice. He'd sounded a little too pleading, and it was time to show the beach-goers who was boss. "You can't swim here! Come in *now*."

He must have nailed the tone, because some people turned to look at him, puzzled. He motioned for them to come toward him. About ten people did, including a family. Cody directed them all up the beach toward the flags. The family were Asian—two adults who were presumably the parents of the two young children in fuchsia bathing suits. The parents shook their heads, brows furrowed.

They didn't seem to speak English, and Cody pointed to the big, yellow *DANGEROUS CURRENTS* sign planted into the sand near the buggy. Then he motioned to the water and made an X in front of his chest, forearms crossed. "No swimming here."

He pointed down the beach toward the red and yellow flags fluttering in the distance, then took a spare flag from his pocket, holding it up and pointing again. The flags were usually near the south end of the beach, but today there was a set toward the middle as well due to the crowd on the first truly hot Saturday of spring.

Fortunately, the mother seemed to get it, realization raising her eyebrows as she nodded. "Xièxiè."

"You're welcome." He waved as they walked off. Grinning now, pride and satisfaction flowing, he turned to Baz, who gave him a slow clap and called, "Only a couple dozen to go."

Cody jogged to the buggy to swig some water from his bottle, and Baz gave his shoulder a playful shove. "Good job, mate. Some days we tell the same people the same thing a hundred times, then have to go grab them out of the rip. It can really get to ya that they don't listen and ignore the signs. Wind ya up good. But try not to take it personally."

"I just don't understand why they don't listen." Cody wiped sweat from his brow. The morning grew hotter, the sun high overhead, beating down. His long-sleeved blue shirt was damp around the collar, but he wanted the sun protection and kept it on. "I know there's sometimes a language barrier, but if I were swimming in a foreign country and the lifeguards were shouting at me, I'd go to shore and see what they were saying. We could be telling them there's a shark heading straight for them."

Baz laughed. "At least the shark alarm clears people out quick smart." He shrugged, his Aussie drawl slow and strong. "Had a couple from Germany yesterday. Utterly clueless—could barely swim. They were climbin' the ladder, let me tell ya. Almost drowned each other after the current pulled them off the sand-bank. People come from landlocked countries and don't know a thing about the ocean, but they know they want to swim at Australia's number one beach. And now that Qantas has more direct flights from Europe to Perth, we're getting a taste of what the East Coast is used to."

"Of course, Barking was named number one because it wasn't crowded like the Sydney spots or the Gold Coast."

Baz smiled sardonically, watching the water. "There's the rub." He shrugged.

Cody gulped more water, his throat dry from all the shouting. "Yeah, I'm not used to this many tourists."

He watched a girl body surfing, making sure she seemed comfortable in the water. Even though the tide was going out, there wasn't a massive difference in the water level. In Vancouver, it could change by three meters or more, and one of Cody's earliest memories was of a trip to Cape Cod, and the fishing boats sitting stranded on the sand, the tide way, way out.

Here, the difference wasn't nearly as stark, which meant people could swim even at the lowest tide. But that didn't mean the rip currents were any less dangerous.

"Mmm."

Cody scanned the sand. "Any sign of that missing kid?" He and Baz had searched the north corner and come up empty.

"Not yet. He'll turn up."

"You're not worried he's drowned? Or been kidnapped?" It made Cody's stomach acidy to think of it.

"Well, yeah. Those are the first things that go through your mind every time. But it happens practically every day in the summer. You'll get used to it. If he was last seen in the water, it'd be more of a worry. No panic stations yet—the mum'll be handling that side of it. We need to stay calm and keep her calm. Still, he's seven, so on the young side. But we'll find him."

The walkie-talkie on the right seat beside Baz came to life. The buggies had the steering wheels on the left side since they were apparently made the same all over the world for whatever reason. Hazza's voice came over the radio. "No sign of him by third gate."

Cody shielded his eyes over his sunnies as he turned. The beach had four entrances, gaps in the low concrete wall that separated the sand from a walkway, the park, and then the bike path and parking lot beyond. They called the gaps "gates" and used them as landmarks to indicate their position. If they were told someone was drowning off second gate, they'd know where to look.

Baz and Cody were between third and fourth gate, the fourth close to the rocks, a spit of rough land that he'd heard called a "groyne," which jutted out at the end of the beach. There were dunes beyond it and then a few smaller beaches up the coast into Freo, including South Beach, near Cody's place.

Through the radio, Hazza said, "Let's hope he found the icy pole his mum said he'd been after earlier."

A memory struck Cody, wanting a Popsicle when he was little on some summer day back in BC, dashing across the street to an ice cream van, his mom hot on his heels. He missed her with a pang even though they'd just spoken.

Baz said to Cody, "Hazza's walking the beach, and Foxy's searching the park and boardwalk. If the kid doesn't turn up in ten minutes or so, we'll get the police onto it. Today's busy—weekends are good training for ya."

Chalkers was stationed in the tower, and his low voice came over the radio. "Foxy's just got him up by the cafe. All good. Hope he enjoyed the icy pole. Mum's absolutely spewin'. She's going to go off after she hugs the shit out of him."

They all chuckled, and Cody figured he meant the "extremely angry" definition of "spewing," not vomiting. Into the radio, Baz said, "Good on ya, Foxy."

The radio went quiet, and Cody's stomach did a little somersault as he remembered how hard he'd come that morning imagining Liam. Thank God no one could read his dirty, dirty mind. He scanned the water. "I should get back on the mega."

"Take a few minutes," Baz said. "Have to pace yourself or you'll lose your cool and start screaming at them to fucking listen for fuck's sake."

He snorted. "Good point."

"You're doing well, Chookie. You and Mia both."

Cody tried not to grin too hard. "Thanks." He'd personally rescued nineteen people his first week, three more than Mia. Not that it was a competition, except it totally was since the odds of two non-trainee positions being available next season was slim. Cody knew his tally was down to being in the right place at the right time to leap into action, but it still felt good to be ahead. He couldn't deny it.

"Foxy said you did really well with that after-hours spinal the other night."

"Yeah?" He cleared his throat, tamping down the surge of giddy excitement. "Cool."

"The surfer'll be fine?"

"Yeah, his wife came to get his board yesterday. Steve's in pain, but it's bruising, no fractures. He won't be catching waves for a while, but could have been a lot worse."

They watched the water, keeping an eye on a few teenagers who'd likely get lifted off the sandbank and pulled out when the Croc started snapping. Cody couldn't resist asking, as casually as humanly possible, "He's been a lifeguard a long time, huh?"

"Who?"

"Oh, sorry. I mean Liam." He shouldn't be poking around. What was the point? Liam Fox wasn't a mystery for him to unravel, and he was only distracting himself unnecessarily with a stupid crush. Yet he'd asked, and he waited eagerly for Baz's response.

"Yeah, he's been on the service a long time now. I've been here nine, so at least ten years, I reckon. After he blew out his knee, it took a couple years for him and the team to accept he'd never play again. He didn't know which way was up. Teddy was here seasonally and encouraged Foxy to join. They've both been full-timers for years now."

"Wow, that sucks about his knee." Cody already knew some of this but played dumb. "You wouldn't know it the way he runs. Did he have an accident?"

Baz glanced at him. "Oh, right, you wouldn't know. You were probably still back in Canada, hey? Liam was a big footy star."

"Oh!" Cody played along, feeling slightly guilty. "Wow."

"First-round draft pick, rookie of the year for the Eagles, the whole lot. He could have been one of the best the game has ever seen. Oh, he had the gift."

"Wow," Cody repeated softly. He could only imagine how devastating it must have been to lose that gift. He was struck by the urge to hug Liam, and not for sexual reasons.

"Barely twenty-two when he got tackled and landed the wrong way. It was a total fluke, but his leg bent back and another bloke crashed on top of him. Brutal. Multiple surgeries and tons of physio, but it was no use. I remember my old man was gutted. We all were. I didn't know Foxy at the time, of course, but he was famous—around here especially since he's a Mandurah boy. It was a heartbreaker. Especially for Foxy, obviously. Footy was his life. He had endorsements and all that. Models on his arm at red carpets. Still has fans wanting selfies. Don't think he likes the attention, though."

"Huh." Cody leaned against the buggy, automatically watching the water. "So he and Cyclone go back to before the service?"

"Oh yeah, he and Teddy are like brothers. Teddy and Foxy's older brother were mates at school, so they've known each other forever. Teddy wasn't the boss here yet, but he got Foxy's foot in the door. Not that Liam didn't have to pass all the tests you did."

"Right, totally. He's super fit."

Keep it casual. Just talking about Liam's body with another lifeguard. No big deal.

"Yeah, didn't grow up surfing like most of us on the service since he was too busy with footy, but he's a beast. Trains constantly. By the way, I saw you out there on your lunch break yesterday. Got a sweet barrel. Surf was pumpin'. You're good, especially for a bloke from Canada."

Cody flushed with pride. "Thanks. I love the water. Took lessons here at Barking for a few summers after we moved. There was always something about this place. The energy, I guess. South Beach is chill and beautiful, but I love it in a different way."

"Yeah, Barking's like that, hey? Something about it. Foxy never planned to stay so long, but he's one of the best on the service now. I've always looked up to him." He laughed. "Literally as well."

Cody chuckled. "Think about how I feel."

"Ah, Chook, maybe you'll still grow," Baz teased. "But you know, despite your nickname, you're strong for your size. You've got fire. Like a little Tasmanian devil. Maybe we should call you Tazzie."

"Could you? *Please?* It would be heaps better than Chook."

Baz laughed. "We'll see. It's hard to shake names once you got 'em. Besides—" He sat up straighter. "See that guy near the rocks? Did he just jump in? He wasn't there a second ago. He might end up out the back if he doesn't get smashed."

Tensing, Cody focused to his right. After a wave crested, he saw the head. "He definitely wasn't there before."

"Shit, he's going already. What the hell? What's he doing out there? Croc's not really pulling yet, but—yeah, hand's up. You're in."

Cody tossed his sunnies and yanked off his shirt, grabbing the thick rope handle on the side of the rescue board and running. Flying into the water, he stroked double-arm on his knees, then flattened out, paddling hard as adrenaline surged.

He punched over the waves, just two-footers, nothing big. Keeping his gaze locked on the man waving his arm for help, Cody went full out. The man must not have been able to swim much at all to be in trouble so fast when the rip wasn't pulling. Had he fallen off the rocks?

Didn't matter. Cody paddled as hard as he could, eyes locked on the outstretched hand. Closing in—twenty meters away. Ten, five, three—

Got him!

As Cody gripped the man's forearm, he simultaneously sat up, straddling the back of the board and hauling the patient sideways over it. He said, "I've got you, buddy. It's okay." The words were out of his mouth automatically as his brain processed what he was seeing a beat later.

What the actual fuck?

Tommy smiled up at him like he'd been conjured from the depths of hell because Cody and his parents had spoken his name that morning. His teeth were sparkling white, dimples activated, green eyes amused, his dark hair wet and dripping over his stupidly pretty face. He winked.

Tommy fucking *winked.*

He said, "Hey, sweets."

As if his hand burned, Cody whipped it away from Tommy's arm, struggling to understand the evidence in front of him. Yes, his ex was actually sprawled across his board, smiling at him like they were sharing a secret joke.

Cody sputtered, "What?"

"My hero! You rescued me." Under the water, Tommy slid his hand around Cody's shin and calf, caressing intimately.

Cody kicked, his skin crawling. It was like having a blue bottle's tentacles circling him. "*Don't.*" He tried to catch his breath, fury boiling through him. Tommy still touched him, and Cody reached down and tore his hand away. "Are you fucking kidding me?"

He knew Baz and Chalkers were definitely watching him, and whoever else happened to be in a tower. When a rescue was happening, especially an urgent one, everyone on duty was usually aware of it and monitoring. Was Liam watching? Nausea and rage battled, and Cody wanted to shove Tommy off the board and leave him there.

Keep your cool. Don't let him win.

Tommy blinked innocently. "What? Sweets, I needed help. It was just my luck you're on duty. My hero." He beamed, and Cody wondered how he'd ever, *ever* fallen for that smile and Tommy's shit. How he'd ever been in love with such a *dickhead.*

He wanted to shout that he knew Tommy was a damn good swimmer and the rip wasn't going off yet, and Tommy was so full of shit, and that *Tommy* had been the one to dump him and who the hell did he think he was showing up at Cody's new job and faking a rescue?

Instead, he gritted his teeth. "Get on the board." He looked behind them at a set coming in. "Hurry up or we'll get smashed into the rocks." The waves should break closer to shore, but the swells were rising.

Smiling coyly, Tommy pulled himself up and promptly put his head practically on Cody's lap, his long legs stretched out toward the front of the board. Cody shoved at his shoulder as he barked, "You know it's the other way!"

"Oh, sorry! I'm all confused." Tommy coughed weakly. "I think I breathed in some water. My head hurts."

Liar. Plus, instead of the boardies he'd always worn in the past, today Tommy wore skimpy little blue bathers, almost a Speedo but not quite, like the trunks Daniel Craig wore in *Casino Royale*. Major spank bank material for Cody as a teenager—which Tommy damn well knew.

Cody pushed and prodded until Tommy squirmed his way around to face the front. Then Tommy rolled the board with a loss of balance so forceful that Cody went in too, dunked under as a wave washed over them.

Gripping the board with his right hand, Cody surfaced and wiped water from his face. Tommy's legs wrapped around him, their crotches brushing.

Underwater, Cody pushed him away violently, hating to touch that lean, strong body that was still so familiar. "Get back on the board and cut the shit, or I swear to God, I'll leave you out here."

Tommy's eyes went wide with faux fear as he coughed weakly again. "But I'll drown, Mr. Lifeguard." He smirked for a moment before blinking innocently.

"This game isn't fun." Cody looked around, making sure no one else was in trouble nearby. The Croc would start biting any time now. Bigger swells were coming in, and he shoved Tommy onto the board on his belly, forced to get on behind him.

He paddled, his head practically in Tommy's ass. This was how they did rescues, stretching out between the patient's legs, and typically he didn't think about it. Having people's butts in your face was just part of the job. But with every stroke of his arms, his cheeks burned. Tommy wriggled his barely covered ass, inching backwards because he was the freaking worst.

Ignoring him, Cody paddled, glancing behind at the swells and judging the timing to get to shore. Looking forward again, he tried not to remember the times he'd been in a similar position, albeit with his face buried in Tommy's pert ass. The humiliation and fury burned his skin all the way down his chest.

When they reached the shallows, he twisted and dumped Tommy in the water. Picking up the board, he stalked past him, Tommy sitting and wiping his face. Tommy coughed dramatically, and Cody ignored him, heading for shore. Baz stood on the buggy's running board, watching, Hazza now beside him and watching as well, hands on hips. They had to know something was off.

Cody glanced back. Tommy was still sitting in the water as a wave rolled him. A few people around were eyeing him with concern and frowning at Cody. One woman motioned to Tommy, clearly puzzled and getting annoyed that Cody wasn't helping him up.

Biting back a growl, he went to crouch by Tommy, who'd been washed onto the sand now and sat up again. Cody hissed, "Enough!" He saw Hazza approaching. "This game is done."

Tommy glanced over at them. "Don't you want to introduce me, sweets?" Then his eyebrows shot up, genuine surprise creeping into his tone as he whispered, "Don't tell me *you're* not out?" The surprise morphed into a superior sneer. "Seriously? You're back in the closet like in year nine?"

"No! I'm out. Also, you were in the closet in year nine too." They'd both come out at sixteen, and sometimes Cody swore Tommy had done it just to be competitive. "It just—" He clenched his jaw, wanting to let loose a primal scream of frustration. "I have a strategy. Also, it's none of your damn business."

He had to acknowledge the tug of fear in his gut. What if the guys treated him differently? What if they didn't like him anymore? What if he didn't get the job next season? He wanted to think it wouldn't be an issue at all, but he couldn't know that for certain. It was a macho, competitive environment, and there was nothing wrong with getting to know people before coming out. He wasn't going to let Tommy guilt-trip him. Fuck that.

He stood and ordered, "Get up. *Now.*"

Tommy pretended to stagger up. "Really letting your bossy flag fly, huh?" He lowered his voice again. "It's pretty hot, actually."

After all the shit Tommy had given him when they were to-gether about being too bossy, the urge to punch him had Cody clenching his fists. He'd never punched anyone in his life, and he wasn't going to start now and lose his job.

"You right?" Hazza asked, and he was looking at Cody, not Tommy.

Cody forced a nod, his body so tense he felt like his neck was going to snap. "He's fine. He's leaving now."

Tommy coughed, his voice suddenly tremulous. "I swallowed a lot of water."

Oh, for fuck's sake. Cody pressed his lips together, exhaling noisily. "You're fine."

As he arrived, Baz was saying into the radio, "—going to find out." He eyed Tommy, then asked Cody, "There a problem?"

Cody knew Tommy was loving this, making him squirm. All right, the strategy was being altered. Defiantly, head held high, Cody answered. "He's my ex. He wasn't in trouble out there. He was one of the best swimmers at school. Second to me," he couldn't resist adding. "He's trying to get my attention for some reason I can't understand given we broke up ages ago."

Tommy played innocent, eyes wide. "I had no idea you'd be here. Codes, it's great to see you again, but..." He lifted his hands. "I'm not sure what happened out there. I'm having an off day, I guess." He coughed weakly.

"Uh-huh." Baz crossed his arms. "Well, you're on solid ground now, so move along. If you're feeling sick later, see a doctor."

"Maybe I can go up to the tower and lay down?" Tommy pressed a hand to his belly. "I don't feel so good."

"Your color's fine," Hazza said, stepping closer to Cody, shoulder-to-shoulder. "You've had your fun, and now it's time to leave us to our job. You may think it's a laugh to pretend to need help and get attention, but we don't think it's funny."

Tommy still played innocent. "Honestly, it was a coincidence." His gaze cut away to the side for an instant before he refocused, his hands up. "Okay, I'll go. No dramas."

Cody had followed Tommy's gaze, and there were several people watching avidly from up the beach, girls giggling behind their hands, guys laughing loudly.

To Tommy, Cody said, "Friends of yours?"

Tommy shrugged. "Yeah, uni mates. One of the chicks has a house down the block if you want to come party tonight." He winked. "If I'm feeling up to it. I might need you to nurse me."

"Hey, *mate*." Baz glared at Tommy, his chest puffed.

Aussies used that iconic word in a bunch of ways—friendly, affectionate, worried, perfunctory, comforting, grateful, for emphasis—and completely ironically. The bite in Baz's tone left no doubt as to his meaning.

Baz waited until he had Tommy's full attention, making him squirm in the silence before he went on. "Piss off. We've told you that if you're not feeling well later, you should go to the doctor. You're not showing any signs of water in your lungs. Our duty of care is complete. And if we see you rock up again and pretend to be in trouble? We're calling the cops, because that's being a public nuisance. While Cody was out there rescuing you unnecessarily, someone else could have drowned. We're telling ya to stop distracting us, because you're putting lives at risk. So get the fuck off the beach. Your ratbag friends too."

Tommy opened his mouth as if to argue, but then lifted his hands in surrender. "No need to be a prick. Just wanted to see how Cody was doing. Got in over my head in the current. It happens." He smiled, that sly lift of lips that used to make Cody's heart soar and now made his fists clench. How had he ever fallen for Tommy's shit? He was sick with shame.

"Talk soon, Codes," Tommy said with that smile. "I just won a fifty-dollar bet, so the least I can do is shout you a beer."

Cody turned his back and carried the rescue board to the buggy, Tommy's too-familiar laughter echoing on the breeze like rusty nails dragged down his spine. He picked up his uniform shirt, losing himself in it briefly as he pulled it over his head and flaming cheeks. He was afraid to turn around and see disgust on Baz and Hazza's faces. He hoped he wouldn't, but it was always a possibility, and—

A hand briefly squeezed the back of Cody's neck, and Baz asked, "Okay, mate?" No irony in his tone now, just concern, and Cody exhaled. Baz added, "You did a good job keeping your cool. I might have knocked his block off."

Cody turned, trying to laugh. "I was tempted, trust me. Sorry about all that."

"Nah, not your fault," Hazza said. "We do get people faking it sometimes, looking for attention. Had to get the coppers down last summer for a girl who kept acting up." He nodded at where Tommy and his friends were packing up. "Was he always such a wanker?"

Wishing the beach was quicksand, Cody said, "I think he was, but I was an idiot and didn't realize it for a stupidly long time."

Over the radio, Chalkers asked, "Everyone happy at north end?"

"Yeah, Central," Baz answered. "It's sorted. Some tosser pretending to be in trouble to impress his mates. Kicked them all off."

Chalkers replied, "Copy that. Bunch of arseholes."

Baz put the radio back on his seat in the buggy and ruffled a hand over Cody's damp head. "Don't worry about it, Chook. We've all got 'em. There's always at least one ex and no bloody idea what you were doing with them."

"For sure." Hazza gave Cody's shoulder a knock. "Don't sweat it." He scanned the water, eyes searching for trouble. "Mine's Nic. She's fit as hell, but fucking nuts."

Cody smiled tentatively, taking a deep breath. "Yeah, Tommy was hot, I guess, and I was in too deep before I realized he's a complete dick."

Baz asked Hazza, "Was Nic the one who wanted you to text her every half an hour? All day?"

"Yep. She said it was because she worried about me with my dangerous job, but when I said no, she went off about how I was flirting with other girls on the beach. Mental."

"Chicks." Baz shook his head. He glanced at Cody as he settled back into the buggy, feet up. "Suppose blokes can be just as bad."

Cody laughed. "Yeah." And shit, the relief was something else, soothing the jagged edges Tommy had left. The guys knew—two of them so far, at least—and they didn't seem to care a bit. Hopefully no one else would, and at least Cody would be out, for better or worse.

Tommy's sneering voice echoed, but Cody held his head high. He'd never *hidden* his sexuality with the lifeguards, and now he'd be out and proud. Tommy could most sincerely get stuffed.

Hazza said, "Hey, that kid who was missing this morning? He'd swiped five bucks from his mum's purse. He was determined to get that icy pole."

Baz laughed heartily. "Now he'll be lucky to get another one before he's a teenager." He nodded to the water. "Haz, you watching those heads? They're going to be out the back before we know it."

"Yep. A couple of us will have to go. They won't be able to get in with the Croc starting to pull. Chook, you're getting wet again any minute, I reckon."

"Good." Cody stripped off his shirt, ready to run and leave the past behind.

A COUPLE OF hours later, Cody and Baz took the buggy up to the tower for their short afternoon break and switched off with Chalkers and Hazza. Cody nuked half a leftover wrap in the microwave by the sink in the corner of the main viewing area. The electric kettle was boiling, switching off automatically.

Taking a bite of powdered donut as he plunked a teabag in a mug and filled it, Ronnie asked, "What happened earlier? I heard a bloke was getting aggro with you?"

"Looked like you were getting aggro with *him*," Liam said, eyes on the beach through the binos where he sat by the windows. He sounded disapproving, and Cody fidgeted. He hated the thought of Liam being disappointed in him.

Damo sat at the far end of the windows watching the water, one foot folded under him, spinning the chair a few inches this way and that. He glanced at Cody, clearly curious.

Aware of Baz watching him, apparently waiting to see what Cody chose to say, Cody cleared his throat. "Yeah, it got a bit tense. He's my ex, and he pretended to be in trouble so I'd rescue him."

"Complete wanker," Baz added after a few beats of silence. "Not Chook's fault at all. He did really well holding his temper. Bloke was a real piece of work."

Cody shot him a grateful smile as Ronnie's mouth dropped open. "He faked drowning to get your attention? Bloody hell!" He paused, ginger brows close as he seemed to process the implication. "Oh. So you're gay, then?"

"Yep." Cody's heart thumped, but he tried for an easy smile. "Hoping my taste in blokes will improve with age."

Damo laughed. "I was just going to say that I hope your boyfriend now is heaps better. Because that one's a tosser, eh?"

Relief flowed, sweet like warm honey. "I don't have one now, actually. Happily single." He glanced at Liam rigid by the window, and the relief soured.

Liam still looked through the binos, gripping them so hard his knuckles were white. He said nothing, not moving a muscle. Did he have an issue with Cody being gay? It was possible, and the thought was so disappointing that Cody's throat thickened for a horrible moment before he caught his breath, defiance returning.

It didn't matter what Liam Fox or anyone thought. He was out, and he was proud, and even if it cost him his dream job, he wasn't going to hide.

Please don't let it cost me my dream job.

The other lifeguards seemed totally cool with it, at least. Cody watched Liam from the corner of his eye, willing him to turn around and smile and say something about how Tommy was a douche.

Through another mouthful of donut, Ronnie asked, "You got something, Foxy?"

Flinching, Liam croaked, "No," and turned to stare at the north end, not lowering the binos or even glancing over. His shoulders were bunched, practically brushing his ears.

Damo and Ronnie shared a confused look. Then Damo shrugged and went back to the window, spinning his chair again—left, right, left, right. He held up the binos with one hand, the other toying with the ends of his long, blond curls.

Ronnie said to Cody, "You live up in South Freo, right? You ever hit that gym over on Hampton? You'd pick up easy as."

Liam stayed rigid and silent, binos to his eyes as Baz chimed in about another gym he knew that was apparently full of gay men. Cody nodded and smiled, grateful to them more than he could say. But he was aware with every heartbeat that Liam was still silent, a dark cloud looming in that corner of the tower.

Didn't matter, though. Cody had learned a long time ago he couldn't control what anyone thought of his sexuality. If Liam didn't like it, he could piss off. Right? Right.

Now Cody just had to repeat this mantra to himself about a thousand more times, hoping repetition would soothe the undeniable knot of *hurt* lodged in his chest.

Chapter Six

THE BIG OLD gum tree came into view as the street curved, familiar white bark and three trunks shooting up from the massive base. Liam supposed they were technically branches, but they'd been thick enough to climb for as long as he could remember.

The orange tile roof of the single-story house was the same as it had always been, although the new solar panels gleamed across one sloping side. Liam's dad had been reluctant to invest in what he'd always called "that hippie bullshit," but he liked the money it saved him on the power bill.

Greg and Cora's minivan took up more than half the driveway, so Liam parked his SUV by the curb. There was no footpath, and his mum's rock garden went right to the edge of the front yard. She'd grown up in leafy, lush Far North Queensland and had yearned for a proper lawn that Dad had declared a waste of time in Perth's dry environment. He was probably right, but Liam thought they should have at least tried like some of the neighbors. The parks managed to have grass somehow.

The white blinds were drawn in the front windows to keep out the sun's heat, and Liam found himself sitting there, listening to the engine tick down. Everyone would be out the back, so they wouldn't know he'd arrived, and he... Well, he didn't want to put on a smile yet. If it wasn't Jamie's birthday and he hadn't promised Cora, he'd have called with an excuse.

"He's my ex, and he pretended to be in trouble so I'd rescue him."

Liam had been replaying it over and over the past few hours, especially "my ex," those two words looping like a gif. *My ex.* The way Cody had said it—like it was nothing. Like he was talking about a chick and not a bloke. Announcing that he was gay like it was no big deal. Like it was normal.

Sitting there at the windows watching the middle set of flags, Liam had been frozen. Barely able to breathe, terrified that he would puke, or worse—*cry.* Terrified that he would be seen. Wanting it at the same time, reckless hope joining in the fear as he sat there listening to the boys talk about gay things with hardly any awkwardness.

There had also been a surge of jealousy that left him with bitter acid in his stomach that still bubbled. He lifted the lid on the center console storage under his left elbow and pulled out a roll of Quick-Eze, tearing the wrapper down to release a few round tablets. He chewed the chalky white pills.

Cody had come out to the boys, and he'd made it seem easy as. Like it was nothing. He'd *laughed* with them about picking up blokes at the gym, and the boys hadn't seemed bothered by it at all. And Liam had sat there, gutless like always, trying not to explode with the confusion of feelings, shocked to his core that the conversation had actually been happening. Jealous that it had seemed so simple.

Was this the difference in Cody that Liam hadn't been able to identify? Was it some instinct that had whispered: *You're like me!* Yet Cody was really nothing like him—he was *out* and braver than Liam could ever hope to be.

Yet maybe there was still some sameness—a bond or link or *something* that Liam had recognized in his bones. Why did any person ever feel a connection to another? Teddy had always insisted he'd known Jill was "the one" the minute he saw her on the dance floor at one of the bars in Claremont. Jill was pretty to be sure, but Teddy said it was more than that. Liam had never understood it, but maybe it was something like this.

He laughed harshly, the sound loud in the SUV, sweat already beading on his skin with the air con off. Obviously, the difference he'd felt with Cody was nothing like love at first sight. They barely knew each other, and Cody was too young, too small. Living in Australia, and a colleague on top of it.

Still, hope sang through him: *You're like me!*

He'd barely met any LGBTQ people in his whole life—at least that he'd known of. No one in school had been out, and in the AFL he sure as hell hadn't known anyone gay. Cora's cousin was a lesbian with a few adopted kids, and he'd met her at Greg and Cora's wedding and a summer barbecue once after that. They'd said hello and that was about it.

The cousin seemed accepted by Cora's family for the most part. Liam's dad had grumbled a few sneering comments, and Liam had kept his distance from the woman even though he'd wanted to pepper her and her wife with questions.

That was it. Well, aside from the men he'd had sex with in America and Europe. A few in Asia. But they weren't...*real.* Which was mental since Liam had had his dick inside them in some cases. But he'd avoided names, and they knew him as Matt123. Those men were almost like dreams he'd had, distant and foreign. Literally.

Cody was *real,* and he wasn't going anywhere. Liam shivered, electricity zipping through him that could have been fear or excitement. Or both.

"He's my ex, and he pretended to be in trouble so I'd rescue him."

Liam had seen the bloke through the binos and had known something was off with the rescue, the rhythms of it not right. The young man had been wearing ridiculously small bathers—

practically sluggos, as Liam's dad would call them. He was handsome and fit, and after Cody had told them he was his ex, Liam had pictured them kissing and fucking despite his best efforts, snapshots of cocks and moans and bare skin hijacking his mind.

The sweat beading on Liam's forehead dripped down his temple. He was breathing loudly, and his dick swelled. He'd seen the fire in Cody during the rescue, getting aggro with this Tommy, and he couldn't deny it'd turned him on. He rubbed himself through his jeans with the heel of his hand while Cody's lean muscles flexed in his mind, taking control of his ex, even though the guy was bigger...

"Run!"

Jolting, Liam almost slammed his head against the roof. He blinked in the rearview at the three kids playing cricket by the curb down the block, using garbage bins to mark off the pitch. An older boy encouraged a younger, telling him to keep running as a third boy retrieved the ball from across the road.

Christ, he was sitting in his car like a bloody perv, close to wanking while kids were right down the street. While he fantasized about a younger trainee who was a hundred percent against his rules. What was wrong with him? He laughed out loud.

"Everything, mate," he muttered. "Everything."

Liam popped a few more antacids before grabbing the wrapped box and beer from the back seat and walking up the driveway. He called out as he pushed the unlocked front door of the house open. "Hiya!"

He was proud of how normal he sounded. He was fine. Everything was fine.

No one answered, but he could hear the distant murmur of voices in the backyard. Shifting the case of Emu he'd brought for his dad, he closed the door behind him. His thongs flapped on the wood floor as he went down the hall, his eyes drawn to the dining room despite himself.

He stopped in the doorway on the left, the kitchen opening up to the right, the sliding doors to the yard on the other side past the round breakfast table. The formal dining table to his left sat eight, was carved of hard red Jarrah, and weighed a ton. Yet it fought for dominance with the display that took up the entirety of the far long wall.

The shrine, Greg called it. The framed picture in the center of Liam was the largest size the local mall's long-gone photo store had been able to print. In it, he ran down the footy pitch with the ball in the crook of his arm, opponents reaching for him, arms outstretched as he evaded them, thighs flexing and an intense scowl on his baby face.

His hair had been blonder and longer when he was nineteen, the swoop of it flying up and back from his forehead as he ran. His face had been clean-shaven, and he looked like a kid compared to the bearded man who greeted him in the mirror these days, wrinkles starting to fan out from the corners of his eyes.

Around the gold-framed picture was a custom-built wall unit with glass-fronted cabinets on either side of the photo. Instead of the fancy china dishes most people would keep in their dining room, countless trophies gleamed. Medals, citations, a picture of Liam shaking hands with the old prime minister. More framed photos—team pictures going back to when he could barely run without tripping, when footy was just for fun.

Fun. Another boy living another life.

"Liam?" Mum called. "That you?" Leanne appeared in the kitchen doorway, her smile tightening momentarily as she saw where he was standing, surely knowing what he was looking at.

"You should really take down the shrine one of these days," he said.

She scoffed. "And break your father's heart? Nonsense. You know how proud he is of you. We all are. Now come here and give your mother a kiss."

He did, choking down what he wanted to say, that perhaps his parents could find something else in the past twelve years of his life to be proud of. Dad probably would tell him not to be a bloody galah, and maybe Liam *was* being foolish, but he hated that damn shrine.

Well, mostly.

He couldn't deny the tug of pride—old and familiar like the house, weathered and faded but still part of him. Looking at the shrine, Liam could almost pretend he was that boy, that young man with the whole world in his hands as he raced down the pitch.

Almost.

His mum tucked a bleached-blond curl behind her ear, not a single gray in sight, sparkly multicolor earrings dangling. In her sixties now, she still wore her hair big, almost like it was the eighties. They'd always teased it was because it made her taller, and Liam bent now to hug her properly after depositing the beer and gift on the counter. She smelled like roses and her famous garlic-soy-lime chicken marinade, and her bright sundress slipped off one tanned shoulder.

"Aren't you a sight for sore eyes!" She hugged him tightly, up on her tiptoes, then slapped his arm lightly. "Didn't you get my messages? Would it kill you to call your mother?"

The guilt that constantly simmered in his gut boiled up. "Sorry. It's been busy at the beach with this warm spring."

"I know you're busy, love." She rubbed his arm where she'd slapped it, letting him off the hook like always. "All right, go on with you. Have a beer with your father while I finish up the salads." Sliced and diced veggies crowded chopping boards on the counter.

"Do you want a hand?"

She scoffed. "Since when have you boys lifted a bloody finger in the kitchen?" She made a shooing motion.

Picking up the gift for Jamie, Liam headed into the yard. The spacious patio had a tin roof for shade, a built-in barbecue taking up the right side. Dad was in his usual spot in his deluxe outdoor armchair in the corner by the barbie, complete with footrest, drinking an Emu from the same faded red stubby holder he'd used for decades, wearing shorts, a short-sleeved plaid shirt, and an Eagles cap. Liam could swear his dad had worn this same outfit his whole life.

There was a table and chairs, with extra folding chairs dotting the space, people scattered around. Beyond the patio was the kidney-shaped pool, Jamie and his little cousins splashing around in it the way Greg and Liam used to. Mum's frangipani were coming into bloom along the fence with white and pink flowers.

"Hi, Dad."

His father's craggy face brightened, and he quickly levered himself up with a grunt, almost toppling over in his rush. Liam strode forward. "Whoa. Had too many already?" he half-joked, grabbing his father's arm, which felt too small.

"Ah, bugger off." Stu shook his arm free, then extended his callused hand, his fingers perpetually stained with nicotine. "G'day, son. Good to see you."

Liam clasped his palm. "Yeah. You too." Stuart Fox had never been a big man, but his shoulders seemed to stoop a bit more each time Liam saw him, which, granted, was only every month or two.

Stu's voice had always been deep and raspy. "Did you watch the game?"

He hadn't, but he'd remembered to check a recap video online. "Yeah, what a goal from Woodbridge! He's bound to be rookie of the year."

Stu grunted. "You were better than him, but he's got speed."

As his dad pressed a beer into his hand and continued talking about footy, Liam nodded and made the right noises. He *could* watch games nowadays, unlike in the years following his accident. It wasn't torture now, although he didn't typically seek out the matches.

There were still a couple of players he knew on the Eagles, although he hadn't spoken to them in years. His teammates had texted and visited for months after the injury, telling him they knew he'd play again, that they couldn't wait to have him back on the field.

But after another surgery, and then another, Liam had known it was useless. He stopped responding to their messages and got Mum to turn them away if they made the trip down to Mandurah. Liam had bought his own condo by Elizabeth Quay in Perth, but he'd spent endless months back in his childhood room being nursed by Mum, Dad lurking in the doorway, saying less and less as time went on and the parade of physiotherapists and experts eventually petered out.

"I think Freo's got a better chance this season than the Eagles. What do ya reckon?" Stu asked.

"Yeah, the Dockers are looking good," Liam agreed. He assumed they were, anyway.

"Yeah." Stu gulped his beer and they stood in silence a few moments before he said, "Been a good spring."

"It has." Liam nodded. "Yeah." As more silence stretched out, he added, "We've had some properly busy days at the beach. About fifteen thousand this arvo."

"That many?" Stu drained his bottle.

"Yeah, decent spring. Hopefully a nice hot summer's coming. Mum's frangipani are looking good," he said, breathing a sigh of relief as Cora approached with a grin.

"Look who it is!" She kissed his cheek and took Jamie's present to add to a pile on a folding table. She was small and blond and curvy—not unlike Mum, which Liam had ribbed Greg about.

"Hey, Cors. How ya goin'?"

"Can't complain. Good to see you." She glanced at Stu, who'd moved away to fire up the grill. She smiled again at Liam, although it was tighter now.

Liam lowered his voice. "You right?"

She rolled her eyes and muttered, "You missed a rant about Australia's biggest problem these days. Spoiler alert: it's immigrants."

He sighed. "Usually is. Look, there's no point in arguing with him. He's not going to change now."

Cora pressed her lips together. "That certainly seems to be the prevailing wisdom."

Greg appeared to give Liam a back-slapping hug and handshake. "Glad you could make it for once." They were about the same height, Greg fit as well, his short hair darker.

"He's real busy up there," Stu said.

"We know, Dad," Greg answered. "We're busy too, for the record."

Cora seemed about to say something, but then smiled. "Jamie's been talking about seeing you all week. He's almost more excited about you than the pressies. Almost." She winked as she called, "Jamie! Look who's here!"

A scream of joy rang out, and Jamie sprang out of the pool, rushing over to give Liam a sopping hug. Liam scooped him up, groaning loudly. "You're getting too big! Who said you could get this big?" Giggling, Jamie hung on, his little arms around Liam's neck. Liam's heart swelled. He really should try to see the kids more. Jamie was growing so fast.

He kissed his nephew's head, tasting chlorine and not caring. "Happy birthday, matey."

"I'm five now!"

"*Five?*" He lowered him to his feet. "Are you sure this is allowed?"

Jamie nodded. "Did you bring me a present?"

"James Stuart Fox!" Cora narrowed her eyes. "You'll be lucky to get any gifts if I hear that kind of cheek again."

Liam crouched and whispered loudly, "You've always gotta make sure your mum's out of earshot when you're being cheeky."

"Not what I meant, Uncle Liam!" She laughed.

"Will you play with us?" Jamie asked him. "*Please?*" He turned to Greg. "You too?"

"How can we say no to that?" Greg said.

Liam greeted his aunt and uncle and a few cousins, along with Cora's parents and sister and assorted family members. He was both relieved and disappointed Cora's cousin and her wife weren't there. This was the family party for Jamie, and Liam was relieved his little friends and their parents weren't present as well. At least he already knew everyone.

He and Greg changed into their togs, and soon they splashed around the pool playing Marco Polo with Jamie and his handful of cousins. Teddy and Jill arrived, and Teddy soon hopped in with his daughter, Chloe. She was four and had a shriek that could wake the dead, but was the cutest thing with her mop of dark curls.

With three grown men, there were really too many people in the pool to properly play, but they still had fun thrashing about, taking turns being it, lunging with outstretched hands or diving out of the way. When Liam caught Jamie once, he ducked down and put him on his shoulders, standing up with Jamie's little fingers clutching his hair, his delighted laughter ringing out.

The sun was dipping under the roofs, the smell of sizzling meat filling the air when Mum called that it was time to dry off. For a moment, Liam could have been right back in his childhood, the years vanishing with a powerful sense of déjà-vu.

He'd tried to buy his parents a new house after he'd gotten his signing bonus from the Eagles, but they'd been determined to stay put. Aside from the shrine, nothing had really changed. Dad still worked as a brickie, and Mum had her volunteer work and activities with her ladies when she wasn't helping Cora with Jamie and the baby.

Pulling himself out of the pool, Liam was struck with a wave of sadness. This was well and truly his home, yet he'd visited less and less. He'd kept his secret for decades now, and as wonderfully familiar as it all was, he was always on guard here. Waiting to get pulled off the sandbank with no warning.

Greg nudged him on his way past. "You right?"

"Uh-huh." He put on a smile as always, reaching for a faded old beach towel and escaping inside to get dressed. His old room was still as he'd left it, but he avoided it and changed in the bathroom. He flipped on the fan, the low hum blocking out any sounds from the house, cocooning himself for a few minutes. Recharging.

As he dried off, his thoughts returned to Cody, and he rubbed at the goosebumps that spread over his arms. Nothing could ever happen between them—nothing *would*. Earlier lapse aside, Liam was not going to think about Cody that way again, or imagine Cody and his tosser ex and those ridiculously small togs.

He took a deep breath, the decision made, his mind clearing. As he'd told Damo, it was all down to discipline. Giving himself a nod in the mirror, he rejoined the party.

The first round of burgers and chicken were being passed around on paper plates when the Holbrooks from down the street arrived with apologies, another case of Emu, a wrapped gift, and a tray of caramel slices Mum popped in the fridge.

Beside Liam at the condiments table, Cora sighed and murmured, "Sorry. I told them not to."

It took Liam a second to understand. Then he focused on the young woman trailing Mr. and Mrs. Holbrook. His heart sank. "Is that... Shit, I can't remember her name."

"Sandra," Cora whispered. "She's twenty-seven and single, and your mums think you two would just be perfect together."

He groaned, squirting too much tomato sauce on his burger. He vaguely remembered Sandy Holbrook as a knobby-kneed girl. She was a very pretty woman, slim and curly haired and with a bright smile, but Liam cringed. "This is supposed to be Jamie's day."

Cora snorted. "Your parents want you to settle down three hundred and sixty-five days a year, let me tell you. You're hardly ever around. It's me and Greg who have to listen to them bang on about it." Her tone lightened. "Although… She does seem lovely. I met her on New Year's last year. Quite smart—a pediatric nurse. So she's caring as well. You could do worse." She slapped the top of the bun on her burger and took a bite. Through the mouthful, she added, "And that's all I'll say, I promise."

"Thanks, Cors. I think the baby's crying."

Cora took another bite and made a zipping motion across her mouth. Greg, Teddy, and Jill sat on chairs by the edge of the patio and pool deck, Jill with Chloe on her lap, cajoling her to eat. Liam quickly squeezed in beside them with another chair, putting his back to the Holbrooks. There were about twenty people around, so it was crowded enough that Liam wasn't being rude by not saying hello.

Jill pushed her glossy, black hair over her shoulder as she struggled to keep Chloe still, sighing heavily at Teddy. "A hand, please?"

Teddy picked up a forkful of potato salad. "Come on, love. Hold still."

"She's the one who should be called 'Cyclone,' huh?" Greg said with a laugh.

Jiggling baby Amelia, Cora joined them and sat, balancing her plate on one knee. Jamie and his cousins ate in a cluster by the gift table. For the moment, no one approached Liam to force an introduction with Sandra.

He'd just exhaled and had a bite of his burger, juice dripping down his chin, when Teddy said, "Heard there was some drama today."

After swallowing, Liam concentrated on breathing calmly. He somehow hadn't expected Teddy to bring it up. He shrugged and took a swig of beer, wetting his dry throat. "Just some d—" He glanced at Chloe on Jill's lap. "Jerk."

Cora asked eagerly, "What happened?"

When Liam only shrugged again, praying his dad was too occupied with the nearby barbie to pay attention, Teddy answered, "Ex-boyfriend of one of the trainees pretended to drown."

Cora gasped. "Seriously? What a tosser. Hope she kicked his arse."

Jill said, "It was Cody's ex, not Mia's." To Liam, she added, "I bet Cody was frothin', hey?"

Liam shrugged again, draining his beer and gripping the foam stubby holder. Teddy laughed and said, "Oh, I bet he went off. Wish I'd been there to see it."

Cora huffed. "Should get the coppers onto that ex if he tries it again. Faking drowning should be a bloody crime. Don't you think?" she asked Greg.

Greg's gaze was on his plate as he took a forkful of coleslaw. "Sure."

"You're telling me." Teddy shook his head. "Cody handled it well, Baz said. He and Mia are tough ones. Lucked out with the trainees this year, I reckon." He grinned and pressed a hand to his chest. "Or I should say the boss chose well."

Teddy didn't seem to have an issue at all with Cody being gay, and Liam sighed in relief. He'd never thought Teddy of all people was homophobic, but had always been too terrified to even hint at the subject. A tentative little ray of hope shone deep inside him. Maybe at some point—

"Bad enough with the birds. You're letting faggots in the service now?"

There it was—the sledgehammer to the chest from his father. Liam had known it would come in one form or another, swung so casually but with deadly aim. His burger felt lodged in his esophagus, his lungs frozen, any ray of light ground into the dirt. His father worked the barbecue, gulping his beer.

"Aw, come on now, Stu," Teddy said, cajoling but firm. "You know we don't discriminate."

Liam's father grunted, flipping a burger as grease sizzled. Barely moving his head, Liam stole a peek at his mother sitting nearby. Her expression was completely unchanged and placid, as if they were talking about the weather. She took a dainty bite of chicken, cutting it with her knife and fork.

"You don't have any fags at the firehouse, do you?" Dad asked Greg.

"Don't think so," Greg answered, still focused on his food.

Cora smiled thinly. "I really wish you wouldn't use that kind of language. The children—"

"Oi! This is my house, girly." Stu adjusted the heat and threw on a pile of steaks. "I'll say whatever I bloody want."

Cora pressed her lips together, jiggling the baby and giving Greg a pointed look that he ignored. Liam's mum said to her sister, "Oh, Lisa! This mango salad is delicious! Is it a new recipe? Everyone, you must try the mango salad!"

Baby Amelia was fussing, and Cora got up without a word, Jill following her into the house with Chloe. Greg ate on, and Liam stared at his plate, pushing potato salad around with his fork. Mum went around dishing out mango salad, insisting that everyone try a little.

"*No fucking son of mine is going to turn out a faggot.*"

Liam's mouth was dry, and he couldn't take another bite.

"How are things at the station?" Teddy asked Greg eventually.

"Yeah, good." Greg glanced at Liam now. "They're hiring

again soon. Not too late."

"Aw, now you're gonna poach my best lifeguard with me sitting right here?" Teddy joked. "Come on, mate."

Greg laughed, but there was a serious edge to his voice. "You'd be closer to home, Liam. Mum and Dad aren't getting any younger."

Liam tried to laugh it off. "Barking's not exactly days away. It's forty-five minutes unless the traffic's crap." Close enough to Mandurah, but far enough as well. "Things are good at the beach. Besides, you don't really want your little brother working with ya."

Greg shrugged. "Not really, but I promised them I'd have a word." *Them* clearly being their parents.

It shouldn't have, but it stung. Liam had idolized his brother growing up, but once he'd become a star, their relationship had never quite been the same. Liam forced a cheery tone. "Well, you've done your duty."

"As usual," Greg muttered.

"What?" Liam asked, clenching his jaw.

Teddy cleared his throat in the silence, but before he could say anything, Mum appeared with an arm around poor Sandra Holbrook, and as much as he loved his nephew, Liam wished he were anywhere else.

Chapter Seven

STANDING BY HIS rescue board, Cody scanned the hordes of swimmers between the flags. Kids screeched and splashed, playing in the shallows, people of all ages body surfing the small swells that crashed on the shore break. Laughter rang in the warm air. Farther out, people swam, bobbing up and down as the waves rolled past.

Another set came in, the waves closer, and a dozen people were dumped on the shore break, most laughing as they surfaced, some sprawled out in the shallows. Cody focused on a balding Asian man in green boardies, facedown as the water washed over him.

Cody's heart skipped.

He was already moving, jogging around a sandcastle as the man rolled onto his back and *screamed*. Cody raced the last several meters, splashing into the water. Kids stood frozen, staring down at the man. Cody's knees sank into the sand, water swirling around.

"It's all right, mate." He grasped the patient's left shoulder— the right one very clearly dislocated, the bone bulging unnaturally to the side. "We're going to help you."

He glanced around at the growing crowd of onlookers. There was no *we* at the moment, there was only Cody. The man was writhing, splashing as he kicked, and Cody had to get him onto dry land. He pulled his radio off his bum bag, realizing he'd almost dunked it.

"Cody to Central."

"Go ahead, Chookie."

"I've got a man with a dislocated shoulder between the south flags by second gate. He's in a lot of pain. Going to need assistance and an ambo."

"Copy that. Central to Baz and Mark, can you boys get down there to help Chook with this dislocation?"

As the radio chatter continued, Cody asked the patient, "Did you hit your head at all? Do you have any pain in your neck?"

Panting, his teeth bared, the man gasped, "No. The wave just rammed my shoulder into the sand." He spoke with a flat accent that sounded American.

The lifeguard in the tower, Tony, asked, "Chook, is it a suspected spinal?"

"Patient says no, he just jammed his shoulder when he got dumped in the shore break."

"Copy. How old is he? Calling the ambo now."

Cody got the basics from the patient, then helped him to his feet with the help of another bloke nearby. The clump of onlookers shifted out of the way as Cody barked at them to move. With Mia on the back, Mark and Baz rocked up in an ATV, narrowly avoiding the sandcastle.

Mark—not Maz or Marko, Cody had noted, was probably near forty, and his dark hair was silver at the temples, his skin on the pale side. He had a quiet air about him that perhaps didn't lend to a nickname. Several tattoos were inked on his arms and chest, with an undulating wave over his ribs.

"Step back!" Baz shouted. He helped Cody settle the patient on the back of the buggy. "John, is it?" Baz asked the patient.

John nodded, wincing and biting back a cry.

"All right, matey," Baz said. "We've got some pain relief for you. You'll be sweet, trust me." To Mia and Cody, he said, "You guys seen the green whistle yet? You know what it is?" He opened a thin box and tipped out a green plastic tube that looked like a kid's cheap musical instrument crossed with a magic marker.

Mia looked like she was about to shoot up her hand like Hermione Granger in potions class. "It's methoxyflurane, an analgesic gas that provides pain relief. Orally administered. If it is administered, an ambo must be called. Trainees can't give it to a patient—only a fully certified lifeguard can."

"Correct, as usual." Baz glanced at Cody. "Anything to add?"

"Well, you get the patient to suck it." Heat flooded his face. "I mean, not *suck* it, not like… What I mean is, they put it in their mouth and breathe in the gas."

Baz smirked as he poured a little vial of the drug into the tube. "That's right. Johnno, you're going to suck on the green whistle and you'll be laughin' in no time." He put the plastic tube into John's good hand, urging it to his lips. "It'll taste a bit funny at first, but keep the whistle in your mouth and breathe in and out. That's it. Nice, long breaths."

Mark mimed inhaling deeply. "Just like that."

John grimaced. "Christ, it hurts." He craned his neck, looking at his misshapen shoulder.

"No, no, don't look," Baz said. "You'll be right. Hopefully the ambos can pop it back in. We've seen many a grown man cry with dislocations." He asked Mark, "Whaddya think?"

Mark had been quietly examining John's shoulder. He said to him, "I'm actually a full-time paramedic. The green whistle should kick in any minute, and then we'll get you to the tower. I don't want to try putting it back in until you've sucked on the whistle a bit longer."

"Mmm. Okay," John said. He laughed. "Wow. This is good shit."

"Yep. You'll be off your head in no time," Mark assured him with a little smile.

"Nah, I'm good. Like a bird in the sky." John's laugh was high-pitched. "If I was a bird, I'd probably be a fat seagull fighting over fries." He inhaled the gas. "No, I'd be an eagle. From California. Or maybe a grizzly bear. Grr!"

"Dad? Oh my *gawd*." A teenage girl appeared. "We've been looking for you! What happened?" Her gaze fell on his shoulder, and she gasped. "What did you do?!"

"I soared like a bear!" John exclaimed.

The girl screwed up her face. "Huh? Dad, are you stoned? Oh my *gawd*!"

Then they were comforting her as well as her injured father, but Baz and Mark kept it all calm and cool. They drove John to the base of the tower, going at walking speed in the buggy so he wasn't jostled, his wife and children crowding around. The ambo came, and Cody was sent back to his post.

After ten minutes, he asked on his walkie, "Central, did Mark or the ambos get John's shoulder back in?"

"Not yet. Focus on the water, Chook. It's out of your hands. He's not your concern anymore."

"Right. I am!" He released the button, feeling like an idiot.

Some time later, Baz stopped by in the buggy. "Just wanted to let you know the ambos did get John's shoulder in before they took him to hospital. Poor bugger. I dislocated my knee once, and the pain was unreal."

"Oh, cool. I mean about John, not your knee."

Baz chuckled, running a hand over his bald head. "Yeah, I know. And it's all right to care. We all do. If we didn't care, we'd be shit at the job, hey? Tony wasn't trying to be a dick on the radio. You just can't get distracted. When you're switched off and worrying about another thing, you could miss something in the water. But you're doing a great job."

Cody exhaled. "Yeah?"

"Yep. You and Mia are both on the ball. Keep it up." He put the buggy in drive and zoomed off.

Later, Cody was perched on the counter by the windows finishing his peri-peri chicken wrap when Mia came out of the little locker room in the back of the tower and hopped up the three steps to the main area.

"So I hear you like cock," Mia said casually, pulling down the sleeves of her blue uniform shirt, which skimmed her hips, her bathing suit barely peeking out.

A stunned silence filled the tower, Bickie and Ronnie in their office chairs by the window turning to Cody. Waiting. Cody's pulse raced, but he played it cool. "Where'd you hear that?"

She jerked her thumb toward the locker room. "Written on the toilet wall."

He sighed with faux relief. "Oh, good. They keep painting over it in the public stalls. I'm running out of Sharpies."

After a beat of silence, roaring laughter erupted, Bickie and Ronnie howling, heads back. Mia smiled, looking rather pleased, and Cody laughed too, exhaling.

On the radio, Hazza said, "Hey, can I get a hand at third gate? Group of school kids from South Korea. I need to move them down to the flags. They can't swim a stroke and there's dozens of them."

Bickie nodded to Cody and Mia. "Get on it, you two. Orange ATV's still in the shop, so you'll have to hoof it."

Cody followed Mia outside and down the stairs to the sand. They took up a light jog, weaving through the growing crowd. He could see Mia glancing at him sideways and gave her a smile.

She spoke quickly, the words tumbling out. "Hey, you know I was just kidding, right? I have no problem at all with you being gay. I think it's awesome."

"No, I know." It was still nice to hear, he had to admit. "I have to say it was unexpected. What you said."

"Right. I was just trying to... I don't know. I thought it might be funny?"

"It definitely was. All the more so because it was the last thing I expected you to say."

"Yeah? It was funny?" Her ponytail swayed, eyes hopeful under the brim of her cap. "Cool. I'm not always great with jokes."

"Well, you went balls to the wall with that one. Go big or go home, right? I get it. It's nerve-racking, trying to fit in."

She made a graceful leap over a stray beach bag. "You're telling me. No one's burped the alphabet yet, but it's coming. They're such...*blokes*. All their teasing and nicknames."

He winced. "I wish they'd pick another one for me."

"Hey, at least you have a nickname."

"Yeah, but it's terrible."

"They only give them to people they like. They like you."

He realized it was true. "But that doesn't mean they don't like you! Honestly, they're probably afraid to offend."

She sighed. "Yeah, probably. That's why I decided to try and fit in better. But I'm glad they've been cool about your sexuality. Pleasantly surprised, tbh."

"Me too. So many of the guys grew up around here, and they're tight. It would really suck if they were homophobes. I guess some still could be, but no one's acted like it." His stomach twisted, his feet digging into the hot sand as they jogged, his breath coming shorter. "Well, Liam seemed...not thrilled. But it is what it is."

And what it was, was crappy, no matter how many times—probably in the thousands—he'd repeated that mantra. *It is what it is. It is what it is.* Of all the people to have an issue with it, it had to be the guy he had a lingering crush on despite best efforts to the contrary.

"Dude, come on." Mia veered closer to the water on their

diagonal run across the beach around sunbathers and families under multicolored umbrellas. "My money's on closet case."

"What?" Cody stumbled, nearly tripping over a sleeping topless woman sunning her back on a bright beach blanket. The smell of coconut lotion filled the air. "I...what? Seriously?"

"It's textbook. Never had a serious girlfriend, right? The boys make noise about how he loves them and leaves them, and 'oh he's such a ladies' man and a heartbreaker.' Uh-huh. I bet he likes cock just as much as you do." She raised her hands. "I mean, I could be wrong. But my gut says he's playing for your team. My gut's usually on the money."

Cody's head spun, stupid excitement zinging through him like a pinball. "But he's worked here a decade. Wouldn't the other guys have figured it out?"

"Possibly, but he was a big footy star. It probably hasn't occurred to most of them that he would be anything but straight and banging hot chicks. You know how ridiculously macho the AFL is. Sure, the league has made noises about being inclusive, but there still aren't any out players. With Foxy, there's something I can't put my finger on about him. Like there's an uneasiness there—some kind of tension. You know what I mean?"

"Yes! I know exactly what you mean! But I never thought..."

"Another reason I think he's a closet case? He could barely take his eyes off you last night while you and Ronnie were on pack-up."

"*What?*" Cody did trip this time, right over his own feet, almost hitting the wet sand on the water's edge.

Mia tugged his arm and helped him up. "I'm telling you, he was *really* interested in you and Ronnie loading up rescue boards on the trailer. You were pulling up the flags, and he was riveted. I volunteered to clean out that revolting fridge, and he didn't realize I was watching him watch you. Through the binos. Mate, no one watches pack-up through binos. I thought he must've seen something in the water, and I came up behind him to take a look, but there was nothing. And when he realized I was there, he went beet red and started filling out the time sheet."

"Are you messing with me?" His heart thumped, belly doing somersaults. The thought of Liam Fox watching him was incredibly hot. "I know you're trying to fit in with the guys, but if this is a prank…"

She shook her head, not smiling anymore. "No. That would be a real dick move. I'm serious. Foxy's got his eye on you."

They were almost there, the gaggle of schoolchildren splashing around and shrieking, safe for the moment on a sandbank. Cody slowed to a walk, Mia following suit.

Mind spinning, Cody said, "Or maybe it's because he's a homophobe, and he's heaps grossed out, but he can't look away. Like those shows on TV with operations. Or Dr. Pimple Popper."

"It's possible." She frowned. "But I dunno. He seems like a good guy. Just wound pretty tight."

Cody gave her a teasing nudge with his elbow. "You'd know a little something about that. I think this is the most I've heard you say in a row, well, ever. That is when you're not answering a question and quoting the lifeguard manual."

She grimaced. "I've been so afraid of stuffing up I've barely talked. I told myself I was going to work on being more personable. Try a few jokes."

He could just imagine she'd set SMART goals and had a dry erase board in her living room detailing her plan of attack. "Operation: More Personable is a ripper so far." He held out his fist, and she bumped it with a grin. "Hey, some of the boys train at the outdoor gym here at sunrise. You want to go with me one morning?"

"Yeah, that would be cool."

"Awesome. It's a completely platonic date. I'll just have to break it to Charlene that I can't take her for our usual morning swim."

"Also a completely platonic date?"

"Definitely. I'm kinky, but beastiality's a bit outside my wheelhouse. Golden doodles aren't my type."

Mia laughed. "Noted. And thanks."

They got to work, wading into the water and shepherding out the school kids, trying to explain to the handful of teachers that it was safer to swim between the flags, especially with the tide turning and rips coming up. It was like herding cats, but Cody couldn't stop smiling to himself.

Liam Fox can't take his eyes off me.

Chapter Eight

A WAIL ECHOED from the beach, and Liam groaned. "Here we go."

"Chook, you're up. You'll have more patience than we will," Baz said, looking through the binos. "Yeah, I can see the blueys washing into shore from here. Heaps of 'em."

"For real?" Cody asked dubiously.

Liam had to laugh. "For real." The boys had apparently sent Cody out the rainy day before to search for a "porpupus," which they'd told him was a rare Australian animal like a platypus crossed with a porpoise, and an injured one had been spotted in the water. He'd circled on the Jet Ski for two hours, thoroughly searching while everyone else stayed warm and dry in the tower, laughing their arses off.

If Liam had been there, he might have called an end to it sooner. He said to Cody, "You know blueys are the real deal."

Nodding, Cody lifted his arms, pulling one wrist and stretching his side, then the other. His uniform shirt rode up, boardies low on his hips. A hint of surprisingly dark hair fanned over his belly, trailing down... Liam caught himself staring and fumbled to pick up the binos. Sweat dampened his shirt under his arms.

Cody opened the door, admitting the wailing boy and his panicked parents. Watching the water, Liam could hear Cody patiently explain to them that it was a bluebottle sting—yes, like a jellyfish—and everything would be okay, and the pain would fade.

Glancing over, Liam saw Cody spray the red welts on the boy's chest with antiseptic spray and tell the parents he'd make an ice pack, and that if they took the boy to the showers by the cafe that might help too. There were tons of conflicting opinions on the best treatment, and really the only thing was to wait.

As Cody put ice in a plastic bag, he glanced over and saw Liam watching him. Liam had to stop himself from whirling around guiltily. Instead, he gave Cody a thumbs-up, as if he'd only been watching to make sure Cody did everything right. He turned back to the windows, cursing himself.

He was the one acting like a bloody fan, and like Cody was some magical unicorn he could hardly believe was right in front of him. Liam internally rolled his eyes at himself.

Yes, Cody was a real live gay man, and he was a lifeguard too. It wasn't a big deal, and it was stupid for Liam to be so fascinated by him. Yet he found himself hanging on Cody's every word, drawn to him with a strange curiosity.

Liam's rules were still firmly in place, but perhaps he and Cody could just...talk sometime. Not about Liam's secret, obviously, but there was nothing stopping them from being friends, was there? No, definitely not. And if Liam was curious about what Cody's life was like, that was fine. It wasn't breaking the rules to find out more about him.

The rules were about sex, and they were *not* going to hook up. If Liam happened to be at South Beach one morning when Cody was there with his landlord's dog, they could go for a coffee. Nothing wrong with that. Mates went for coffee.

The stung boy's wailing continued, and soon he was joined by a parade of children and adults who'd ignored the big yellow warning signs they'd dug into the sand. When the wind came in from the open ocean at a fast enough clip, inevitably the bluebottles invaded, drifting on the current. Thousands of them could fill the water, their long, barbed tentacles waiting to wrap around swimmers. The venom traveled to the lymph nodes and glands in the groin and stung intensely.

"I know it hurts, mate," Cody told a screeching little girl. "Be brave. It'll fade in half an hour or so, I promise. An hour tops."

She gulped and sobbed, her face bright red. A man, presumably her father shouted in a Brit accent, "What was that thing? Christ, call an ambulance!"

"It was a bluebottle," Cody answered calmly. "It's also called a Portuguese man o' war. The sting isn't usually dangerous. She doesn't need an ambo. All these people have been stung today too. The only thing—"

"Look at her! She's in horrible pain! You need to do something!"

Liam shared a glance with Baz and turned to monitor the situation. He didn't want to step in too early. It was good for Cody to get the experience dealing with unreasonable people. Unreasonable and worried parents, especially.

Cody held up his hands, trying to placate the man. He kept his tone even. "Sir, I've explained to you that there is really nothing we can do except rinse in warm water, spray the affected area with antiseptic, and apply an ice bag to soothe the pain as you wait. Waiting is really the key. I know she's in pain, and it's scary and confusing, but this happens to thousands of people every summer. You can take her to the shower block and try a warm shower and wait there. We only call an ambulance if there's an allergic reaction or breathing is affected in any way."

The girl wailed, her lungs clearly working at full capacity.

"So that's it? You're kicking me out and telling me to just *wait* while my child suffers?" The man was beet red, veins in his neck bulging as he got in Cody's face. "That's ridiculous. I want your name. I thought you were supposed to help people!"

Liam was up in a flash, stalking to the top of the steps, using his height to his advantage to loom. "I'm Liam Fox, the senior lifeguard on duty. Cody's done everything we can do. You're welcome to take your daughter to the shower block as suggested. Sometimes it helps—it really depends on the person. Time and patience is the only surefire solution. Our priority is the water. Bluebottle stings are a painful nuisance, but we can't fix them. I wish we could. Now you've made enough of a scene. It's not helping your daughter."

Tears streamed down her face. Liam wanted to tell the dickhead to comfort the poor girl, but instead he added, "Thank you for your understanding. We need to focus on saving lives."

As the man opened his mouth to argue, sputtering, his fists clenched, Baz called, "Foxy! Confirmed shark sighting. Launch the ski."

Because it just wouldn't be Barkers without everything going to shit at the same time. Biting back a groan, Liam pointed at Cody. "You're with me. The bluey stings have to wait. Get down there." He hustled back to Baz, who was still on the radio.

"Yep. Copy that. On it." Baz said to Liam, "Chopper spotted a great white. There's a massive bait ball out there. I'm flipping the alarm. You'll do the sweep on the ski?"

Liam nodded and raced out of the tower, blocking out the angry father and the exclaiming bluebottle victims who demanded attention. As he hit the sand, the shark alarm blared to life, a piercing siren that sent gulls flapping into the air, the beach-goers whipped into a frenzy of excitement and activity. *At least this'll get 'em away from the blueys.*

Wearing his life vest, Cody was already driving an ATV out of the garage, towing the Jet Ski. Liam leaped into the buggy, and Cody went as fast as he could, laying on the horn like a pro as people clustered on the sand. Cody had put a vest for Liam in the back, and he buckled it on.

"You sure you want to go out?" Liam yelled over the siren. "It's a great white. I can get Bickie to come."

Cody didn't even glance at him. "I'm going."

Liam grinned as they reached the shore. Bickie and Mark were there shouting at people over the siren and clearing a path. It was tricky to get the buggy deep enough into the water to launch the ski without getting bogged, and Cody didn't argue when Bickie told him to get out so he could take over behind the wheel, executing an expert turn on the sand and backing the trailer and ski into the surf as thousands watched, swimmers streaming in from the water as the siren blared.

As soon as they were clear, Liam fired up the ski, Cody jumping on the back before they faced into a crashing wave. Had to get head on and out of the impact zone. If a big-enough wave hit them side on, the Jet Ski would be knocked over—and possibly land on top of them, all five hundred kilos of it.

"Hang on tight!" Liam shouted.

A wave loomed, frothing furious white as it broke and Liam gunned the engine, head down and over the crest. Cody followed instructions, pressing against his back, arms locked around Liam's waist as they sped out past the straggling swimmers. Cody's groin was snug against Liam's arse. It was a hot day, but Liam shivered.

Focus on the bloody shark.

He concentrated on the water, making sure no one was in their path. The Jet Ski towed a long, wide mat with rings for hand-holds to bring back patients, and it dragged behind them, just as much a danger to swimmers if Liam clipped someone with it. He headed for the rocks jutting out from the south end, then turned north to do a sweep along the limits of Barking.

His walkie-talkie was in a waterproof bag clipped to his life vest. Baz's voice said, "Central to Jet Ski."

Wind in his face, Liam reached up to hit the button. "Copy, Central."

"Chopper says it's about a hundred meters out from you. There's a distance swimmer by third gate, almost a kilometer out. Bloke must not be concerned, but you'd better grab him."

"Copy that, Central." Liam drove north, parallel to the beach. To Cody, he shouted, "You see the swimmer?"

"Not yet!" Gripping Liam's shoulders almost painfully, Cody stood. Liam kept hold of the handlebars, keeping the ski steady. Cody's knees dug into the top of Liam's ribs over the life vest. He was pressed against him, both of them leaning forward into the wind and salt spray. Liam's heart pounded, and he told himself it was only the adrenaline of the moment—a Great White nearby and a swimmer possibly in danger.

"Got him!" Cody yelled. "One o'clock."

The fit, dark-haired older man wore a short-sleeved wetsuit and a snorkel, stroking steadily with his face in the water. There were many capable swimmers who did laps of Barking far out from the beach, although Liam always wished they'd stay closer to shore.

As they neared, Cody sat, and Liam eased off on the petrol, shouting, "Hey!"

Finally, the man looked up from a few feet away, clearly annoyed. "I'm fine! Don't need rescuing. I'm an excellent swimmer."

"Didn't you hear the shark alarm?" Liam asked.

The man scoffed. "It's probably a seal or a dolphin."

Liam pointed up. "Chopper confirmed it's a Great White."

Now *this* got his attention, and Liam almost laughed as the man jerked, his eyes widening. "Bloody oath!" He was at the mat in a few strokes, pulling himself up, Cody reaching back to give him a hand. "What are you waiting for!" the man yelled.

Liam gunned the engine, Cody chuckling in his ear with a gust of warmth, his arms wrapping around Liam again. There wasn't anything out of the ordinary about it—you had to hold on when you were on the back of the ski. Liam had told Cody to hang on tight, so that was all it was, even if the other guys didn't typically press *this* close.

As they headed back to shore, Liam was hyperaware of Cody's thighs tight around his hips. Although he was smaller, Cody really was muscular and fit. His arms circled Liam, and for a mad moment, Liam wanted to lean back into that embrace.

The beach was packed with people, the water clear aside from a few surfers at the north end who'd decided to take their chances, knowing the odds were in their favor. Liam beached the ski, the swimmer stumbling off the mat with hurried thanks, almost tripping on his flippers.

Liam headed back out, looping around to make sure all was clear, Cody hanging on. Cody shouted, "Can we keep the swimmers on the sand and just stay out here all day?"

"Sounds like a plan," Liam agreed.

But soon enough the chopper confirmed the shark had moved south and gave them the all-clear, moving on to follow it. Baz blipped the alarm twice to indicate that it was safe to go back in the water, and Liam angled for shore. But then another radio call came in.

"Hold up, Jet Ski. Member of the public called triple-0 from one of the apartments. Saw a bloke walking over the rocks, and he seemed to slip. Haven't seen him now in ten minutes. They're afraid he's bashed himself or fallen in the water."

Liam looked to the south end of the beach, where the craggy rocks jutted out, a breakwater where people liked to fish. On the other side the dunes rose up, a few condo buildings up atop the hill. "Copy that, Central. Chopper didn't see him?"

"Nope, but they were focused on the shark."

It could end up being a body retrieval, and Liam hesitated, debating whether to bring Cody back to shore and take one of the guys with more experience. No. Would take too long.

"Central, we'll go take a look." He gunned it for the south

end, Cody pressed against him. If someone was in the water or unconscious—or worse, both—seconds counted.

When they came around the edge of the rocks, Liam slowed. "No sign!" Cody shouted. "Oh, wait! Got him."

As Liam squinted to the left, he saw the bloke at the base of the rocks, surf foaming white as swells crashed. The young man looked conscious and alert, balancing on the top of a flatter boulder, water rising around him before receding. He sat with his leg out, holding it gingerly.

But Liam couldn't get too close to the massive boulders or risk damaging the ski and stranding all of them. "You right?" he called over the pounding surf, which knocked them around as it swirled and broke on the rocks, the tops of which loomed a couple of stories high. The bloke said something, but Liam couldn't hear it.

The tide was rising, and Liam calculated the odds of the patient being able to climb up with what looked like a bum leg, or wait for rescue before the swells smashed him. Nope. Wasn't going to happen.

They were out of view of the tower now, and Liam knew Baz would be waiting for an update. "Jet Ski to Central. We've got eyes on him. Looks like he might have broken his leg or busted his ankle. We've got to get him off the rocks."

"Copy, Jet Ski."

Liam shouted to the man, "Can you jump out to us?" He motioned toward them with his arm, but the bloke shook his head, eyes going wild.

"I'll get him!" Cody shouted, and before Liam could react, he leapt off the back of the ski and into the pounding surf, a wave covering him completely for a terrible moment. Then he emerged, his orange life vest reassuringly bright, swimming hard for the rocks.

"Fuck!" Liam's heart was in his throat as he watched Cody fight the frothing water. He hadn't even had a chance to brief him on procedure, and frustration warred with concern. He said into the radio, "Jet Ski to Central. Cody's in getting the patient. It's a tricky one."

"*Chook's* in? Okay, copy. Need an ambo?"

"Yeah, just in case. Over." No time to explain that he would have gone in, but Cody jumped the gun.

A swell thumped the rocks, lifting Cody and practically spitting him out by the patient. Cody was speaking to him and urging him to the edge, and this was definitely beyond what a trainee should have been doing his first month. Liam could only watch and wait powerlessly with the ski ready to speed to safety. He hated every second that Cody was in danger.

Watching a big set near, Liam shouted, "You've got to jump! *Now!*" He understood the patient was afraid, but there was no time to be gentle. The waves were only getting bigger, and they were all going to get smashed. "Jump!"

Cody did, hauling the man with him into the swirling water, towing him as he swam hard back to the mat. Cody shoved him on and gave Liam the thumbs up, clinging to the mat as Liam gunned the engine and took them in an arc away from the brutal rocks. He slowed when they were safe from the next set of waves, giving Cody time to scramble up to sit behind him again.

Turning to check on the patient on the mat, Cody held onto Liam's hip, and Liam felt like all his nerve endings were suddenly centered there. "Took a tumble?" Cody asked the patient. His hand rested on the crease where Liam's leg bent. A dozen of the guys had probably held onto Liam the same way over the years, yet now he was breathless.

The man nodded. "Could not get back up. I lost my camera." He had a thick accent—French, maybe. "My ankle hurts very much."

"You're right now," Cody said. "No drama. Hold tight, and we'll be on solid ground in no time." He circled Liam's waist, leaning into him again as Liam gunned the engine. In Liam's ear as they sped to shore, salt-spray wind in their faces, he said, "That was awesome!"

Liam wasn't sure whether to laugh or glare, but he was immensely relieved to have Cody safe and sound and wrapped around him. And relieved to have the patient safe on the mat as well. That was the most important thing, of course.

Mark was waiting for them with a buggy, and he helped the man hobble to the back, peppering him with medical questions. Cody's grin faded as he looked at Liam. "Did I do something wrong?"

"Yes. You jumped before I could even tell you what to do. Before we could even discuss it."

"Oh. Shit, sorry."

Liam was antsy thinking about all the ways it could have gone wrong, imagining Cody getting smashed by the ski or into the rocks. "You're the trainee—I was in charge out there, never mind that I was driving the ski. The driver calls the shots. What if you'd jumped and I didn't realize it? I could have been about to maneuver the ski—I could have hit you."

"Right." Shoulders slumping, Cody nodded. "I didn't think of that."

"I know. *I* should have been the one in the water. That was your first rescue off the rocks. If we'd done it properly, you would have taken over on the ski, and I would have gone in for the patient. And we'd have communicated all the steps before jumping."

"You're right. I'm sorry." Cody rubbed a hand over his wet head, his hair curling at the ends. "I really didn't mean to step on your toes."

Standing by the beached ski, Liam unzipped his life vest, adrenaline still flowing. "It's not about my toes. It's about your safety, and mine. And the patient's."

"Totally. That makes sense."

"I know you're young and not afraid of anything, and you think you're invincible—"

"It's not that." Cody shook his head. "I'm not a daredevil or anything. I mean, I surf and whatever, but I don't think I'm invincible. He was really scared. I wanted to help him, so I didn't stop to think."

Any lingering frustration melted away in a rush of something new and tender that Liam did not want to identify. "I get it." He reached out to pat Cody's shoulder. Cody's skin felt warm and wet in the sunshine. "You did a good job. Next time just make sure you're following procedure."

The dimples appeared in Cody's cheeks. "Look before I leap. Got it."

And Liam felt like he was taking a leap of his own, *looking* far too much at Cody, enjoying touching him far too much as well. The hand on Cody's shoulder was innocent, but Liam stepped back, fiddling with his life vest straps. He needed to get in control and remember his rules before he fell any deeper.

Chapter Nine

CHARLENE'S TAIL WAGGED so hard it could take out an eye, and she strained on her leash like a giant muppet, her golden, curly fur sopping wet. Bent over to pick up her poop, Cody laughed. "See something you like?" It was his day off, and he was making it up to his favorite girl for skipping their morning dates to train with Mia and some of the guys.

"Uh… G'day."

Cody bolted upright, and yes—Liam Fox was actually standing there on the grass at South Beach's dog park. "Hey!" He held the taut leash in one hand and raised the other before remembering he held a green bag of warm shit. He whipped his hand down. "Good morning." Cody only wore his boardies. His running shoes and tee were in his backpack.

Charlene butted against Liam's bare knees below his dark plaid shorts eagerly. Smiling, Liam transferred his weight to his right leg before crouching and settling more evenly on the balls of his feet in his thongs. "Who's this?" He held a paper coffee cup in one hand. His tanned skin looked phenomenal against his white T-shirt.

Before he started drooling, Cody said, "Charlene. She's my landlady's dog." As Liam scratched her ears, she licked eagerly. "She likes you. To be fair, she likes literally everyone who will pet her."

Liam chuckled, and *Jesus*, he was handsome. And *here*. He lived down in Barkininy, so what was he doing up in Freo? "Interesting name for a dog."

"Yeah, when I call her, sometimes a middle-aged woman will look over, all confused. She's named after Kylie Minogue's character on *Neighbours*. Like, from the eighties or something? Puffy blond curls."

"Ah." Liam petted Charlene a bit more before standing, again shifting his weight to the right. "Your knee bugging you?" Cody asked.

"Huh? Oh, no." He shrugged. "I got so used to favoring my right side. The physio was always after me to stand evenly."

"Doesn't seem to bother you at work. I've seen you fly across the sand."

He shrugged again. "Probably all in my head when it acts up." His smile faded, tension visibly creeping through him. He sipped his coffee, scratching behind Charlene's ears when she head-butted against his free hand.

"Oh, is that from the new cafe on South Terrace? The Pink Elephant?"

Liam's brow furrowed. "How did you know?"

"Um, the pink elephant on the sleeve."

"Oh!" Liam looked down at the cup. "Right. I guess that's a hint."

"Nothing gets by me, clearly."

They laughed awkwardly, and *what was happening*? Cody cleared his throat. "Is it good? I've been meaning to try it."

"Yeah, it's great. Bickie's sister owns it. Want to support her, so I drove up."

"Oh, awesome! I'll definitely try it out."

As Liam fidgeted, rocking on his heels, Cody suddenly *knew*. All his instincts agreed, and he couldn't deny what his gut was telling him—that Liam Fox hadn't come here for the coffee. He'd come to find Cody. They played for the same team.

Mia had pegged Liam as a closet case, and he sure seemed nervous now. Cody wanted to take his hand and tell him it was okay and to breathe. Just how deep in the closet was he?

What the hell—Cody was going for it. "Hey, are you busy this morning?"

Liam hesitated, taking a gulp of his coffee. After he swallowed, he said, "Not really. Rostered day off."

"Oh yeah? Me too. I was wondering if you know anything about leaky faucets. My kitchen tap's driving me nuts. I don't want my landlord to have to spend money on a plumber. I've got a toolbox and a YouTube video bookmarked, but I honestly have no idea what I'm doing." Well, he had some idea, but that was irrelevant.

As Liam hesitated again, Cody motioned, "My place isn't far. Just up South Terrace."

Liam turned to look, as if he could see it beyond the concrete Sealanes fish market, its red neon sign announcing a deal on fresh pink snapper. He turned back to Cody, his chest lifting with a deep breath. "Sure. I know enough."

"Cool, thanks. Brekkie's on me. Or lunch—whatever."

"I don't mind helping."

"Cool," Cody repeated. He lifted the bag of poop. "Let me just..." He handed over Charlene's leash to Liam and jogged to the nearest bin, Charlene barking and whining. Laughing, he ran back to pet her. "I'm still here, Char. I know you love me best."

Sitting on the grass, he took out his towel and rubbed lingering sand off his feet before putting on his socks and shoes. Normally he'd put on his tee, but he left it balled in his backpack. Liam had certainly seen him shirtless before, but...hey, why not?

"We were going to run back. Do you have your car, or...?"

"Yeah." Liam nodded to the parking lot near the street. "I can give you a lift."

"Are you sure? Wet dog isn't the air freshener most people go for."

Liam smiled, and a thrill rippled through Cody. He wanted to see more and more and *more* of that smile. And the rest of this gorgeous man. Liam said, "I'm sure."

Charlene stuck her head out the SUV window, thrilled to be in a vehicle since Mrs. Delfino couldn't drive anymore after breaking her hip. Cody directed Liam to turn up the laneway that sloped up between South Terrace and Manning, then left on the lane that ran behind the houses. Most of the garages were closed, although a neighbor worked on his motorcycle in one, and Cody gave him a wave as they passed.

"Who's that?" Liam asked sharply.

"A neighbor. I don't know his name." He pointed. "That's mine on the right." Getting out his keys, he pressed the button for the remote, the door rattling up with a mechanical hum to reveal the narrow, empty garage. "Probably easier if you back in. "I'll get out first." He grabbed his pack and opened the back door for Charlene, who bounded out and through the garage.

The back end of the garage was open to a short walkway to the patio, a multi laundry line installed just under the edge of the garage roof to keep the clothes from being bleached in the sun. Cody ducked under his drying uniform and beach towel as Liam backed his SUV inside.

It was a tight squeeze, the back window brushing the laundry. Liam shimmied out and around after Cody pressed the button again, the motor rumbling as the garage door came down.

Cody opened the gate to Mrs. Delfino's yard and shooed Charlene away. "Go get treats from your mummy! Good girl."

Liam stood just beyond the laundry, peering up suspiciously at Mrs. Delfino's house beyond the tall passionfruit vines and the neighbor's massive pink bougainvillea, which spread over the top of the fence along the right side of the property. Mrs. Delfino's back deck was just visible, more bright flowers in planters along the thick railing. The steeply sloping yard below the deck was mostly scrubby bushes.

"Your landlord lives up there?" Liam asked.

"Uh-huh. She's in her seventies. Her husband died a few years ago, and her kids are all married and stuff. I moved in last year, and I try to help her out. She broke her hip, so she can't go any farther than the deck right now. I trim the bushes and exercise Charlene. Mrs. Delfino can walk well enough now to take her out a bit, but it helps if I go for a run and swim with her to get out most of her energy."

"That's good of you."

He shrugged. "It's a pleasure." Nodding to his covered patio on the left, he said, "This is my place."

Liam followed him past the wooden table and chairs that sat against the outer wall of the studio beside the glass door. It opened with a big old-fashioned key that Cody had to use from the inside as well if he wanted to lock it at night. He led the way inside. The same key opened the matching glass door on the far side of the studio. Through the open curtains, the growing sunflowers by the laneway fence were visible. The TV sat on the wall to the right of that glass door in front of a coffee table and love seat.

The floor was pale wood, and there was a wide window alongside the studio to the right, but the view was only the windowless concrete of the garage next door beyond a narrow, shaded path leading from the front gate to the back patio.

"Home sweet home," he said, flipping on the ceiling fan. He'd left the big screened windows over the patio open to get air in. The studio had AC, but he preferred the fresh breeze unless it was scorching hot and humid.

Liam gazed around warily. From where he stood in the doorway, the queen bed was directly on his right. He stared at it, and

Cody was glad he'd at least pulled up the sheet and thin duvet, even if nothing was really tucked in.

Adam's apple bobbing, Liam croaked, "It's nice."

A dark thrill of lust spiraled through Cody. Yes, Liam Fox was *thirsty*. But Cody had to play it cool and not spook him. He felt like a spider luring its prey into a web, and he couldn't deny it excited him. He'd never, ever do anything Liam didn't want, or pressure him, but if Liam *did* want this—if he actually wanted *Cody*... His heart thumped.

Calm down. Fix the leak and see what happens.

"You want another coffee? I've got a machine. It's Mrs. Delfino's old one. I don't use it very much, but there are some pods." On the kitchen side of the studio, he opened a drawer.

"Sure. Thanks." Liam slid off his thongs by the door and tentatively walked over.

While Liam looked at the collection of coffee types, Cody took off his running shoes and socks and made sure the bathroom was clean enough. He should probably put on a shirt, but...didn't. As he puttered around, he asked, "Did you grow up in Barking?"

"No. Mandurah." Liam held up a pod. "I'll have hazelnut."

"Cool. The mugs are there." Cody motioned to another drawer. There was a pantry, but no cupboards, so everything was in drawers. A microwave and toaster sat on the counter beside the coffee machine. "You know how to use it?"

Liam nodded, and Cody continued puttering, finding the toolbox. Cody said, "You live by Barkers now, right?" Liam nodded again, and Cody kept talking, trying to play it casual.

"I looked for a place there, but this one was too good to pass up. I love Freo. When my family moved to Perth from BC, we went all around and did the sights. Barking Beach, Fremantle Prison, the Roundhouse, the Maritime Museum. Check, check, check, check. Took the ferry over to Rotto to see the quokkas. Did

Elizabeth Quay, although it's heaps nicer now. The zoo, Swan River cruise, all that."

Cody paused as he opened the toolbox, putting it on the dining table in the middle of the studio. "Hey, can you do me a Milano after? Thanks." He didn't really need another coffee since he'd had a flat white earlier, but he wanted to give Liam something to distract him. He could sense a ball of anxiety in Liam and wanted to tell him it was okay, and they didn't have to do anything. That Cody wouldn't bite. Much.

He considered whether he was completely misreading the situation, but honestly couldn't figure out why else Liam would be so nervous and tense. Cody kept talking.

"So once we hit the major items on the list, my family rarely came south of the river again. But I fell in love with Barking and Freo right from the start. Don't get me wrong, Mullaloo and the northern beaches are spectacular. But there's something about the energy of Barking. And Freo is so chill and artsy. I love that there are literally four cafes within a two-minute walk, and there are hardly any chains around. Ben and Jerry's near the market, but that's about it. I guess there are more fast food places east, but I don't have a car."

"I was going to ask. You ride your bike down to Barking, right?"

"Yep. But it's great to have the garage here in case I rent a car for whatever reason, or if someone's over."

Standing by the kitchen counter, Liam stiffened, jerking his gaze down to the coffee machine. Cody almost clarified that he didn't just mean hookups, that once in a while he saw his family on his dad's side. Although his aunt and uncle and cousins lived inland in the Swan Valley where his dad had grown up, and it had been almost a year since they'd come for a day to catch up and go to Cicerello's for fish and chips.

Instead, he kept talking as he unnecessarily rearranged the

toolbox to give himself something to do. "You know, the first time I went to Barking, I got caught in the Croc."

"Really?" This teased a little smile out of Liam. "Do you remember who pulled you out?"

"Not his name, but he was older. Blond hair, buff, really tanned. Very white teeth. He had a tattoo on his chest—a dolphin. He was like the poster boy for an Aussie lifeguard." *Not unlike you.*

"Ah, Muggsy. He's a contractor in Coogee. Used to be casual at the beach, but then business was too good. Nice bloke."

"He was like a knight on a stallion. I'd been stupidly trying to swim back to shore instead of sideways out of the rip, panicking. And then the lifeguard was there, the rescue board appearing over the crest of a swell like out of thin air. I'd felt so alone and terrified, and he pulled me up over his board like I weighed nothing."

He didn't add that as a scrawny, gawky, horny-as-hell thirteen-year-old, he'd turned Muggsy into his go-to spank bank favorite. "You'd think it would have put me off Barking Beach forever, but I was hooked. It was fun and scary, and Muggsy was so reassuring. It really made me want to be a lifeguard. That combination of excitement and helping people."

A smile tugged at Liam's lips as he toyed with the pod of coffee he'd pulled out for Cody, the machine pouring his first. "Thought you weren't a daredevil."

Cody laughed. "No more than you are. I mean, I like the thrill of the ocean. But I'm not crazy like Baz. Holy shit, some of the waves he's surfed? I saw an old competition on YouTube. It was *insane.* Or the break down near Walpole, 'The Right'?"

Liam whistled. "Oh yeah. One of the biggest in the world. I wouldn't dream of it, mate."

"Me either. I did surf school down in Dunsborough last year. The swells are sick. Got absolutely smoked a few times. Then once

I was in a vortex, and it was dumping me over and over." He shuddered. "I thought my number might have been up."

Cody remembered it as if it were yesterday, the sensation of being pounded down by a breaking wave, then sucked back to the rim of the shallow sandbank, then thumped down, sucked back—like a rag doll in a washing machine. Holding his breath, praying he'd be able to gasp in another before the next swell crashed him down.

"I was lucky the waves let up and the Jet Ski could get in and grab me. Never been so happy to see another human being in my life. That's when I *really* knew I wanted to do this job. I've dreamed about it since I was a kid, and worked hard toward it, but in that moment, after the relief... It was like I knew it in my soul." He scoffed. "That sounds stupid."

"Nah. I get it. I totally get it."

"Was it like that for you and footy?"

Liam looked back at the coffee machine, his shoulders tensing. He was silent a few moments, and Cody was about to apologize for bringing it up when Liam said, "Kind of. I always loved it, and I was so good at it. I worked my arse off, but I was born with the gift too. It made my dad so happy. Mum too, but...especially dad."

He sounded so wistful, and Cody almost held his breath waiting for him to go on. Liam said, "Making him proud motivated me even more to be the best. Footy was my life. It was...*me*."

Silence stretched out as Cody tried to think of the right thing to say, fighting the urge to reach out for Liam and reassure him that whoever he was now, it was okay. As much as he wanted Liam sexually—and holy shit, did he ever—it was the mystery of him as well, the depths of sadness and longing that Cody wanted to soothe.

The coffee machine popped up the empty pod, and they both jumped, then laughed awkwardly. Cody moved to the sink.

"Better get started. So I unscrew this first, right?"

Liam sipped his coffee and gave Cody instructions where necessary, nodding and not saying much else. Soon enough, the tap wasn't dripping, and Cody drank his coffee and tried to think of another reason for Liam to stick around. He scanned the studio, then a light bulb went off—or didn't, more to the point.

"I need to change a bulb in the track lighting too. I've been meaning to get to this stuff for weeks." He went to the wall by the patio door and flipped the right switch to remind himself which light had burned out. Then he got the spare and climbed up on the solid dining table. "It's a pain in the ass. These bulbs are fiddly."

Liam chuckled. "Pain in the *aaaass*. You sound so American sometimes. Canadian, I should say."

"Pain in the *arse*, excuse me. See? If I say it like that I sound pretentious. Like to-*mah*-to. It doesn't work with my accent." He screwed in the bulb on the track.

"Fair enough. It does sound strange now that you say it."

"Can you flip the switch?" he asked. Liam did, and the bulb came on with the others. "Cool, thanks," Cody said, still standing on the table.

Well, that didn't take long.

Mind working for yet another excuse for Liam to stay, he moved to step down onto the chair, watching Liam under his lashes. Then he did something he wasn't exactly proud of, but what the hell.

He was going for it.

"Whoa!" Cody faked losing his balance, arms out, and Liam was right there with strong hands spread over Cody's bare waist, steadying him on the wooden chair. Cody grabbed Liam's shoulders, looking down at him—although not that far since Liam was a giant.

"Thanks," Cody said, the word coming out breathier than he

intended. He felt light and tingly all over, and *fuck*, he really wanted Liam Fox.

And he swore Liam wanted him too. If Cody was wrong, he'd be embarrassed as hell at work tomorrow, but his instincts screamed it, and the evidence was right there—parted lips, big pupils, Liam's hands still hot on Cody's bare skin above the waistband of his boardies hanging low on his hips. Liam stared up at Cody, swallowing hard with an actual little *gulp*.

"I'm looking before I leap," Cody said. He waited for a response, but Liam seemed frozen in place. He was breathing too hard to not be aroused—or afraid. Cody ached to sooth those sharp, jittery edges, to kiss them away and tell him there was nothing to be afraid of.

He understood being on the down-low—he'd fucked some guys who weren't out to their parents yet—but Liam's fingers trembled where he clutched Cody's waist. He'd never been with someone this hesitant and skittish.

Slowly, he slid one hand from Liam's shoulder to his face, skimming over his neck and the pulse fluttering there. Cody cupped his rough cheek, giving Liam all the opportunity to pull away. "If I kissed you—"

With a groan, Liam dragged Cody's head down, their mouths crashing together. *Yes, yes, yes!* Joy and lust exploded as they kissed. It was clumsy, Cody bending to taste him—coffee and a hint of hazelnut sweetness—their lips parting on gasped breaths. But it was perfect.

The need to climb inside Liam's skin set fire to his blood, and Cody tipped against him, Liam grabbing his ass now, Cody's hardening dick jammed against his broad chest. Tingly pleasure lit up Cody down to his toes.

Liam's light beard scraped Cody's face as their mouths moved together, and it was *everything*. He licked at Liam's tongue, practically climbing on top of him, desperate for more. Not breaking the kiss, he reached down, straining, needing to feel that Liam was as into this as he was.

His fingers brushed the hard bulge in Liam's shorts, and Cody moaned. To feel the evidence of Liam's excitement thrilled him on a cellular level. There was no denying that erection. Liam was really here in Cody's home, every walking-wet-dream inch of him, his strong hands clutching Cody, little moans escaping his lips.

Cody was on the edge of the chair, bent and straining and kissing Liam like his life depended on it, and suddenly they were tipping. They both cried out in surprise, muffled by their kisses, as Liam staggered back.

Luckily the bed was only a few steps away. Liam crashed onto the mattress, Cody tumbling on top of him with a burst of laughter. With an absolutely stunned expression, Liam laughed too, and he was *beautiful*.

Then fear flickered across his face, his eyes widening and breath catching. Cody rubbed against his hardness, straddling him and diving for his hungry mouth, determined to kiss away every doubt.

Chapter Ten

W*HAT ARE YOU doing?!*
   The voice in his head jolted him, and Liam felt like a naughty child with his hand in the jar of lollies Mum still kept in the pantry for his nephew. Then Mum and Dad and their shrine were in his head, and he was ashamed and afraid, yet desperately hard. He was all wrong.

Cody broke the kiss, voice breathy as he asked, "Is this okay?" His long-lashed, chocolate eyes searched Liam's face, and Liam had no idea what he'd see there. Desperation? Lust? Terror? *Wrongness?* He tightened his grip on Cody's hips and had to look away, gaze flicking around the room.

The drapes over the glass doors and big windows were open, and Liam realized with a terrifying jolt that they could be seen. *He* could be seen. Cody followed his gaze and smoothed his hands over Liam's chest, sending shivers rippling over Liam's skin.

"It's okay. Someone would have to be right there to look in," Cody said. But he rolled off Liam and the bed, hurrying to yank the closest drapes shut, his erection tenting his boardies. "You're safe here." He moved to the other windows.

Liam looked around the studio, squinting to make out a telltale red light, even though he knew there were plenty of cameras now without them. If Cody had hidden one…

"Hey, it's okay." Cody frowned down at him. Standing at the foot of the bed, he tentatively smoothed his hand over Liam's good knee. "What are you worried about?"

"There's no camera, right?" Liam blurted before he could lose his nerve.

Cody flinched, his eyebrows shooting up. "A *camera*? You mean to, like, secretly film you? Jesus, no." His face creased in disgust. "*No.* Do you think I'd do that?"

Liam was flat on his back on Cody's bed with his erection straining against the fly of his shorts. That morning, he'd decided to take a drive up to South Beach, telling himself he was supporting Bickie's sister. And sure, he was—but he was also looking for Cody, and he knew it. When he'd found him, and Cody had asked him to come home with him, Liam had told himself he was only going to help with the faucet.

But he'd known deep down this was where he'd end up. That this was where he wanted to be—in Cody's bed. Maybe he'd live to regret smashing his rules, but he'd never have considered it if his gut didn't tell him to trust Cody.

Cody was frozen in a scowl, waiting, and Liam shook his head. "No. I don't think you'd do that. It's not you. It's me. I'm..." *Pathetic. Terrified.* "I'm sorry."

Face softening, Cody crawled onto the bed, straddling him. He took Liam's hands, and Liam realized his own fingers were shaking. Cody spoke softly. "You're safe here. That's a big fear, huh? Being filmed?"

Liam nodded, his throat thick. Even though he had no reason to think Cody or any of his foreign hookups would film him, the idea of it had panicked him for years. He could imagine the video being spread around the internet, strangers watching him. Judging him. His breath stuttered.

"Hey, it's okay." Cody gently squeezed his hands. "I get it. I'd never, ever do that to you. Please believe me. If you can trust me, I think we can have a lot of fun together."

"I do. I wouldn't—I never do this. But you're... I—" He broke off, gasping, as Cody rocked their hips together.

"I want you so bad, Liam." Cody bit his own lower lip, his gaze dark with intent. "Do you want me?"

"Yes," Liam rasped.

As Cody tugged off his boardies, his thick, uncut cock springing up from a trimmed nest of brown curls, Liam's mouth actually watered. Cody grinned at him, leaning close and kissing Liam deeply, his tongue eager. Liam had never wanted anyone this much, not even Biggsy that long-ago day on the pitch.

That hadn't really been about Biggs himself—the want had been far deeper than that. But as Cody rubbed against him naked, repeating against his open mouth, "You're safe here," Liam wanted so much more. He wanted to believe.

Cody tugged up his shirt, and Liam raised his arms, the tee going flying. Scooting back, Cody unfastened Liam's shorts and peeled them off his legs. His prick bulged in his dark boxer-briefs, and Cody teased his fingers over the straining cotton. He licked his lips. "I've been wondering if your cock is as spectacular as your ass." He grinned. "Excuse me—*arse.*"

Liam laughed, a burst of joy almost wiping out the panic. Cody was *funny*, and gorgeous, and kind, looking at Liam with a sweet smile and gentle patience. It was pathetic that Liam was the one needing reassurance when Cody was half his size and barely an adult.

Yet when Cody took Liam's face in his hands and kissed him softly, Liam wanted to disappear into him and be truly safe. He was breaking all his rules, and part of him wanted to run with a surge of horror. His chest heaved, lungs tight.

Cody kissed him again, his thumbs slowly stroking Liam's cheeks, the motion soothing over his light beard, the scrape of stubble strangely calming. "We can stop anytime," Cody whispered.

Another burst of fear—this time that Cody really would stop. "I can't," Liam gasped, not sure what he was saying anymore. He couldn't do this. He had *rules*. Rules kept him safe. He'd been swimming between the flags all these years, and now he was ignoring the danger signs and paddling into the rip.

Yet when Cody whispered, "You need to come, don't you?" and straddled him again, rolling his hips, their hard cocks grinding through cotton, Liam could only kiss him frantically, their teeth clacking.

It truly was pathetic, a grown man so desperate and off his head, but Cody didn't laugh. Instead, he said, "It's okay. I've got you." He squirmed backward, breaking the contact of their pricks and easing down Liam's underwear, tossing it away.

Liam sat up, reaching for him, desperate for more contact. Cody pushed Liam's legs open, his knees bending and heels digging into the mattress. With a wicked grin, Cody ducked down to swallow the tip of Liam's cut cock, sucking hard. Liam clamped his mouth shut, panting through his nose and choking down his moans. He leaned back on both hands, arms straight and bent legs splayed.

One of Cody's thumbs pressed into the crease between Liam's groin and hip, holding him steady as he explored with his tongue, tracing Liam's shaft. He pressed along the ridge, hard then light. With his other hand, he circled the root of Liam's cock, squeezing then releasing.

The sensations were unpredictable, and Liam closed his eyes and trembled with anticipation and sweet pleasure, zeroing in on the wet pressure of Cody's mouth and the teasing of his tongue. He was alive and rooted in his body—absolutely on fire despite the gooseflesh the breeze from the ceiling fan spread over his skin—sure he would rocket to the stars without Cody's mouth and hands grounding him.

As Cody swallowed him almost to the root now, slurping loudly over the hum of the fan, Liam watched his bent head, wanting to run his fingers through the curling ends of Cody's brown hair.

But he might shatter into a million pieces if he moved, so he pushed his fingers and heels into the bed. For a moment, he could back off in his mind, as if he stood a few feet away staring down at himself and the display he was making.

He was stunned to see himself so shameless, sitting there with Cody's head between his spread thighs. He was naked and splayed, and it was the middle of the morning, sunlight glowing around the drawn curtains, the drapes over the patio windows rippling in the breeze.

Cody slurped and moaned around his prick, looking up at Liam under his eyelashes—seeing him, *knowing* him. Liam whimpered as his balls tightened, helpless to do anything but come.

White dots exploded in his vision, and he jolted, shooting into Cody's eager mouth, tasting blood as he bit his lip to stop from shouting. It felt so damn *good*, surrendering to the release he'd needed more than he'd known. Chest heaving, Cody lifted his head, licking at the spunk dripping from his mouth. Liam shuddered with another pulse of sweet pleasure.

Liam reached for him, collapsing back on the bed and pulling Cody with him, fingers finally in those pretty curls. The fear lurked on the edges, a big set of waves heading for shore that he could see in the distance and didn't want to face. Not yet.

Not when Cody was straddling him again, kissing him messily, deeply, his tongue still coated in Liam's own spunk, the salty taste melded with lingering coffee.

"You taste so good," Cody mumbled, squeezing his hand between them, his prick throbbing against Liam. "Wanted to do that since I first saw you. Wanted to climb you and suck you and fuck you."

A spark of joy and *want* rocked Liam, another pulse of release twitching his spent dick. Cody spit into his palm and jerked himself fast. Then he leaned his left hand on Liam's shoulder, straining, surely for leverage. But the result was that he pinned Liam down, looming over him, lips parted as he stroked himself.

Even though Liam could surely get free and overpower Cody in a blink, a fresh pulse of desire—of release—crashed through him, his arms dropping to his sides. He wanted to lift his legs around his ears and beg Cody to fuck him, rough and merciless, to fill him with cum until it dripped out, to paint him with it and pour it down his throat until he felt nothing but glorious surrender.

But all he could do was gasp, his cock twitching as Cody held him down. Then Cody muttered, "Fuck. Gonna come all over you."

Unable to swallow a moan, Liam laid motionless, eyes glued on Cody's dick as it erupted in milky bursts onto Liam, in his chest hair, over one nipple, down his belly, which was helplessly quivering now. Liam couldn't come again so soon, but his balls tingled with fresh aftershocks.

Bending, Cody licked that stained nipple, sucking it gently before biting playfully. Liam was boneless, waiting for the panic to hit him. Cody caressed him and kissed up his chest and neck gently, murmuring, "That was amazing."

Liam found he could only agree, staying flopped out on the bed as Cody padded to the bathroom and returned with a damp cloth to wipe up any remaining mess. The wet cotton felt good, his skin cooled by the fan blades thumping steadily overhead.

Cody hooked a leg over Liam's and stretched out on his side, propping his head in his hand. With his other, he idly traced patterns over Liam's chest and belly.

"I never do this," Liam said, surprised by the sound of his own rough voice saying the words aloud.

"Mmm. Define 'never.'" Cody's fingers drifted over Liam's ribs.

Acid bubbled in his gut. What was he doing? He needed to get the hell out. Get back in control. Yet he found himself confessing, "I go overseas once or twice a year and hook up with strangers. But I never do...*this*. Linger afterwards. And I never do it here in Australia. Or with an Australian. Let alone someone I actually know."

Cody's eyebrows shot up. "Wow. Okay." He circled Liam's bellybutton with his fingertips. "Do you usually have sex with women?"

"Not since I played footy. I never..." He looked at the high wooden ceiling. "It was what I was supposed to do, so I did."

Cody's foot rubbed gently over Liam's shin. "I understand."

"Do you?" Liam met his patient, kind gaze. "How? You're so open about it." He waved a hand. "About...gay things."

"We all have our own journey." Cody laughed. "That sounded really new-agey or some shit, but you know what I mean."

Liam closed his eyes, fear returning and tension tugging at him. "I'm breaking all my rules. I shouldn't be here. I can't ever—you don't understand. I—I—"

Warm lips met Liam's, covering his in a tender kiss. "Shh. You're safe here, remember?" Cody smoothed his hand over Liam's chest and flanks.

Opening his eyes, Liam sucked in a breath. "You can't tell anyone. No one knows. Not Teddy, not anyone. I shouldn't be here!"

"Hey, hey." Cody was half on top of Liam now. "Look at me." Liam realized he'd squeezed his eyes shut, and slowly opened them to find Cody watching him seriously. He caressed Liam's cheek. "I'll never tell anyone. I'll never out you. I promise."

Liam's breath whooshed from his lungs, the press of Cody's

warm body as reassuring as his words. "I'm not supposed to do this."

"We don't have to do anything." He nuzzled into Liam's neck.

"I should go. I have to go."

Sighing, Cody eased away and sat up. "Okay. I'll open the garage for you."

But Liam found himself tugging Cody back down, holding him close and fiddling with the curly ends of his hair. He *never* did this. They were *cuddling*. Liam had never stayed in bed with anyone, male or female, always getting up and dressed and showing them the door with a tight smile.

But he'd already obliterated the rules, and it was so comfy and warm in the dim light of the studio, the fan humming, Cody's breath tickling his throat. He was heavy and solid and real, and Liam wanted to hang on and say something to bring out his dimples again.

Just this once.

Chapter Eleven

L IAM'S STOMACH GROWLED, and Cody chuckled, stretching with a sleepy groan. They'd dozed, and now Cody reluctantly peeled himself off Liam and the bed. He was afraid Liam would bolt, but he had to piss, and he was hungry too.

From the bathroom, he called through the open door, "I can go over to Mod Cafe and bring back brunch. They do great sandwiches and salads. Whatever you like." He tried to keep his tone light and casual.

Liam Fox is naked in my bed. No biggie!

He added, "The beer and bottle of ketchup in the fridge aren't going to cut it."

Liam was sitting bolt upright on the bed now. He looked toward the laneway, the door still covered by the curtains. He was skittish AF, and Cody had never been with anyone so nervous. He decided to keep talking normally. "It only takes a minute since I can cut through the alley behind Galati's during the day. You can come with me, or I'll get whatever you like."

"I can't come with you." Liam looked at him like he was insane.

Cody said, "Okay. Is there anything you don't like?" He didn't point out that no one would think anything of them simply walking down Wray Avenue together. There was no reason for anyone to think they were more than friends.

Not that Cody could put any other label on them yet. It was still surreal that Liam was actually in his bed. The taste of him lingered in Cody's mouth, and he didn't want to brush it away with mint. He was going to savor sex with Liam every second he could.

"Uh, I don't fancy tomatoes."

"Cool." Cody pulled on shorts and a T-shirt, not bothering with underwear. Liam watched him closely. Cody grabbed his wallet and keys and slipped on his flip-flops. He opened the curtains over the door by the laneway enough to squeeze through.

"I'll lock the outer gate behind me. No one can get in." The fence and gate were made of dense wood, and the only way to see into the studio would be to climb up. The only people who used the laneway were other residents accessing their garages, and normally Cody wouldn't bother locking his gate if he were only running over to the cafe. He looked squarely at Liam. "Promise you'll be here when I get back?"

After a heartbeat, Liam nodded.

Cody practically skipped through the back of Galati's and across the street to Mod Cafe. He ended up doing four kinds of sandwiches and a selection of sweets for dessert. Nutella caramel slice, mint-choc slice, raspberry muffin, Chelsea bun. He hoped Liam had a sweet tooth, or he'd be hopped up on sugar.

As he waited for the sandwiches, he tried not to grin like an idiot. He'd sucked Liam Fox's dick, and it had been spectacular. He had no idea what to make of Liam's confession that he only had sex overseas. Wowsa. That was taking being on the down-low to a whole new level.

Liam was clearly terrified of anyone knowing. Cody could only imagine how stressful that was. How *lonely*. He hated it and wanted to make Liam smile and feel good and not be afraid ever again.

One step at a time.

He held his breath as he opened his door and squeezed through the heavy navy-blue drapes. He almost dropped the bulging paper bags, his heart plummeting at the empty studio. Shit, he shouldn't have left Liam alone with time to think. "Fuck," he said.

Liam appeared in the bathroom door, wearing his shorts and nothing else. "What?" he asked sharply.

"Oh! Nothing!" Cody managed a laugh. "I forgot to get an extra pickle."

Liam visibly exhaled, although he held himself stiffly. "You can have mine."

"Yeah? Thanks." It was only a pickle, and he actually could take or leave them, but affection flowed at Liam offering.

They stood looking at each other, Liam shifting awkwardly—anxiously, clearly out of his depth. Cody dropped the bags on the dining table and rounded it. "Hey," Cody whispered, slipping his arms around Liam's waist and lifting up on tiptoes to kiss him softly.

With a low sound in his throat, Liam kissed him back, big hands strong on Cody's hips. Shit, Cody wanted to forget lunch and get Liam back in bed and never leave it, but he was aching for more than that too. He eased away with a smile.

"Want to sit on the patio?"

But Liam looked at the closed drapes with suspicion, still fluttering in the breeze. "We should stay inside."

"Right. Cool." Cody nodded to the leather love seat and the TV in the corner. "Did you watch *Travel Guides* last night? I recorded it."

"Sure. Okay."

"Have a seat." Cody kissed him again lightly and got out plates. He made a spread on the thick Jarrah coffee table and flipped on the TV while Liam perched with a straight spine on the right-hand side of the love seat. The only other thing in the fridge was beer, and he offered Liam a bottle of Great Northern. "Drink?"

"Yeah, thanks. Wait—no." Liam rubbed his face. "I don't drink if I'm…"

"Is that one of your rules?"

He nodded, looking away guiltily. "But I've already broken the others, so why not."

Cody popped the bottle into a stubby holder and brought it over with his own, settling beside Liam. The love seat was relatively spacious, but Liam was huge, so his thigh pressed against Cody's. Cody fiddled with the remote and told Liam about the sandwiches, which he'd had cut in half so they could share. Liam went for the turkey and brie first, and Cody took note for the future. Not that he should be getting ahead of himself.

The TV was a good distraction, and they laughed at the Fren family complaining about climbing a ton of stairs to the top of a temple in Asia. They ate and drank, and Liam's spine relaxed bit by bit. It was nice just being together, and Cody couldn't resist watching him from the corner of his eye sometimes, loving the wrinkles around his eyes when he really laughed at something.

Cody switched to Netflix when the show was over, and they watched a couple of episodes of *Brooklyn Nine-Nine* and had a few more beers. The day had grown hot, and Cody's skin was moist, the fan keeping them cool enough with the drapes blocking the sun in their warm cocoon.

Suddenly Liam blurted, "Your parents don't mind?"

Cody blinked. "Oh, about me being gay?" At Liam's tight nod, he said, "Nah. Mom's totally supportive, and so are my sisters. I don't think it's my dad's *favorite* thing in the world, but… No, I shouldn't say that. When I told them, it felt like he was thinking, 'Here we go again—Cody insisting on being difficult. Being different.' But that's probably not fair of me either.

He's never been squeamish about it or anything. He didn't like my boyfriend Tommy, but I don't like him much either."

Liam half-smiled. "Fair enough."

Cody paused the show with the remote. "My dad and I don't really connect, but it's not about me being gay. He hates that I'm not going to uni. Haaates it. He's such a snob you'd think he was a classics professor or something and not science. My mom has accepted that being a lifeguard is my dream, at least."

"You have sisters too, right?"

"Yeah, Gwen and Lucy. They're cool. Gwen went back to Vancouver five years ago, and she's in postgrad now. Lucy's going to UBC too. When I was in year twelve here, my parents decided when I graduated, we'd move back to be close to my sisters and the mountains for my mom. Dad got a good position, so it was all set."

"Except you didn't want to go?"

"Nope. This is home now. I mean, Canada's awesome, but this is the place I'm meant to be. Living on the water, swimming, surfing, lifeguarding, being in the *sun*. It's rainy as fuck in Vancouver, and the rest of Canada is way too cold in winter. So I decided I wasn't going. Got my citizenship last year."

"How did your folks take it?"

Cody half-laughed, half-grimaced. "Not great at first. My dad's face got so red, I thought his head might pop clean off his neck." He made an exploding motion with his hands. "I told him it was his fault for moving us down here in the first place. Honestly, I don't understand what my mom sees in him. Not that I don't love my dad, but they're just so different. They make it work somehow, I guess. He gets his way most of the time from what I can tell, although there are some exceptions. He wanted to call me 'Bartholomew,' but Mom won that battle. Thank God."

"You'd be Barty or Barto." Liam laughed.

"Exactly! My dad grew up as Robbo, and he swore when he

went to Canada he would be Robert from that day forward. He never would have come back to Perth if he hadn't had such a great offer from UWA." Cody shrugged. "He did everything he could to convince me to go back with them, but living here is what I want."

"Do you talk much with your sisters?"

"We text and stuff. We get along great, but we're not super close. I miss them, but not enough to give up my dreams, which are totally different from theirs. They're really smart like my parents, but I was average at school. Not amazing, not terrible—in the middle."

"I didn't try much in class. Footy was all I needed. Mum and Dad didn't go to uni. Didn't even go to TAFE. Dad's been a brickie since he left school."

"Honestly, I'd rather be a tradie than an office drone. The idea of working in a cubicle is so depressing, and forget academia. I miss my family, but I have to live my own life, you know?"

After a pause, Liam nodded, but he dropped his eyes, his shoulders high with tension. Cody hesitated—should he even try to bring it up? Seemed like too good an opening not to. "What's it like with your parents?"

"Me?" Liam shrugged, eyes on Andy Samberg frozen onscreen. "All they ever expected was that I'd play footy. Tore them up when I had to retire, but there was nothing any of us could do about it."

"They don't know anything about this?" Cody motioned between them. "About you?"

Liam went rigid. "No. They can't know. No one can. This is why I have rules, why I shouldn't be here."

"It's okay," Cody soothed, not touching him aside from where their thighs pressed. "You're safe here, remember?" He quickly shifted the subject before Liam panicked and made a run for it. "And you knew Cyclone from when you were kids?"

"Yeah, Teddy was mates with my older brother Greg. Greg's a firey. Mum and Dad tried to convince me to join up, but I didn't want to stay in Mandurah. Had money, so I bought a little house in Barking. Nothing fancy, but it's all I need."

"Is it?" Cody asked, slipping his hand over Liam's knee. Liam went rigid, and Cody realized he was touching the scarred knee, skin ridged below his fingertips. He almost whipped his hand away but didn't. "Does it still hurt?"

"In my head," Liam rasped. He gripped his beer in his right hand and finished the bottle before thunking it on the table. "Do you want me to fuck you?"

Cody stuttered at the abrupt change of gears. "Uh—what? Um, yeah. Hell yeah." He loved fucking any way he could get it, and if this was what Liam needed, he was all in. He kissed Liam hard. "How do you want me?"

"Uh…" Something passed over Liam's face. Not exactly indecision, but a moment of uncertainty, a tremor of…what? Fear? "However you like it best."

Cody turned toward him on the love seat and flattened a palm over Liam's broad chest, stroking lightly over the hairy flesh with his thumb, teasing a nipple. Not pinching, but soothing. "I like it all sorts of ways. How do you like it best?"

A blush reddened Liam's face above his beard, and he laughed uneasily as he lurched to his feet. The beer was light, so there was no way it had affected him much, although he seemed unsteady. He tugged Cody's hand. "Come on."

Cody followed him around the love seat to the bed. "We don't have to fuck if you don't want to."

"What? No! Of course I want to. It was my idea." He stripped off, then tugged at Cody's clothes. Once Cody was naked, Liam spun him around, urging him onto his hands and knees on the bed. "I'll fuck you so good you'll feel it tomorrow."

"Mmm. Yes, please." Cody leaned across the mattress and

rooted around in the bedside table drawer, fishing out the lube and condoms. He passed them back to Liam and waited eagerly. When Liam's slick finger circled Cody's hole, Cody dropped to his elbows, arching his back and moaning. "*Yesss.*"

He'd meant it when he'd said he liked it all sorts of ways. With his ass up in the air, he felt deliciously slutty, presenting himself, submissive and ready to get drilled. When he got the chance to top, it made him so hot to be totally in charge, to fuck his partner hard and take control over him. Then ease off and make him beg for more. Make him beg to come.

It made his dick throb just to think of it, and if this was what Liam needed, Cody wanted to give it to him. He pushed back on Liam's finger impatiently. "I can take it. Come on."

So much for submissive.

He laughed to himself, dropping his forehead to the mattress. As much as Cody loved topping, he *did* like dick inside him, and the thought of Liam's thick cock was a major turn-on. Foil ripped, and he wriggled his ass eagerly. He wanted sweat and slapping skin, motion and rhythm.

Not saying anything, Liam took hold of Cody's hip and nudged at his hole. Cody bore down, groaning. "Fuck, that feels good. You're so big."

Liam grunted and pushed inside. The stretch burned almost too much, but Cody breathed through it, loving the sensation of fullness. He was being impaled, Liam inside him so deeply he might break. But it was so fucking *good*, and he cried out, eager to be rammed until he couldn't think straight.

"Shh!"

Cody tensed, disbelief flooding him like a cold shower. He lifted his head. "Did you seriously just *shush* me? In my own bed?" He looked back incredulously.

"Sorry." Liam screwed up his red face, pulling out and sitting back on his heels. He glanced at the glass doors to the patio. "I don't want her to hear."

"Huh? Mrs. Delfino? She can't hear us down here, and even if she could, I don't care! I like to make noise when I fuck. We're both grownups. We're allowed to do this. We're allowed to enjoy it."

"I know." Liam hung his head, rubbing the back of his neck. "I'm sorry."

The burst of anger faded. Liam was tied into so many knots, and Cody suspected being closeted was only part of it. "I get it. Let's try again. Okay?"

Nodding, Liam repositioned himself. He began thrusting in and out, and Cody stuck up his ass, pushing back. But he couldn't catch the fire he craved. Liam was silent aside from his breathing, and it felt like he was going through the motions. The connection between them had vanished, and they might as well have been in two different rooms even though their bodies were joined.

Cody twisted his head to look back at Liam. Eyes screwed shut, Liam grimaced as he fucked Cody's ass. He could feel that Liam was hard, so he had to be enjoying it well enough, but the magic was missing. Frustrated, Cody pushed up on his hands and reached back to grab Liam's thigh.

His eyes popping open, Liam stuttered to a stop. "Are you okay? Am I hurting you?"

Not in the way that feels good. "I'm fine. I just... Are you sure you're into this?"

Liam's face creased in what seemed like genuine pain. "I'm sorry. It's not you." He grunted in frustration. "I mean that—I don't mean—" He shook his head, squeezing his eyes shut again.

"Hey, it's okay." Cody eased forward while gently pushing him away, Liam's cock softening and slipping out. He urged Liam onto his back and straddled his hips, smoothing his hands over that hairy chest. "No dramas. We're good."

Eyes shut, Liam rubbed his hands over his face, his beard

scratching audibly. "I don't know what's wrong with me."

"There's nothing wrong with you." He leaned down and kissed the hollow of Liam's throat, rubbing his face against his stubbly neck, liking the roughness. He didn't know what the problem was, but maybe they could reconnect. It was like a loose wire in a cord of Christmas lights, and you just had to move it the right way and hit the right angle, and *boom*, the lights were back on and you were in business.

Cody started with kissing, nibbling his way up Liam's throat and chin and jaw, moving to his cheeks, one and then the other, before capturing his lips in a surprise move. He swallowed Liam's little gasp with a rush of satisfaction. Thrusting his tongue into Liam's mouth, he took charge of the kiss, weaving his fingers into Liam's short hair and angling his head.

Liam moaned now, and it was different than other sounds he'd made before. There was something...vulnerable to it, Liam underneath him, letting Cody take control. Excitement bubbled up, and he kissed Liam fiercely until their lips were swollen and his face was raw with beard burn.

Their chests heaved, and Cody muttered, "That's more like it."

Liam clutched at Cody's thighs, lips parted and spit-wet. In the dim light, his eyes looked black with lust. "Uh-huh," he rasped.

"Can I ride you?" Cody grinned. "Gonna come with you inside me whether you like it or not."

Liam sucked in a breath, and his cock, which had come back to life, swelled *hard* against Cody's ass. Cody's heart skipped. He wasn't sure why he'd added the last part. He'd only been joking—if Liam didn't like something, he would stop immediately. He'd meant it as a tease, but... Hmm.

Hmm.

Not sure exactly what he was doing, going on instinct, Cody

took Liam's wrists and pushed his arms over his head on the mattress, pinning him down.

Liam lifted his hips, his rock-hard cock seeking pressure.

Fire tore through Cody like scrub igniting in the dry season. Did he want Cody to take charge? It sure seemed like he did. Cody licked his lips, and Liam watched the movement, his hips jerking again.

Cody kept hold of Liam's thick, corded wrists against the bed. Liam was far stronger than he was—he could toss Cody off him anytime he wanted. Yet he didn't. He stayed put, breathing hard. Waiting.

Cody leaned down and whispered in his ear. "I'm gonna ride you so hard. Gonna come all over you, then feed it to you until you swallow every drop. You can't touch me. Don't move unless I say you can." Still holding Liam down, he leaned back, heart in his throat. Had he gone too far? Was Liam going to shove him off and leave?

Liam nodded breathlessly.

"Yes?" Shit, was this really happening?

"Yes," Liam croaked. He swallowed thickly and his eyes fluttered closed. Not the screwed-shut determination of earlier, but a release. "Please," he whispered.

Cody could hardly breathe, relief and anticipation battling. Part of him wanted to take his time, tease Liam relentlessly until he begged to be covered in Cody's jizz, but he was too desperate to come. The excitement of Liam submitting had him shaking as he lowered himself on Liam's cock, releasing one of Liam's wrists so he could reach back and get that gorgeous shaft inside him.

Liam didn't move his arm. He hardly moved a muscle, only lifting his hips to help Cody maneuver him inside. They both moaned as Cody sank all the way down, squeezing Liam's cock with his ass, eager for the burn. Liam did move now, his free hand reaching for Cody. Cody grabbed his wrist and held it down

138

again. Liam moaned even louder now.

"No. You can't move unless I tell you. Can't come until I tell you." At Liam's nod, Cody kissed him lightly, slowly. "Or next time maybe I'll tie you up." Liam gasped, his cock throbbing inside Cody. "You want that?" Cody asked. Liam didn't answer, sweat glistening on his forehead and dripping down his temple. "I think you do. I think you'll do everything I say, and you'll love it. And so will I."

He fucked himself on Liam's thick cock, crying out as he hit his gland. "And I'm going to be so loud when I come all over you, and there's nothing you can do about it."

Liam *whimpered*, and the sound almost sent Cody right over the edge without even touching his own dick. He did now, using his right hand, giving Liam a glare to remind him not to move. Liam watched him, mouth open, panting, his hips making little desperate thrusts. Cody stopped to grab the lube, accidentally squirting it all over both of them.

But he got some on his dick, and he moaned, because it was just what he needed. Liam's eyes shut, and Cody ordered, "Look at me." His eyes popped open.

Grunting and twisting, Cody found the right angle, the friction on his gland sending up fireworks, white spots in his vision, his hand flying as he came, crying out shamelessly, spurting in long threads over Liam's hairy chest, even onto his chin. "Fuck! *Yes.*"

As the pleasure subsided, Cody squeezed Liam's cock inside him, wanting to hear that whimper again. Liam panted softy. "Please."

Cody took hold of Liam's free wrist with slippery fingers and lifted higher, bringing up both of Liam's arms over his head and crossing the wrists so he could hold him down with one hand. With the other, he scooped up his jizz, bringing it to Liam's mouth. Liam licked it up with little lapping sounds of pleasure.

Some of it was still stuck in Liam's chest hair, but good enough. Gripping his wrists, Cody squeezed the iron rod of Liam's cock inside him. His ass was sore since it had been a while, but he didn't care. With his finger in Liam's mouth, he rocked his hips. "You've been so good. You can come now."

Moaning around Cody's finger, Liam thrust helplessly, his head slamming back on the mattress as he strained, the muscles in his taut arms bulging. Cody squeezed his ass, giving him the friction he needed, and Liam shook violently with his release.

They panted together, Cody dropping his head to the crease of Liam's neck, loosening his grasp on Liam's wrists. He and Liam were wet and getting sticky, and Cody reluctantly eased off to get rid of the condom and dampen the washcloth, his feet quiet on the wooden floor.

When he returned, Liam still had his arms over his head, wrists crossed. His legs flopped open, that big body boneless. He watched as Cody cleaned him.

Cody asked quietly, "You liked that?"

Liam nodded, a blush creeping down his chest. Cody kissed him deeply. "You were so good for me. Thank you."

"I shouldn't—" Liam shook his head.

"Like *hell*. That was incredible, and we are definitely going to do it again."

Tossing the cloth wherever, Cody stretched out, snuggling into Liam's side. He reached up and tugged Liam's arms down, wanting that warm strength wrapped around him now. Liam might run away soon, so Cody burrowed close while he had the chance.

Chapter Twelve

THE STACCATO KNOCK echoed through the tower, and Liam
shared an apprehensive glance with Bickie. Knocks came in
different types—hesitant, casual, friendly, urgent. The tenor of
this one had Liam hurrying to answer, the edge of franticness to
the raps getting his blood pumping.

A boy of about twelve stood at the top of the steps, leaning
back to let the door swing wide as Liam opened it. The blond kid
was panting, his fingers twitching as he shifted anxiously like he
was standing on burning hot sand. His blue boardies and black
short-sleeved rashie looked dry, but his hair was damp. He
blurted, "I can't find my sister!"

"Okay, buddy." Liam patted his trembling shoulder. "Come
inside. It's all right. We'll find her." He ushered the boy in,
guiding him up the few steps to the viewing area. "What's your
name?"

"Jake."

"Okay, Jake. How old's your sister?"

"Ten. I told her to swim between the flags. I wanted to surf
with my mates up the north end. Mum only lets me surf when it's
little swells like today, so even if I'm smoked, I won't get too
hurt." His words tripped out.

"That makes sense." Liam had to refocus him. "And you last

saw your sister going into the water at the flags? Or heading toward that area?"

"Yeah, she was walking that way. I didn't want to bring her, but Mum made me." He fidgeted. "I can't find her!"

Liam slung his arm around Jake's thin shoulders and pressed him into one of the desk chairs. "No worries. We're going to find her. What's her name?"

"Emily."

Bickie said, "Breathe, buddy. This happens every day. We'll find her. What's she wearing? Is she blond like you?"

"Uh-huh. And, um, pink bathers. Pink with white dots."

Liam asked, "What about a rashie or hat?"

He shook his head. "She's supposed to, but she left them on the towels. They're there, but she's not. I looked for her by the flags, and my mates did too, but we can't see her anywhere."

Crouching by Jake's chair, Liam patted his knee. "How long since you last saw her?" He blocked out Bickie on the radio, spreading the word to search for Emily.

"We surfed for a while. An hour, I think." Jake shivered. "I thought she'd be there when we got back. We started looking, and she wasn't by the flags."

"And how long did you look before you came here?"

"Twenty minutes, I guess."

Shit. Almost an hour and a half, give or take. "Mate, she probably came out of the water and couldn't find where you left your gear. Beach is crowded, and it's easy to get turned around, especially kids. Is she a good swimmer?"

He nodded. "We both did Nippers."

Bickie asked, "You're sure she went between the flags?"

Jake gnawed on his lower lip, turning it white. "I'm not sure. That's where I told her to go! And she knows. But I was concentrating on the swells."

"The tide's in; the rips are quiet right now," Liam said. "I'm sure she's somewhere on the sand."

On the radio, Bickie said, "Pete, get the ski and have a good look out the back. Take Mia with you. Chook, you copy at south end?"

"Copy," Cody said. "I'm looking for her and asking around."

A secret little shiver shot down Liam's spine at the sound of Cody's voice, memories of yesterday cartwheeling through his mind. It was entirely inappropriate that his balls tightened when he was at work—dealing with a missing kid!—but his body had a mind of its own.

He still couldn't believe yesterday had actually happened. When he'd finally left after they ordered in supper, Cody had held Liam's face in his hands and stared at him intensely, up on his tiptoes.

He'd promised again that he'd never out Liam—that this was their secret. Liam knew the safest thing was to go back to his rules and never, ever see Cody outside of work again. He should get back to normal. Back to safety.

He also knew he couldn't.

He knew it in the thrill down his spine and the little spot of tenderness on one of his wrists where Cody had squeezed. He knew it in the fact that he'd woken hard and fantasizing about Cody fucking him. They'd only scratched the surface, and there was an endless need in him for more. He should have been scared out of his mind—and he was. He was caught in a rip, and fighting against it wouldn't help. He had to ride it out.

All morning, he'd wished they could run away and lock themselves back up in Cody's studio. But they had work to do. Kids to help. To Jake, he said, "It's okay. She'll probably rock up any minute saying she can't find you and that *you're* missing."

Jake smiled weakly, nodding. "Me mum's going to kill me if anything happens to Em." Tears welled in his blue eyes. "What if some pervert grabbed her? I was so annoyed with her coming along. I was *mean*."

"Aw, mate, we've all been there." Bickie rolled closer on his chair and squeezed Jake's shoulder. "Little sisters do your head in, eh? But of course you still love 'em. Look, we're going to find her. You sit here with me for a few minutes, and Foxy'll go check the park and cafe."

Liam nodded and gave Jake a sympathetic smile before hurrying out of the tower with his sunnies and cap. The park's grass was soft under his bare feet as he jogged along, hoping to spot a miserable little girl looking lost. He got on the radio to Damo by the flags.

"Any sign there? This poor kid's beside himself." Eyes peeled for any pink, Liam headed to the walking and biking path that passed the cafe and stretched out kilometers in both directions.

"Nothing. The ski's out, but the brother said she could swim? They're locals?"

"Yeah." Not that capable swimmers couldn't drown, but it was less likely when the rips weren't pulling. If she'd been between the flags, she shouldn't have had any problems, and a local was less likely than a non-swimming tourist to get into trouble.

Liam said, "If we can't find her in fifteen, we call the coppers. I'll get the brother out of the tower and keep him busy. Don't want to upset him any more. We'll have to call the parents too."

"Copy that. There's heaps of people on the beach. I reckon she's just been swallowed up by that crowd and she'll come good. They always do."

"Yep, let's hope so."

Every missing child at Barking since Liam had started work had been found safe and sound. Usually took a few years off the parents' lives with the worry, but otherwise no harm done. Yet every time, the thought circled his brain like a shark: *There's a first time for everything.*

He made his way back to the tower and was just taking Jake

outside so Bickie could call the police and the kids' mum when Cody's voice came over the radio. "Central, I've got her. Bringing her up to the tower now."

"Ah, sweet as," Bickie said. "Did everyone catch that? Stand down—Emily's been found."

"She's okay?" Jake asked, still pale and looking like he didn't quite believe it.

Liam shepherded him onto the sand. He pointed at the ATV winding toward them through the sea of umbrellas and people. "She'll be here any minute." He patted the boy's scrawny shoulder.

Emily was surprisingly dry-eyed as she climbed out of the buggy but burst into tears when she saw her brother. "I couldn't find you!" She hiccupped, and Jake pulled her into a hug that was all awkward, skinny limbs.

"I'm sorry," he mumbled miserably, patting her back. Then he blurted, "Don't tell Mum!"

Liam said, "Next time you'll swim with your sister between the flags, right?"

Jake nodded as he stepped away from Emily. He looked up at Liam. "Thanks. Sorry for being so..." He waved his hand and grimaced.

"Mate, you handled it better than I did." Liam lowered his voice like he was telling a secret. "I once lost my sister at a shopping center. Cried my eyes out."

Jake and Emily's eyebrows shot up, and they laughed disbelievingly, Emily swiping at her wet cheeks. Jake's pals ran up, talking over each other in their clear relief that Emily had been found. One offered to buy her a yellow Calippo, and the prospect of the frozen treat had them all running off to the cafe with a final wave for Liam and Cody.

Cody blew out a loud breath, taking off his sunnies and polishing them with his shirt. "That's a relief." He gazed at Liam thoughtfully. "You don't have a sister, do you?"

"Nah, but…" He shrugged.

"But you wanted to make him feel better. Both of them."

Liam nodded, suddenly tongue-tied at the secret little smile Cody was giving him, his gaze dropping to Liam's mouth and back up like he wanted to kiss him. Liam admitted, "I remembered how you said you fin chopped a girl to make that bloke feel better for crashing into another surfer. That night with the spinal."

"I remember. You're really sweet," Cody murmured, and Liam wanted to kiss him desperately, basking in the glow of Cody's tender gaze.

Keeping his voice calm, Liam spoke into the radio. "Central, I'm going to ride back with Cody. Do a sweep." He climbed into the passenger seat Emily had vacated. It wasn't smart, but he was dying to be near Cody. Just for a few minutes.

Behind the wheel, Cody spoke softly as he drove. "I wasn't sure you'd want to talk to me at all today."

"Me either," Liam admitted.

"I wanted to text you this morning, but I knew you were opening, and I thought… Maybe you'd get pissed off."

"How do you have my number?" The idea of texts from Cody made him equally excited and nervous.

"That group chat with the other guys on WhatsApp."

"Oh, right. Maybe we should just keep everything professional."

Cody glanced at him as he tapped the horn. "In writing, you mean? Or all the time?"

A hundred percent he should have replied, "*All the time*," but Liam said, "In texts and emails or whatever."

"Cool." Cody parked at the south end of the flags, and they watched the water in silence.

From the corner of his eye, Liam could see Cody tracing idle patterns over the steering wheel with his fingers. He could almost feel it on his skin, all his nerves on alert. After years of shutting down, especially at work—ignoring shirtless colleagues and blokes on the beach—Liam was hyper-aware of Cody's body.

The hair on his legs was tawny. His bare right knee was only a few inches from Liam's left, and Liam imagined he could feel the heat of Cody's skin. Cody pushed up the sleeves of his blue uniform shirt, his corded forearms strong.

There were freckles dotted on his arms amid a scattering of hair. Liam itched to trace a fingertip over the clusters, which would probably get darker over the summer and the long, sun-filled days. Cody had gotten wet earlier, and his hair had curled at the tips above his ears.

Liam imagined Cody naked and stretched out on a bright towel on pale sand, somewhere on their own without another soul around. He'd be glistening all over, his freckles stark, a tan line around his narrow waist…

Idly tapping the steering wheel, Cody said, "I'm off a couple hours after you. I could come over. Your house is close by, right?"

Bang! Liam's heart went like he was doing a rescue, his fantasies obliterated by panic. "Too close!" He shook his head. "Hazza lives in the next block, and Teddy's right around the corner, and you'd pass Baz's place. No. I'll come to you."

"Oh. Okay." His tone was flat, and Cody's reflective sunnies hid his eyes completely. He was holding onto the steering wheel now even though they weren't moving. There was a freckle by his ear that Liam wanted to press his lips to.

"It's not that—it's not you. I just can't—I shouldn't even be doing any of this. I don't want…"

Cody's shoulders relaxed an inch, his hands sliding away from the wheel. "I understand. Really." He smiled, a sly little curve of his pretty mouth as he dropped his voice. "There's so much I want to say to you right now."

Before Liam could start to imagine what that might be, another buggy pulled up. Teddy hopped out, and talk about feeling like a kid with his hand in the lolly jar. His face burned, and he shifted in his seat as Teddy leaned in his side. Liam jerked when he patted his shoulder the way he had a million times.

"Whoa!" Teddy smiled. "Didn't mean to sneak up on ya." Liam crossed his arms and laughed it off as Teddy added, "Good job on finding the girl, Chookie."

"Thanks," Cody said. "I was getting pretty worried."

As Teddy and Cody chatted, Liam concentrated on calming himself the hell down as he scanned the water. This was exactly why he'd followed his rules for so many years, and it should have been a reminder of why he had to end it with Cody immediately and never so much as glance at him again outside of work.

Yet now that the door had been opened, it felt impossible to shut. Not yet. He had to find out what Cody wanted to say, didn't he? It was only polite.

Liam barely resisted snorting to himself. *Polite.* He was so full of shit. He—

"That kid's struggling, hey?" Liam said. Sitting up straighter, he focused on the boy's awkward, flailing arm strokes. "Not far from shore, but..."

Cody was already dropping his sunnies and hat in the back. "Should I go in? Yeah?"

They always tried to give people a chance to get back in themselves, but with kids, Liam was quicker to say, "Yeah. Get him." He kept watch on the boy as Cody whipped off his shirt, grabbed the board, and ran. Teddy stood on the running board on the driver's side watching, and he and Liam didn't say anything aside from radioing Central to tell them Cody was in the water.

When Cody had the boy on his board and was paddling him in, Teddy slouched behind the wheel, propping a bare foot on the side mirror. "Good rescue. He's a natural."

"Mmm," Liam agreed, afraid if he said more he'd give himself and Cody away in a heartbeat.

After a minute of quiet, watching Cody chat to the boy at the shoreline, kneeling and speaking to him kindly, Teddy said, "Too bad your old man's still in the dark ages."

Liam really should have put some Quick-Eze in his bum bag. He kept his voice even. "Yeah. He's not gonna change now." If there was one thing in the world Liam was sure of, it was that.

"Probably not. Still. Jill said Cors was pretty upset."

Guilt flooded Liam as he thought of the way his father had snapped at her, calling her '*girly*.' "Shit. I should've said something." He'd been too cowardly, too afraid to draw any attention to himself while the other F-word was still echoing in the air.

Teddy shrugged. "Greg should've said something. She's his wife."

The question was one Liam had asked himself a million times. He recklessly said it aloud before he could lose his nerve. "Do you think he agrees with Dad?" Liam wasn't sure he wanted to know the answer.

"About that homophobic crap?" Teddy hesitated. "Nah. I mean… I can't remember him ever saying much about gay people. I'm sure we all said some ignorant shit when we were kids. Stupid jokes. But I wouldn't think Greg's like that. Hope not. Honestly, we don't hang out much these days unless Jill and Cora set it up, or it's something with your family. Just busy."

"Yeah. I don't see him much either." Truthfully, it was only when he had to.

Teddy took off his sunnies and polished them on his shirt, his gaze on the water. "Did you two have a row at some point?"

"What?" Liam scoffed. "'Course not. Like you said, just busy." The fact that he'd distanced himself from the family over the years had nothing to do with Greg.

"Once you have kids there never seems to be time for anything." He gave Liam a friendly poke with his elbow. "You'll see. So... That Sandra seemed all right? You going to ring her?"

Liam watched Cody walking towards them with the rescue board. Water dripped down his bare chest, and a secret little bolt of excitement shot straight to Liam's dick. "Maybe," he lied. He'd been forced into half an hour of small talk with Sandy at the barbecue, and that was enough.

Teddy laughed, but his brow was creased. "What are we going to do with you?"

As Cody slid the board back in the rack on the side of the buggy, he asked with a smile, "About what?"

"Nothing," Liam answered.

"About you being the pickiest bastard on Earth!" Teddy exclaimed. "You must've dated hundreds of gorgeous girls by now. Every time someone tries to fix you up, you say you're seeing someone else. Yet we never meet them. What are you looking for? Bloody perfection? You'll end up old and alone." Teddy gave him another friendly nudge. "You can only play the field for so long, mate. Find a keeper and leave the fucking around to the young blokes." He nodded at Cody.

Cody smiled—without dimples—and suddenly looked off at the water. "Is that a head out the back?" He climbed up on the buggy, and Liam and Teddy straightened up, peering intently at the water.

Teddy was all seriousness. "In front of us? Or toward third gate?"

"Yeah, toward third," Cody answered from above where he leaned over the roll bar. "Ah, wait. It's okay. She's swimming strongly. Sorry—wasn't sure for a second. False alarm."

"No, it's all good," Teddy said. "Always watching and questioning." He clapped his hands once. "Right, I'd better get back on patrol. It's a busy one. All hands on deck." He hopped out of the buggy with a wave.

Liam exhaled slowly as Teddy drove away. "Thanks for the distraction," he said quietly, glancing up at Cody.

Cody looked down and winked. "Anytime. See you tonight?"

The dark thrill returned, and Liam nodded. "Tonight," he whispered.

Chapter Thirteen

L IAM HUNG AROUND the beach after his shift ended, going for a surf. Growing up, he'd been consumed with footy, but he'd still surfed sometimes with Teddy and Greg. As a lifeguard, he'd improved his skills vastly.

When the lineup got too crowded, he dried off in the park, pretending to sun bake. Finally, Cody wheeled his bike down the ramp from the tower and rode off along the bike path that linked up to Freo. He hadn't glanced Liam's way, although Liam couldn't tell if that was on purpose or whether Cody hadn't noticed him.

It wouldn't be a long ride, and Liam counted off the seconds and minutes, the late-afternoon sun dipping lower. The fresh, shorn grass of the park was soft and springy, tickling his bare skin where he stretched out, the earthy smell filling his nose.

Ten minutes. One, two, three…

When he reached twelve, he sprang up and hurried home, his bare feet thudding on the footpath as he told himself not to run. He didn't change out of his gray boardies or put on a shirt. He only went into the house far enough to drop the bag with his dirty uniform, slip his feet into thongs, and grab his car keys.

He had a squat little driveway in the shade of a couple Catalpa trees, and no garage. His few seasons in the AFL had left him with a ton of money, but he'd bought a squat little place with only two bedrooms, not wanting to rattle around in some McMansion.

The leather seats of the SUV were hot, and he fired up the air con as he headed north, tapping the wheel, not bothering with the radio. A voice in his head dutifully advised him to turn around and recover from this dive into insanity before he could be towed out to sea any farther.

He ignored it, thinking about Cody and getting hard as he navigated the roundabouts and speed humps.

When he pulled into Cody's laneway, it occurred to him that he might have to ring him to open the garage door. But it was open and waiting, Cody's bike against the far wall. Liam backed in, forcing himself to go slowly.

He squeezed out, avoiding a hanging mop handle on the wall. The garage door rumbled shut behind him, and he realized Cody had ducked under the laundry, standing between T-shirts and a beach towel. A few pairs of boxer-briefs hung there too.

"Hey," Cody said, spinning the remote for the garage around his finger on a key ring. He'd changed into shorts and a tee when he'd left the tower—none of them were allowed to wear their uniform while off duty. Now he was only wearing the shorts, the tee gone.

"Hey." Liam sounded breathy and high-pitched, and he winced a bit. He stood there squeezed between the SUV and the concrete wall. Waiting.

A little furrow knitted Cody's brows. The light bulb in the ceiling was apparently on a motion timer, since it went out. Now Cody's face was in shadow, the fading light behind him and the laundry.

"C'mere," Cody whispered.

Heart in his throat, Liam scraped along the wall and ducked under a blue uniform shirt that reminded him he was breaking the rules. *All* the rules. He ignored it as Cody tugged his head down for a hot, wet kiss, his fingers rough in Liam's short hair, his tongue demanding entrance in his mouth.

They were hidden in the laundry under the lip of the garage, and he relaxed into the kiss, moaning. Cody pulled back, licking across Liam's bottom lip, his hands flattening on Liam's bare chest and teasing his nipples. Liam shivered.

"Been dying to do that all day," Cody said.

Liam nodded and kissed him again, chasing more contact. But Cody slipped out from the clothes, giving Liam's hand a tug before letting go. Liam followed him along the short footpath. When he looked up, he could only see the orange reflection of sunset in a few clouds, and the sprawling bougainvillea over the neighbor's fence. The passion fruit vines obscured the detail of Mrs. Delfino's house.

You're safe here.

He followed inside the studio, relieved to see that Cody had already tightly shut the other curtains, and that he locked up behind them and pulled the drapes closed. The air con was on low, the ceiling fan thumping. Liam stood by the dining table, waiting.

Leaning against the navy drapes that covered the windows and glass door, Cody tilted his head, brows close again. "Are you afraid to touch me?"

"Uh... No?" Liam shifted. He was doing it all wrong, clearly.

"Do you want to kiss me?"

Was that a trick bloody question? He nodded, fidgeting.

"Then come here. You're allowed to kiss me."

No, I'm not. I'm really not. He said, "I know."

"Then why do you look like you're waiting for the firing squad?" Cody held out his hand, and Liam made his feet move, reaching out to catch it and let Cody pull him down into another kiss. This one was softer, Cody nuzzling against him, Liam's beard rasping. He pulled back and asked, "Want a drink?" With another kiss, he eased away and went to the fridge. "Beer, Coke, wine—"

"No wine!" Liam blurted, cringing at how strident he'd sounded. "Uh, beer's good."

"Okay." Cody looked as though he was going to ask, but thankfully he let Liam off the hook. He put a bottle of Great Northern in a stubby holder and passed it over before opening his own. "I'm glad you're here." He motioned Liam to a chair at the table as the microwave beeped.

"Hope leftover pad thai's okay." Cody scraped noodles onto two plates.

Were they going to sit there and just...have dinner? Sure, they'd had lunch the day before—was it really only yesterday?—but that was before...

Cody put the plates on the table and sat across from him. There were a few bowls of snacks as well—crisps and caramel popcorn. But Liam was distracted by Cody's lean, muscled chest. There was only a bit of hair, and he was captivated by the swirl of it around Cody's reddish-pink nipples.

Cody asked, "Is this okay? Sorry, I need to hit the grocery store tomorrow."

Liam forced himself to eat a few crisps—honey soy chicken, he thought. "No worries." He poked at the leftovers on his plate, not sure he could get it down, his stomach knotted. Were they going to go to bed? They *were*, weren't they?

"I like that print." Liam needed to say something to drown out the doubts. He motioned to a framed retro style poster of the Fremantle port, shipping cranes in a colorful row in the illustration.

"Thanks. I've always liked the cranes. They're strangely beautiful, you know? They remind me of birds you'd make with origami. Either that, or a cross between giraffes and Imperial Walkers."

Liam sipped his beer and smiled softly. "Yeah. I can see that."

Cody flicked out his tongue to catch a bit of peanut from the corner of his mouth. Yesterday, those lips had been wrapped around Liam's cock, and now they were sitting at the table eating leftovers. He'd never even learned a hookup's name before. Had always shown them the hotel room door once the condom was in the bin. Had been too afraid to ask them for what he really wanted, but Cody knew.

As if reading his mind, Cody said, "That was really good yesterday. Being in charge. You liked it, right? When I told you what to do?"

Liam squirmed. Were they actually going to *talk* about it? Cody had been...*vocal* before, but that was in the heat of the moment. This was over beer and crisps and pad thai! Couldn't they just get to it and stop with the talking? He opened and closed his mouth, trying to come up with a reply.

"It got me so hot."

Now Liam sputtered, looking anywhere but at Cody. "You—" He threw up his hands. "You talk so much!"

Cody jerked his head as though Liam had slapped him. "Okay. And I guess that bothers you?" He sounded hurt and a little angry.

"I didn't mean it like that. I'm saying this all wrong. I don't— I'm not used to talking about all this." He waved his hand.

"Sex?"

"Yes!" Sweat prickled the back of Liam's neck, and he shoved a mouthful of noodles in his mouth. He'd been too anxious earlier to eat lunch, and even though his stomach growled, he could barely chew. After he swallowed, he added, "I've never talked about it, but you'll say anything and everything."

A smile tugged at Cody's lips. "It's true, I will. I love sex. Thinking about it, talking about it, doing it. Sex is awesome." He sat back in his chair and took a swig of beer. "When was your first time? With a man?"

Shame flooded him, and he jammed a fistful of sickly-sweet popcorn into his mouth. He shrugged.

Cody's face creased with concern, but he said mildly, "Mine was with Tommy. I was seventeen. He hardly ever let me top." He rolled his eyes. "Tommy's such an *aaasshole*."

Liam found himself smiling a bit. "He is." He hesitated, then casually asked, "You like doing that?" before gulping more beer.

"Topping? Oh yeah." Cody grinned, and there were the dimples. "I've experimented with a bunch of stuff. But I definitely like topping. I haven't done it a ton, but I dig it." He idly ran his finger around the rim of the bowl of popcorn, gaze on his hand. "Do you want me to top you?"

Liam's throat went dry as Cody met his eyes, the question hanging, the fan blades going *thump, thump, thump*, cool air dancing over Liam's bare chest. His nipples tightened, along with his balls.

"I shouldn't," Liam whispered.

Cody's spine snapped straight, his face screwing up. "Says who?"

"I don't know. Everyone." He picked up a crisp but was pretty sure he'd choke on it. He shouldn't like being held down and told what to do. "I should be the one on top." He crumbled the crisp with stiff fingers.

"*A man like you? No, no, no.*"

Liam could hear the mocking voice and thick Italian accent as if Lorenzo sat at the table with them now. More than mocking— *disgusted*. He could imagine the grass of Paris's Bois du Boulogne damp under his knees, seeping through his jeans. When they'd first taken a cab to the park, Lorenzo had snickered at Liam's struggle to pronounce the name, but Liam hadn't minded the ribbing. He'd been so excited.

"Did someone say that to you?" Cody pressed his lips into a thin line. "Did someone say you shouldn't want to be fucked?

Because you're big and strong?"

"Well, yeah. Look at me."

Cody's nostrils flared, and he leaned forward, hands flat on the table. "I don't know who the fuck he was, but that's bullshit. Bull. Shit."

That night, Liam's head had spun pleasantly with a bottle of red—he hadn't been sure what kind since he didn't know red wine beyond the sparkling Shiraz his mum bought at Christmas. He liked to blame the wine for dropping to his knees in the stand of thick-leaved trees and tugging at Lorenzo's belt, begging to be fucked.

Shame burned his cheeks, and he didn't know what to do with Cody's anger. "But a man like me..."

He remembered the curl of Lorenzo's lip. Lorenzo had been pretty and tall with glossy waves of hair, and Liam had wanted his cock inside him so badly he'd been ready to bend over on the footpath outside the cafe where they'd eaten mussels and chips with their wine. *Frites*, the French had called them. They were thin and delicate, the fanciest chips Liam had ever had.

"It's bad enough I'm gay," Liam explained, but Cody's nostrils flared.

"There's nothing wrong with being gay," Cody insisted.

"No, not for you." Liam wasn't saying this right, but more memories invaded.

He'd waited until they were hidden in the park before dropping down. Lorenzo had been bossy as hell the whole day since they'd met by the Eiffel Tower, and Liam had grown more and more excited. Lorenzo definitely didn't follow AFL—he'd claimed to barely be interested in soccer. He'd been bloody perfect.

Until he'd sneered down at Liam, stepping back and shoving Liam away. "*I thought you were a real man, no? It should not be like this.*" He'd waved his hand at Liam. "*A man like you should be strong! This is... No, no. It's pathetic.*"

Cody's blunt nails dug into Liam's forearm as he leaned forward. "Are you listening? That's bullshit, Liam. That's what my sisters call 'toxic masculinity,' and they're so right. Are you saying it's okay for me to want to get fucked because I'm smaller? You realize misogyny has its grubby fingerprints all over this, right?"

"I…" Liam wanted to run. He wanted to whip his arm away and run. This was why he'd had rules. He couldn't be sitting here *talking* about this.

The shame still burned more than ten years after Paris, the embers flaring to life reliably. Sometimes when he tried to sleep at night, his brain would replay it all endlessly—the wine, the wet knees, the begging, Lorenzo's disgust. Then his pity, which was even worse, and the stabbing, horrible pain when Lorenzo had briefly tried to give Liam what he wanted.

"I'm sorry." Liam didn't know what else to say.

"Fuck," Cody muttered, letting go of Liam's arm and rubbing his hands over his head, leaving a few chunks of hair askew. His cheeks puffed out. "I'm sorry. I'm not mad at you. I'm mad at our fucked-up society. I'm mad at whoever told you that you shouldn't want what turns you on." He slowly pushed back his chair and stepped close around the edge of the table, standing between Liam's legs as he leaned down to kiss gently.

It was only a press of lips this time, tender and apologetic. Liam held onto Cody's legs just above his knees, fingers wrapping behind, seeking the warmth and strength. Cody took Liam's face in his hands, peering down at him seriously.

Cody asked, "Have you ever been fucked the way you want?"

"No. Not until you." He gripped Cody's legs, needing an anchor. "I tried once. He… He was the one…" Liam had to close his eyes, not able to look at Cody. "Didn't last long. It hurt."

"Oh, baby," Cody murmured, pressing sweet little kisses to Liam's cheeks.

Liam stiffened. "You shouldn't call me that."

"Why?" Cody stroked Liam's cheeks with his thumbs. Liam still didn't open his eyes, and Cody whispered, "Because I'm younger? Smaller? That's bullshit too." His thumbs moved rhythmically. "When did that happen to you? When it hurt?"

He dug his fingers into Cody's legs, eyes still squeezed shut. His voice almost sounded like it was someone else's telling this story. "Just before I joined the service. Footy was over for good. I went to Europe. I'd been there a week, in Paris. I went to clubs. Made out with some blokes for the first time. Hand jobs in the toilets—that kind of thing. It was all new. Exciting. Then I met Lorenzo."

Liam gave Cody the short version, ending with, "I never asked again. I realized I'd been reckless, going to gay bars, even in Europe. I'd been fantasizing about telling everyone back home. About having a new life. But I'd been bloody stupid to think..."

His eyes were still shut, and his stomach heaved. He couldn't believe he was actually *saying* any of this out loud. That he was telling Cody what a coward he was. "No one can know. I only used apps after that. Quick hookups in my hotel rooms."

After a few moments of silence, his warm hands still steady on Liam's face, Cody asked, "And that's the way it's been the last, what? Ten years?"

Steeling himself for Cody's disgust at just how pathetic Liam was, he opened his eyes. His heart stuttered. There was no repulsion in Cody's eyes. There were *tears*, a sudden wetness that Cody blinked away. Maybe Liam should have hated to see that pity, but it was nothing like Lorenzo's had been.

Taking a shuddering breath, Cody leaned down and kissed him again. Gently at first, and then Liam opened his mouth, gasping, pulling Cody to sit over his lap, needing more. Cody clung to his shoulders, turning his head and diving into Liam's mouth with his tongue in a way that felt like wonderful penetration.

Soon they panted, both hard and sweaty where any bare skin touched, Liam's palms flat on Cody's back. Cody grinned at him, and Liam's heart soared.

Cody promised, "When you're ready, I'm going to fuck you. And there won't be anything wrong with it. Or you." He claimed Liam's mouth again, licking inside, spit slicking their swollen lips.

"God, please," Liam begged, thrusting up his hips. "Now." Tomorrow this could all disappear, and he couldn't wait. It might have been stupid to trust Cody—had it only been a day since they'd first touched? But he *did* trust him, and he needed this too much to deny himself a minute longer.

Cody leaned back, looking seriously into Liam's eyes. "Yeah?"

"Yes."

"On the bed. Now." Cody sprang up, his hard prick tenting his shorts.

They got naked, and Liam crossed to the bed, head spinning, as if he was outside himself. Then he was on his back, Cody straddling him, and Liam was back in his body with a vengeance, his skin too tight, lust burning through his veins.

"When did you first think about having a cock in your ass?" Cody toyed with Liam's nipples, sending sparks over his chest.

"Year eleven. Got tackled hard on the pitch."

Cody bit his lip, eyes lighting up. "I watched some of your footy highlights on YouTube. You were always so in control, hey? Even if you got a bullshit call from the ref, you never let it shake you. It must have taken a lot of discipline."

Lungs tight, Liam could only nod.

"I bet it felt good to fantasize about someone else being in control for a while. I bet you'd love it, getting on your hands and knees. Being fucked so hard you can barely stand it. But you *can*. You can take it, can't you?"

"Yes," Liam breathed. "Please."

"Mmm. So pretty when you beg." Cody crawled back and

stood at the foot of the bed. When Liam shifted to follow, he said sharply, "No. Don't move."

Liam was sitting up, his legs out and slightly open. He nodded.

"Tell me. Tell me what you want." Cody walked around to the side table, drawing out the lube and condoms, then bringing them back, standing by Liam's feet again. "Tell me how you've always imagined it."

Liam's face flushed red hot. "Um, different ways."

After squeezing lube onto his palm, Cody stood there and stroked himself slowly, teasing his foreskin. His cock was flushed almost purple, his gaze focused on Liam as if there was nothing else in the world. "Tell me." When Liam could only stammer, Cody murmured, "How about on your back? With your legs up."

Liam felt foolish and ashamed and thrumming with lust all at once. He nodded.

"Oh, I bet you'd be gorgeous like that. Showing me your tight little hole, ready for my cock. Opening up for me and waiting so patiently. Hmm?"

Liam nodded eagerly, reaching for his cock as it swelled even more. He jerked as Cody barked, "*No!* I'll tell you when you can touch yourself. And it's definitely not yet. Not even close."

Fisting his hands in the sheets, Liam nodded.

Cody frowned, taking his hand off his cock. "Do you want it like this? Me in control? You know you can say stop at any point. Maybe your first time, we should go easier."

"It's not. I told you." He shoved away the echo of Lorenzo's sneering laughter.

"I mean your first *real* time." Cody smiled softly. "It's going to be awesome. We don't have to do this dom/sub stuff. I think we both liked it yesterday, but this can be different. You can take the lead."

"No." That thought made him itchy and fidgety, his erection

flagging. "I want… Please."

"Okay." Cody kneeled on the end of the bed but didn't come closer. He traced circles over Liam's shins, teasing the hair there. "Tell me more."

"I don't… I don't let myself think about it very much."

Cody's brows met, but then he exhaled a long breath. "But I bet you've fantasized about getting down on your hands and knees. I bet you've thought about being fucked like a dog until you couldn't walk. Getting rammed by every inch of a long, thick cock. Powerless to do anything but take it. Until you come. Getting filled up. Being owned by that cock."

Gasping, Liam nodded, lips parted and mouth gone dry. He was fully hard again. Waiting. Burning for more.

Cody's touch on Liam's shins was still feather light. "I bet you want to be pounded. What other fantasies do you have? Maybe you want a cock in your mouth at the same time as your ass? Being fucked at both ends like in a porno."

Fear slashed him like claws, and Liam jerked back. "I can't!" Yet his dick throbbed, his nipples peaking at the thought of being overpowered and filled like that, completely dominated. It thrilled him, but that would mean two men, and he could never trust anyone else.

He was already out of control, going under with Cody, trusting him and risking everything. What the fuck was he doing? He was off his head. He was going to ruin everything—his job, his family, his whole pathetic life.

"Hey." Cody was closer now, crawling between Liam's legs, stroking palms over his shoulders and pressing him back to the mattress gently. "It's okay. You're safe here. We're not doing anything you don't want. We're only talking." He kissed Liam gently, pressing their lips together, eventually teasing his mouth open, soothing and calming with the sure strokes of his tongue.

Liam should have been ashamed to need comforting—*What*

kind of man are you, the voice in his head hissed—but he was eager for the weight and warmth of Cody's body. Part of him still couldn't believe this was even real as he caught his breath, the panic fading.

But it was very real when Cody's breath tickled Liam's ear with his whisper, his hands making circles on Liam's waist. "I bet you'd like it if I told you how I want to fuck you the first time."

Liam groaned, a strangled sound that came out as a raspy, "*Nnngh.*"

"Did you clean yourself for me?"

Now he squirmed with embarrassment, closing his eyes. "This morning. Just in case." He was certain he could feel the heat of Cody watching him. He cracked his eyes open, and sure enough, Cody smiled down at him.

"Good," Cody said.

"How do you do this?" Liam blurted. At Cody's raised eyebrows, he added, "*Talk* about everything."

"I dunno." He propped himself on Liam's chest like a Sphinx, fingertips teasing Liam's chest hair, his elbows digging in a little, but not painfully. "It's nothing to be ashamed of. I love sex, and sex has certain practicalities. Like shit and cleaning out assholes. Enemas. I mean, I'm assuming you didn't do a full enema this morning? That would be pretty intense if you're not used to any of this."

"Oh, mate." Liam squirmed again. "Do you have to say that out loud?"

Cody shook with laughter, his elbows making little jabs into Liam's stomach. "Say what?" He widened his eyes innocently. "Enema?"

"Stop!" Liam was laughing too, and as Cody opened his mouth, undoubtedly to say it heaps more times, Liam pulled his head down for a kiss. They kissed and laughed some more, and Liam could hardly believe he was laughing at all.

When they parted, Cody licked his lips and whispered in Liam's ear again, a hot gust. "Do you want to hear about how I'm going to eat your ass?"

Lust returned like a flash rip, and Liam spread his legs, hips thrusting.

Cody's low chuckle had Liam's balls tightening. "I'll take that as a yes," he murmured. "Maybe I'll show you, hmm?"

Thrusting again, Liam nodded so hard he knocked Cody's temple. "Fuck! Sorry." He froze up. He was so awkward and stupid.

But Cody only laughed. "I'll live." As he lifted himself off Liam, his tone lowered. Darkened. "Now roll over."

Shivering, Liam did, stretching on his belly, rubbing his dick against the sheets. He waited. His legs were spread, and he looked back to see Cody kneeling between them.

"How do you think I've imagined this?" Cody asked.

"I—I... I don't know," Liam stammered. He could feel his face burn but didn't look away.

"Oh, I bet you do." Cody traced tingly, barely-there circles on the backs of Liam's calves. "I bet we're on the same page. I bet you'll love it."

"Yes," Liam whispered.

"Get your knees under you. *Aaass* up in the air."

Heart drumming, Liam did as he was told, propping himself on his elbows, his arse sticking up. He was sure he had to be red all over.

"God, look at you."

Part of Liam wanted to tell him to stop looking, shame threatening to surface, but then Cody was spreading Liam's arse with his hands, his thumbs rubbing up and down along the crack.

"Is your knee okay?"

"Yes," he managed.

Cody smoothed his palms down Liam's shaking thighs. "I've

got you. Don't move."

Liam could barely breathe, let alone move. He held himself rigid. Exposed. Neck straining, he watched Cody get off the bed and disappear from view. When he returned, he had a towel and a thick pillow tube like the ones people used to prop themselves up in yoga. He pushed the tube under Liam's stomach, and Liam raised up as Cody arranged it under his hips with the towel draped over it.

"Relax. Let the bolster take your weight. You don't have to hold yourself up now. You can let go."

Arse really in the air now, Liam folded over, gravity pushing his chest and shoulders into the mattress. He turned his head so he was resting on his cheek. His cock pressed against the bolster, the towel giving a bit of rough friction that he wanted to hump against. Cody's fingers trailed down his spine like a whisper.

"You don't have to do anything now. Just relax. I'll take care of you." Cody's lips followed his fingers.

Fighting a reflexive spasm of resistance, Liam exhaled and let himself go boneless. It was strange to be propped up like that, with his arse so exposed. He flattened his hands on the bed, waiting. As Cody teased his crack, Liam held his breath.

The gasp punched out of him, his hips jerking at the first touch of Cody's wet, textured tongue. A slow swipe. Then another. And another. It was weird and wonderful at the same time, and Liam moaned so loudly he froze up.

Cody stroked his hips, his breath tickling Liam's hole. "It's okay. It's just us. No one can hear. No one can see."

Of course that filled Liam with a bolt of panic, his mind spinning with imagined viewpoints, secret cameras that might capture him like this, his arse up and moaning like a slut for Cody's tongue. *Imagine if everyone saw this—Mum and Dad, the boys at Barking, Teddy, Greg, Cora—*

Cody gripped Liam's hips. "*Liam.* Be here with me. You're

safe. I promise. Okay?"

Opening his eyes, Liam stretched his neck so he could see Cody—see the promise in his gaze, the confidence and control. Forcing a breath, he exhaled, willing himself to relax. "Yes."

"Okay," Cody repeated, relaxing his fingers and petting his thighs tenderly. "Do you want to stop?"

"No." The words tripped out. "Please—please don't stop. I want you to… Please."

Leaning over, Cody kissed him, their mouths straining to find each other. "Don't worry. I'll fuck you so hard you won't sit for a week."

Then Liam's arse was spread wide, Cody burying his face in his crack, pushing inside, fucking him with his tongue. It was wet and humid with Cody's breath, and unlike anything Liam had ever felt. He was almost unbearably vulnerable, tensing as Cody eased a slick finger inside.

Yet it wasn't anything like it had been that night with Lorenzo—the rough, jagged pain, Liam's arse dry and burning. Lorenzo's impatient disdain, his disinterest. How he'd left Liam alone in the park afterward with a careless "*Ciao!*"

No, Cody was right there with him, murmuring praise against Liam's flesh, opening him with his mouth and fingers. The stretch was painful, but Cody was gentle until Liam was almost howling with need.

When he heard the foil condom wrapper rip open, Liam trembled, turning his head to press against his other cheek, his neck sore. His arse smarted with the stretch of fingers, and now the push of Cody's cock head stole the air from Liam's lungs. His body seized despite himself.

"Can't!" The word exploded before Liam could think twice.

Cody stopped moving, his cock still stretching Liam's hole open. "I know, baby." He'd been holding Liam's hips tightly, and he relaxed his grip to circle lightly. "I know it feels like that. Like you can't take another millimeter, like you're going to break. But you won't. You're made for taking cock. Aren't you?"

Liam whimpered, fighting the panic, sweat dampening his hair. "Yes!"

"Oh, you really are. You've fantasized about this for years. When you let yourself. Late at night. In the dark."

"Yes," he whispered. His hole was so stretched and painful, but he imagined what it would be like to have Cody slide home, to finally feel a cock filling him properly, not the brief, short stabs Lorenzo had made before giving up and abandoning him. To feel *Cody* filling him. "Please. Don't stop."

"That's it. Bear down." Cody tightened his grasp on Liam's hips again, pushing. "Fuck, you're so tight. You feel so good. There!"

They cried out together as Cody pushed inside, Liam bearing down until Cody was all the way in. Cody breathed hard, caressing Liam's back and hips, before teasing the stretched rim of Liam's hole. "Feel that? Feel me inside you?"

Liam could only moan and nod, his cheek rubbing the rumpled sheet. It still hurt like hell, but the satisfaction of being so full was something he couldn't describe. Bit by bit, he relaxed, letting the bolster support him—letting Cody comfort him with touches and kisses to his spine.

"What does it feel like?" Cody asked, his voice ragged.

"Like... Splitting me open. But...so full."

Cody stretched out over him, a comforting, intensely satisfying weight. Cody's heart pounded so hard Liam could feel it on his back, and he kissed Liam's neck and murmured, "Baby, you've got me shaking. Holy shit. You feel amazing. I love being inside you."

Knowing that Cody was just as affected made Liam's heart swell in a way he couldn't explain. He felt *seen*. Lorenzo had taken such little care, and much to Liam's shame, hadn't even come.

He'd yanked out, half-hard, and shaken his head, muttering something in Italian, and Liam had felt so incredibly wrong and bad.

With the nameless men on holiday, he'd never had the guts to ask for what he craved. To beg for it. Yet Cody had *known*. Liam's head spun, his arse on fire, gratitude and need overwhelming him.

"Fuck me," he pleaded.

"Oh, I will." Cody smiled against Liam's sweaty shoulder blade. "Relax. Don't touch yourself. I'm going to be the one to make you come."

As Cody eased out and back in, moving more and more as Liam relaxed, they grunted and groaned. Liam pushed his cock against the towel on the bolster, needing more pressure as he hardened fully again after softening from the initial pain.

"Made for taking my cock," Cody muttered, their skin slapping loudly as he thrust.

"*Yes*," Liam moaned. He jerked with Cody's movements, giving himself, taking every bit given to him. He clutched at the sheets, straining, needing more.

Cody's weight covered him, his hands coming to circle Liam's wrists, squeezing, pinning them to the bed, making Liam cry out. The thrusts were shallower, but at a new angle, and Liam almost screamed, bucking as Cody hit his gland. Cody tightened his grip, then yanked Liam's arms up so he could pin his crossed wrists with one hand.

Liam knew he could break free at any time, but he didn't, reveling in being held down. Cody's hand squeezed under and wrapped around Liam's cock, working him hard. "You're made for this," Cody muttered. "I want to come in you forever."

Liam's sudden orgasm shook him with great spurts, gasps and moans wrenched from his throat as Cody fucked him through it mercilessly. The smell of sex and sweat was thick in the air, his cock jerking in Cody's hand. Cody shook too, crying out so loudly that Liam should have been cringing. Instead, he spurted again, a last gasp of sweet pleasure.

Panting, Cody released Liam's cock and wrists, then pulled out gently and collapsed beside him, half over the bolster, his leg over Liam's. "Fuck," he mumbled, his face pink and dimples showing. He dragged his hand over Liam's head as if he barely had the energy to lift it. "You're amazing."

"I didn't do much," Liam protested. He was still displayed over the bolster, and he should have been ashamed. But when Cody spread his hand over Liam's arse cheek, caressing, he was almost proud.

Cody laughed, but not cruelly. He wriggled closer, murmuring against his lips, "The way you gave yourself up like that? Opened up for me?"

He kissed Liam more deeply with a sweep of his tongue before easing back to look in his eyes. "I feel like—" He swallowed hard, then repeated, "You're amazing."

As they kissed, Liam could almost believe it.

Chapter Fourteen

"**B**ROUGHT YOU SOMETHING." Cody passed the paper bag to Damo, who sat by the tower window and opened it with an eager grin.

"Awww, *maaaate*." Damo pulled out the tart, displaying the treat to the other guys. "Bakewell tart from Mod Cafe in Freo. My fave! Thanks. You're a legend!"

"What about the rest of us?" Chalkers asked, spinning in his chair and scratching his coarse salt-and-pepper hair.

Cody shrugged. "I didn't know what you'd like."

Chalkers stared at him, his lined face incredulous. "Are you fair dinkum? You didn't get us anything?"

"Oh, the old sea dog's gonna have your balls for brekkie!" Ronnie howled with laughter, looking between Chalkers and Cody. "I know who's scrubbing the toilet block later!"

Cody tried not to smile, but he couldn't keep a straight face. He pulled a bigger paper bag out of his backpack. "Didn't know what you'd like, so I got a bunch of stuff." He handed over the bag of squares and tarts and cookies. He had an extra mint-choc slice saved for Liam in the fridge at the studio.

A smile broke through Chalkers' scowl as he took the bag and peered in. "Caramel slice is mine, boys." Then he ruffled Cody's hair, and Cody couldn't stop grinning. Every day he loved the job more.

Bickie came up from the back and happily grabbed a big oat-meal biscuit. He watched something through the glass. "Mate, it's never going to happen."

"I believe in the power of their dreams!" Damo insisted, swallowing a big bite of tart and mumbling, "Ten bucks says they nail this pyramid."

Cody stood behind Damo's chair, finding the source of debate about thirty feet away on the sand. A group of female backpackers, who were possibly drunk already at eleven a.m., were trying to make a human pyramid. They scrambled on top of each other in bikinis, boobs swaying.

It was a cloudy day with not much happening on the beach, although the weather was supposed to clear. There were people around, but it wasn't crowded yet aside from surfers at the north end enjoying the big swells.

"You're on," Bickie said. "Gotta love the Pommies. They're always up for it no matter the weather."

Liam came in from patrol, and he joined them by the glass, shooting a shy little smile his way, so quick Cody might have imagined it, making his heart swoop. Seeing the women's shenanigans, Liam laughed, his face alight in a way that made Cody want to take him into the toilet or down in the garage or *anywhere*, really, and kiss him until they could barely breathe.

He wanted to fuck him again and hold him and wake up with him. He wanted Liam safe under the blankets, sleep-muddled with bedhead, stretching his big limbs, kissing him with morning breath.

So far, Liam had insisted on going home and not staying past midnight. Apparently in his mind, that was a respectable time to be leaving a mate's place. Any later, and they'd *clearly* be found out. Which was ridiculous, since Cody's neighbors surely didn't give two shits about who visited him.

But Liam got so jumpy, and Cody hated that haunted— *hunted*—expression. Liam wasn't at all what people thought, and Cody wanted to keep him close and safe and kick the shit out of that Italian bastard who'd done such a number on him.

It'd been almost a week of visits, and he'd had Liam every night, so far only taking him the same way he had the first time, with Liam over the bolster. Liam was getting used to it, his movements feeling less nervous and jerky with each encounter. There was so much Cody wanted to do with him—*to* him—but he'd decided patience in all things with Liam was the best strategy.

Chalkers said, "Ten bucks says the first aid kit will be needed."

"Then we'll send Foxy down with it." Bickie waggled his eyebrows. "Girls'll love it. He's the resident heartbreaker."

Liam's smile faltered for such a short moment that Cody might have imagined that as well—but knew he hadn't. He wanted to snap that Liam was *his*, and the girls could get stuffed. It took effort to hold his tongue and look cool as he waited for Liam's reply.

He had mixed feelings, though, when Liam said, "I'm too old for this lot. They'll want Damo." Cody tried not to overthink it, but he was about the same age as the girls.

Damo grinned. "Too right." He gave his long blond hair a toss.

"Ohhhhh!" The shout came up in unison from all of them as the pyramid tumbled down.

"Tragic." Damo shook his head solemnly.

Bickie was about to say something when his smile vanished and his head whipped to the left. He grabbed the binoculars. "That kid shouldn't be that far out on his own. South end. First gate. He's going to start copping waves on the head."

Like a switch had been flipped, everyone looked to where Bickie watched, all laughter and joking about bets vanished. It still gave Cody mental whiplash the way the guys could get serious in an instant. Damo and Liam grabbed binoculars, and for a few moments, Cody could only hear the distant sound of beachgoers and his own thudding heartbeat.

"Don't see any parents around," Damo said.

Bickie was still staring at the boy. "Chook, you're in. Damo, drive him down."

Damo jumped up and was out the door and flying down the stairs, Cody on his heels, his heart really pounding now. He still wasn't used to how things could go bad in the water in an instant. As Damo gunned it for the shore, honking and yelling at stragglers to move, Cody stripped off his blue uniform shirt and tossed it in the back of the buggy.

Bickie's voice came over the radio. "Go, go, go!"

Shit. That meant the kid was going under. Adrenaline flooded Cody, and he wanted to leap from the moving ATV.

"You remember the sign for resus?" Damo asked.

Cody nodded. "Arm up and three pumps down with my fist."

"You got it. If he's unconscious, even if you're not sure if he's breathing or not, give the sign and we'll be waiting with the defib." He braked by the edge of where the sand turned wet. "I'm ready to back up if you need help. But you've got this!"

Cody leapt from the buggy and yanked at the rescue board's rope handle, his feet digging into the damp sand, salt filling his nose as he waded in. He couldn't actually see the kid at the moment over the rise of a wave, but Bickie's urgent tone had said it all. He threw the board at the water, kneeling on it and rowing with both arms.

Over the whitewash, he glimpsed the boy's head before the boy disappeared. He reappeared after several heartbeats, bouncing off the bottom. Cody paddled with all his might, staring at the last spot he'd seen him, praying he wouldn't have to find him on the ocean floor.

His muscles shook as he fought the power of the incoming

tide, gritting his teeth, blinking seawater from his eyes as he climbed over the lip of a wave about to break. He sailed down the back, the next set coming right behind it, the boy out of sight. Sucking in a breath, Cody rolled the board under the wave and came out the other side.

Only a hand extended from the water, and he grasped for it, sitting up and straddling the back of his board as he hauled the kid over. Coughing and gasping, the boy clung to the board sideways, legs still in the water. He was about ten and ginger, his face far too pale under his freckles.

"You right?" Cody held the boy's shoulder. "It's okay. Catch your breath."

But *fuck*, another set loomed, and for a second, Cody wasn't sure whether to paddle hard and try to get over it, or risk rolling the kid under. And in that breath's hesitation, it was too late, and the wave crashed onto them. The world became the swirling, smashing force of the water, ripping the board away and pushing Cody down to the dark bottom, spinning him in a torrent— *down-up-down-back-side-up.*

The kid ripped away, wrenched from his hands.

Finding the surface, Cody gulped a breath, searching, his chest about to explode. He saw a flash of red hair and lunged toward the boy, kicking as hard as he could, grabbing his arm. The board was gone, being washed into shore in the tumult of water. Cody watched it helplessly, cursing himself. It was his job to keep hold of the boy and the board, and he'd totally, completely failed.

"It's okay!" Cody lied, hoping the kid wouldn't panic and pull him under. It was dangerous as hell to be with a patient in the water without the control of the rescue board—practically the first thing on the list of *DON'T EVER DO THIS AS A LIFEGUARD.*

Now Cody was in the impact zone with a patient. He knew they'd all be watching in the tower—that Liam was watching— and he burned with shame and anger at himself, but most of all with the fear that this kid clinging to him could still drown them both.

The boy seemed too exhausted to panic, coughing and gray-faced. Another set was coming, and Cody swam hard toward shore, dragging the boy with him, hoping they could body surf in. They didn't catch the wave, but at least they weren't smashed by it either. Then Damo appeared, arms stroking confidently through the water, and Cody could breathe again.

Cody heaved the kid onto his belly on Damo's board, glancing behind and telling Damo, "Go!"

Damo had the big board turned on a dime, paddling fast. Cody dove under the wave and came up, relief flooding him as he watched Damo catch the wave and surf the kid into shore. Liam waited there, and Cody's stomach knotted. Shit, he'd messed that up. The kid could have died because he'd stupidly hesitated. He body surfed the next wave in, afraid he might actually vomit on the sand.

He choked the bile down and splashed over to where Damo and Liam crouched with the boy. Liam was saying, "Did you swallow a lot of water?"

The issue was actually inhaling the water into the lungs—secondary drowning could kill days later. But patients often didn't know if they had, but they knew if they'd swallowed the horrible, salty water. If a patient had swallowed a lot, chances were they'd inhaled it too.

The boy nodded, and a bit of froth bubbled around his gray lips. Damo spoke into the walkie-talkie. "Yeah, definitely get the ambo. We'll get the oxy on him and bring him up to the tower."

Cody stood by uselessly as Damo and Liam worked, putting the mask over the boy's slack face. The portable oxygen should help pink him back up, but he definitely needed a trip to hospital.

A middle-aged man in shorts and a sweatshirt raced toward them, shouting, "Billy!" He stumbled to the sand, reaching for the boy.

Liam gripped the man's shoulder. "Is this your son?"

"Yes! Is he all right?" The man raked a hand through his hair, shaking. He sounded like a local. "I was having a coffee, and he said he was going for a swim. He's a good swimmer!"

"He almost drowned." Liam urged the man to his feet. "Ambo's on the way, and we're going to take him up to the tower. You can ride with us."

Cody replayed it all in his mind, cringing. He had totally fucked up the rescue and lost the board, and if the kid had gone under again and Damo hadn't been able to back up...

"Cody, get the board," Liam said. "Keep an eye on this end."

"What? Right. Yes." Cody nodded and ran over to where the board bobbed in the shallows, a few kids gathering around. He dragged it back to the sand, his skin prickling with shame—and fury at himself—feeling like the kids were staring at him and judging.

The ATV Liam had driven down remained, and Cody thunked the board in the rack on the side. There was a spare towel in the back, his shirt in the other buggy that was back at the tower now. He rubbed the cotton over his head, practically ripping out his hair, then sat rigid behind the wheel, watching the water, the back of his mind replaying the fucked-up rescue again and again.

The other buggy neared with the low hum of its engine, and Cody wasn't sure how to feel when Liam climbed out and slid into the passenger seat next to Cody, his blue eyes unbearably kind. He handed over Cody's uniform shirt and quietly asked, "You right?"

Cody almost ripped the collar as he jammed the shirt over his head. "Fuck!" He clenched his fists, a scream clawing at his throat as his arms got tangled for a second.

"Hey, hey. You did your best." Liam's big palm glanced over Cody's knee for the barest of moments.

Cody huffed in disgust. He might have knocked Liam's hand

away if it had lingered. "Don't patronize me. I fucked up."

Liam was quiet a moment. "I'm not patronizing you. You don't—you can't be perfect."

Cody ignored that. "How's the kid?"

"The ambos are checking him out now. Oxy's helping. He'll be fine."

"I should have been faster getting him on the board, and I was angled the wrong way. It was a shit-show."

"*Hey.*" Liam took Cody's shoulder now, squeezing. "The ocean is in charge. We've all been dumped, or lost our board, or even rolled the Jet Ski. Happens to the best of us." He let go of Cody's shoulder. "This is why you're a trainee. You're learning."

"But I should know better! I've read books and watched videos and studied the manual. Mia hasn't lost her board, has she? I should have handled that." He squirmed. Liam was making sense, but it was still humiliating to have fucked up the rescue. Humiliating that *Liam* had been there to witness it.

"You can't always be in control. No matter how hard you work, you're going to make mistakes."

"But I like being in control!" Cody blurted. In the silence, Liam stared at him with eyebrows raised, and after a beat, they both laughed. The knot of tension in Cody's chest loosened.

Liam glanced around and murmured, "And you can be. Later."

The promise in that word—*later*—sent a pulse of lust through Cody, the fury fading. He tried to smile. "You'll still be able to take me seriously after this?" He meant it as a joke. Sort of.

Liam's brows knit. "You think this would affect…" He glanced around before finishing, "Us?"

Hearing that word—*us*—was more thrilling than it had any right to be given how deeply Liam was in the closet. "No. I don't know?" In that moment, Cody felt unbearably young and raw and exposed. He'd failed in the water, and even though the dom role was new for him, he realized how desperately he wanted to continue exploring it.

"You think it would change how I think of you? Because you stuffed up?"

Cody sighed. "No." Although he was tempted to ask what exactly Liam did think of him. In detail. "I just hate being *weak*."

Liam looked away, crossing his arms. "What must you think of me, in that case?"

Shit. "No! That's not what I meant. You're not weak!" *Shit, shit, shit.* The beach on patrol wasn't the place for this conversation, even if it was quiet and the people in the water in front of them were fine for the moment. But the idea of Liam hurting because of him was unbearable.

Cody whispered, "Being submissive isn't weak. There is so much strength in it." Liam snorted, and Cody persisted. "There *is*. Giving yourself over takes guts. And just because you like it in bed doesn't mean it's the same in the rest of your life."

Liam exhaled slowly. "Then the same goes for you, right? You're not perfect. You don't have to be. You *can't* be. It's the ocean. The only way to learn is out there. You've surfed in big swell—you know you can watch a million videos of other people doing it, but until you're out there being smashed by a ten-footer, you can't really know what it's like. The conditions are tough today. And sometimes the ocean will show you who's boss no matter how long you've done this job."

"You're right." Cody rubbed his face. "I'm sorry. I just hate fucking up."

"We all do, mate." He said that last word tenderly. Softly. Affectionately, the way he might have said *sweetheart*. "You're so kind and patient with others. With me. Give yourself a break."

Before Cody could respond, Hazza and Teddy arrived in a buggy. Hazza gave Cody's back a slap. "Okay, Chookie? Don't sweat it. You'll be sweet as next time."

"Did I ever tell you about my first rescue?" Teddy asked. He whistled. "It was a disaster."

Cody laughed for real as Teddy told his story, but his mind still lingered on how he'd messed up, and how he would be better and stronger next time. How he would prove himself. He kept his gaze away from Liam, afraid he'd get hard thinking about Liam's promise.

Later.

"Ow!" CODY HOPPED on his left foot in the hot sand later that day, lifting his right. "Fuck." He was too far from the parked buggy to lean on it, and he tightened his core, throwing out his left arm for balance as he squinted down at his foot.

He put his sunnies on his head, squinting in the bright, clear glare after the cloudy morning. There was a thin, amber-colored shard of glass sticking out from the bottom of his heel.

"Okay?" Liam called, running toward him, shirtless, dripping wet, and carrying the rescue board like it weighed nothing. The couple he'd rescued were hugging each other in the shallows.

Butterflies flapped in Cody's belly, and if he hadn't been wearing his blue lifeguard shirt, he imagined their wings would have been visible against his flesh. He tried to remind himself that Liam would have been concerned for anyone in pain, but his heart still soared as Liam raced over and dropped the board—then dropped to his knees.

Dropped to his knees at Cody's feet.

Lust seared Cody's veins, obliterating the pain in his foot. After the intense frustration of the failed rescue that morning, he'd tried to put it behind him with varying degrees of success. The echoed promise of *later* had helped.

During his lunch break, he'd gone for a hard swim and imagined the things he might do with Liam once they escaped to the studio and locked themselves away from the rest of the world.

Liam bent low at Cody's feet, big hands gentle on his right ankle. "Let me see."

Cody let him, managing to squeak, "Beer bottle."

Liam practically growled. "Bet it was those bogans you pulled from the Croc earlier." He lifted Cody's foot higher, and Cody grabbed his damp shoulder for balance. Head bent, Liam gently twisted his foot to get a better angle, humming under his breath.

Shit, Cody was going to get hard if he didn't start thinking about anything else but Liam kneeling at his feet, and what they could be doing if they were safely inside Cody's place.

Liam gazed up at him. "Should be able to get it out." His brow furrowed after a moment. "You okay?"

"Yeah." It came out all breathy, and realization flickered over Liam's face. His Adam's apple bobbed. He still held Cody's foot, and now they were just staring at each other like there was no one around for miles.

"I—we—first aid kit," Liam croaked. "In the buggy."

"Uh-huh." Cody couldn't stop himself from stroking Liam's warm, wet skin, his thumb caressing just an inch from the edge of Liam's collarbone. It was such a small movement that no one would notice.

Liam dropped Cody's foot and shot to his feet, and Cody hopped again, putting down his right big toe in the sand before he fell on his ass. Liam strode to the buggy, then returned with the kit. He dropped down again, not meeting Cody's eyes.

An ATV pulled up next to them, Ronnie behind the wheel. "You okay?"

Cody cleared his throat. "Yeah. Just a bit of beer bottle. Liam's got it under control."

"Bet it was those bogans, hey? Wish they were still here so we could kick 'em off." He asked Liam, "No ambo?"

"Nah." Liam's head was still bent, and he had the tweezers out. "It's barely more than a sliver. Won't need stitches, I don't reckon. Definitely not an ambo." He wrapped a hand around Cody's ankle, sending a helpless shiver over Cody's skin. "We'll look to see if there's any more glass. Let us know if anything comes up."

"Will do." Ronnie gave Cody a sympathetic smile. "Heard you had a crap morning. Happens to all of us."

Cody fought a grimace. "Yeah. Thanks." The guys were all being so supportive and encouraging, and it made him itch with the need to prove himself. He waved as Ronnie drove off.

He had to touch Liam's shoulder again for balance, but this time he didn't indulge in any caresses. Liam's wet hair gleamed in the sun, and Cody yearned to run his fingers through it. Instead, he winced as Liam snapped on the blue gloves, tweezed out the glass, washed the wound, then pressed a large Band-Aid over it. He finished by wrapping a bandage around Cody's foot.

"Just to keep the sand out," he said briskly. "Try putting some weight on it."

Cody did. "Yeah, that's good. Hardly feel it now." Truthfully, it stung like hell, but he'd live. He didn't need his foot on the rescue board, at least. Getting to the water would hurt, but it could have been worse.

"Good." Liam got to his feet, peeling off the gloves, towering over Cody. He seemed about to say something, but then scooped up the first aid box and strode back to the ATV as the couple he'd rescued approached, holding out their hands and thanking him profusely.

It was Cody's turn to drop to his knees, combing carefully through the sand and collecting the rest of the broken bottle, which was thankfully mostly in one piece. The assholes had buried it, because that's what assholes did, he supposed. This shift could not end soon enough.

Of course, they had to do an hour's overtime because it was too crowded to simply leave. Finally, as the sun went down, the beach cleared out for the most part, and the lifeguards went off duty. Cody volunteered to help Liam with pack-up, and he drove an ATV, towing the trailer behind.

The trailer held six rescue boards, three stacked lengthwise on each side. Liam pulled up the dangerous current signs and the flags, slotting them into their metal holder above the boards. They'd both gotten wet in rescues near the end of the day, and neither had put on their shirts. The evening breeze tightened Cody's nipples, anticipation snaking through him.

Soon after what Cody had started thinking of as the *on-your-knees* incident, Liam had been called to supervise at the north end of the beach. He and Cody had been all business during the pack-up, barely looking at each other. Liam hopped off the ATV by the tower. As Cody backed into the garage, his pulse raced.

Later.

He wanted it to be *now*. His body thrummed with restless—*reckless*—energy despite the long day of work. Ronnie gave him a wave at the foot of the tower as he passed by, earbuds in place and wearing a faded Queen T-shirt. Cody was pretty sure he and Liam were now the last lifeguards.

He hopped out and backed up onto the sand so he could see the tower. The metal shutters were down over the windows. No one was in sight.

Turning, he did an automatic scan of the water. A few surfers remained. There were a handful of swimmers, but no one looked to be in trouble. Liam was also scanning the water, and now he turned to Cody, and they stared at each other for a heartbeat.

Without saying a word, Cody returned to the musty garage, shimmying past the buggy and full trailer until he was in the back, where wetsuits hung and various equipment was stored. Shovels leaned in corners, buckets stacked. In the other half of the garage with its front door closed, the Jet Ski waited on its trailer, the ATV with orange on its roll bar parked in front.

Cody lifted his foot and prodded at his heel. It still hurt a little, but nothing serious. The bandage was dirty with wet sand now, but it had done the trick. He stood on the dank concrete and waited, toying with the sleeve of a damp wetsuit hanging against the rear wall.

His breath caught as footsteps approached. He smiled as he watched Liam maneuver his bulk past the buggy and trailer and come to stand in front of him, blocking out the world.

"Hey," Cody said, trying not to grin.

Liam swallowed hard, his voice gruff. "Hey."

Cody let his gaze slide down Liam's body and back up again. He licked his lips as he took in Liam's broad, hairy chest and taut nipples. "Hey," he repeated softly. "We're the last ones?"

Liam nodded and glanced over his shoulder. "But we shouldn't. Not here."

"I know." But Cody noted that Liam hadn't said they *can't* or that they *couldn't*. They probably *shouldn't* have been fucking at all, but that ship had sailed. He decided to push it and see how far he'd get.

Yes, the door to the garage was still open, although they were largely hidden from view by the buggy and trailer stacked with rescue boards and signs. Neither of them had flicked on the florescent overhead light, and the pink-gold of sunset filtered through the damp, dim space, beaming around Liam's wide shoulders.

Heart in his throat, Cody reached down, barely grazing Liam's crotch with his fingers. "I bet I could make you hard without even touching you."

Liam froze, his gaze unreadable with the sunset behind him.

Cody leaned in, not touching him, but leaving his hand half an inch away. On his tiptoes on the gritty cement, ignoring the faint twinge in his heel, he whispered in Liam's ear, "Bet you'll get hard just at the thought of what I want you to do for me. Right here, where anyone could see."

Liam's exhalation was more of a shudder. He still didn't move a muscle. Their bare chests didn't touch, only their shoulders pressing together as Cody leaned close.

"Bet you'll get hard thinking about dropping to your knees and sucking me." Cody lowered his heels, reaching up with his left hand to grip the back of Liam's neck, bringing his pliant head down, lips still at his ear. "You'll get so hard thinking about swallowing my cock right into your throat. Swallowing my cum."

Whimpering, Liam thrust his hips against Cody's waiting hand, and *fuck*, he really was hard already. Cody gave him a brief squeeze, then only held his palm flat against him, hardly giving any pressure. "That's it." He tightened his fingers in Liam's hair, which was just long enough near the crown of his head to get a good grip. "You want that, don't you? To get on your knees for me? Choke on me?"

Chest rising and falling, Liam nodded, pushing his crotch against Cody's hand. His dick strained in the confines of his board shorts, and Cody couldn't resist giving him a long stroke, loving the sensation of that thick shaft so hard already. His confidence soared, the rush of power like what he imagined drugs must be like.

"That's good," he whispered in Liam's ear, nipping the lobe and making Liam jerk. "What are you waiting for?"

The thud of Liam's knees hitting the cement made Cody wince internally, and he almost told him to be more careful not to hurt himself. But bit his tongue as Liam tore at Cody's board shorts, the *rip* of the Velcro loud in the small garage. Cody groaned as Liam's callused hand wrapped around his throbbing dick.

"See how hard you make me?" Cody asked. He loosened his

grip on Liam's hair for a moment, brushing a palm over his head gently. "You're so hot like this. So strong and brave."

Liam gazed up at him, his face flushed, blue eyes dark and needy. He licked his lips and sucked at the head of Cody's dick, so tall even on his knees that he had to bend. The suction was heaven, and Cody let the pleasure ripple through him before urging Liam away. He pushed at his shoulders, and Liam obeyed, sitting back on his heels. Now he was at a better angle, and he looked up at Cody, waiting.

"You want to suck me?" Cody traced the shell of Liam's ear. Cody's shorts hung open, his dick standing tall, the tip glistening in the light of the sun, fiery right on the horizon, sinking out of view in a blink.

Liam nodded vigorously, and Cody grasped at his hair again, ordering, "Say it."

"I want to suck you," he rasped. "Please."

Cody grinned. "Well, when you ask so—" His words were lost in a moan, and he snapped his mouth shut. The buggy and metal trailer with the shelves of blue-and-white rescue boards still blocked them from sight, and no one passed by. He knew they were the last two lifeguards on shift, but as Liam sucked him, slurping loudly, Cody was aware of how dangerous this was.

Risky and stupid at the very least, but he only clutched Liam's hair tighter, gasping. "Fuck," he muttered. "That's so good."

Liam had reached up to hold the base of Cody's dick, his lips meeting his twisting fingers, his other hand digging into Cody's hip. Cody leaned back against the damp wetsuit hanging from a hook on the wall.

Liam's mouth was so hot and perfect, his beard rough when it brushed Cody's belly and balls. Spit dripping from his full lips, Liam pulled back and heaved a breath before diving lower, fondling Cody's balls directly and sucking one into his mouth, and then the other.

"Jesus," Cody mumbled, biting his lip hard to stop from shouting. He was going to come already, and he didn't want this to end yet. Giving Liam's head a hard tug, he pulled him off.

Liam sat on his heels on the cement, long fingers clutching Cody's hips. Licking his swelling lips, panting, he stared up with pure lust. Cody tore his gaze down to Liam's crotch, where that big cock tented his shorts. "You haven't touched yourself yet, have you?"

Lips parted, Liam shook his head, Cody's fingers still tight in his hair.

"I bet you want to, don't you?"

The answer was a moan, his eyes flickering shut for a moment.

"Bet it'll make you even harder if I fuck your mouth, won't it?"

Jolting, Liam dropped his hands, opening his jaw, his body shivering while going loose and wonderfully submissive at the same time. Cody ran his thumb around Liam's wet, wide lips. "You're so beautiful. Don't touch yourself until I tell you."

Liam's nod became a jerk as Cody pushed into his mouth, forcefully enough to shock him and make him choke for a moment. Then Cody eased back gently, setting a steady pace, not hard at first. He held Liam's head in both his hands now, thumbs on his cheeks, feeling his own cock filling Liam's mouth. His balls tingled, and he wasn't going to last long, but he kept the pace moderate, slowly speeding up.

When he was fucking Liam's mouth in earnest, his balls slapping Liam's chin, the beard friction amazing, Liam began moaning low in his throat, little whines that made Cody want to shout at the top of his lungs. He had to press his lips together, folding them in on themselves, breathing loudly through his nose.

Liam's lips were stretched around him to the limit, spit dribbling from the corners of his mouth, his face red, body still loose, totally under Cody's command, their eyes locked.

"Fuck," Cody muttered. "Look at you on your knees for me. You love it, don't you? You're so good. Is this what you need? You're gonna make me come so hard. Gonna come inside you, and you're going to swallow it all, and then you can come too."

Cody was sure that if his mouth hadn't been shoved full of cock, Liam would have cried out. *Loudly.* It was muffled, but the sound was so sweet it made Cody's balls draw up tight. He shot down Liam's throat, holding his head in place, gasping and flinching, the pleasure so white hot his balls practically exploded.

Panting, he released Liam's head, flopping back against the wetsuit-padded wall, his dick slipping out of Liam's mouth, trailing spunk over his swollen lips.

Liam swallowed again, gasping, the tear of Velcro on his shorts making Cody jump. Looking up at Cody, Liam stroked himself twice before coming, eyes closing as he shook, splattering Cody's feet and shins.

Then Liam toppled against him, breath hot on Cody's bare hip where his boardies hung open, arms wrapping around the backs of his thighs. It was all Cody could do to stay upright. He pushed his fingers softly through Liam's hair, caressing his shoulder with his other hand. They were in near-darkness now, only splashes of red remaining on the horizon, fading into the night.

"Whoa," Cody whispered.

Liam nuzzled against his hip wordlessly, sweat on his temple damp on Cody's skin.

When they pushed and stumbled to their feet, they laughed, but Liam kept his head down as they tucked themselves back into their shorts and cleaned off as best they could. He turned, gaze anywhere but on Cody.

But Cody ducked around him, flattening a hand on Liam's broad chest, the hair tickling his palm. He gazed up steadily until Liam met his eyes. Cupping Liam's cheek with his left hand, Cody went up on tiptoes again.

Slowly, he licked the remnants of himself from Liam's lips, then slid his tongue inside, exploring tenderly. Liam was stiff for a few moments, and Cody kissed patiently until Liam snaked his arms around him, holding Cody so strongly his feet no longer touched the ground.

Chapter Fifteen

"SWIMMER IN FRONT of me!" Liam shouted through the buggy's megaphone. "Go to your right!"

The rips were pulling midday, the Croc flexing its jaws in particular. Swimmers who'd started between the flags, or at least near them, drifted across and were sucked out before they knew it. Liam watched a man who was in his late twenties or maybe early thirties start to go.

He got on the megaphone again, leaning forward in his seat. "Swim to your right, to the sandbank where people are standing."

The man seemed like a capable swimmer, but he didn't even look over, completely ignoring the message. Liam gritted his teeth and tried again. "Attention! Swimmer right in front of me! Listen to me!" There were no landmarks in the water, and there was no good way to single out a person so they knew lifeguards were addressing them. "Bloke with the brown hair" wasn't exactly going to narrow it down.

Jumping out of the buggy, Liam took off his sunnies, hat, and shirt before reaching back in for the microphone. "Come back to shore! Swim to your right toward the flags."

Suddenly an older bloke in green boardies appeared beside Liam, his face pink beneath his ginger hair and beard. He gripped two ice cream cones, mint choc chip dripping over his fingers in the heat. "Ethan?" He shook his head and said to Liam, "He can't hear you! He can't wear his hearing aids in the water." The man threw down the cones and charged toward the surf without a moment's hesitation.

"Whoa, whoa, whoa!" Liam raced after him, grabbing his freckled arm tight. "I'll get him. You'll just need saving as well. It's all right."

The bloke yanked powerfully against Liam's grip, gaze locked on this Ethan, who was suddenly getting more distant now as the rip clamped hold, capturing him in the channel of water being funneled out to sea.

The man on shore didn't seem old enough to be the swimmer's father, but he was clearly frantic with worry. He was solidly built, and Liam looked around for another guard to give backup to keep him on shore.

Liam got in front of him, propelling him back with hands on his shoulders. "Mate, I'm going to get him right now. Stay put. I mean it. You'll only make things worse."

The man's wild gaze tore from the distance to Liam. Breathing hard, he nodded.

Unhooking his walkie-talkie from his waistband, Liam spoke as he reached for the rescue board. "Going in by third ramp. Got a head being sucked out the back." He dropped the radio, not waiting for a response.

When he wheeled around, he half expected the ginger man to be back in the water and trying to punch through the waves in the impact zone, but he was frozen where Liam had left him, watching the sea.

Liam whipped past him, splashing into the surf and paddling hard, veering to the right, away from the shore break to use the rip himself to get out fast. The patient's head was staying above water, and Liam kept him in his sights as he paddled.

The rip hauled him out between the breaking waves, roaring

at two or three meters per second. Liam barely had to stroke, and soon he was out the back, straddling his board and grabbing the patient's arm.

"Thank god!" Ethan shouted in an American or Canadian accent as he clung to Liam's board. He was breathing hard as he looked up at Liam. "Thank you!"

"Can you hear me?" Liam asked loudly.

"I can read your lips if you go slow."

Nodding, Liam pointed to the end of the rescue board. He tried to enunciate. "Get on your stomach. Head up that end."

"Head that way?" Ethan asked loudly. At Liam's nod, he pulled himself up, arms shaking. Liam helped him wriggle onto the board.

Once he was balanced, Liam stretched out and paddled them sideways out of the rip, looking for a wave to catch back in. He could see the ginger bloke waiting in the shallows, Cody with him now, likely reassuring him.

When they were safely ashore, the man hauled Ethan into a fierce hug that went on several moments. He drew back and said loudly and clearly, "You scared the bloody crap out of me." Then he kissed Ethan hard, and Liam almost lost his balance, gripping the board's rope handle.

He couldn't look away as the men kissed. It wasn't particularly sexual, but they pressed their lips together with such...*caring* and devotion. Right there on the beach in front of anyone, like it was no big deal.

Sure, Liam knew gay people came to Barking, but he'd never seen a display of affection like that. He could hear their little gasps for breath as they parted, could see the clear love shining in their eyes, the trembles in their bodies as they hugged tightly.

He could feel the heat and weight of Cody's gaze on him. He glanced around to see if people were staring, but aside from a few giggling kids, no one seemed to care that two men had kissed.

The ginger took a little zippered case from his pocket and passed it to Ethan, who wiped his hands on his wet boardies and inserted small beige hearing aids into his ears. Ethan said, "Man, that was intense." To Liam, he added, "Thank you so much."

Liam nodded, his throat dry. He had to sound normal, but could only manage, "Uh-huh."

"This is my husband, Clay."

Husband! The way Ethan said it so casually—so normally—gave Liam a thrill. "I'm Liam." He shook Ethan's outstretched hand. "And, uh, this is Cody."

Cody smiled, not seeming affected at all. "Great to meet you both. You're feeling all right?"

Ethan laughed. "I think so. A little shaken up. When I realized how far out I was, I freaked for a minute and started swimming in. Went nowhere fast, and then I remembered that getting tired won't help in a rip."

"You'll be right, mate," Liam said. *Be normal. This is all normal.* "Good job on not panicking. Makes all the difference. Did you swallow much water?"

Ethan shook his head. "A mouthful when I panicked."

Agitated, Clay paced a few strides on the sand. "You could have drowned! Just like that!"

Liam said, "I barely stopped him from going after you."

Ethan laughed with fond exasperation. "Clay, I was fine." He rubbed Clay's arm, his thumb stroking, touching like it was nothing. Like it was normal. Liam's heart pounded even though the rescue was over.

"Well, what was I supposed to do? Stand there and watch you float off to Africa?" Clay shook his head and muttered, "*Strewth.*" He definitely had a strong country accent, and Liam wondered how an Outback bloke had ended up married to a younger North American. Probably quite a tale.

"I'm sure I would've hit Rotto first," Ethan said, winking at

Clay.

"Or Carnac Island," Liam blurted. "Chock full of tiger snakes. You'd be better off in the rip."

Ethan frowned. "Did you say snakes?"

Liam nodded and spoke more clearly. "Tiger snakes. Deadly. Carnac Island looks pretty from a boat, but I wouldn't step foot on it."

"Good to know." Laughing, Ethan shook his head. "I've lived here seven years now, and I'm still discovering delightful new things. An island full of snakes!"

"That's Australia, for you, right?" Cody said. "Seven years for me too, and sometimes it leaves me speechless."

"Not too often." The affectionate words in Liam's head came out of his mouth, and when Cody laughed and elbowed him playfully, Liam found himself grinning. He turned that grin on Ethan and his husband—*husband!*—Clay.

The four of them standing there on Barking Beach were all like each other, and even though Liam had fucked men he knew were like him, it was different to be on Barkers, talking and joking.

Cody and I could have this.

The thought was terrifying and thrilling and impossible, and Liam was afraid he might spew or cry, just like the first time he'd heard Cody and the boys talking about that dickhead ex in the tower.

"Say, did you play footy?" Clay asked. "Liam Fox, isn't it?"

Liam jerked, the sensation of ice down his spine flooding away the warmth. He nodded, shoulders tensing.

"That was a tough break you had. Good to see you on your feet." Clay chuckled. "Guess that was years ago now, though."

Ethan said, "If you were a cricket player, he probably would've been more worried about you than me out there." He winked at Clay.

"All right, all right," Clay said with a laugh. "Although Liam was a legend. Not surprised to see you saving lives, mate. Thanks again." He extended his hand, and Liam took it.

"Seriously, thank you," Ethan said, then groaned. "Is that my ice cream?" He pointed to the melted pale green mess on the sand.

"I'll buy you another." Clay threaded his fingers together with Ethan's. "Come on. Not letting you out of my sight."

Smiling at Clay—beaming, actually—Ethan gave Liam and Cody a wave and called, "Thank you!" as he and Clay headed off to the cafe beyond the park, hands clasped and bare arms brushing.

Liam watched, eyes glued to them even though he told himself to turn around. Get back to work. He jumped when Cody grabbed his arm and said, "We've got another head out the back."

"What? Yes." Liam stumbled away from Cody, even though Cody hadn't touched him in a way another lifeguard wouldn't. Liam focused on the water. "Yep. No way she can get back on her own. Go grab her."

Cody glanced at him as he picked up the wet board. "You right?"

"Go!"

Flying down the sand, Cody didn't look back. Liam scooped up his radio and called the tower so they knew Cody was in. Liam watched Cody perform the rescue, the woman putting her head the wrong way on the board and Cody pushing at her shoulder. Ethan and Clay were probably out of sight anyway, but Liam didn't let himself look again.

Still, in the back of his mind, he imagined them with fresh green ice cream on sugar cones, holding hands and smiling at each other, their kisses sweet. Eventually going home to their own house, wherever that might be. Sleeping in each other's arms and waking up together in the morning for another day.

Liam's throat was painfully tight as he watched Cody paddle

in with the patient, *want* and horrible, gut-churning fear battling.

"DAD!" LIAM BLINKED in confusion, dread flooding him at the sight of his father shuffling into the tower an hour later in his old thongs, shorts, and a short-sleeved plaid shirt with a fresh grease stain on his round belly. How? What? *Why?*

The pizza pocket Liam had just nuked was warm in his hand through the paper towel, and he squeezed it too tightly, sending a spurt of hot cheese over his knuckles. "Are you..." His gaze shifted to his uncle's weathered face and wiry gray hair. "Hey, Uncle Wally."

"Well, here he is! Missed you at dinner on Friday. Your aunt made your favorite, too."

"Oh." Liam stared at them, his father and uncle's presence in the tower all wrong. He could feel the curious gazes of Hazza and Damo and Ryan, one of the casual guards. "I, uh... Sorry. I had to..." His mind was blank. Which lie had he told? He'd spent the evening at Cody's, sneaking home in the early hours.

Uncle Wally chortled. "I bet you had better things to do, eh? Can't blame ya." He came close and shook Liam's hand.

"Look at all the birds," his old man said, whistling. "Boy, you're tripping over 'em." He shook Liam's hand as well, nudging him in the side.

Uncle Wally added, "Nice work if you can get it."

The guys all laughed good-naturedly, but Liam cringed, forcing a smile and chuckle. "Not watching the girls while I'm working."

"Aw, come on." Dad elbowed Hazza. "Don't tell me you lads aren't sticking your wicks in every chance you get."

Hazza raised his hands in surrender. "Not me. Have a girlfriend now. But yeah, the eye candy's not bad. Damo probably has some thoughts on the matter."

More laughter, and Liam prayed for a rescue to come up so he could race out into the water and far, far away. Instead, Teddy walked in, shooting Liam a quizzical look before smiling and calling out, "Stu, Wally! To what do we owe the honor?"

Wally answered, "Bloody Bunnings is out of the garden fountain me wife wants at all the stores around Mandurah, so here we are. Thought we'd drop in and see the lad. Don't see him enough. Maybe he's finally found the right woman, eh?"

Teddy laughed. "Maybe!"

"About bloody time," Stu grumbled, but he elbowed Liam again with a smile. "How's my boy doing?" he asked Teddy. "You're keepin' him busy, eh?"

"Don't know what we'd do without him," Teddy said, and even though Liam knew he'd say the same to anyone's mum or dad, warmth flowed through him to see the smile crease his father's tanned, wrinkled face under his Eagles cap. He felt twelve years old again, Coach Norton praising him after practice, telling Dad that Liam could be the best. The very best.

The tower door swung open, and Cody appeared with a patient, a teenage girl holding her nose. Liam went hot and cold, panic whooshing through him. No, no, it was all wrong—Dad and Uncle Wally and Cody in the same room. Liam wanted to grab his family and hustle them outside and back to Mandurah and the corner of the world where they were allowed.

Cody was speaking, and Liam could barely hear him over the rush of blood in his ears. "Asshole backpackers kept playing footy even though I told them not to. Hit Jess here in the face." Cody urged her to sit on the medical bed in the back area.

Ryan said, "Keeping an eye on a couple heads up north. Fourth gate."

Liam forced himself to move, picking up a pair of binos and focusing on the water. "Yeah," he croaked.

"We'd better get out of your hair, son," Stu rasped, probably wanting another smoke. "Good to see you, Ted." He shook Teddy's hand and gave the others a wave. To Liam, he said, "Your mother could use a hand with her rocks. With my back…"

"I'm sure Greg can help," Liam said distractedly, watching the two swimmers at the north end drift farther out.

"Right. See ya, then." His father shuffled down the few steps to the back area, then stopped. "You're one of the new ones."

With horror, Liam wheeled around. Jesus, his father was talking to Cody. *Fuck!* Cody gave his name and stuck out his hand for Stu to shake, saying, "Good to meet you, sir."

Liam's father didn't move for an agonizingly long time, finally taking Cody's hand for a quick moment with nothing more than a grunt. His smile faltering, Cody shook Uncle Wally's hand too. Stu eyed Cody with a flinty, narrowed gaze Liam had seen before, and god, if his father *said* anything to him…

"Shouldn't you be back at north end?" Liam barked at Cody as Stu opened his mouth. He gripped the binos, trying to stop himself from fidgeting and showing the whole room that his nerves were jumping like live wires. "Two heads out the back. You'll be in soon."

Forehead creased, Cody said, "Um, yeah. I'll drive back now."

Uncle Wally laughed, a throaty wheeze. "Gotta keep the young turks on their toes, eh?"

Liam said, "Yep." Hazza was tending Jess's nose, and he glanced at Liam with a frown as Cody left, even though he hadn't been stationed at north end.

Stu grunted again, muttering and shaking his head. Teddy said, "I'll walk you out," shepherding Stu and Wally through the door.

"Whoa!" Damo exclaimed. The word was short, a punch of sound, unlike an amused "*Whoaaa!*" that you might hear in the tower watching one of the boys nosedive on the way back into shore.

Liam took the steps up to the main area in one bound, eyes on the water as he stopped behind Damo, forcing everything else from his mind. "What?"

"Five kids just got pulled off the sandbank between the flags. Flash rip." In the radio, Damo said, "Orange ATV, get out the back of the flags. Five—six!—kids panicking. You're both in right away. North end is okay for the moment." He glanced at Liam and nodded, and Liam was already turning and speeding out of the tower and into another buggy waiting at the bottom of the stairs.

He laid on the horn, weaving around clumps of people on the sand. It had started as a day of run-of-the-mill rescues, and then there had been Ethan and his husband, and then Stu appearing, and now it was full on.

Liam got there just after Baz and Cody, and he paddled hard with both arms, kneeling on the board. The swells were small, so he could see the heads on his way out, hair plastered over faces and skinny arms flailing. Baz and Cody went for the ones farther out, and Liam scooped up a girl by the arm, sitting up and hauling her over the board like she weighed nothing.

"I've got ya." Liam patted her shivering back. "Catch your breath. You right?"

Not more than eight, the girl nodded, gasping. Liam bent over to see her face. It was always more intense with kids. They were so small and defenseless, and as much as the thought of losing anyone on his watch frightened him, the idea of losing a kid was a fear like no other.

They got them all back in, and then Cody and Liam had to race up north for the two people Ryan had been watching. They clung to boogie boards and could barely swim, and Liam was terse with his patient as he paddled in. He rubbed a towel over his head back at the buggy, trying to catch his breath.

"What was that?" Cody asked, low and sharp.

Liam played dumb, ashamed of himself the moment he said, "What was what?" There was no reply, and he dropped the towel to find Cody by the back of the buggy, glaring with a clenched jaw.

Cody hissed, "That shit with your dad. What did you think I was going to say? 'Hi, Mr. Fox, great to meet you. Boy, do I love fucking your son's tight hole. Did you know he sucks cock as well as he used to punt a football?'"

"No!" Still, Liam shivered, the cold fear followed by a flush of heat. Cody would never say anything like that, but hearing the words aloud made his stomach churn. "Jesus, don't talk like that here!" He glanced around. "We'll speak later."

"Don't you trust me?" Cody asked, holding his hands out from his sides.

Anger exploded through Liam like a grenade, but he kept his voice to a whisper, "How can you ask that? The things I've let you do—of course I trust you."

Cody's arms dropped, his clenched jaw releasing as he exhaled. "It really sucked that you treated me like that. I would never out you. Not to anyone, and least of all to your dad."

"That's not why. I was afraid of what he'd say to you. He knows you're gay. It came up at my nephew's birthday. It was the same day that arsehole was here. You know—Tommy." Jealousy and resentment battled at the thought of Cody's ex. "Anyway, I was afraid... I didn't want him to say something nasty to you."

Cody blinked. "Oh." He took a gulp from his water bottle. "You think he would have?"

"I don't know. Maybe not with Teddy right there, but Dad usually says exactly what's on his mind. I didn't want you to have to hear that. Having you in the same room, I was afraid of what he'd say, and... I was afraid he'd see. That he'd know somehow."

Cody visibly softened. "I get that you're afraid to come out.

Especially to your dad. I understand." His voice was a low murmur. "But you can't keep living this way. With or without me."

Those words—*without me*—stabbed fresh terror into Liam's heart. It was the first time either of them had mentioned the future at all. He knew it was inevitable, that it was something they had to discuss, but he didn't want to face it. He didn't want it to exist—only wanted the *now* with Cody and to keep tomorrow at bay indefinitely.

"Central to orange ATV. Foxy, can you go down to the flags? We've got an injury. Probably need to bring the patient to the tower."

"Copy that," Liam said into the radio and climbed into the buggy, giving Cody a nod, their conversation mercifully over for the moment.

An hour later in the tower, Damo said, "These guys are getting a bit much again, hey?"

Liam stood and peered to the right where Damo pointed. The young men were close enough to the tower that Liam didn't need binos to make out the roughhousing. Some kind of group wrestling match that was kicking up sand and making noise, the families nearby on the crowded beach clearly uncomfortable.

Baz came over from the medical area. "Yeah, enough of that."

Damo got on the radio. "Central to Chook. Can you stop by those backpackers between second and third gate and tell them to knock it off?"

"Copy that," Cody said. "I already told them up north to stop playing footy when they broke that girl's nose. Looks like they just moved down the beach. I'm definitely keen to have another word."

Liam frowned, eyeing the group of young men. To Damo and Baz, he said, "I'll go down and back up."

"Nah, he'll be fine. Cyclone's down there, not far away. Besides, Cody's tough. For a small guy, he's strong as hell." Admiration was clear in Baz's voice and shining from his eyes as he watched Cody pull up to the troublemakers in the buggy and stride toward them.

Liam had the sudden urge to punch his old friend right in the face, a possessive fury gripping him even as he simultaneously appreciated that someone else recognized what he'd discovered about Cody. That he was strong and tough, and so much more.

He was confident, giving Liam exactly what he needed, while also being dependable, a rock to lean on. Caring and sweet and *fierce*, but gentle. Funny and *fun* and beautiful—so damn beautiful it stole Liam's breath. Not that Baz had even hinted at any of those other things.

Through the glass, Liam watched Cody speak forcefully to the backpackers, his finger jabbing the air, then pointing to the boardwalk as he undoubtedly threatened to kick them off the beach. Most of them held their hands up as if puzzled by Cody's vehemence, as if they hadn't been causing a scene.

But after another exchange, Cody standing firm, they nodded. Cody nodded too, turning to go back to the buggy when one of them sprang, shoving Cody with so much force he hurtled through the air for what seemed like forever before crashing face-first on the sand.

Liam was already flying down the stairs, Damo and Baz's shouts of disbelief disappearing in the roar of blood in his ears. His feet barely touched the wood, and he was powering across the sand, not caring who was in his way, ramming through the crowd that had instantly gathered.

Cody was on his feet and whirling around as Liam barreled in. The long-haired backpacker who'd shoved Cody was saying something, his mates tugging him away. His sneer transformed, his lips making an "O" as Liam grabbed his tee in both hands and lifted him clear off his feet.

Liam wanted to scream, "*Don't you ever touch him again! You hear me, you piece of shit?*" He wanted to slam the bastard down and punch him until his smug face was red with blood. He felt his own face go hot with rage, and then Teddy was there, wrestling with Liam's grip, the cotton tearing and the backpacker staggering away.

"Coppers are on their way," Teddy announced loudly. "You all sit tight."

"We just met him this morning at the hostel!" one backpacker protested. "It's nothing to do with us!"

As Teddy spoke, he was patting Liam's chest and backing him away. "You've all been causing drama and you were asked nicely to stop. Now you're going to sit down and shut up and cooperate with police."

Then Teddy was muttering to Liam. "Hey! People are filming. Calm the hell down."

Fuck. Liam dropped his head, his skin crawling at the thought of all the little lenses probably pointed at him. Maybe it would go viral:

EX-FOOTY STAR WHO COULD HAVE BEEN THE BEST IS A BIG QUEER; WATCH HIM GO MENTAL ON BACK-PACKER WHO SHOVED HIS BOYFRIEND

He swallowed convulsively at the thought of everyone knowing, even though he told himself they'd likely just think he was a meathead with rage issues. Maybe he was. And Cody wasn't his *boyfriend*, although the thought made his heart sing for a ridiculous moment before he locked himself down.

This is why I have—had—rules.

If Dad and Uncle Wally had still been there, what would they think? Would they slap his back and tell him they hadn't seen him move so fast since the finals his last year? Would Dad be proud? No. Not if he knew the truth.

Teddy was saying more to the backpackers, but Liam's ears

buzzed, and he didn't care about those ratbags—he had to see if Cody was hurt. Cody was standing with Baz, and Baz had a big hand on his shoulder, and the rage flared again before Liam was able to catch a breath. He wanted to shove Baz aside and scoop Cody into his arms and carry him away even though he could clearly stand and could very likely walk.

There was a full "ring of death" gathered around them, the circle of beachgoers watching the drama unfold. In this case it wasn't a drowned patient at the center of it, and no CPR being done. Cody was nodding to something Baz was saying, and then he called, "Liam."

Liam stopped a few feet away, his fingers twitching. He nodded.

Cody smiled tentatively. "Thanks for the backup. I'm fine."

Liam nodded again, aware that he was breathing too hard. Baz said, "You look like your head's gonna blow." He laughed as he slapped Cody's back. "Chookie can handle himself, hey? Maybe we *should* call you Tazzie from now on. Tough little devil."

"Yeah, I'm good." Cody smiled at Baz, and then said to Liam carefully, "I'm good. That asshole just took me by surprise."

"You're not hurt?" Teddy asked, appearing beside Liam.

"Nah." Cody waved it off.

"All right, folks!" Baz shouted. "Go back to your towels and work on your tans! Nothing to see here." Into his radio, he said, "Central, Cody's fine—don't need an ambo."

"Copy that. Coppers are arriving any minute."

The siren wailed in the distance, and Liam's heart thumped. Then he realized Teddy was also patting him on the back, a little harder than necessary. "You get up the north end. Croc's snapping. Cody and I will deal with this. Yeah?"

"Yeah," Liam grated out.

Teddy ruffled Liam's hair even though he had to reach way up to do it, unlike when they were kids. "Drink some water, mate."

His voice lowered. "You sweet?"

"Uh-huh." He despised leaving Cody unprotected, but Liam escaped in the nearest ATV.

Stationed at north end, he rubbed the phantom ache in his knee and thought of that man, Clay, and how he'd looked watching his husband in the rip. Liam wondered if he'd looked as frightened when Cody was shoved, or if he'd been all red-faced fury.

He wondered if the fear and rage at the thought of Cody hurt came with love, and if he could stem this reckless tide before it was too late.

Chapter Sixteen

*H*EARD YOU COPPED *it from some douche today*, Mia wrote. *You right?*

Cody had gotten a dozen texts from other lifeguards as well, and it was nice to know they had his back. Pacing his patio under the new colored lanterns he'd strung, with Charlene mirroring his steps as he idly scratched her head, Cody replied:

Yeah, thanks. It was nothing. I'm good.

He brushed his fingers over the graze on the bottom of his chin. It smarted, but really was nothing. The shove had shocked him more than anything else, and it had tied up the rest of his shift giving a statement to police and all that crap. He'd been off a few hours before Liam, and he fidgeted, anxious to have Liam back in his arms. The brick was cool under his bare feet with night settled in, and with each minute, he worried this would be the first night Liam didn't show.

Damo said Liam went off his head. I swear I'm right. He's into you.

His belly fluttered. The image of Liam's red-faced, protective rage had been playing through his mind on a loop. Maybe he shouldn't have enjoyed it *quite* so much, but fuck it. His fingers twitched with the urge to reply that *YES, YES, YOU'RE RIGHT! WE'RE BONING AND IT'S THE GREATEST THING EVER!*

Obviously he couldn't, although not being able to talk to anyone about Liam was wearing on him. He'd considered his sisters, even though he'd never spoken much with them about dating and that stuff. The guilt had stopped him anyway. He'd promised Liam, and even if his sisters were in Canada and totally trustworthy, it still felt like a betrayal. Confiding in Mia was definitely out of the question, as tempting as it was. In the end, he replied:

LOL, I wish. See you tomorrow. ☺

Staring at his phone, Cody opened a new text to Liam, even though they'd agreed not to put anything in writing. He typed and retyped a short message, second-guessing every word.

Hey. Coming over?

Hey. See you soon?

Hey. Everything okay?

Hiya. Was it a late pack-up?

Yo, what's up, bro?

Grunting in disgust, he put his phone back in his pocket without sending anything. Not that Cody would have said anything incriminating—and ugh, he hated that he even *thought* about that word in connection to their relationship.

Or whatever this was.

As an engine approached in the laneway, Cody practically did a cartwheel, and Charlene wagged her tail enthusiastically, sending a ripe passion fruit that had fallen onto the low brick retaining wall flying. It rolled through the dry scrub at the foot of the vines, making her yip and wheel around to investigate the noise. In the dim light of the patio lanterns, she eyed the dried leaves suspiciously.

Cody laughed, some of the tension ebbing. "You're not that bright, but you're pretty." He gave her a good scratch before shooing her through the gate and up into Mrs. Delfino's yard. "Go on. We don't need an audience." She barked, but he knew after a minute she'd go in search of her mom up in the house.

He had the garage door opener ready in his pocket, and he hit the button as soon as Liam tapped his horn, the SUV's red taillights bright as Liam backed in, the lane pitch black beyond.

Along with the affection and lust and excitement at being alone with Liam again, Cody had to admit that the way Liam had rushed him away from his father still ate at him. Liam never really said anything about his family, aside from the fact that he couldn't come out to them. Cody was dying to ask a million questions, but he reminded himself that he had to be smart about it.

When the garage door rumbled down, Liam squeezed his big body out of the SUV and along the concrete wall past the hanging mop and pail, his dark T-shirt catching on the handle for a moment.

They met under the laundry as usual. Liam had to stoop, and as usual, he waited hunched there awkwardly for Cody to close the distance between them. Even though he'd come over every night for weeks, each time he seemed tied up into knots that Cody had to loosen and release.

"Hey," Cody said, smoothing his palms down Liam's bare arms and peering up at him, the bulb in the garage ceiling casting harsh light. The sleeve of one of Cody's damp uniform shirts was caught on Liam's head. "That was a hell of a day, huh?"

He hugged Liam tightly, up on his tiptoes. Liam crushed him with his thick arms, and Cody exhaled. *Jesus*, Liam smelled good—like salt and sun and coconut.

"Are you sure you're okay?" Liam asked, his gaze roving over Cody's face and zeroing in on the graze. He ducked even more, angling Cody closer to the garage entrance and the harsh light. "Is that a bruise?"

"Barely a graze. It's nothing."

Liam's jaw clenched, his eyes flashing, and Cody had to admit it sent a shiver of delight to his balls as Liam muttered, "I should have flattened that bastard."

"You almost did. But I'm okay." He drew down Liam's head for a kiss. Their mouths opened, Liam's beard scratching. Cody breathed him in, tasting something chalky and possibly vaguely minty with his tongue. He pulled back. "What kind of lolly is that? Not very sweet."

Shrugging tightly, Liam laughed, his gaze dropping. "It's Quick-Eze."

"Oh! Is your stomach upset?" He caressed Liam's head, brushing back the swoop of blond hair. "Do you need ginger ale? I think I have a Bundaberg in the fridge." He pressed the back of his hand to Liam's forehead. "You don't feel hot."

"Nah, I'm sweet."

"You are." Cody kissed him again. "Also, for the record? Almost ripping that guy's head off today was really, *really* hot. Even though I'm fine, and I can take care of myself, blah, blah, blah." He whispered in Liam's ear and traced Liam's nipple through his thin tee. "It was extremely hot."

Adam's apple bobbing with a *gulp*, Liam glanced beyond Cody, craning his neck. "We should go inside."

Cody led him to the patio and into the studio, closing the glass door behind them and pulling the thick drapes. Liam eyed the door on the other side of the wooden building, that one open wide and the screen in place.

It was black beyond. There were no streetlights in the laneway, and Cody was still surprised at how country dark it got in Fremantle, which was technically a city. He locked it all up and pulled the drapes, and he could practically see Liam unclench.

Cody joked, "The perimeter is secure."

Liam's smile was half-hearted. Cody knew he shouldn't tease—not about protecting Liam's privacy and his secret. Even if it was getting harder and harder to stop wondering about the future.

How long can we keep this up?

He shoved away the worry. Liam was worrying enough for the both of them, and Cody needed to make him feel safe in the studio. He almost suggested that maybe Liam would feel safer in his own home, but Liam didn't want to bring him there. That pang of hurt lingered as Cody forced away that thought as well.

Taking a deep breath, he asked, "How was the rest of your shift? Pretty crazy day." As much as he wanted to fuck Liam, lust scratching at his skin, he wanted more too. Something comfortable and domestic.

"Nothing else out of the ordinary, thank God, although we had to stay late with so many people still there. A bag thief, tourists caught in the Croc, a newbie surfer with a fin chop in his thigh from his own board. It was deep. Poor bloke."

Cody went to the fridge and took out two bottles of beer, passing Liam one in the Cicerello's stubby holder, the top of the bottle sweating already. With his finger, Liam traced the red letters on the white plastic proclaiming Cicerello's: *WA's No 1 FISH 'N CHIPS—est. 1903.*

Cody asked, "Did you catch the bag thief?"

"Red-handed. Hazza stopped him by second gate. You'll never believe what he told us."

"Hmm. Did he think it was his friend's forgotten bag?"

Liam smirked. "How did you know?"

"They seriously need to come up with a new story. Why are so many people randomly leaving their bags at the beach and asking their friends to go grab them? And gosh, somehow these loyal pals always take the wrong bag by mistake."

"And they're just trying to help their mates!" Liam shook his head solemnly, a little smile tugging on his lips. "Poor blokes, hauled off by the coppers. So misunderstood."

They laughed and sipped from their bottles, standing in the space between the fridge on one side and the bed on the other.

Cody wondered if he should usher Liam over to the loveseat, although even there, the bed was only a few feet behind them. But maybe if they sat there and talked, it wouldn't seem as though Liam was only there for sex.

But maybe he *was* only there for sex? Liam had one hand shoved in his jeans pocket, and he held his beer in the other. He fidgeted a bit, his eyes flicking around. Was he nervous? Impatient? Bored? Cody had no idea.

He decided to go for the loveseat, walking over and putting his beer on the thick wooden coffee table and settling into the leather. Brow furrowed, Liam followed and sat beside him, taking up more than his half of the small couch, his denim-clad leg pressing against Cody's.

"Are we going to watch telly?"

Cody shrugged. "I thought it would nice to relax? We've watched TV before."

"Right. I don't mind." He still looked vaguely puzzled.

So Cody turned on the TV, and they sipped their beers and watched the last part of an old *NCIS*. During a commercial, Liam said, "I was thinking about those blokes from earlier."

"Don't worry about that asshole."

"No, I mean..."

He trailed off, and Cody realized who he meant—the adorable married guys who were totally relationship goals. He waited.

After a few more beats, Liam said, "Er, the couple? Ethan and Clay, I think their names were."

"Oh, right. Why? Pondering a foursome?" As soon as he said it, he cursed himself. Liam tensed so much he practically knocked Cody off the loveseat. Cody squeezed his knee. "Only kidding."

"Right." Liam gave him a watery smile.

"I want you all to myself." Cody waggled his eyebrows.

Liam rested his big hand over Cody's on his knee. He laughed, but it was short and forced. "You've got me."

Do I? For how long?

He was dying to ask it out loud, but instead he gave a faux-diabolical laugh and spoke in a terrible, vaguely Eastern European accent with extra V-sounds, "Oh yes, right where I want you."

Liam's laugh was genuine this time, a sexy rumble. Cody took Liam's wrist and kissed the pale, soft skin by his pulse point. Liam's smile turned bashful, and he dropped his head, and *God*— Cody was falling in love with him. This big, beautiful man with so much shame was filling Cody's heart the way no one ever had.

He almost said it out loud but stopped himself. It was probably the quickest way to get Liam to run for the hills. The fact that Liam was having sex with him was a massive step forward, and Cody had to be patient. It hadn't even been a month—he couldn't start talking about love.

Hell, *most* guys would probably run for the hills. He would have in the past, although aside from Tommy, he'd never dated anyone long enough to even think about the L word.

To nudge Liam back to the married couple from that morning, he asked, "Do you ever see people you've rescued again?"

"No, usually not. Sometimes they come back. A few years ago, there was a local woman who had a heart attack during her morning run on the beach. We did CPR and got the defib on her. Brought her back just before the ambos rocked up. She baked us about twenty tins of biscuits. Still see her around. Her name's Sylvia. I'll point her out next time."

"That must feel good, seeing her doing well."

"Yeah. It really does. But most of 'em go on their way, and that's that."

"That couple today were really cute together, huh? Pretty big age difference, I guess, but they seemed so happy. Age is just a number." The fourteen years between he and Liam had never really come up, probably because Liam had more than enough issues already. If they went public, some people would probably comment, but fuck them.

But you're not going public anytime soon. Or ever.

"Yeah," Liam said. He sounded like he wanted to say more, and Cody waited until Liam added, "It was nice talking to them. I don't usually… I don't really know any gay people. Until you."

"What about the guys overseas?"

"No, that was different." He'd tensed up again, and Cody kissed his cheek.

"I get it. How's your beer?"

"Low." Liam drained the bottle.

After getting them refills, Cody traced the faded ink on the swell of Liam's bicep, his fingertip outlining the tattoo. Liam laughed and said, "A football with my team number inside it. Startlingly original, I know. Let's just say I wasn't famous for my subtlety."

Laughing, Cody traced over the twenty-seven. "You were still a teenager, right? You're forgiven for lack of tattoo originality." On the TV, an obnoxious right-wing political ad came on, and he jabbed the mute button on the remote. "Look, at least it wasn't an appropriated indigenous symbol or a ring of barbed wire around your arm or whatever."

"And what about you? No tattoos yet?"

"Nope. Although perhaps you should conduct a thorough search."

"Hmm. Perhaps I should."

"Do you still have your uniform?"

"My Eagles gear? Somewhere at Mum and Dad's." He paused. "They kept all my footy stuff. Trophies and all sorts. Dad was always so proud. There's still a big display—the shrine, my brother calls it. It's embarrassing."

Hmm. "Must be a little nice to make your dad so proud."

Liam shrugged, his shoulder brushing Cody's. "That's not me anymore, though."

"Right." *And you don't want to destroy that image your father loves so much. Even though you won't let him know the real you and he's got to come to your work to even see you.* "You and your brother aren't close? You never mention him."

"What? No, 'course we are," Liam said too quickly and completely defensively. "Just busy. He's got Cora and the kids, and I've got Barking." He glanced at Cody. "And...well..."

"Right," Cody repeated.

"I'm sorry about earlier when Dad and Uncle Wally showed up. He's just... He's always had an issue with gay people. I guess it's the way he grew up. My grandparents were outback folks. Not that that's an excuse. But my dad, he..."

Liam gulped his beer, and Cody was motionless, waiting. He imagined he could see the riot of confusion and mixed emotions under Liam's skin, like waves crashing and swirling, like being stuck in the vortex, gasping for breath before being sucked under, back and forth like a doll. Liam had kept it all bottled up for so long. He was drowning, and Cody had to time it perfectly to jump in and pull him to safety.

Finally, Liam said, "When I was about six, the coach wanted us to go to a ballet studio for dance lessons. He'd heard it improved footwork, and that American football players were doing it. Figured it couldn't hurt. Mum was for it, but Dad went all red. We were outside by the pool, and he said, '*No fucking son of mine is going to turn out a faggot.*'"

Cody cringed, sucking in a breath. "God." He gripped his beer, not sure if he should touch Liam now or not. He held off.

"It's the first time I remember hearing the word. And I sure as hell didn't want to be whatever that was since it made Dad froth like that. I was mad at Coach for even suggesting it, and Mum for thinking it was a good idea. Then when I was older and really understood what it meant, I..."

Oh, baby. Slowly, Cody stroked Liam's thigh, the muscles

bunched and jumping under his palm. "You must have been so scared."

Liam's throat worked as he swallowed more beer, his left hand fisted. "It was the one thing I wasn't supposed to be," he whispered, as if his dad could hear somehow.

"So you kept it totally secret." Cody stroked Liam's right thigh. "I understand. They don't care that you're not married or whatever?"

Liam shook his head too hard. "It's fine. It's good."

"You know, for someone in the closet, you're a terrible liar." Cody smiled, but Liam went rigid.

"Telling them is not an option. Yes, they keep trying to fix me up with girls, but it's fine. I tell them I'm seeing some woman, but it never works out. It's fine."

Cody nodded, although he was dubious, to say the least. This was his first experience with someone this deep in the closet—at least that he knew of. Sure, he'd been nervous to come out at home and school, but he'd drawn on his inner defiance. Anyone who didn't like who he really was for whatever bullshit reason wasn't his problem.

It had been something he and Tommy had shared that had bound them together tighter than they ever really should have been. They weren't ashamed of being gay and weren't going to hide.

Liam was still looking at the floor. Tentatively, Cody said, "They might surprise you. If you told them the truth, they—"

"*No.*" Liam raised his head now, eyes blazing and jaw tight. "Don't try and talk me into it. I'm not telling them, and you're not going to convince me. I can't tell them. You don't get it."

He lifted his palms again. "Okay. I'm not trying to talk you into anything, I swear."

"And you can't tell anyone about this." Liam motioned his hand between them almost violently. "Not anyone!"

"I won't." *But how long can I do this?* Having a secret affair was fun and exciting on one hand, but at a certain point it would start feeling dirty in a crap way. Still, Cody added, "I promise." Liam's chest rose and fell rapidly, his eyes wide, and Cody needed to reassure him. "You're safe with me. Always."

Liam nodded, closing his eyes and hanging his head. Cody slowly reached for him, sliding his hand over Liam's back and up to his neck, rubbing his thumb over the jumping pulse point.

"I promise," Cody repeated, kissing his cheek and forehead, drawing Liam down, that big body seeming impossibly small as Liam curled against him. His fear broke Cody's heart.

"It would ruin everything," Liam whispered so softly Cody barely heard him. "I can't do that to them."

But what about you? What about living your own life? Not being ashamed of who you are? Loving yourself? What about being proud of yourself? Of us?

Kissing Liam's head, Cody held him, knowing he'd have to ask out loud, but not today. After a minute, Liam sat up and reached for his beer. He sipped silently.

"I want..." Liam drank again. "It's not that I don't..." He cleared his throat, body clenched. "After my career was officially over, I went to Europe to get away. It was a whole other world where no one knew me, and I thought maybe... That first week, going to bars and meeting men, it was so exciting. I wondered if maybe I could eventually be in the open here too. Then—" He jerked, knuckles white on the stubby holder.

"Then that asshole Lorenzo shamed you." Fuck, if Cody could find that piece of shit... He spread his fingers on Liam's knee.

"He was disgusted by me. And if I told my family and friends and bloody Australia the truth, they'd be disgusted too."

"Not everyone." Part of Cody wanted to shake Liam for giving Lorenzo so much power over him. For giving his father so much power. "And what you like in bed is no one's business but yours."

He couldn't resist adding, "Ours."

But clearly the encounter with Lorenzo had left deep scars, especially coming at such a pivotal moment, being the first man Liam had ever asked to fuck him. It had clearly traumatized him deeply to be rejected for his desires, and Cody ached to *fix* it.

He eased the beer from Liam's iron grip, loosening his fingers until he could put the beer on the table. Then Cody took his hand, their palms tight. He said softly, "You don't disgust me. You delight me. You make me so happy."

He was edging into dangerous territory and put the focus back on sex. "Fucking you is better than I ever could have imagined. You're helping me discover new things about myself."

"I am?" Liam's voice was hoarse, his blue eyes lighting up as if he didn't think it possible that *he* could be doing anything for Cody.

"Absolutely. I've never explored this dominant side of myself so deeply. With you it's all new and exciting."

Liam clung to Cody's hand, their knees pressing together. "It is?"

"Oh yeah. You make my imagination run wild. Take your old uniform, for example. Boy, do I want to see you in those short-shorts."

"What?" Liam's laughter burst out of him, his face blushing an adorable pink. Cody could sense some of the tension draining. "Come on!" Liam protested, but he was still laughing, his grip on Cody's hand not releasing, but relaxing. "The uniform'll be awfully tight on me now. I'm not in fighting shape like I was back then."

Cody snorted. "Oh yeah, you've really let yourself go. It's shocking."

"Piss off." He elbowed Cody, still blushing. "I was slimmer then." He patted his belly with his free hand. "I try to keep in shape, but being a professional athlete was a whole different level.

And I could eat whatever I wanted when I was twenty."

"So those short-shorts will be even tighter, hmm?" He waggled his brows. Liam had opened up, and Cody's instincts said if he pushed any further, he would bolt. Time to completely shift gears. "Sounds like a win-win. Your poor cock will be trapped under that tight fabric." He lowered his voice, stroking Liam's thumb with his own. "You'll be so hard, but you won't be able to touch yourself."

Licking his lips, Liam asked, "Why not?"

"What if you were tied up?"

Mouth opening and closing like a fish, Liam shuddered, his fingers twitching against Cody's.

"You'll be helpless." Cody flicked his eyes down Liam's body and back up. "I could do anything." Liam gulped so loudly it made Cody smile and ask, "You've fantasized about that, right? Being bound?"

Liam fidgeted, looking at the silent TV, which was now showing a bad US sitcom. "Sometimes."

Hmm. I bet you have. "Did you like thinking about it?" Cody let go of Liam's hand and snaked his arm around him, the leather of the couch squeaking. He rubbed circles onto Liam's waist, stealing under his T-shirt to find bare skin.

"I dunno," Liam mumbled, head dropping.

"I know you like it when I hold down your wrists. What about more? Actually being tied up? I bet you've jerked off thinking about it. Haven't you?" Liam shrugged. "Tell me," Cody ordered evenly, not raising his voice, but putting a hint of steel in it.

Liam shuddered and met Cody's eyes. "I've watched videos. I've wondered. Wanted, but... The idea of doing it for real?"

"Scary, right?"

Half-laughing, Liam nodded. "Pathetic, I know."

"Not at all." Cody kissed his cheek softly. "I've never done it before either. It's only an idea. There are heaps of other things we can do."

"Right." Liam's hands clenched and unclenched in his lap. "Although when you said before—I mean, if you—" He broke off with a shaky laugh.

Cody thought back. "You mean when I said if I tied you up, I could do anything?"

Liam nodded. "Like what?" he whispered, his lips parted and blue eyes wide.

The lust that had been simmering in Cody roared to a full boil. Oh yeah, Liam wanted this. "Hmm, where to begin? We don't have your little short-shorts here, so I guess you'll have to be naked. There are so many ways I could tie you up. I could make you spread-eagled on my bed on your back. Your wrists and ankles bound at the four corners. Or you could be standing with your arms over your head." He nodded to the top of the IKEA wardrobe. "I could loop the rope up there."

"Uh-huh," Liam murmured, his chest rising and falling rapidly as he followed Cody's gaze.

"Or, hmm." Cody had had a fun little fantasy the other morning when he'd woken lonely in his bed. Maybe it would be too much? But Liam was waiting for him to say more with such naked desire, his cock bulging in his jeans. What the hell.

"I had another idea."

Chapter Seventeen

L IAM'S MIND SPUN, watching Cody get up and take out a reusable hessian grocery bag from the wardrobe. He tipped it onto the dining table. Several packages of braided blue cord tumbled out, and Liam stared at the coils, blood pumping.

Cody held up one of the packages. "First things first. This is braided polypropylene. It's soft and smooth, but there's weight to it. It'll hold you."

Liam's throat was dry, his knees trembling as he stood and crossed a couple strides to the table. "Where did you...? Online?"

"Bunnings, actually. I'd been meaning to buy a square screwdriver so I can tighten Mrs. Delfino's door handle."

Liam laughed at the absurdity of buying sex ropes at bloody Bunnings of all places. "Did you have a sausage sizzle in the car park?"

Cody scoffed. "Obviously."

Excitement and fear swirled through Liam. Was he really going to do this? Was he going to let Cody *tie him up*? He eyed the rope.

Cody said, "I've been researching, and this rope should be perfect. If you want me to tie you up, that is."

"How?"

Taking a deep breath, Cody picked up one of the rope packages. "We can start with something simple. Put you on your knees, and I can tie your hands behind your back with a single column tie."

"Uh-huh." The mental image sent blood rushing south. Liam didn't care if he used a pretty little bow. "Then what?"

"We could start with the rope. I had another idea, but it might be too much at once."

"I want to know." He felt like he'd scream if Cody didn't tell him. His dick was aching, and he shivered with anticipation.

"Remember when we talked about fantasies, and I mentioned you getting fucked by two cocks at the same time?"

Liam's arousal evaporated, and he glanced around the room, irrationally afraid another man was going to appear. The curtains were still closed tightly over the locked doors. "I don't want anyone else."

"Hey, hey." Cody kissed him, taking Liam's chin in his hand and meeting his gaze seriously. "It's just you and me. I promise. No one else. You don't need to be afraid."

"I'm not," he lied.

"Okay." Cody caressed Liam's head, sending tingles down his spine. "Have you ever fucked yourself?" In the silence as Liam tried to understand, Cody smiled. "Not in a 'go fuck yourself' way. I mean, literally. With a dildo."

"What?" Liam laughed, shuffling his feet. "That would be too…" It was a crazy idea. Mental!

Wasn't it?

"There's nothing to be afraid of. I had an idea, but if you don't like it, we can stop."

"I'm not *afraid!*"

Cody's thin eyebrows rose. "If you say so."

"I'm not!" Liam huffed indignantly.

With a sly grin, Cody said, "Prove it."

"What, you double-dog dare me?" Liam laughed.

He lifted his chin. "Triple-dog dare you."

"Fine. As soon as I get a dildo, I'll fuck myself with it."

Smirking, Cody opened the drawer on the bedside table and tossed a bottle of lube and—*holy shit*—a massive dildo on the mattress. "I assure you it's fastidiously cleaned."

Liam couldn't tear his eyes away from the foreign object that was all too familiar. "Wow. You've got one right there. It's blue. And it has balls."

"Yeah, when I was experimenting, I went for the realistic look. The balls, I mean. Not the blue so much. Aside from the obvious blue balls joke."

Liam stared at the blue rubber. "You... Wow. So you've..." He waved his hand.

"Shoved it up my ass? Absolutely."

"You always have a way with words." Liam stared at it, not moving closer. "Where did you get it?"

"At a sex shop in Freo when I turned eighteen. I'd had sex with Tommy, but neither of us really knew what we were doing in high school. I wanted to explore."

"So you just walked in, and..." He motioned to the dildo. "And boom."

"Yep."

Liam half-laughed, scratching his beard and shifting restlessly. "You didn't worry about being caught? Or seen by someone you knew?"

"Nope. Granted, I wasn't a massive footy star."

He could just imagine the headline: *Pervy Foxy—Former AFL Rookie of the Year Likes it up the Arse.* Dread spiraled even though he knew it wasn't real. Suddenly he imagined his Mum and Dad with the weekend edition spread out at the breakfast table, shocked at the picture of him with a massive blue dildo.

"Hey." Cody was in front of him now, looping his arms around Liam's waist, his hands bare and warm on Liam's back under his shirt. "No one knows. You're safe."

"I know." Liam tried to laugh. "Weren't you embarrassed? I mean, the clerk would know you were probably going to use it on yourself."

"Oh, she definitely knew—she took me through the options in great detail. She was cool. One of those funky grandmas with short hair, bright colored glasses, and a tie-dyed sundress."

"You discussed dildos with a strange old lady?" Hands on Cody's slim shoulders, Liam stared down at him in complete shock. "And you didn't care what she thought?"

"She works in a sex shop. She doesn't judge." He laughed. "I'm blowing your mind, I know. Look, we don't have to use it. I can put it back in the drawer."

Liam's gaze stole over to the bed. "Uh…"

"It's a big blue fake cock, not a brown snake," Cody teased.

"You like it? Doing that? F—fucking yourself with it?"

"Yeah. It felt good. It was fun to experiment."

"Do you still use it?" *Don't be jealous of a big blue cock.*

"Not for a while now." He went up on his tiptoes and kissed Liam. "Like I said, it was just an idea. You don't have to do anything you're not comfortable with."

Liam didn't know whether to be relieved or embarrassed or thrilled as he eyed the sky-blue shaft. Not to mention the balls. "Hey, a dare's a dare." His voice pitched up sharply as he added, "I'm not afraid."

"Okay, this was clearly too much. It's cool, we totally don't have to do it." Cody picked up the dildo, and Liam practically leapt to the bed to snatch it from him.

"I'm not afraid."

Who are you trying to convince?

"It's okay if you are. Bondage and dildos weren't what you were expecting. Not that I was planning this for tonight, for the record."

For a second, irrational anger surged in Liam. *I'm sick of being a coward!* He took a deep breath and gripped the veined, curving shaft. "Huh. It's soft on the outside, but still hard."

"Yeah. They try to make them like real dicks. There's a suction cup attachment if you want to stick it to a chair or the shower wall or the floor. Wherever. Or you can just hold the balls."

"Right." He grasped it by the round sacs, getting a feel for it. His heart thumped, which was dumb, since this wasn't a big deal. *Mate, just shove it up your arse and call it a day.*

"Tell me more about what you had in mind." He'd been excited by the rope, and now he felt like Pandora with an open bloody box and no going back.

Unmistakable heat flared in Cody's brown eyes, and lust zipped through Liam's veins at the sight. Cody cleared his throat. "We'll get you used to it first. Play with it. Make friends." He peeled off his T-shirt and unzipped his shorts. "Let's get naked."

Liam hurried to follow the order, and they kneeled together on the bed. Cody took the lube bottle and squeezed the clear gel into his palm. His nipples were deliciously red, and Liam wanted to lick them. Cody's eyes locked with Liam's before he smoothed the lube over the dildo, coating it generously.

They both breathed heavily in the quiet of the room, the ceiling fan humming, cocks hard as they watched Cody lube up the fake dick. Cody took hold of Liam's free hand and smeared the cool gel on his fingers.

"Get yourself ready," he said. "Start with one finger. And let me see."

Shifting to the side and reaching back with his right hand, Liam poked at his arse. He'd had Cody's tongue, fingers, and cock inside him, but it felt different when it was his own finger. It felt different when Cody was watching, his lips parting and pupils dilating as Liam pushed inside. Adrenaline spiked through him as he fucked himself with one finger and then two, stretching his arse.

That it clearly turned Cody on sent a rush to Liam's head. He loved seeing Cody so hard his dick was purple and leaking. One of Cody's hands drifted up to play with his own nipples, and Liam wished Cody was touching his instead. He had half a mind to ask, but no. He was supposed to be fucking himself.

When he was ready, he grabbed the dildo and pushed forward onto all fours, making sure Cody had a good view. He gripped the balls of the glistening dildo. Some of the lube smeared on the sheets before he reached back and tried to push it into his hole, jabbing awkwardly.

"Widen your knees," Cody ordered. "That's it."

For a second, Liam pictured what he must look like—fucking *displayed*, about to shove a blue cock in his ass while Cody coached him and got off on it. It was crazy, but there was no way Liam was stopping. Not when his dick was hard enough to cut glass. Not when he wanted to make Cody come just by watching him.

Grunting, he shoved the head of the dildo inside him. Or he tried to, but there was no way. He huffed out a laugh. "I don't think it'll fit. This thing is massive."

Cody laughed too, a shaky exhalation. Liam turned his head to look at him where he still kneeled, sitting back on his heels. Cody ran his palm over Liam's ass and down his thigh. "Just go slow. Bear down like you do with me. It'll happen. Trust me."

And *fuck*, Liam really did. He had to trust Cody to even be considering this, let alone doing it. He dropped his head. His heart actually hurt to see the concern and understanding and endless patience in Cody's eyes along with the desire.

Cody caressed Liam's hip, his hand warm and strong. "You can stop anytime."

"No way." Liam pushed at his hole, gripping the springy fake balls. Arse on fire, he got the head of the dildo past his tight rim.

After that, it was a little easier, and he groaned as he pushed. Cody's hand was still spread on Liam's hip like it was grounding him. Blinking at the white sheets beneath him, Liam pushed in the dildo. It hurt so much, the toy probably twice the size of Cody, who had a good, solid cock.

"You like that?" Cody asked, barely a whisper.

"Burns. So...full."

"I know. You'll stretch."

Liam roughly plunged the dildo deeper and then back a few inches, not taking it all the way out since he wasn't sure he'd want to get it back in past his sore rim. His cock had softened, and he grunted in frustration. Muscles straining, he jabbed harder.

"Easy," Cody said, rubbing Liam's hip gently. "Can you find your prostate? It'll feel so good, baby."

Liam's wrist was cramping where it was twisted up behind him, and he swore with a sharp exhalation. He tried to change to his left hand, but it was too awkward, and sweat gathered on his skin as he struggled to get it.

"Here." Cody's hand covered Liam's on the fake balls. "Can I?" Liam dropped his hand to the mattress, nodding. Cody must not have seen that, because he asked, "Yes or no?"

"*Yes*. Fuck, I want... It's not... I need..."

Cody twisted the dildo inside Liam, moving it slowly. "You need me to make you come?"

On his hands and knees, Liam closed his eyes and pushed back. "Please."

Cody started gently, and Liam wanted to scream, but the pain and frustration faded, heat spreading to his toes and fingers where they dug into the mattress. The way Cody moved it, the curve of the dildo started to feel better inside him, not just a blunt instrument. In Cody's hands, the sensation was more careful, more purposeful, and it rocked Liam to the core.

His balls tingled, his dick going painfully hard as Cody found just the right place. "Oh, fuck! There." Liam could hardly recognize his own wrecked voice.

"You like it?"

Liam growled. "You know I do."

Cody's huff of laughter brushed over Liam's bare butt cheek, and goosebumps spread over his skin. The dildo was stretching him painfully, but the bursts of pure pleasure from his gland made it hurt so good. "Need to come," he muttered.

"I know. But not yet."

Liam whined helplessly. "Why not?"

"I have something more in mind, remember?" With that, Cody pulled out the dildo without warning, making Liam yelp.

"Fuck," Liam muttered.

"Feel really empty now?" At Liam's nod, he said, "It's a strange sensation, huh?"

Liam sat back, still on his knees. He squeezed his arse and circled his hips. "Yeah."

"Don't worry." Cody kissed him swiftly. "Soon you'll be so full you'll hardly be able to stand it. You'll be helpless, and you can't come until I let you."

A thrill skittered through him like water sprinkled on a hot pan. His cock strained, and he almost touched himself without thinking, moving his hand before stopping and putting both hands behind him. Liam's arse ached, but curiosity burned. Cody's eyes widened, a smile on his wet lips.

"Look at you. You're perfect. You want the rope?"

"Yes." Fuck, yes, he wanted it. He wanted anything Cody would give him. *Everything.*

Face brightening with those adorable dimples, Cody asked, "Yeah? We can stop whenever you want. You can say... Flash rip. That can be your safe word. Unless you hate it."

"I don't hate it." Liam could barely breathe for the building anticipation.

That was how he found himself on the floor between the bed and the bathroom, standing up on his knees with pillows under them, the blue dildo suction-cupped to the wood below. Cody had applied more lube to it, shifting it a few times before he decided it was in the right place. Now he finished tying Liam's hands behind his back, binding his wrists.

"Feel good?"

Liam tested the soft, smooth rope. "I really can't get free." His heart skipped, cock growing harder.

"You really can't." Cody ran his hand over Liam's head as he walked around him, scraping with his blunt nails, sending tingles down Liam's neck. "Unless you say your safe word. Otherwise, I'm in control. You're going to take what I give you."

He shuddered. "Yes."

"And here." Cody gave him a big metal spoon from the kitchen, sliding it into Liam's grip behind his back where his wrists were bound. "Hold tight. But drop the spoon if you want to stop and you can't speak at the time."

Buzzing, he remembered he wouldn't be able to speak during part of it because Cody's dick would be filling his mouth. Liam nodded, wrapping his fingers around the cool metal handle.

Cody drew whisper-light patterns over Liam's head and shoulders, making him tingle all over. "You're helpless. Blameless. Going to be filled by two cocks, and there's nothing you can do. Although you can make yourself come. Maybe. Can't touch yourself with your hands, and I'll be too busy fucking your mouth. But if you can get the angle right with the dildo, I'll let you get yourself off."

Liam moaned. "Please."

Without warning, Cody grabbed Liam's chin and held his mouth open. Feeding in his swelling cock, he rocked shallowly. Liam swallowed and sucked eagerly at the head, tonguing at the foreskin. The sensation of his arms restrained behind him, of being about to topple over helplessly, fighting for balance, made him tingle all over.

"You love it, don't you?"

Nodding as best he could, Liam moaned.

Cody eased free, holding the root of his shaft and circling Liam's parted lips. "Now sink down on that other cock. I bet it's sore, hmm? Your *aaass*." They both grinned at his pronunciation.

"But you have to fuck yourself on it," Cody added. "Or you won't come."

His arse was indeed on fire, but Liam ignored the pain, chasing that fullness, trying to get the dildo inside him when he could barely use his fingers with his wrists bound together and the spoon in his hands. He grunted in frustration—then satisfaction as he got the head against his hole. Using gravity, he sank down, gasping.

"Oh, fuck!" His thighs flexed as he stopped his momentum. His hole burned, the stretch too much.

"That's it. Look at you." Cody's voice was soft, filled with awe.

Liam opened his eyes, not realizing he'd closed them. His head was thrown back, his mouth open as he panted. Hands bound behind him, a thick dildo splitting him open. His muscles jerked, and despite the pain, his cock throbbed, leaking from the red tip.

Staring up at Cody—at his flushed nipples and wet lips, his pupils huge, cock dripping with Liam's spit—Liam held that intense gaze as he sank farther down, impaling himself completely on the dildo, the fake balls against him.

He tugged at the ropes again. He really, truly couldn't get free even if he wanted to. He was hot and cold all over, more vulnerable than he'd ever been, except perhaps when he'd lain on the footy pitch in Melbourne, the rival team's supporters stunned into silence as Liam writhed, knowing his knee was destroyed, tasting blood as he bit down on his own tongue, trying not to scream.

That knee twinged now, but he ignored it.

Gripping Liam's head, Cody bent and kissed him, thrusting with his tongue, bruising his lips until they both gasped. Then Cody was fucking his mouth again, choking him on some strokes, and Liam was so full he was going to explode. But unlike on the pitch in Melbourne, here it was only Cody watching him fall apart. Taking him apart piece by piece.

And though Liam's nerve endings screamed at all the sensations, he wasn't afraid. He was safe with Cody, who saw him so low and bare, yet kissed him like he wanted to devour him whole. Liam kept his jaw relaxed, letting him fuck his mouth, Cody groaning and muttering about how good it felt, and how Liam was made for his cock.

Gathering his courage, Liam lifted himself, bracing with his feet, toes bent against the wooden floor. He inhaled sharply through his nose and started fucking himself on the dildo.

Cody rocked his hips, filling Liam's mouth with steady strokes, musky fluid dripping down Liam's throat. "That's it. Find the right spot. I'm gonna come inside you, and you're going to swallow every bit."

Liam wanted to say yes, to fill him up, but he could only mumble. Cody pulled out, breathing hard. Tracing Liam's swollen lips with his thumb, he asked, "Okay?"

"Yes," Liam croaked, his voice hoarse and jaw sore, lips tingling from being stretched around Cody's shaft. He realized Cody was making sure he hadn't said the safe word. "Yes," he repeated, fucking himself harder on the dildo, fighting for leverage, gripping the spoon. "Come inside me."

Smiling so sweetly, Cody filled his mouth again, stroking Liam's head lovingly. "Won't take long. Do you think you can make yourself come on that cock? You're made to have all this meat inside you. You take it so well. God, you're sexy. So beautiful and perfect."

Liam could only moan and lean forward, pushing with his forehead so he could get the angle to fuck himself better. Cody's dick almost in his throat, pubes tickling his nose. He could barely breathe, his head getting light, barely withstanding the ripples of panic as he worked himself desperately. His cock leaked, and he was close. He just had to—

He shook violently as he hit his prostate, crying out around Cody's shaft, spit leaking from the corners of his mouth and dripping down his chin. It was messy and wet and amazing, and Liam was almost crying, his whole body straining for release.

He swallowed, whimpering, and his mouth flooded with salty spunk, Cody's cry echoing so loudly they could probably hear it clear into the Swan Valley. For the first time, Liam truly didn't give a shit.

Choking, he swallowed as much as he could until he coughed and gurgled. Cody slid out, holding Liam's head and muttering, "Oh, fuck. That's it. You can do it, baby."

With his hands useless behind him, the spoon tight in his grasp, Liam leaned his forehead harder so he could push off for leverage, pressing against Cody's waist. Cody stumbled, and Liam's stomach dropped as he tipped forward.

But it was only a few inches before he was safe again. Cody held tight to his shoulders, spreading his legs for balance, solid and rooted. Liam knew Cody wouldn't let him fall.

He worked the dildo in his arse, panting and moaning as he hit the right spot again. He needed to come so badly, every muscle tense, sweat slicking his skin, dripping into his eyes and stinging. He needed to touch himself. If he could only get some friction on his dick, he would explode.

"You're so close," Cody murmured. "I know you can do it. You're beautiful, Liam. That cock is huge, and you're taking all of it. I'm so proud of you."

He finally got the angle right, the pressure against his prostate almost too much. The pain and pleasure and Cody's pride threaded together, Liam's balls drawing up, helpless against his orgasm like he was going over the falls of a crashing wave, tumbling into the swirl of white water. White hot pleasure burned through every pore, his hands twitching behind him as he gasped and dropped the spoon with a clatter, his cock pulsing with spurt after spurt.

He slumped against Cody, who dropped to his knees and eased Liam off the dildo and onto his side. They were both sweaty, Cody's hands damp as he stroked Liam's flank and hip. "You're amazing," Cody told him, and Liam closed his eyes, boneless as his wrists were released. Cody brought his stiff arms forward gently, and Liam flopped onto his stomach.

Everything was sore, but in the best way, like after a grueling workout. Cody gently examined his wrists as Liam caught his breath. The wood was sticky under him, but he didn't care. He was wrung out, his eyes closing, but a lump of emotion had lodged in his throat—gratitude that he could have so much more than he'd ever even let himself imagine.

Cody skimmed his fingertips over Liam's used, stretched hole. "Does it hurt too much?"

Liam wanted to say no, but words seemed so very far away. His eyes were too heavy with unshed tears, his throat too thick, jaw aching.

"*Liam?*"

He could hear the clear worry and opened his eyes, eager to reassure, fumbling to touch. He squeezed above Cody's knee. "It's just right," he slurred.

"Okay." Cody was bent close, examining Liam's face. He sat back and exhaled noisily, caressing Liam's arse cheeks and hips, down over his thighs, kissing his fevered skin, his breath hot. "The thing is, there's no way I can lift you onto the bed."

Liam groaned, a smile lifting his lips irresistibly. "You could try."

Cody did, and soon they were laughing, sweaty and slippery, stumbling up to the mattress and into each other's arms with grateful sighs. Liam couldn't keep his eyes open...

Gasping, he woke with a start. The TV was still on, Formula One cars zooming silently around a winding track. The lights were on too, the fan beating gentle air over their sticky, naked bodies. Cody stretched sleepily and tugged Liam closer, but Liam slithered free, lurching to his feet.

"I should go. It's late." Past two, according to the green display on the microwave. He found his jeans and T-shirt on the floor.

Cody yawned. "Just stay. Please? You can leave before sunrise. You're opening tomorrow, right? It's only a few more hours."

Liam kept his head down, searching for his boxer-briefs, suddenly unwilling to look Cody in the eye. It was so, so tempting to crawl back into that bed and pull the covers over them. He ached for Cody's warmth.

But if someone saw him leaving now, it was still in the realm of possibility that they'd simply been two mates having a few beers. If he crept out at dawn...

His stomach heaved, cold sweat breaking out as he struggled to catch his breath.

"Liam—"

"Goodnight," he blurted, unable to even glance at Cody. "You're rostered on tomorrow arvo, right? I'll see you then. And I'll come over in the evening around eight, yeah?" He eased open the door to the patio, slipping between the curtains before stopping dead. His voice was too high and tight as he asked, "Uh, the garage?" He had no choice but to look back.

Cody sighed heavily from where he now sat up naked in bed, his hair mussed. "The opener's there in that bowl. Leave it in the laundry basket. I'll close it once you're gone." His voice was flat, and he didn't look angry, just terribly defeated, which was far, far worse.

"It's not—that was—" Liam hated himself for not being able to find the words. For not being brave enough to stay.

"I know. Sleep well."

"Thank you," Liam whispered, fishing out the garage door opener and clutching it with sticky fingers as he slipped out into the darkness. He didn't deserve Cody's understanding, but he was profoundly grateful.

He'd completely given up control earlier, his body still aching perfectly. He'd been safe and protected and understood, but now Liam couldn't shake the fear that if he stayed the whole night, he'd be too far out to sea. Too exposed and endangered. He couldn't do it. He had to get home.

The streets were empty as he drove south, chewing a handful of Quick-Eze. He reached Barking before he knew it. The ocean was a dark, teeming presence to the right, the lifeguard tower empty, a lone security light glowing on top of the stairs. Before long, he'd be there, pushing up the shutters on the windows, checking the medikits and defib, filling the ATVs with petrol.

There wasn't a soul in sight now, and he stopped by the curb. He considered parking under the Norfolk pines and...what? Unlocking the tower and sitting there alone instead of going to his empty house? It had felt imperative to get home, but now the loneliness was unbearable.

"Feeling bloody sorry for myself," he muttered.

Still… He could go back.

Cody wouldn't be angry. He *should* be, but he wouldn't. He'd kiss Liam sweetly, up on his tiptoes, his hands warm and gentle on Liam's arms. He'd welcome him back into bed, curling around him in a tangle of limbs.

Raw with regret, Liam almost turned around. But no, Cody would be sleeping now, and it would be even more selfish to disturb him than it had been to leave. No, it was better this way. Liam had broken all his other rules, but this one he could follow—he wouldn't sleep over at Cody's. It was simple. It kept everything under control.

Liam drove inland and jabbed on the radio, turning up whatever song was playing even though he'd be back to the dark house in half a minute. He didn't want to hear himself think a moment longer.

Chapter Eighteen

T HE EASTERN SKY was pale as Cody yawned. It was quarter to five, and the cafes weren't open yet, so he had to make do with a thermos of instant brew rather than his usual flat white. Bickie had unlocked the tower, and he and Damo were down in the garage making sure the Jet Ski and buggies were fueled and ready before they pulled out the trailer of boards, flags, and danger signs.

In the first aid corner of the tower, Cody checked that the medikits were stocked and the oxy cans were ready to go. The defib battery was on and flashing, ready for action that Cody hoped they wouldn't see. While part of him was curious to see a resus, it filled him with dread to think of someone being dead right there up close.

Once he finished checking the equipment, of course Cody's mind returned to Liam. Liam and the mind-blowing sex they were having. It had been a week since the dildo, and Liam had returned every night.

Every night, Cody had fucked him, the evening before securing his wrists to the posts of the bed frame, sucking him mercilessly and making him beg, finally lifting his thick, heavy thighs and pounding him.

Every night, Liam ran away as though he'd turn into a pumpkin.

Every night, Cody pretended it didn't bother him.

Luckily, the day was hot and busy, summer setting in, the crowds growing exponentially. Cody saw Liam in passing on patrol, his stomach wriggly at the mere sight of him, lust zipping through him for sweet seconds before he refocused completely on the water. He racked up rescues, the Croc snapping fiercely and tourists ignoring warnings, truly not understanding the danger of the ocean until the rip had them in its jaws.

"Mia!" Hazza called late afternoon, waving her over to where he and Cody tried to help an agitated woman who was motioning at the water. Mia raced across the sand, and Hazza said, "Can you translate?"

She turned to the woman, asking her something, presumably in Malay. The woman stared at her blankly, replying in a language that sounded like Chinese to Cody, although he was far from an expert.

But sure enough, Mia glared at Hazza. "I'm still not Chinese. Or Korean. Or Japanese. My family is Iban from East Malaysia. For the record."

Hazza winced. "Sorry, mate." He turned to the woman, speaking loudly and slowly. "Is someone missing?"

The woman pointed to the water urgently. "No swim!"

They all followed her finger, and Cody tried to spot anyone in the waves who looked to be in trouble. He asked her, "Is it your son or daughter? Child? Children?"

Hazza lowered his hand, palm down and waving to indicate a short height. The woman nodded hard, pointing to the water again. "Daughter," she said, fighting tears.

"Hazza to Central," he said into the radio. "We've got a worried mum. Think it's her young daughter in the water who can't swim. Mum doesn't speak very much English, so we're not sure, but can you have a look?"

Mia patted the mother's arm. "It's okay. We'll find her."

The woman probably didn't understand the words, but hopefully the tone was reassuring. Cody had asked Teddy why they didn't carry smartphones so they could use translation apps, but apparently it had been deemed too much of a potential distraction. They had to keep their eyes on the water as much as possible.

Cody repeated to the mother, "We'll find her."

They did—the little girl had wandered up the beach, only wading up to her knees. In the end, Cody worked fourteen hours, staying late after Mia went to the ER under protest, Teddy insisting she get tested after she nosedived and the board clunked her head, opening up a gash that needed stitches. She'd bitten her tongue too, blood on her lips.

"You'll be right," Hazza had said as he and Cody had driven her up to the tower in the buggy. "I hear lemons and jalapenos are the best thing for it, eh, Maz?"

Cody smiled now as he left the tower, thinking of Mia's bloody grin at the teasing and finally getting a nickname. He hadn't minded finishing out the day for her, but the idea of riding his bike home was too big a mountain to climb, so he left it locked under the tower. He felt like he'd run a marathon, his shoulders aching from all the paddling.

He'd whispered his request to Liam earlier, and now he waited a few blocks north, out of sight of the beach, for Liam to go home and get his SUV as the sun set. When Cody climbed in, Liam was looking around guiltily, and Cody bit back an annoyed comment.

For fuck's sake, it wasn't as if they couldn't be *friends*. Plenty of the lifeguards were buddies. In fact, Cody had said no to multiple invitations to grab dinner and a few drinks after shifts because he had to rush home and hide away with Liam.

"I'm starving," he said now. "Can we stop for hot dogs? Rum Amuk is on the way."

"Can't we just order in? I don't want to stop. I've had enough of people today."

Cody's jaw tightened, irritation sparking. *Or you just don't want to be seen with me.* "It'll only take a minute. You can wait in the car if you're scared."

Liam scoffed. "I'm not scared." Still, he didn't meet Cody's gaze. "Just don't feel like talking to anyone else. I'm beat."

"I'm tired too. You don't have to talk. We'll place our order, they'll make the food, we'll say thank you, and that's it. And no one will think we're gay."

"*Fine.*"

"Great."

They drove in silence, Liam flipping stations on the radio. Finally, he said, "I like this song."

Cody actually didn't recognize it, but he took the olive branch. "Me too. It's fun. My sister Gwen sent me a nineties playlist yesterday. She's really into retro. That was your era, right?"

"Kind of. I was still a kid. I'm not *that* old."

"You sure?" Cody teased.

Liam found a spot across the street from Run Amuk, close to East West Design, a massive home store warehouse with colorful murals of beach life and Fremantle along its building. The day's warmth lingered, and the patios of the restaurants on South Terrace were crowded and buzzing. Cody half-expected Liam to wait in the SUV after all, but he came.

As they crossed the street, the urge to take Liam's hand, to thread their fingers together like any other couple, was so strong that Cody had to shove his fists in his shorts' pockets.

They placed their takeaway orders for gourmet hot dogs and sides of fries in the small, colorful restaurant. There were a few tables, each decorated with pages of *Where's Waldo* books. Glued-together toy cars formed a thick sort of wall paper on the upper half of the walls, white tile underneath. Cody loved Run Amuk's food and its fun vibe. He was about to suggest to Liam that they actually stay and grab one of the tables when a grating voice rang out.

"No way! Dude, it's Liam fucking Fox!"

Cody's heart sank, Liam going stiff next to him. The guy who'd spotted Liam was in his thirties and had a sunburned nose and beer on his breath. "How ya goin'?" he asked as he lifted his hand for a bro shake, Liam having no choice but to clasp his palm.

Liam's smile was entirely fake. "Good. Thanks." He turned and picked up a menu even though they'd ordered.

The guy ignored this silent cue. "What've you been up to? Man, it sucks what happened. You were incredible. I wish you could've played longer. Bet you'd still be playing now, hey? You were the best, mate." To his friend, the guy said, "You remember Liam Fox?"

He did, and so did an older woman behind the counter, and the three of them exclaimed about how wonderful Liam had been, listing off ancient accomplishments, and Cody cringed with every word, knowing Liam's soul was being shredded.

When that man Clay had mentioned it on the beach after Liam had saved his husband, it had been a brief acknowledgment. He hadn't gone on and on and *on*. Cody hadn't really thought anything of it.

But now, he wanted to jump in front of Liam with his arms out, screaming at these people to *shut the fuck up*. They meant well, but the way they were talking—couldn't they see they were hurting him? Couldn't they tell Liam didn't want to rehash the details of the life he'd lost?

But all Cody could do was stand silently, and the fans *did* give him curious looks, clearly wondering who he was, probably especially curious since he was so much younger than Liam.

He decided it was weirder to interrupt and proclaim that he and Liam were *friends*, that they worked together, you see? Nothing more! So Cody kept his mouth shut, gratefully taking the paper bag of food when it was finally ready, nodding and smiling as he and Liam left.

They climbed into the SUV in silence. Liam didn't start the ignition, his gaze distant on the dark street through the windshield. Cody cleared his throat. "Are you okay?" His fingers flexed, almost taking hold of Liam's hand where it was fisted against his thigh.

"I didn't want to go in there," Liam snapped.

"I know. I'm sorry. But I'm sure they didn't think anything of it. Of us, I mean." Although he knew it was more than that—it was feeling vulnerable and being recognized for the millionth time and reminded of all the wonderful things that were lost. Witnessing it firsthand, Cody understood how painful it was for Liam in a way he hadn't before.

Liam's jaw clenched, and sweat beaded on his temple in the stuffy vehicle. Cody wanted to ask him to turn on the engine and AC but didn't. Instead, he said, "I know this is difficult for you in ways I can only imagine. I really am sorry."

"It's not your fault." But Liam still didn't look at him.

With a sickening twist of his stomach, Cody could see the future stretching out before them. Maybe it was too soon to even think about that, but the reality of Liam's fear and choices hit Cody so hard he could barely breathe. The bottom of his knees stuck to the leather, and he felt anxious and hot all over.

He blurted, "I know it's only been a month or something, but I really like you. I mean, the sex is great. Better than great. Amaz—"

"Can we not *talk* about that right now?" Liam nearly shouted, rubbing his left knee violently.

"Okay." Cody had been clutching the paper bag of food, and he put it between his feet. "I realize it hasn't been long, but I want…" He didn't know how to put it into words that wouldn't send Liam running. "I understand why you've kept who you really are a secret, but—"

"I have to." Liam looked at him now, his knuckles white on his knee.

"I get it. I'm not saying we should—" He struggled to get it right. He needed to get this *right*. "I understand why you're afraid to come out."

"It'll be on the *news*. People will debate it. Dissect it. Dissect *me*." He was breathing hard.

Cody wanted to soothe him, but about this, Liam was totally right. "They will, and it'll suck. Strangers will have all kinds of opinions about you and your life. I can't pretend to have a clue what that's like. I've obviously never been famous, and you have. You'll be under the microscope, and girls you had sex with a million years ago will probably come out of the woodwork and give the tabloids interviews. Maybe some of the men from overseas too, if the media really digs. It'll be the worst."

"Exactly."

"But people will support you as well. People you might not expect. The world is changing. Yes, you'll get some hate, but you'll get love too. And eventually, the attention will fade, good or bad. There'll be another news story, and another, and life will go on."

Liam seemed to be contemplating it, but then he shook his head stubbornly. "How can I go to work? The boys..."

"They don't seem to have an issue with me."

"That's different."

"Why?" Cody asked quietly, trying to be patient. "They're your friends. They accept me. There's no reason they wouldn't accept you."

Liam shrugged violently. "But my family won't. I'll lose them."

Cody bit back an impatient huff, keeping his voice even. "You can't be sure of that."

"Oh, now you know them better than I do?" Liam motioned

with his hands, whapping his right fingers on the window.

"Of course not. But look at Cyclone. You've known him since you were a kid, right? He'd help you."

"Teddy's different. He's always been different."

"Then why haven't you told him?" He held up his hands. "I don't mean that to sound…accusatory or whatever. I just want to understand."

Liam shrugged. "Dunno. Besides, since he married Jill he's been busy. The baby and all that."

Cody didn't comment that Teddy's daughter was at least three. "What's the worst that can happen if your family found out who you really are?"

Liam scoffed. "Are you serious? They'll never look at me the same for starters."

"That doesn't have to be a bad thing. If they knew the real you—"

"The *real* me? What, I should tell them I love getting down on my hands and knees? That I'm—" He exhaled sharply, slashing the air with his hands and nearly hitting the windshield this time.

Cody grabbed Liam's left hand, squeezing tightly. "That you're what?" he asked softly. When Liam didn't say anything, Cody added, "That you're not a real man?"

He nodded, clinging to Cody's fingers.

Keeping his voice soft and calm, Cody said, "First off, that's bullshit. Submitting has nothing to do with being a man or a woman. And no one needs to know anything about what you like in bed. That's for us, and no one else. Do you know the details of your brother's sex life with his wife?"

"What? No." Liam screwed up his face. "That would be weird."

"Right. Because it's private. It's their business. So why would it be any different for you?"

"Because I'm…" He grunted, clearly frustrated. "They'll never accept me."

Get it right. Stay patient. "Okay, let's say they won't."

"Thanks for humoring me, mate," Liam snarled.

"I'm not!" Even though Cody maintained that Liam couldn't know for certain how they'd react. "What I'm trying to say is... Okay. This is just a scenario. Let's say you tell them, and they react like you thought they would. My question is: What are you really losing?"

Liam sputtered. "My family!"

"But you don't have them now. Not really. You see them, what? Once a month? Sometimes less? You avoid them. Your dad said as much when he came to Barking. You won't let them know you. You moved away from Mandurah, and you said you've pretended to be sick to avoid family events. So what exactly are you holding onto? What would you truly be losing? If they could know the real you, it might change everything for the better."

"I told you, if they knew 'the real me,' they'd be disgusted. A man like me wanting *that*."

Cody groaned in frustration. "I'm still not talking about sex!"

Liam's brows knit. "Then what? They know the rest of me."

"Do they? You barely talk to them. Barely see them."

"Your family lives on the other side of the world!"

"Yeah, and there are times when it really sucks. I Skype my parents every week, but sometimes I'm busy and it goes two weeks. I text with my mom and sisters about random shit, and with the time difference, it's hard to really connect. But I need to live my life. If they didn't accept that I was gay, it would hurt like hell, but I'd go on. I'm creating the life I want. I'm making my dreams come true. Don't you want that? Don't you *need* that?"

"I have what I need," Liam insisted, crossing his arms and staring ahead.

Bullshit. "I don't think you realize how much you've closed yourself off. And maybe if you tell your family who you really are—who you've *always* been—maybe they'll turn their backs on you. That would be devastating. But you've already made them strangers. It hurts all of you. How long can you keep this up?"

Liam stared out the windshield. "My nephew and niece—there's too much at stake."

"But how often do you see them now?" He was repeating himself, but clearly it wasn't getting through. "Your dad came to the beach the other day because he wants to know his son. He's making an effort."

"And you know what he was probably thinking when you met him?" Liam snarled. "He was thinking, 'It's that little faggot.'"

Cody tried not to flinch. He lifted his hands. "Then why do you care what he thinks? Fuck him!"

"He's my father!" Liam shouted. "I want him to be proud of me! I was everything he wanted in a son, and I ruined it all. If he knew, it would kill him."

"Or maybe it would just kill the image of you in his mind. You said you hate that shrine your parents have, right?"

"I do!"

"Do you? Or do you actually like it, deep down? You still want to be their perfect son, but you're robbing them of actually having a relationship with you."

"You don't know anything about it. You don't know them at all."

"Of course I don't!" Cody took a deep breath, trying to rein in his temper. "You won't even let me in your house, let alone theirs."

"I told you from the start no one could know. You promised!"

"I'm not telling anyone!" He grasped Liam's forearm. "Baby, I won't do that to you."

Liam snatched his arm away, looking around, eyes wild with panic. A woman walking a terrier went by, gaze on the bright screen of her phone. He shouted, "I told you I didn't want to come here!"

"I know," Cody muttered, wiping sweat from his forehead. An awful hopelessness washed through him. They couldn't go on like this forever. *Cody* couldn't, at least. Yes, it had been barely a month, but he already wanted so much more. "I know you're scared, but please just think about it. I want to be with you."

"You are!" Liam was still looking around, that hunted expression creasing his beautiful face.

"I want…" *Everything. I want to love you.* "I want to wake up with you. Just the two of us. Stay over tonight. All night. *Please.* No one will know."

Liam swallowed hard, not meeting Cody's eyes. "I can't. This is too much."

Cody swallowed a surge of panic. "Okay. I know this is all new. For both of us." It was still hard to believe he'd only known Liam such a short time. "Let's just go back to my place and relax and—"

"I need to go home. I'm opening tomorrow. Should have an early night. I'll drop you off."

He sighed. "Come on."

"I want to be alone."

With a burst of frustration, Cody threw up his hands. "Aren't you sick of being alone? Taking your little sex vacations where you pray no one recognizes you, and you can't even be real enough to ask for the sex you actually want?" He pressed his lips together, wishing he could yank the words back. It was a dick move to throw that in Liam's face. "I'm sorry."

"I'll drive you home," Liam said flatly, his gaze on the road. He started the engine.

Cody couldn't bear the thought of being in his studio alone. He opened the door. "I need some air. I'll walk." He slammed the door and strode off, hoping he'd hear Liam call his name, or that Liam would drive up and ask him to get back in.

But when Cody finally looked back, the SUV was gone, the spot where it'd parked empty in the glow of a streetlight. He didn't care when he realized he'd left his hot dog. He couldn't choke down a bite anyway.

Chapter Nineteen

"**B**RR!" MARK HUGGED himself with an exaggerated shiver. "Going to need a bloody space heater in here today! Feels colder than winter and it's practically summer."

Five of them crowded into the glassed semicircle of the tower's main section, extra chairs brought up from the locker room. Cody perched on the counter at the right edge of the window, winding the drawstring of his hoodie around his finger. He peered at the steely sky, the clouds impenetrable, rain coming and going and the wind whipping. A few surfers braved it up at the north end, but other than that, the beach was deserted.

Everyone was bundled up, aside from their bare legs and feet. Sitting in the center of the desk by the phone, Bickie had actually put on his socks and sneakers. You knew it was cold when a Barking lifeguard wore shoes. Cody considered it, but figured he had to hang tough.

He said, "People in Canada would laugh their asses off at us thinking fifteen Celsius was cold. But shit, this is *cold*."

Ronnie, who'd just come in from a cursory patrol in the ATV, brushed back damp ginger curls. His navy uniform jacket glistened. "It is seriously freezing. It's the wind. Hard to believe it was thirty and sunny yesterday."

Liam had a rostered day off, and Cody was glad he could stay warm and dry at home, as desperate as he was to see him after their fight. Cody had taken forever to fall asleep after choking down a bowl of leftover noodles. Charlene had barked at his gate early as usual, and he'd ignored her for twenty minutes until guilt had gotten him moving.

Was Liam upset too? It was worse to think that he *wasn't*. Did he want to talk to Cody and make things right between them again? This was all happening so fast, and Cody was falling deeper and deeper. He couldn't pretend it wasn't killing him to be stuck in the tower, the minutes crawling by with nothing to do in the shit weather.

What was Liam doing? Did he think about texting Cody, even though they'd agreed at the start to keep it all offline? Cody had typed and retyped a hundred apologies that morning. It wasn't that he thought he was particularly wrong—in fact, he was still sure he was right.

But he was desperately sorry that they hadn't made up. It was the first night they hadn't had sex, and his skin felt too tight, his limbs stiff. Being at odds with Liam was just all *wrong*.

He stared out at the gray, choppy water. Was Liam watching TV? What kind of couch did he have? What was he wearing? Did he have a throw blanket to keep warm? What did his house look like? Would Cody ever get to come over?

He'd looked up the address in the staff directory weeks ago and checked out the front of the house on Google's Street View. He realized that was creepy, but honestly gave zero fucks. Liam's house was a cute little bungalow with a couple of leafy trees out front and a postage stamp yard with yellowish patches of struggling grass.

Fuck, he wanted *in*.

"How's the water looking down there?" Damo asked Ronnie.

"Murky *as*," Ronnie said. "That storm this morning churned it up really good."

"Sharky water," Bickie muttered, picking up the binos and peering north. "Those boys better keep an eye out. Sharks'll swim right into them in conditions like this. Can't see shit."

Chalkers said, "We'll do some training drills later this arvo." He was the senior lifeguard on duty, Teddy taking the quiet day to catch up on paperwork in his office beyond the park. "Get the weighted dummy out so Chook can practice bringing in an unconscious patient on his own again."

"From the sharky water?" Cody asked dubiously before he could bite his tongue. He and Mia had drilled with the dummy for two days before they started, but he had to admit he'd rather stay in the relative warmth and safety of the tower today.

Of course, this garnered a round of hearty laughter, and Chalkers raised a grayish brow. "Where's that gung-ho attitude, Chookie? I'll ring Mia and get her down here. You know she won't hesitate."

"I didn't say I wouldn't do it!" Cody laughed, shaking his head. "Just asking for clarification."

Bickie groaned, still looking through the binos. "Ohhh, man. That bloke just got smoked. Went right over the falls."

They all turned to watch, and Cody picked up his binos. The waves were three feet, so not huge, but they were pumping one after the other. Not as powerful, but relentless. The swell period, the amount of time between the cresting waves, was only a few seconds. These waves were shitty compared to big sets with twenty seconds between them, when you could really get a quality ride through the tube.

"Don't know why they bother," Damo said. "Can hardly get a decent turn." He stared through binos. "*Oof.* Those waves are just coming down on his head one after the other."

Mark stood. "Should we go?" The light atmosphere had grown serious in a blink.

"Maybe." Bickie still watched through his binos. He sat back.

"Nope. He's right—walking into shore now. Looks okay."

"Good," Mark said. "I don't want to go outside."

They all laughed, the swell of tension receding. They chatted about this and that, and Cody gnawed over the argument with Liam. Things between them had become serious so quickly, and he told himself it was good to have a cooling-off period, to go a day or two without having sex.

He told himself that, but he didn't believe it.

It wasn't just about the sex—he hated to leave tension between them, to think that Liam was hurting and that it was Cody's fault. Liam had clung to his insane rules for years, and Cody had pushed his boundaries and knocked down his fences with a bulldozer. Liam was definitely freaking out.

And of course he cared what his dad thought, even if his dad was a homophobe. It was easy for someone else to say you shouldn't care what your family thought.

Cody wound and unwound his hoodie drawstring, watching the few brave/foolish surfers at the north end. If someone else was in his shoes, he'd tell them they were getting way too serious about this guy, way too quickly. Just fuck him and have fun. See other people. Don't get too attached.

He rubbed the knot at the back of his neck miserably. Already way too late for that. And shit, he knew coming out was up to each person, and that everyone had their own journey, and he had no right to tell Liam what to do. But it still broke his heart to think of Liam living a shadow life for years to come.

When Cody was sent out to do a patrol, there was only a mist of rain left falling, but the wind still whipped. A figure up ahead walked near the water's frothing edge. As Cody neared in the ATV, he realized a small dog—a pug?—was trotting alongside the woman, who wore a red raincoat with the hood up.

Cody picked up his radio from where it sat with his bum bag and binos on the empty seat beside him. He slowed as he said,

"Central, there's a lady walking a dog. Should I say something?"

Despite the fitting name, dogs weren't allowed on Barking and had to stay on the dog beach to the north around the headland. Bickie drawled, "Nah. If there's a council ranger out in this weather—which I've never seen in my life, for the record—they can tell her to move on. Not our job, mate. We only step in if it's a nuisance. Certainly no one out there complaining today."

"Copy." Cody continued on, giving the woman a wave as he passed her. At the south end, where the outcropping of rocks jutted out, there wasn't a soul around. Fishermen often clambered out on the boulders, but not today. He started a wide turn to the left to head back up.

What was that?

Stepping on the brake, Cody squinted at the water. The rocks were on the left, but there had been something—*there!* Eyes locked on the dark object floating in the foamy water past the outer break, he felt on the seat with his right hand, grasping the binos and jamming them to his eyes.

Clump of seaweed?

Heart drumming, he focused the lenses. There was a dark, weedy clump, but—*shirt! Skin! Person!*

Cody tossed the binos and fumbled for the radio. "Unconscious patient!" Dropping the radio, he jumped onto the wet sand and ripped off his jacket, hoodie, and blue shirt, his fingers clumsy and cold.

"What?" Bickie's voice punched through the air. "Are you serious?"

He lunged for the radio, words flying. "First gate!"

Then he had the board out of the rack on the buggy's side, and he splashed into the water, adrenaline thundering through him, not feeling the cold, keeping his eyes locked on the person as he paddled with all his strength over the waves, losing sight of the patient over and over as he punched through the constant swells.

When he reached the person floating face down, pulled by the current, he grunted and groaned, heaving with all his might to get them onto his board. Knowing they were watching in the tower, and just in case it hadn't been clear, he held up his fist and pulled it down three times. His brain zoomed through the check list.

No rigor mortis—good. Could still get her back. No froth around her lips—bad. Been in the water a while, dragged around by the current. She was an average size, but dead weight was truly almost impossible to lift. It had been a struggle with the dummy, and now with a real person, there was no way he could get her on the board the way he would a typical patient. The constant little swells were chipping away, and he clung to her, terrified that if she was torn from his grasp she'd go under.

His back to shore, he positioned the board between them, swells washing over. Reaching over and holding her lifeless arm by the wrist, he kicked up and rolled the board toward him as they'd been taught, using momentum to drag her on, her head on the upside-down board now, the edge at her armpit. Digging his fingers into her shoulder, he rolled the board again so it was right side up.

Now she was sprawled across the top. He tugged one leg up first, her jeans sodden and making her even heavier. But he got the right leg up so she was safely on top, her head toward the nose.

He was continuing the checklist when he remembered to check the swells. *Boom!* A fresh spurt of adrenaline burst through him, and he flopped down, getting her legs under his armpits as he paddled as hard as he could to catch the incoming bigger wave and not be smashed by it. He shouted in relief as the water surged up beneath them, that unmistakable lift as they rode the wave to shore.

People were there—Chalkers, Ronnie, and Damo splashing out to help him. The four of them lifted the board like a stretcher and waded onto the sand. Mark had the defib and oxy ready. He cut through the young woman's clothing to bare her chest, Ronnie ready with a towel to dry her skin before attaching the defib pads.

As the machine whirred up, assessing, Damo performed chest compressions. They all waited for the female electronic voice to tell them whether there was a shockable rhythm. Part of Cody couldn't believe this was real—that they were doing a full-on resus. He stood with his hands on his knees, panting, his head spinning.

The minutes ticked by, Mark leading the resus while all Cody could do was watch. When Chalkers wrapped a towel around him, rubbing his back, Cody realized he was shivering, his teeth actually chattering.

"Good job," Chalkers said. "You did a damn good job. It was textbook."

Then why wasn't she waking up? Why wasn't the defib working? It was shocking her, and they were taking turns with CPR, Mark on the oxy, but there was no pulse.

What was her name? Did she have a family? Parents, siblings? Friends? Even kids? A boyfriend? Girlfriend? Cody thought she looked in her twenties, but he wasn't sure because her skin was so horribly gray. Her long, dark curls were snarled around her head, snaking out over the sand. Her fingernails were painted in chipped bright purple, her earrings limp hoops caught in her hair.

Teddy arrived in a buggy with the ambos, and they took over. The mist of rain continued, and Cody felt like it was snow, and that his feet were in ice, not sand. The boys tried to get him to go back to the tower, but he was immovable.

No, he was going to wait until he knew—although he did. He *knew*. He was going to wait until the ambos said it, and finally one did, a middle-aged woman with bleached hair that had a pink streak over the top of her ponytail.

"We're calling it. The time is…"

Cody tuned her out. The police had arrived too, and at least the beach had been practically empty and there were no onlookers. When he looked back at the patient, she had vanished under a sheet, and the absurd thought struck that he hadn't had the chance to say goodbye.

"What's her name?" he croaked. He realized Chalkers was still standing beside him with a comforting hand on his back.

Teddy approached, grim-faced in his raincoat and cap. "Hey, mate. No ID on her, so the police will investigate. I know this is rough, but the boys said you did it all perfectly. We're damn proud of you. Come on, let's get back to the tower, hey?"

"But she's dead." It was far from *perfect*.

"I know, Chookie." Teddy rubbed Cody's head. "It's part of the job, but that doesn't make it easy. It's never, ever easy."

For an awful moment, Cody thought he might burst into stupid, childish tears, but he breathed deeply and nodded. He knew Teddy was right, and as a lifeguard he'd have to do body retrievals, and that a resus sometimes failed.

Still, he was numb as he plodded up the stairs to the tower, accepting the praise and sympathy of the other guys, having a shower in the little locker room that didn't seem to thaw him at all. Teddy had told him to dress in his street clothes, and he pulled on his jeans and hoodie.

Damo was in the locker room when Cody emerged. "How ya goin'?" He winced. "Stupid question, I know."

"It's okay." Cody was surprised he was able to talk, and that he even sounded fairly normal.

"That was a rough one. And I know you probably don't want to hear it right now, but you did everything you possibly could. Everything any of us could do. She was already gone." Damo's brown eyes filled with tears, and he shook his head, wiping his eyes. "When you go home from work and you've saved a life, it's a hell of a feeling. The best feeling in the world, hey? But when you don't, it's a real kick in the balls."

There was something about seeing easygoing, jokey Damo get emotional that released one of the knots in Cody. He realized he'd been breathing shallowly, and now he inhaled a full breath. He nodded. "A real kick in the nuts with steel-toed boots."

"Too right," Teddy said as he appeared in the doorway. He leaned against it and rubbed his sun-worn face. "We'll do a full debrief tomorrow with everyone who was here. In the meantime, you can head home, Cody. We'll be packing up in a couple hours anyway, and the rain's back. Or you can stay and hang out. Talk. Whatever you need. You have the number as well for the counseling service? It's completely anonymous, and you can call them anytime. For any reason."

"I'm good, I think." He needed Liam.

Teddy asked, "Did you ride your bike down? You can leave it in the garage, and I'll give you a lift home, or anywhere else you want to go."

Cody hesitated. There was nowhere else he wanted to be than in Liam's arms, but he couldn't say that.

"Or hey, Jill's making fried chicken tonight," Teddy said. "Come home with me now. It's not far, and I can whip back and finish up. Jill would love the company. She's always whinging about needing grownup time." He raised his hands. "Not that I blame her! Our daughter's an angel, but sometimes you just need to talk in complete sentences."

Cody chuckled, surprised to find that he could, guilt quickly hammering him. "God. I shouldn't be laughing."

Mark squeezed into the doorway, his serious face kind. "If there's one thing I've learned as an ambo, it's that you absolutely need to keep laughing. Some patients will break your heart, but you've got to keep going. There are more people to save tomorrow. But that doesn't mean you shouldn't be sad. Okay?"

"Yeah." Cody nodded, blowing out a long breath. "Yeah."

Teddy said, "Let me ring Jill, and I'll pop you over."

"No, no. It's okay. Thank you, though. Really. I'm going to go to my—friend's house." He only hesitated a split second, but Damo's eyebrows shot up.

"Ohhh, a *friend*, hey? You found a new bloke?" He grinned. "I expect to hear everything next shift."

"No, it's not—I mean—he's, well—" Cody groaned. "I'm leaving now."

Teddy squeezed his shoulder. "I'll ring you later to see how you're getting on. With today, I mean. Not how you're getting on with your boyfriend, although a good fuck is what the doc ordered."

Mark nodded seriously. "Studies show that—"

"Okay, I'm leaving now!" Cody headed for the door, getting back-slapping hugs and head rubs from everyone in the tower.

He was soaked before he reached the park, but he didn't mind. His sneakers squeaked on the pavement as he crossed the street and left the beach behind. He looked back but didn't see anyone around. If someone was watching, they'd see him disappear down the main road into the streets of Barking, the neat houses and tall gum trees a maze.

They'd have no idea where he was going. In the miserable weather, what were the odds anyone would spot him? Even if he was home, Hazza surely wouldn't see Cody pass his house on his way to Liam's. Just in case, Cody took the long way, walking down and then around and coming at Liam's address from the other direction.

Soon enough, he found himself at Liam's door, soaked to the skin, his backpack drenched and hanging heavy on his shoulders. What if Liam turned him away? His heart clenched at the thought. Maybe he should just go and not give Liam the chance to hurt him like that. He should be strong and deal with it on his own.

Fuck, Cody hated to fail. He hated it more than anything, and normally he wanted nothing more than to be alone to work through his anger at himself for stuffing up.

But this time, after regaining a bit of calm, he felt like he was suddenly cracking in half, grief far more powerful than his frustration. Grief for a stranger whose name he didn't even know. But he'd touched her. She'd been real, and now she was dead, and he couldn't ever, ever change it.

This time, he needed Liam. He needed him in a way he'd never needed anyone. The longer he stood on Liam's doorstep, the more chance for someone to see him, so he had to shit or get off the pot, and—

Ding!

His finger pressed the little round button of the doorbell, and it echoed inside beyond the wood and opaque glass panels of the door. A shadow inside moved, footsteps thudding. Liam opened the door and stared at him.

"Cody?" Liam continued staring, his brow creasing.

"She's dead," he blurted, and his eyes burned again.

"Who?" Liam reached for him. "Oh God, what happened? Who's dead?"

Cody tripped into his arms, and Liam was so wonderfully big and strong and warm as he hauled Cody inside.

"I'm sorry. I know I shouldn't have come. You don't want me here, but I…"

"Shh." Liam eased off Cody's pack and hugged him so tightly, lifting him off his feet. "You're okay. You're safe."

It was something Cody had said to him a dozen times, and hearing it back had him choking on a sob. "She's dead," he mumbled, and he let the tears fall, secure in Liam's arms.

Chapter Twenty

LIAM REALIZED THE tap had been running in the bathroom for minutes. "Cody?"

The door was ajar, and Liam nudged it open with his toe, not sure if he should intrude. Cody hunched shirtless over the sink, his body jerking as he scrubbed his hands. Liam crept next to him at the sink, his gaze flicking between the mirror and Cody himself. Cody's head was down, and he stared at his hands.

After crying for a few minutes, he'd breathed deeply and told Liam what had happened. There were probably texts flying about it, but Liam had been napping, miserable after the quarrel with Cody the night before, feeling angry and guilty and basically a giant mess as usual. Now he didn't give a shit about any of that. He just wanted to help Cody feel better. Dealing with death on the job never got easy, but the first time was brutal.

"I can smell it."

Liam's stomach dropped. He knew that stench—a putrid sort of smell that clung to your hands for far too long after handling a body. "It's okay." He wanted to hold Cody again, but didn't touch him yet, his hand hovering in the air as Cody slammed down the pump on the plastic container of aloe soap from Woolies.

Lathering the soap, Cody rubbed harder. "I swear to God, I

can smell it," he muttered, finally turning his head to look up at Liam. "Am I losing it?"

"No." Liam spoke calmly although his heart thumped. He squeezed Cody's damp shoulder, which shook as he continued scrubbing. "It's real. I've talked about it with the boys. The patient's skin gives off...something. I don't know if it's oils or an aura or what. It takes a while to fade, no matter how much you wash." He reached for Cody's hands, stilling the frantic scrubbing. Cody tried to jerk away, but Liam held tight.

"It'll get on you!" Cody exclaimed.

"It's okay. It'll fade. I promise."

He stared down at their hands, then back to Liam. "Are you blowing smoke up my ass? Have you guys really noticed the smell before?"

"Honestly. I don't know if it's something about being in the water, but that odor on your hands is a real thing. It should be gone by morning."

"Really?" His voice was so *small*, and *young*, and Liam's heart clenched. He honestly usually forgot that Cody was only twenty.

Liam made his tone deep and confident, with no room for doubt. "Absolutely."

He kissed Cody's head, rubbing his back, wanting to erase his pain like chalk from a blackboard. He murmured, "It wasn't your fault."

"But I—"

"*No.*" Taking Cody's face in his hands, he gazed down at him, making sure he was listening. "It wasn't your fault." He kissed away the fresh tears that spilled, then hugged him tight. Cody clung to him, snuffling against his throat. Liam wanted to hold him forever and keep him safe and—

His heart skipped.

Forever.

That was mental. Wasn't it? But for a few seconds, he clung to that word as tightly as he did Cody, letting himself imagine.

"Do you have condoms?" Cody asked, his mouth wet on Liam's neck. He lifted his head and stroked Liam's cheek. "I know you like... But will you fuck me? I don't want to think. I just need..."

"Yes. Yes." Liam kissed him hard, Cody sighing into his mouth, sagging against him.

Cody had been so patient and kind and in control with him, giving more than Liam had even known he'd needed. Protectiveness swelled, and he ached to take care of Cody now, to keep him warm and safe and never sad or doubting again.

Liam bent and scooped him up, one arm under his knees. Cody's eyes still glistened, but he smiled, a little huff of laughter brushing Liam's face. He wound his arms around Liam's neck as Liam carried him into the bedroom and lowered him carefully to the mattress. He kissed Cody until they were breathless before hurrying back to the bathroom.

He rooted around behind the cleaning supplies and first aid stuff and the random crap under the sink. He'd fucked men on his holidays over the years, each time telling himself it was enough and that he shouldn't want more, even though he craved it.

He'd never been able to shake Lorenzo's disgust, or the memory of how painful it had been when Lorenzo had reluctantly tried to give Liam what he'd begged for. So at least topping had gotten him off, even if it usually left him with a nagging, hollow feeling.

But back in bed with Cody now, taking off their clothes and covering his body completely, kissing him until their lips were wet and raw, Cody's chin red with beard burn, his fingers digging into Liam's back and shoulders and hips, it was entirely different. Liam was bursting at the seams—full and *necessary*.

Face-to-face, he worked Cody open, and it was so different from the first, aborted attempt at fucking him. That had ended with Cody topping from the bottom, but this time, as Liam pressed into him, he had purpose. Cody's lean, muscled legs bent up, moans falling from his parted lips, and Liam wanted to give him everything. Give him the release he needed.

Cody's eyes flickered open and shut, his hands roaming over Liam's shoulders and down his arms, Liam's name on his tongue, his cock like iron between them. Eventually, his arms dropped, fingers loose around Liam's corded forearms, and Cody gave himself over completely, eyes shut as he grunted and groaned.

Slowing his strokes, Liam leaned down and kissed Cody's face all over, tasting his salty sweat where it dampened his temples. Liam had never had a man here in his bedroom, in his bed. The women had been in his old condo by Elizabeth Quay, a lifetime ago. Here, in his plain room with dark curtains and mass-produced ocean art, he'd only ever been alone.

Cody cried out as Liam fucked him hard again, balls swinging, their skin slapping. For a horrible moment, fear gripped Liam, and he almost told Cody to be quiet, shushing him like he had the first time he'd been inside him.

No. He'd never do that to Cody again. It was just the two of them in the world, their bodies straining, breath short, pleasure building. He angled deeper, ripping another beautiful cry from Cody's open mouth. They were safe, and no one ever had to know.

But they will. They have to. You can't go on like this. They have to know you.

Liam drowned out the torrent of voices with his own moans, concentrating on the tight heat and taking hold of Cody's cock, determined to make him come, putting all his focus on achieving that goal. It amazed him that Cody had wept so openly and didn't seem ashamed or embarrassed at all.

Not that Liam thought he should be, but the way Cody was able to expose himself like a raw nerve, crying and then begging to be fucked when usually he was the one in control—it both boggled Liam's mind and made him want to keep Cody sheltered from anything that could hurt him again.

"Fuck," Cody muttered, his head thrown back, the tendons in his neck straining, veins standing out. "Yes. God, Liam. Please."

"I've got you." He stroked and squeezed. "That's it."

Liam fucked him through the orgasm, pounding his arse and milking his cock, the spunk pale against their tanned stomachs and chests. Only when Cody was spent could Liam let go himself, pleasure flaring hot and then sapping him sweetly.

He kept Cody in his arms, surrounding him, rolling a bit to the side to take his weight off and toss the condom. But as soon as he had, Cody wrapped his arms around him and pulled him back down, their damp skin sticking together.

Liam wasn't sure how long it was until his leg cramped. He pressed a kiss to Cody's forehead, then went to the bathroom and brought back a wet cloth.

"Was that okay?" Cody asked quietly after Liam had cleaned him. He turned on his side, looking up at Liam sitting beside him. He ran his fingers over Liam's knuckles, back and forth, back and forth.

"More than okay."

"Do you want to do it more often?" Cody's flaccid cock curled against his thigh. Liam was naked too, and it still gave him a jolt that it felt so natural. Of course, now that he was thinking about it, he stood and reached for his boxer-briefs to pull them on.

What was the right answer? Was Cody tired of topping him all the time? Liam had felt so connected to him just minutes before, but now he wanted a Quick-Eze. Did they always have to *talk*?

Cody said, "I just realized that I'd assumed you didn't like to top at all, since it seemed like you hadn't been getting what you needed when you went away."

"Right." On his so-called *sex vacations*. It wasn't that Cody had been wrong, but the way he'd spat it had still hurt. "I don't… Can we not…" He wrung the cloth, water dribbling down his hands. "This was good, but I like it the other way more. I shouldn't, but—"

"*God.*" Cody groaned, rolling on his back and rubbing his face. "Please stop saying that. Stop thinking it!" He dropped his hands. "No. I'm sorry. I'm sorry." He sat up. "That was a dick thing to say. I know you can't just turn off decades of internalized homophobia."

"Internalized homophobia," Liam echoed dully. He didn't have a clue what to think of that.

"We can talk about that another time. It's been a hell of a day."

Concern swelled, washing away everything else. "I know." Liam sat back down on the bed, taking Cody's hand, knee pressing against his thigh. "You didn't do anything wrong. It's not your fault."

Cody gave him a shaky smile. "I guess I should practice what I preach and not blame myself."

Liam smiled back. "Definitely." He squeezed Cody's fingers. "You hungry? I'll make my famous cereal for dinner."

"Okay. Thanks."

Padding into the kitchen, Liam breathed more easily. There were probably a dozen things they needed to talk about, but…not yet. For now, they could just *be*, couldn't they?

The *rap-tat-a-tat* knock was so familiar that for a moment, Liam actually smiled as he automatically turned for the front door. Then ice water crashed over him, and he jolted to a stop in the corridor. The house was too small for Teddy to come in and not know that Liam had company.

His gaze darted around, cataloging the evidence—Cody's shoes by the mat, far too small for Liam, his soaked backpack discarded on the floor. He could see Teddy's sloping-shouldered shape through the frosted glass panels, and then the door swung inward because Liam rarely locked it when he was home, and Teddy never waited for him to actually answer it. Liam stood there as Teddy filled the doorway and stopped short.

Teddy's brows met, then smoothed out, and he lifted the six-pack of Toohey's. His old Rip Curl hoodie frayed at the neck over his boardies and thongs. He rubbed his shorn head with his free hand and said, "I can't stay long before dinner, but are you up for the usual?"

It *was* usual, especially after a death at work. How many times over the years had Teddy shown up at his door with stubbies and sometimes greasy food. They'd eat and drink and talk about nothing, and then work their way up to whatever bad thing had happened. Sometimes they left it off and just sat on Liam's patio listening to the crows caw and talking about nonsense, being together because they knew the other understood the pressure of the job.

Liam's throat was too dry, and he croaked wordlessly.

The furrow returned, and Teddy laughed. "You gonna chuck a sickie tomorrow? Or are you really crook?"

"No," he managed. "I…" He cleared his throat. "This isn't…" Glancing over his shoulder, he was relieved to see the short corridor still empty.

"Ah." Teddy laughed, but it wasn't his usual loose sound, this time rounding up to a higher pitch. "You're not alone." He was still in the door's threshold and hadn't seemed to notice the shoes or bag.

Be normal. "Sorry."

The furrowed brow morphed into a full frown, Teddy's tanned face creasing. Then his eyebrows sailed up. He mouthed the word, "*Chook?*"

Just like that, Liam's carefully constructed reality collapsed in on itself like a wave crashing on the reef. His ears buzzed. Did

Teddy—how did he *know*? He knew? How? *How?*

Liam had apparently dropped his head, because he blinked at his bare feet and the worn brown floorboards, uneven beneath him. Did Teddy actually *know*? Forcing a desperate breath, he lifted his head and looked his oldest friend in the eye.

Yes. Teddy knew, without a shadow of a doubt. An automatic denial was on Liam's tongue, but he choked it down. Nausea rising, he tried to catch his breath. It was happening. This was real.

He nodded.

Eyebrows still high, Teddy nodded too. "Right. Okay." He thrust out the beer. "We'll grab a drink tomorrow, yeah?"

"Yeah," Liam croaked. "Thanks." His feet moved, and he took the stubbies.

Lips quirking, Teddy whispered, "Don't look so bloody grim. No one died, mate." He winced. "Well, you know what I mean. Chook doing okay with that?" At Liam's dazed nod, he added, "Good thing he's here with you." He turned away, calling back as he walked down the little concrete path, "If you chuck a sickie you'll be on shower-block duty for a week." He climbed into his Jeep with a wave and drove off.

Liam stood in the open doorway, his hands full, staring at the empty street. The rain had stopped, and a young mum pushing a massive stroller glanced at him, then again. She sped up. His feet moved, and he was closing the door and walking into the kitchen, putting down the beer on the round little table.

He stared at a scrawled crayon drawing of himself at the beach that Jamie had made him the year before, the "Uncle Liam" in a haphazard mix of capital and lowercase letters. In the drawing, he had a big smile on his misshapen head, and Jamie had added "I love you" to the blue sky on top. Had his drawing improved? Liam wasn't sure. Cody was right that he barely saw Jamie. He barely saw his family.

Teddy knows.

Would he go home and tell Jill? Then would she tell Cora, who'd tell Greg, who'd—what? What would Greg do? Liam's heart was in his throat, his lungs seizing up. He didn't fucking know what Greg would do because he had barely spoken to his brother in years. Not about anything that mattered.

As a teen, footy had been his everything, and Greg had cheered him on. But by the time he'd played professionally, Greg had been off becoming a firey, and after the injury, after goddamn Lorenzo, Liam had shut the door.

Cody appeared, wearing his wet clothes and a solemn expression. "That was Teddy?"

Liam nodded. Teddy knew. Teddy *knew*. Would Greg find out? Would he tell Mum and Dad? He didn't know what would happen. He'd kept it all locked down for so long, and now it was truly out of his control.

"I'm sorry," Cody whispered.

Teddy knew, and Liam couldn't change it no matter what. Couldn't take it back. Liam would have to *talk* about it with him, and even if Teddy supported him, it was *happening*, and he couldn't stop it. It was too soon. No. He wasn't ready.

Images seized his mind—all the things he'd done with Cody, the things Liam had let him do, the things he'd loved doing. He'd broken all his rules, and now everyone would know, and *he couldn't stop it.* Shame rose up, burning hot and icy cold.

"No fucking son of mine is going to turn out a faggot."

"A man like you? No, no, no."

Blood rushed in his ears, a howl tearing at his throat as noise exploded. Amber glass covered the stovetop and floor, foamy liquid splashed everywhere, over the crayon drawing, dripping down the fridge. For a moment, Liam stared at the chaos, baffled. He shook, his fists clenched, and he looked down at his hands, at his arm that had just swept the case of stubbies off the table.

Cody stood frozen in the doorway, the whites of his eyes stark in his stunned, beautiful face. Then he was gone, backing up and disappearing, the door thudding distantly. He was running away, and Liam wanted to scream for him—beg him to come back—but he couldn't.

He was panting, harsh, painful breaths, coming apart, his guts spilling over the broken glass.

Chapter Twenty-One

THE SKY WAS blue. The sun beat down as noon approached. Kids splashed and shrieked. Families set up picnic lunches under bright umbrellas. Fully dressed tourists stepped off sandbanks meters from shore and had to be rescued.

Everything was normal.

Liam waited for the axe to fall, but somehow it didn't. He'd been tempted as hell to chuck a sickie after all, but after the day of unseasonable cold and rain, it was a hot and sunny Saturday, and over fifteen thousand crowded onto Barking's golden sand already.

He'd seen Teddy briefly in the tower, and Teddy had greeted him as usual. Liam imagined he could still feel where that familiar, friendly hand had squeezed his shoulder like countless times before. He could see Teddy's flash of a smile and could almost pretend that yesterday hadn't happened at all.

But as he helped a woman with a dislocated knee into the tower, Cody was there, and Cody didn't meet his eyes. Regret slashed at Liam again, a familiar sting. Was Cody angry? Hurt? Worse—afraid of him? The broken glass still littered the kitchen. He'd retreated to his bed that smelled of sex and Cody, unable to deal.

It seemed impossible that it was less than a day ago Cody had wept in his arms, that they'd been huddled together in Liam's bed for the first time. Now the world was still operating as usual, but everything had changed. Except it hadn't. The only messages on Liam's phone that morning were group chats from the boys to Cody, checking in on him and reassuring him that they had his back.

There was nothing from Greg or Cora or Mum and Dad. Everything was normal. Almost. Teddy still knew. It had to be more than Cody's mere presence in Liam's house. Teddy had guessed and hadn't been shocked. A little surprised, perhaps, but not shocked. The conversation would have to come, but for the moment, the world kept turning.

Except that as Liam held the green whistle to the injured woman's lips, telling her to breath in the gas, promising her it would take away her pain, Cody didn't so much as glance over. Yes, he was watching the water through binos, doing his job, and maybe it didn't mean anything. But Liam still ached to haul Cody into his arms and kiss him, to drop to his knees and plead. He wasn't even sure what he wanted to beg for.

Everything was normal, except it never would be again, and Liam didn't know how to go forward.

By three p.m., it was full on, so hectic that Teddy called in extra guys for a few hours. Liam stood by the windows in the tower, scarfing down a microwaved burrito, salt water drying in his hair after being out on the ski doing dozens of rescues. The swell was up and the tide low, the Croc pulling hard.

Bickie was manning the tower, and he groaned, watching something through the binos. "Get that leash off!"

Liam picked up another pair of binos and looked north. He asked, "Third gate?"

"Fourth. Chook's got a beginner surfer out the back in the Croc. Bloke won't take off his leash. Probably saying that the board's a rental and he'll lose his bloody deposit." Bickie groaned again. "Better than your life, mate!"

Burrito forgotten, Liam peered out, focusing on Cody. The patient was clinging to his board in the water, shaking his head, and Cody was yelling something, slapping the rescue board with his palm. The surf was rough, crashing over them, and Cody had just got the young man on the board, the rental surfboard still tethered to the patient's ankle, when they were smashed.

"Shit!" Bickie got on the radio. "Damo, you free? Chook needs a hand. Oh, wait—he's sweet." He paused. "But still might need an assist."

Cody was back on the rescue board and paddling to the flailing patient. Liam said, "I'll go too. Just in case."

It felt like an eternity getting there, the beach so crowded he had to drive the buggy along the back by the low stone wall, the park just as packed beyond. When he got to the shore, Damo was helping Cody drag the patient out of the surf, onlookers gathering.

Liam jumped out, shouting, "Get back! He doesn't need you gawking!"

The patient was barely on his feet, and he coughed as Damo and Cody sat him down. Damo crouched by him. "You swallow a lot of water?"

Liam didn't hear the answer, because his focus was on Cody. Cody, who leaned heavily on his knees, his face too pale, breathing too hard.

"What?" Liam asked, reaching for his wet shoulder. He was partly relieved simply to touch Cody again, but the rigid, trembling tension had his pulse rocketing.

"'M fine." But Cody gasped as he straightened, his hand going to his ribcage.

"You hurt?"

He grimaced, leaning on his knees again. "His board," he gritted out between clenched teeth.

Fuck! This was exactly why they were taught to discard a patient's surf or boogie board during a rescue—it could crash into you or the patient and cause serious damage.

"My board!" The man lifted his head. "It's a rental!"

It was all Liam could do not to tell the patient to go fuck himself and his deposit. He slowly walked Cody to the buggy, Damo waving over Ryan and leaving the patient with him. Cody was breathing in shallow little bursts, his fists clenched and whimpers in his throat as Liam lowered him to sit on the back of the buggy, the easiest place to get on when someone was injured.

Liam perched beside him, their legs dangling, and shouted for Damo to drive. With the force of the water, a surfboard could be a dangerous weapon, and a crack to the ribs was agonizing. Cody needed an ambo. Now.

He could hear Damo radio it in, honking on the horn to move all the damn people who were everywhere and blocking their progress. Liam held the back of Cody's neck, steadying him, Cody's head bent, his pulse fluttering under Liam's thumb.

It was nothing out of the ordinary—he'd have steadied any patient or injured lifeguard the same way to make sure they didn't tumble off the back of the buggy. But he was dying to press his lips to Cody's wet cheek and tell him everything would be okay.

They got him up the tower stairs, Cody stoic but for the little gasps of agony. Bickie ushered them in. "His board got you in the ribs, eh? Ambo's coming. You'll be right. I've got the whistle ready."

Cody had the shakes, squirming on the first aid bed, sitting up against the raised back, his foot going restlessly. He was clearly in a world of pain, moaning now, and Liam wanted to hold him close. But he couldn't. Would Cody even want him to try? He stood back as Bickie held the whistle for Cody, telling him to breathe deeply.

Damo went to the windows to do a sweep with the binos, and Liam should have gone back on patrol. The ambo was coming, and there was nothing he could do. Yet he didn't move, watching as Cody sucked on the whistle, his eyes squeezed shut and foot kicking.

"That's it." Bickie said. "Breathe in and out. Any better?"

Cody nodded and mumbled, "A little." He kept breathing the methoxyflurane, and when he opened his eyes again, his grimace morphed briefly into a beautiful smile. "Liam!" He held out his trembling hand. "I missed you."

Bickie and Damo, who'd hopped back down the few stairs from the main area, laughed heartily, and Bickie said, "Here we go. The whistle's working its magic."

But Cody's smile faded completely as Liam remained rooted to the spot. "Why won't you stay with me?"

"I'm right here." Liam's jaw was so tense he could barely get the words out.

"But you're not really." Cody dropped his hand.

"Suck on the whistle, mate," Damo said, patting Cody's shoulder. "You'll be sweet as."

Cody did, breathing in and out with the green plastic tube between his lips. His smile returned. "Hey, Damo. You have cool hair. I bet the dolphins like it."

"I bet they do!" He flipped his long, blond curls with a flourish, laughing with Bickie. "Keep sucking. Ambo'll be here soon."

Bickie said, "Yeah, any minute. He's off his head now, hey?" He laughed. "God love the green whistle."

But when Cody caught sight of Liam again, he jolted as if he'd forgotten Liam was there. "Will you stay with me tonight? Please?" He shook his head, saying to Damo, "He never stays the whole night with me. I always have to wake up alone."

As Damo and Bickie laughed more uncertainly, giving Liam quizzical looks, Liam tasted bile. He couldn't move or speak or breathe.

"He's afraid of what everyone will think," Cody slurred. "I know some people would be the worst, but I don't think you guys would care." He sucked the whistle, exhaling with a groan. "Would you, Damo?"

"Nah, mate." Damo peered between Liam and Cody, his brows knit. "We wouldn't care a bit."

The door opened, and Teddy marched in. "How's he doing?"

"High as a kite now," Bickie said, glancing at Liam. "Talking nonsense like they usually do."

Teddy's gaze bounced between them all, probably sensing the strange tension.

Then Cody spoke again.

These new words hung in the sun-warmed air, the AC unit rattling in the silence that followed, all eyes swinging to Liam. Liam couldn't breathe. Had he heard right? Had Cody actually just said...

Teddy, Bickie, and Damo stared at Liam, waiting for him to acknowledge Cody's declaration, to make sense of it all.

But Liam backed away, almost tripping on his arse at the foot of the steps up to the main tower. He was burning and cold all over at the same time, his ears buzzing, holding his breath like he was deep under water, the pressure crushing his lungs.

He lurched to the door, shaking off Teddy's hand. As he crossed the threshold, the sun's glare blinding, Cody made another sound. Not words this time, but a horrible gasping breath. Liam stopped, the wet wheezing noise blocking out everything else but the hammering of his own heart. He spun back around.

Cody's eyes were squeezed shut as he wheezed horribly, his face too pale. Paler than only a minute ago.

"Get the oxy on him!" Teddy was saying. "I'll have the defib ready just in case."

Liam stood in the doorway watching as Damo held Cody down on the bed by the shoulder while Bickie put the oxy mask over his face and Teddy unzipped the red defib bag. The *defib*.

No, this wasn't happening. Cody wheezed, and Liam registered somewhere in his mind that the lung was probably punctured, and it could be collapsing. He might stop breathing.

"No!"

It was his own voice, but it sounded like it had echoed up from the beach. Then he was moving, this new fear obliterating everything else. He was reaching out, crowding into the treatment area, and Cody's hand was damp and small.

Liam threaded their fingers together, probably gripping too tight. "It's okay. You'll be right." His throat was hoarse, his own words still sounding distant.

Cody's teary eyes were wide over the oxy mask, and he clung to Liam's hand. Writhing, he groaned. Sirens wailed, drawing closer, and sunlight flooded in from the back door, someone probably rushing down the ramp to meet the ambo. There was warm pressure on Liam's shoulder, and he realized Teddy was beside him like he'd been for years.

Other voices were talking, but Liam ignored them. He kept hold of Cody's hand, telling him to keep his eyes open and breathe. "I'm here," Liam said. "I'm right here."

Chapter Twenty-Two

E VERYTHING HURT.
There was a tube in Cody's nose, a machine beeping rhythmically. A room slowly came into focus. Beige walls with generic flower art in cheap frames, a TV up near the ceiling. He breathed shallowly, the right side of his chest aching. Someone was moving around the room, but he was too tired to focus. His head was stuffed with cotton balls, and he shut his eyes.

When he opened them again, he had no idea how much time had passed, but the fuzz in his head was fading. Everything still hurt, and he was so thirsty. Was Liam there? Was Cody in the hospital?

He wanted Liam.

"Cody?" a female voice asked. A nurse? No, strangely familiar... Dark ponytail swinging and Mia's face appearing to the right. "Hey. You good?" She screwed up her face. "I mean, obviously you aren't—you had a punctured lung."

A plump, older nurse barreled in, big smiles and efficiency, giving him sips of water through a bendy straw. "You had a pneumothorax, which sounds scarier than it is, really. Managed to crack two of your ribs, and part of a bone punctured your lung— just a nick, really."

"Fixed it up with some Blu Tack, I reckon," a familiar voice said, Damo appearing in shorts and a tee like Mia, his long curls damp. "Hiya, Chookie. I'm supposed to be the drama queen on the service. Look at you, going and getting your lung punctured by a surfboard. That is a proper injury." He scoffed playfully. "Show-off."

Cody was quivery with nausea, and his whole body ached with every breath. But worse than that, his mind was frustratingly blank. "Was it during a rescue?"

Damo and Mia exchanged a glance. Mia carefully asked, "You don't remember?"

Standing on his left side now, the nurse patted Cody's shoulder with the barest of touches. "You're probably a little fuzzy, dear. Morphine can make you awfully drowsy and confused, but don't worry, the worst is over. The doctor inserted a chest tube to drain the excess air from the pleural space outside the lung. We're going to keep you overnight for observation and another X-ray in the morning, but you'll be right. Don't fiddle with the tube." She gave him an encouraging smile. "I'll tell the doctor you're awake. Don't stress yourself trying to remember. Rest. You lucked into a private room since the wards are full."

But he *had* to remember, because there was something he was missing, and it was big. Was it about Liam? Was it—

Chipped nail polish, gray skin, a dead weight in his arms. Wet hair in his face, the waves hitting them as his muscles screamed, trying to get her on the board.

She was dead, and he couldn't remember her name. Had he learned it, or…no. No ID. She was gone, and he'd been so cold. But then Liam had been there, warm and powerful and sweeping Cody into his arms like it was a movie.

His gut twisted, saliva flooding his mouth as more memories surfaced. Liam red-faced and shaking amid broken beer bottles, glass and foam, his worst fear realized. Cody walking all the way back to Freo in soaking clothes, cuddling with Charlene when he finally got home.

He'd invited himself over even though Liam had always been clear about his boundaries, and Cyclone had guessed about them. Cody had promised over and over that he'd never out Liam, and then he'd run away rather than stay and face it together.

Fuck, Cody was ashamed of himself.

But how did he end up in the hospital? It was like when you couldn't remember a certain word, or who starred in some TV show, and the information was right there in your mind, skirting the edges, just beyond grasp.

"…thirsty?"

Cody realized Mia had been saying something. She held a pitcher of water and poured more into a little cup with the bendy straw, her face pinched in concern.

"Is it Saturday?"

"It is," she said, nodding encouragingly. "Almost eight p.m. Don't worry about anything except getting better."

Oh Jesus. "What happened? Tell me." Had he been injured during a rescue? Damo had said it was a surfboard. "Is a patient hurt?" *Don't be dead. Please, please don't be dead.*

"No, he's fine." Damo rolled his eyes. "Wouldn't take the leash off his rental board. You were arguing with him and a wave smashed you both. Surfboard broke your ribs, but you kept hold of the rescue board and got the idiot in."

Relief flooded him. "Thank God."

"You… You don't remember anything else?" Damo asked.

"Uh-uh. Was I unconscious? Did I hit my head or something?"

Another glance between Damo and Mia. Damo said, "Nah, you were still talking and on your feet. You had the whistle, then stronger drugs, like the nurse said. Does a number on your brain. No worries."

Fresh unease snaked through him. He tried to push it aside

and think of a casual way of asking about Liam. God, he wanted to see him. Needed to make sure Liam was okay. Cody shouldn't have left like that. Running off like a chicken shit. *Maybe the nickname fits after all.* "Thanks for coming. That's cool of you guys."

"Of course," Mia said. "I was down at south end with some friends today, and when I heard, I figured since your family is in Canada, you might need some company."

"Right." He missed his mom with a deep, painful pang that made his lungs burn. "Thank you."

Damo said, "All the boys are worried. I came as soon as I could. Today was mental, and we couldn't leave to come with you in the ambo. I was an opener and I did almost fourteen hours. Cyclone and Foxy'll be here soon."

Hope filled him. "Is he—Liam—" Cody's brain was too muddled to be casual.

But there it was—another weighted glance between Damo and Mia. Cody's stomach thudded with a sickening lurch. "What? What aren't you telling me?"

Mia shook her head. "I wasn't in the tower, so…"

"Oh God. What?" He stared at Damo, who twisted his hair around a finger and grimaced. "Is he all right? Did he get hurt somehow?" Cody tried to push himself up, his middle section screaming, head spinning. He was giving too much away, but if Liam was hurt, if Liam needed him—

"No, no!" Damo exclaimed as he and Mia urged him back down. "He's fine."

"Then what?" Cody's ribs burned, saliva pooling in his mouth.

Damo said, "Most people talk nonsense on the whistle."

Oh Jesus. "What did I say?"

Mia looked decidedly uncomfortable now, shifting and frowning. Damo grimaced again.

"What did I say?" Fuck, had it been something about Liam?

Cody reached toward them, and just lifting his hand now made him moan, the adrenaline and fear not enough to combat the pain.

Shoulders slumping, Damo pulled a chair close to the bed and sank into it. "From what you said, it sounded like you and Liam—it sounded like you two are…together?"

He squeezed his eyes shut. "Fuck." He wanted to disappear and wake up and have this all be a nightmare.

"Is it true? You and Foxy? Because damn, son. Strong work." Mia smiled tentatively. "I told you he was into you."

He couldn't smile back, misery choking him. He'd apparently well and truly outed Liam, the one thing he'd promised he'd never do. No point in lying to Mia and Damo now. "It's true."

"Hey, it's okay." Her hand lifted, and after a hesitation, hovering in midair, she took hold of his fingers gently. "Everything will be okay."

"Did I say anything else?" he asked. Damo winced—*winced*—and Cody braced. "Tell me. Please."

Damo bit his lip. "You said that you love Liam, but he doesn't love you."

Tears burned Cody's eyes now, spilling over his cheeks before he could hope to get control. "Oh my God. Oh my fucking God."

"It's okay," Mia said. "Not optimal, I grant you, but don't freak out. Maybe Liam *does* love you. He looked like shit when I saw him, and that's not easy for someone that good-looking. Sorry. Joking. Still not very good at that."

Damo cracked a smile. "Mate, he was off his head worrying about you. Held your hand and everything. I honestly never saw it coming, but I probably should have."

"Well, yes, tbh," Mia said. "He's a classic closet case."

"And I outed him." Cody's cheeks were wet, his voice gravelly.

"You didn't know what you were saying!" Damo insisted. "Foxy won't blame you."

"You don't understand. He's so afraid," Cody whispered. Shit, he was saying too much again. He pressed his lips together as if that would stop any other betraying words from ever escaping.

Mia held out a tissue, and when he didn't move, awkwardly dabbed his eyes and cheeks with it. Cody let her, exhaustion winning. He had to see Liam, but his eyes were unbearably heavy…

"YOU'RE HERE."

Cody's voice was hoarse and sleepy, and he blinked at Liam to his right—far too big in the chair, scrunched up and listing to the side, his chin on his chest, neck undoubtedly stiff and sore. Indeed, Liam jolted, his head shot up, and he winced. He was still wearing his lifeguard uniform, which they weren't supposed to do when they weren't on duty.

Liam leaned over Cody. "Are you thirsty?" He poured a cup of water and held the straw to Cody's dry lips.

"Thanks," Cody mumbled, sighing in relief.

Liam opened his mouth, then closed it. Finally, he asked, "Are you in pain?"

"Yes." He'd never experienced his body so battered and weak.

"Where does it hurt? Your ribs?"

"It hurts everywhere." His eyes burned.

Liam examined the tubes and equipment by the bed. "Aren't they giving you morphine? I'll get the nurse—"

"No. They are, I think. It's not—Liam, I fucked up so badly. I'm sorry."

"*You?* No."

"Knock-knock." Teddy appeared in jeans and a tee, whispering as he shut the door behind him, "I snuck in to see how you're going." He stood beside Liam, clapping his shoulder as he peered at Cody.

"What time is it?" Faint light edged the browny-pink curtains. Cody realized he had no idea where his phone was, his usual clock.

"Just gone six a.m.," Teddy answered.

The openers would have the flags planted and equipment checked, ready for another day at Barking. "I'm supposed to work at eight." It was still surreal that he was in the hospital.

"Don't worry about any of that," Teddy said. "Concentrate on getting better."

A surge of panic registered in his fuzzy brain. "How long is that going to take? What about my job? The traineeship?"

"Mate, I just told you not to worry." Teddy's smile froze. "Shit, are you going to spew?"

Liam suddenly had the bedpan, and he held it to Cody's chest, his left hand supporting Cody's head. Cody swallowed the extra saliva that had flooded his mouth, breathing deeply. "I'm okay. But thank you." The fact that Liam had been ready to catch his puke made his heart swell. He asked Liam, "Have you been here all night?"

Teddy grinned. "Couldn't tear him away if I'd tried." To Liam, he said, "Sorry I had to run. Jill and Chloe had bad prawns. I've been dealing with spew all night. They're finally settled down and sleeping." He shook his head. "That was a hell of a day." He pulled over another chair, Liam sitting back down in his.

Teddy said, "Like I told you, don't worry about your job. I'll speak to the council, and I'm sure we can extend your traineeship. It'll probably be months before you're cleared for active duty. Broken ribs and a punctured lung are nothing to sneeze at. I'd also avoid sneezing."

Cody tried to smile. "Right."

"Look. I shouldn't be telling you this, but the council just approved more hiring for next season. Full-time, seasonal, and casual since the crowds are getting bigger and bigger. You and Mia have excelled, and the seasonal positions are yours. Possibly a full-time spot, but I'm not sure yet. Once you're up and around, you can work in the tower. Not alone since you're a trainee, but you can help monitor the beach, and you'll be paid. If you were injured off the clock, it might be trickier, but it was on the job, so you don't have to worry."

Cody exhaled, his ribs aching. "Right. Thank you so much. Shit, I need to tell my parents what happened." He thought of his mom again with a deep pang.

"I rang your mum last night," Teddy said. He lifted the Barking tote bag he'd been carrying. "Your phone and stuff from your locker's in here. She said she'll talk with you later. She's worried, but I told her you're a tough one. Baz says we should call you Tazzie since you're a fierce little devil." To Liam, he asked, "What'd'ya think, Foxy?"

Liam nodded. "Definitely." He sat rigid in his chair, clearly on edge.

Teddy said to Liam, "We haven't had a chance to talk properly yet." He glanced at Cody. "You two are a couple, yeah?"

A couple. Were they? Cody nodded, hoping the answer was still yes. Not that they'd officially been a couple before, but… Whatever. Fuck, he needed it to be a yes. He watched Liam, who swallowed with an audible *gulp*.

Liam said, "I didn't know how to tell you. About me, I mean. I never told anyone until Cody." He stared at his hands in his lap, his fists clenched.

Teddy's cheeks puffed as he exhaled noisily. "I knew it was something. After the end of footy, of course that was a massive shock, and it made sense that you would have to grieve it. Find your way in a new career. A new life. And you did, but as the years passed, I guess I felt like something wasn't quite…clicking. That you were holding back. Was it this all along? That you're gay?"

Liam nodded.

283

Teddy held up his hands. "I have to admit, I don't get it. Not about being gay—obviously I've got no issue with that. Not at all. But hiding it this long? Look, it won't be easy with your folks, but the world's changed so much. Not to say there aren't hateful pricks out there, but hell, we've got marriage equality now. Is it *that* scary to tell the truth?"

Liam still stared down at his hands, fidgeting with his fingers now. His Adam's apple bobbed. "It shouldn't be. Other people do it. I don't know why I couldn't."

"Because you were afraid they'd hate you as much as you hate yourself," Cody said, wishing he could pull Liam into his arms, wanting to climb out of bed and put himself between Liam and the world. "You built a wall to protect yourself, and then you were trapped." To Teddy, he added, "It's easy for you to say it's not scary anymore. Or for me to say it. Coming out is different for everyone."

"You're right," Teddy said. "I'm sorry." He took Liam's shoulder. "Brother, you know I've got your back. At least, I hope you know it."

Liam nodded, grating out a wobbly, "Thanks." He was silent a moment, then said, "You didn't seem shocked. When you came by the house, and Cody was there, and... You seemed to know."

"Not until recently, but the thought occurred when that backpacker shoved Cody on the beach. The look on your face? I've never seen anything like that before. You were bloody ferocious! Thought you were going to knock his block off. We all wanted to, but with you there was something more. I told myself I was imagining it, but I paid more attention, and my gut said maybe Liam Fox is finally in love." He looked at Cody. "Seems the feeling's mutual, hey?"

Liam and Cody shared a wary glance, Cody's head feeling light again. *Liam Fox is finally in love.* Cody said, "Um, we haven't actually talked about that yet."

Does he love me?

"Well, that's my cue to bugger off." Teddy stood and slapped Liam's back. "You two do your thing. Liam, your shift this arvo's covered. Cody, feel better soon. I'll ring later to see how you're going." With a wave, he shut the door behind him.

Silence settled over the small room aside from the steady beep of the monitoring machines. Liam was looking down again, and Cody wished he could see inside his brain.

Finally, Cody said, "I'm sorry." Then the words were spilling out. "First, I showed up at your house uninvited, and I sobbed all over you, and then Teddy found out. I wanted to stay, but I was afraid you'd tell me to go, and that it would crush me. So I ran away. And then a day later I outed you at work. Fuck, I'm sorry. I promised you a hundred times I'd never, ever tell anyone, and now they all know." His voice broke. "Because of me."

Liam leaned forward in his chair, taking Cody's hand between his, his voice insistent, dark circles under his eyes. "It's not your fault."

"You made your boundaries clear, but I came to your house anyway."

"Because you needed me." He drew his brows together. "Well, you needed comfort."

"No, I needed *you*. And then I outed you. I promised you I'd never tell. I'm so sorry."

"It was the whistle. It's not your fault."

Cody swallowed the lump in his throat—a swell of emotion and hope. Liam was still holding his hand. "You're not freaking out?"

"Oh, I'm definitely freaking out." He smiled tentatively before gazing at Cody with such seriousness that Cody thought he really might puke waiting to hear what Liam was going to say.

"I…" Liam shuddered. "I'm sorry I lost it and broke the bottles. I'd never hurt you. Not like that. Please believe me."

"I know. Did you think I was scared of you? Oh, wow. No, I didn't think you'd hit me or anything. Honestly." He reached for Liam with his left hand, rolling toward his right and gasping with agony, fire in his ribs.

"What is it?" Liam jumped to his feet. "I'll get the nurse—"

"No. Stay." Cody clung to his wrist. "I think it's normal to hurt like hell with broken ribs."

Liam sat again. "I wish I could fix it."

A warm flow of affection eased the pain a fraction. Enough for Cody to smile. "It helps, having you here."

"I'm not leaving. When you're discharged, I'll take you home with me, or I'll sleep on your couch. Whatever you want."

"You are way too big for my loveseat." Cody threaded their fingers together. "You'd want me to stay with you? Even if people know?"

"Yes." He took another shuddering breath, a tremor rippling through him. "I have to go forward. I have to tell my family. I can't hide who I am anymore. With or without you." He gripped Cody's fingers so hard it hurt, but Cody didn't mind at all.

With an earnestness that made Cody's heart sing, Liam added, "I hope it's with you, because you're wrong. I do love you. I love you more than I thought I could love. And I'm terrified, but I can't imagine living without you now. I want to wake up with you. Tomorrow, and the next day, and every day that you'll have me."

His throat was too thick to talk, so Cody nodded and pulled down Liam's head for a kiss. Their lips were salty with tears, and it made him think of the sea, boundless and beautiful and everything he ever wanted.

Chapter Twenty-Three

"Ow. Ow, ow, ow."

Liam hovered in the doorway, watching as Cody shuffled toward the toilet, the bandages around his bare torso stark against his tanned skin. "Are you sure you don't need a hand?" Liam asked.

Lips pressed tight, Cody nodded, but as he bent to pull down his trackies, he gasped. Liam lunged, holding Cody's arms in case he was about to fall. "Let me help you." He knelt and eased down the soft cotton pants.

Cody groaned. "I can't believe I need help to sit on the can." He stood balancing on Liam's shoulders, bunching up the material of Liam's T-shirt as he grumbled, "Having you on your knees has never been less sexy."

Hands on Cody's bare hips, Liam helped him sit gingerly. "Well, you're the one who talks about enemas and the like."

Cody giggled softly, then winced. "Don't make me laugh. You're not allowed to make me laugh for at least two weeks." He relaxed his hard grip on Liam's shoulders and dropped his hands. "Okay. I'm good."

"I'll wait outside."

"Fine, but I am wiping my own ass."

"No arguments here." Laughing, Liam closed the door behind

him. He padded into the kitchen and took another swig of coffee, thinking about fetching another pod to make more. No, he didn't want to be jittery at work.

He stared at Jamie's scrawl of a drawing on the fridge. The edges were yellowing, a tear a few centimeters long through the top. Maybe he should ask for a new piece. Jamie would probably be delighted.

If I get to see him again.

He unwrapped a new roll of Quick-Eze and chewed three. It was going to be fine. Greg and Cora surely wouldn't cut him off? Mum and Dad... Well, he wasn't sure. He knew he had to tell them, and whatever would happen would happen.

He popped three more chalky tablets.

First, he had to go back to Barking. Teddy had assured him that the boys supported him and Cody. Liam prayed it was true. He'd gotten a bunch of nice texts. No one had written to tell him he was a disgusting pervert, so that was something.

"Okay!" Cody called.

After Liam got him standing again and pulled up his trackies, Cody washed his hands and shuffled slowly back into the living room, Liam at his heels just in case. The sky was bright blue through the window at the front of the house, shaded by the Catalpa trees. Like the bedroom, the art was generic, here some random geometric designs he'd bought framed and nailed up years ago simply so the walls weren't blank.

For the first time, Liam thought that maybe he should get some art he actually liked.

Inhaling sharply, Cody got settled sideways on the saggy old couch, and Liam rearranged the pillows under and around him. Then he tucked a soft blue blanket over Cody's lap. It had been a Christmas gift from Cora and Greg, and Liam loved its cozy softness in the winter, or when he was ill.

"You right?" Liam asked.

"Uh-huh." Cody smiled softly, laughing about something to himself. Then he shifted, gritting his teeth.

Liam nudged the glass and iron coffee table closer, a wide corner of the surface within Cody's reach covered with supplies. "TV remote, sandwiches, snacks, your phone, laptop. Air con remote. Oh!" He hurried to the kitchen and returned with an esky, which he'd filled with ice and the variety of bottles he'd grabbed early that morning at Woolie's. He left the esky on the floor right by the couch.

Cody lifted the lid. "Wow. Water, pop, juice—ohh, orange Gatorade. Just need some stubbies and I'm set. Joking, joking. No booze until I'm off the pain meds, I know."

"This you can have, though." Liam dumped a shopping bag into the esky, various packages settling over the ice and drinks. "You need choccies to get better. It's a proven fact."

Cody gasped in delight. "Oh, is that Reese's? Cherry Ripe, Violet Crumble, peppermint Tim Tams. I'm going to gain ten pounds." He grinned. "And it'll be worth it."

Liam grabbed a small plastic bin that was typically unused in the corner of the guest room and put it next to the esky. "Garbage." He put a stack of napkins and wet wipes on the table and then held up an empty plastic bottle. "You need to stay good and hydrated, so piss in this if it hurts too much to get up."

Cody grimaced. "Ugh."

"I know, but when I blew out my knee, it was a lifesaver. I don't want you up and down without me here. What if you fell and hurt yourself more? What if you couldn't get up?" Liam paced back and forth. "I should call Teddy and tell him I can't come in today."

"Hey, hey." Cody reached up for Liam's hand. "I'm going to be just fine. You already missed yesterday getting me here from the hospital. Judging by the brightness outside, it's going to be a hectic day. Think of the tourists who ignore the dangerous current signs. They need you."

Liam huffed out a laugh, but his chest was still too tight, his smile too brittle.

Cody stroked Liam's knuckles with his thumb. "I know you're scared. It'll be okay. The guys won't let you down."

"Yeah." He exhaled and bent to kiss Cody's slightly stubbly cheek. "Ring the tower right away if you need anything. I should go. Gotta fill up at the servo on my way to your place."

"Thanks so much for taking Charlene out for her run. Mrs. Delfino's really not up for it. I worry about her alone with me out of commission."

"It's okay. I'll check in on her every day. Do whatever she needs. You concentrate on getting better. I'll look in on you when I bring the car back."

It was great to run off some of his tension with Charlene, whose bright, perpetually happy, daffy face was a balm. Liam made sure Mrs. Delfino was right, although he didn't quite believe her that she didn't need help with groceries. He and Cody would have to convince her.

He parked back in his driveway, hurrying inside to check on Cody before walking the couple of blocks to the beach. He eased the door open, tiptoeing inside when Cody didn't call out.

Sure enough, Cody was dozing against the pillows, his lips parted, hair mussed, a sci-fi show playing softly on the TV. Liam watched him, wishing he could lift Cody into his arms and hold him safe and close until he was healed. Or maybe forever.

Something exploded onscreen, and Liam considered pausing the show so Cody didn't miss any more. Although he found it strangely comforting to nap while the TV murmured, and maybe Cody did too. After a while, Netflix would pause itself anyway.

Both of them had barely slept the night before, Cody because he was in pain with every breath, and Liam because he was afraid of jostling him and because his mind hadn't stopped spinning and worrying.

Maybe he should call Teddy and hope a sub could come in last minute. He and Cody could snooze together on the couch, gorging on sugar and then snoozing again. Avoiding the world, safe in their bubble.

Sighing, Liam changed into his uniform. He couldn't bail last minute, and he told himself Teddy was right that the boys supported him, and it would be a shift like any other.

He popped a few more Quick-Eze.

The climb up the tower stairs was as familiar as being in his own house. His thongs slapped the worn wood, and he pulled open the door before he could stop and talk himself out of it.

By the windows, Baz and Ronnie sat talking. They fell silent as Liam climbed the steps up to them. The acid in Liam's gut surged, and he tasted black bile. His mouth watered, and for a horrible moment he thought he might actually spew.

They know. They know I'm gay.

This was the moment he'd dreaded for years. Hell, for almost his entire life.

They know. What if—

"Foxy!" Ronnie exclaimed, hopping to his feet and drawing Liam into a half-hug, slapping his back before stepping back. "How ya goin'? How's Cody?'

"Yeah, good." Liam stood with a rigid spine, his bad knee suddenly threatening to give out because his legs were trembling so hard. "Hurts to breathe, but he's surviving."

"Oh, mate, ribs are the worst," Ronnie said, rubbing a hand over his red hair. "And he punctured his lung, hey? Scary."

Liam nodded, pushing away the memory of Cody's wheezing, horribly ragged breath, that beautiful face far too pale beneath the oxy mask, holding his hand, waiting for the ambo.

Baz grinned. "He's a tough one, still getting the patient in and staying on his feet." Baz stood and hugged Liam, slapping his back. "Tell Tazzie we'll see him soon." He kept his hand on Liam's shoulder. "How ya goin'?"

Liam nodded, trying to smile, his throat not working right.

Baz's hand didn't move, firm and warm through Liam's thin uniform shirt. "We've got your back. Always."

The fist of pressure released, and Liam might have toppled over without Baz's steadying hand. They knew, and it was going to be okay. It really was. He was grateful beyond words and could only nod again.

"Too right," Ronnie said. "We're all behind you and Cody. Well, maybe not *too* close behind." He laughed, but then wrinkled his nose. "Sorry. That was a bad joke."

Baz rolled his eyes at Ronnie. "Didn't even make sense." He slapped Liam's shoulder. "There might be more dumb jokes, but you know the drill. No harm intended. I'm sure Damo'll say something spectacularly stupid at some point."

Liam had to laugh. "Probably," he croaked, then cleared this throat. He thought of Damo beside him as they waited for the paramedics to assess Cody, Damo giving Liam's back the odd pat as he shot him worried glances and murmured reassurances that everything would be all right. "But he's a good bloke. It's a good team here. I'm grateful." He reached for Baz's shoulder the way he had a thousand times before. "Thank you."

"Bloody hell, look at these girls on boogie boards," Ronnie said, peering through the binos. "Just past the flags south of second gate. Bet you anything they can't swim a stroke. They're going too far out."

Liam hurried to grab his bum bag from his locker and stash his phone, turning on the screen for a second to make sure Cody hadn't called or texted. He pulled on his cap and sunnies and grabbed a radio.

Baz was looking through binos beside Ronnie. "Yeah, they'll be in heaps of trouble when they lose their boards. Not if, when."

Even though the boys knew he was gay, it was another typical day at Barking, and Liam had never been more grateful.

"HEY." CODY STIFLED a yawn and winced, his laptop sitting on his belly. He'd eaten way, way too much chocolate, but only slightly regretted it.

His mom clucked her tongue onscreen. "Oh, darling. Are you in much pain?"

Gwen said, "Mom, he punctured his lung and cracked his ribs. Obviously he's in pain."

Beside her, standing behind their parents, Lucy rolled her eyes. "Can we make this about Cody and not you two bickering?"

Their father said, "Capital idea. Cody, the doctors say you only need time to recover? No surgery?"

"Right. I just have to be patient." He realized they were all in pajamas and asked, "Wait, what time is it there?"

"It doesn't matter," Michelle said. "Sweetheart, we all wanted to see you with our own eyes." She frowned. "Are you at home? Is someone looking after you?"

"I'm—" Cody supposed there was no reason not to tell them. "I'm staying with another lifeguard. His name's Liam. We're dating."

Their eyebrows went up in hilarious tandem, and Cody laughed before gasping, screwing his eyes shut as the pain in his side flared sharply. He muttered, "I'm fine—hurts to laugh."

Robert said, "Well, tell us about this Liam."

"You can Google him. He was a footy star before getting injured. He's been a lifeguard for the past ten years or so."

His parents now wore matching frowns, Gwen tapping at her phone as she asked, "AFL player? Liam what?"

"Yeah, and Fox."

"Already a lifeguard for ten years? How old is this fellow?" Robert asked.

"Thirty-four. Yes, he's older than me. No, I don't care. No, it's not inappropriate, and no, he isn't taking advantage of me."

"Whoa." Gwen's eyes were wide, a grin on her face as Lucy crowded in to see the phone.

Lucy gasped. "He's gorgeous! He could take advantage of me anytime."

"Geez, Codes." Gwen whistled softly. "Nice catch."

Their mom snatched the phone and peered at it, Robert pushing down his glasses and tilting his head as he leaned in.

"He's certainly handsome," Michelle said. "Or at least he was in his youth. I presume he still is?"

"Uh, yeah. I'll take a pic and send it." Cody realized with a start that he didn't have a single picture of Liam on his phone. Would Liam permit it now? He hoped so. "Oh, but don't tell anyone. He's not out."

Four matching frowns. Gwen readjusted her glasses. "So... You're keeping your relationship a secret? That doesn't sound like a good fit for you."

"Just for now. Look, it's a really big deal for him. He was this superstar, and he's always been terrified of coming out. Has a lot of internalized homophobia."

His mom and sisters softened, but Robert grumbled, "I'm not surprised. Sports in Australia are steeped in machismo. In most countries, true, but AFL is—"

"Dad!" Cody and his sisters chorused. Lucy added, "We know."

Michelle asked, "Is he taking good care of you? I spoke to the pharmacy, and I can take a leave to come down."

"Mom, I'm good. I promise. Liam's taking excellent care of me." Affection for her flowed warmly. "But thank you."

"Is he there now?" Robert asked. "We could say hello."

Thank God Cody could truthfully answer, "Sorry, he's at Barking. He'll be home soon. His house is only a couple blocks from the beach. I have everything I need." And then some, including a gross piss bottle, which he didn't mention, but which had indeed come in handy.

"Well, we'd like to say hello another time," Michelle said. "I'm glad he's there to help you. Even if he's worryingly older. And I'm sure you won't let him take advantage. You've always known your own mind."

Cody rolled his eyes. "I promise he's not taking advantage of me. We really like each other." He didn't tell them he and Liam already loved each other, as that would definitely—understandably—set off alarm bells. He knew it was right with Liam, and in time his family would too.

"Oh, I think they *really*, really like each other," Gwen teased. "Look at that moony face."

"Shut up!" Cody said, but couldn't stop smiling. "It's the drugs."

"And your job is secure?" Robert asked, ever-practical.

"Yep. Guaranteed."

Robert sighed. "I wish you'd take this as a sign to seek higher education in a safer field, but I know you won't. So I'm glad the council is treating you right, at least."

He smiled. "Thanks, Dad." A wave of emotion filled him. "I miss you guys."

"We miss you too, darling," Michelle said, her eyes glistening.

He napped more after signing off, then finished the mint Tim Tams even though he was full. Then napped again.

The next time Cody woke, it was dark outside, and a figure loomed over him, backlit by the TV and floor lamp in the corner. He jolted, cringing at the pain.

"It's me!" Liam knelt by the couch, pushing the esky aside. "Sorry to frighten you."

"S'okay." He stroked Liam's damp beard. "How was work?" *Please have been okay. Please, please, please.*

"Good," Liam said. He smiled. "Great, even."

"Yeah?" Despite the throbbing pain in his ribs, Cody sighed with relief.

"It was just…a normal day. They know, and it's okay. Everyone seems okay with it. With me." He shook his head. "It doesn't seem real."

"Believe it." He caressed Liam's head, pushing his hair back, ignoring the twinge in his ribs.

"I was so afraid of them knowing, but it's okay. Teddy was right. I've been stupid to keep it a secret all these years. Going to all those lengths—" His face went red. "Stupid."

"Hey. Teddy never said you were stupid. You're not. Everyone has to come out in their own time."

A smile quirked Liam's lips. "I'm on my own journey, right?"

"Right. And it's not stupid or wrong. It was what you needed at the time. So don't beat yourself up. You've been doing that for your whole life."

"I guess I have." He rubbed his face. "Hard to stop overnight."

"Impossible, I'd say. Just try to be as kind to yourself as you are to me. Now c'mere and kiss me. Gently."

Liam did, rubbing their noses before pressing their lips together. He still vaguely tasted of salt, and Cody chased it, sliding his tongue inside Liam's mouth before pain rocked him.

"Easy," Liam murmured.

"If this was a movie, we'd totally be making tender love right now as the music swelled. Why does Hollywood have to lie?"

Liam smiled. "Soon enough. Are you hungry? I was thinking I could go up to Freo and get hot dogs. Since you didn't get yours that night."

Cody caressed Liam's throat through the open collar of his Polo shirt. "Aww, thank you, baby. How about tomorrow? I have eaten way, way too much junk. I need to digest. But you go ahead."

"Yeah, nah." Liam opened the esky and took out a Cherry Ripe. "Junk sounds good to me."

Cody knew there were things they needed to talk about—how long Cody was staying, him contributing financially for food and utilities, when Liam was going to come out to his family, when Liam was going to come out publicly, or if he even planned to. So many questions rattled around Cody's brain.

But it could all wait. Because as Cody carefully stretched his legs over Liam's lap, and they snuggled together under the blue throw blanket and watched *Travel Guides* while eating chicken crisps and chocolate, they were together. Their journey needed a pit stop.

Chapter Twenty-Four

"IT'S NICE."

Cody parked the SUV in the shade of the gum tree. The engine ticked down as he ducked his head and peered up. "Bet you and Greg had a lot of fun climbing that."

In the passenger seat by the curb, Liam looked at the gum tree, its branches shooting up impossibly high. "Yeah. I was always trying to keep up with him." Scraping palms and knees as he scrambled after his big brother, woozy moments as the ground got farther away. Another memory surfaced, and he frowned.

"Until I wasn't allowed to. I'd made the top youth footy team, and there were already scouts watching me. Couldn't risk getting injured. Greg had to climb on his own. Maybe if I'd blown my knee out then, things would have been different." He scoffed. "That's stupid."

"It's not." Cody rubbed Liam's thigh. "Remember, no matter what happens, I'm here." He quirked a smile. "Turning on the AC intermittently so I don't melt."

"I'm sorry to leave you out here. I can take a cab home. You should go."

"*No.* First off, I'm going stir crazy in your house. And I know you have to do this on your own, but I want to be here. Unless you want me to leave."

The fist of pressure in Liam's chest loosened. "No. Don't go."

In the three weeks since Cody's accident, it had been joyful having him stay. Taking care of him, watching TV with him, gingerly sleeping beside him, careful not to jostle his healing ribs. It was like opening a disused drawer and finding something he hadn't even realized he'd been looking for.

He loved Cody. He trusted him in a way he'd never trusted another human. Cody *saw* him and wanted him for who he really was even when Liam had fought his true nature. Liam loved him savagely yet reverently all at once. He wanted to haul Cody into his arms and never let go, but then bow at his feet and submit, give himself over to Cody's strength and fire.

These truths had made a home in him now, settling into the nooks and crannies between bone and muscle, flowing through his veins like undeniable ocean currents.

"You can do this." Cody took his hand. "It's terrifying, but whatever happens, in an hour it'll be done."

Greg and Cora's minivan was parked on the driveway. Everyone was inside waiting for him, so Liam took a deep breath, squeezed Cody's fingers, and went inside through the always-unlocked door. He didn't stop to even glance at the shrine.

His parents, Greg, and Cora waited in the backyard on deck chairs with mugs of coffee and apprehensive expressions. Liam kissed his mother and Cora and shook Greg and his dad's hands. Leanne insisted on brewing a fresh pot of coffee for him and bustled back with a tray of biscuits and sliced fruit.

They sat around a table, and as soon as Liam had a hot mug— an old Eagles one that had been his favorite as a kid, the blue faded and a chip in the top—Greg said unsmilingly, "So what's this about? We took the kids to Teddy's since you said not to bring them. So?"

"Hon." Cora gave Liam an apologetic smile, her small hand on Greg's arm. "Let's hear him out before we get into anything else."

"Anything like what?" Stu grumbled. He gummily chewed a choc Tim Tam, smacking his lips.

"Like the fact that you need to see the dentist about fixing your dentures," Greg said.

"Oh, he's fine," Leanne said, shifting and smoothing the skirt of her brightly patterned sun dress. "You worry too much."

"Well, someone has to," Greg muttered.

Stu glared. "Boy, what crawled up your arse this morning?"

"I resent being summoned. But we're here, so let's do this." Greg stared at Liam. "What is it? Are you moving even farther away?"

"Barking's not that far," Liam automatically replied, Greg's unexpected prickliness putting him back on his heels.

"Right, but it's far enough that you don't have to pull your weight."

"That is *enough*," Leanne snapped. "Liam's here now, so let's not be ugly."

Greg snorted. "Right, God forbid I criticize precious Liam. Life has been so hard for him because he was a big star and his injury was so bloody tragic. So he gets to live up in Barking and hang out at the beach and do whatever it is he does up there. Meanwhile, I'm the one who's here. Cors and I are here."

Jaw clenched, Greg addressed Liam directly. "I'm the one Mum calls to help Dad unclog the drain. I'm the one who visits every week and makes sure they're taking care of themselves, although they're both stubborn *as*, and won't see the doctor when they should."

Greg ignored the outraged huff from their parents. "I'm the one who has to listen to dad's bigoted rants about whoever is destroying Australia this week. When Dad needs help with the pool cover, I come over. I dug the holes for Mum's frangipani because Dad's back is killing him and he refuses to even consider physio or stretching or exercises. I'm the one who's *here*. You couldn't even stick around after Amelia's christening. I know you weren't really sick, so don't give me that crap."

"You're right." Liam forced himself to look Greg in the eye. "You're right," he repeated.

Cora made a little sound of discomfort, looking between them anxiously. "To be fair, after Jamie came along, we hardly ever got up to Barking, and we didn't invite you down nearly as much."

"He always said no anyway!" Greg exclaimed.

"Well…" She sighed. "Yes."

"We don't need no one looking after us," Stu spat. "You've got some nerve, boy," he said to Greg. "If we're such a burden, you can bugger off."

"Thanks, Dad. Appreciate that, mate." Greg pressed his lips into a thin line. He hadn't shaved that morning, and when he rubbed his face, his dark stubble scratched audibly.

Leanne's hands fluttered, her bracelets jangling. "Oh, let's have a nice morning!"

"No, Mum," Greg said. "Can we be real for once?" He looked to Liam. "What *do* you do that keeps you so busy? You always say you're dating some woman, but we never meet one. Is that what today's about? You finally settling down?"

Leanne gasped, a tanned hand to her freckled chest. "Liam, that would be wonderful! We could—"

"I'm gay."

Insects buzzed, the shrieking and splashing of a neighbor's children in a pool echoing from nearby. Liam's family gaped at him.

Finally, Greg snapped his jaw shut, his forehead creasing. "What?"

"Oh! *Oh!*" Cora pushed at a golden curl that had slipped over her forehead. "I'm such an idiot. Oh, Liam. I should have realized."

His parents remained speechless and terrifyingly still, staring at him like he was a king brown that had slithered onto the patio. Liam could hardly breathe, his heart breaking at the horror in their faces. But he'd survived it. He'd told his truth, and he was on the other side.

"I never…" Greg shook his head. "*What?*"

Words were coming out of Liam's dry mouth. "I was so afraid of losing you all. I made myself a stranger. I—I hid from everyone. But I'm seeing someone now." His face was hot with the weight of all eyes on him, and he said it all quickly, ripping off the Band-Aid. "His name's Cody. He's a trainee lifeguard. He's originally from Canada, and he's really helped me with all this."

His father jolted, his voice a growl. "That *kid?*" His weathered face creased with disgust. "What are you, some pervert? One of those kiddie fuckers?"

"Oh!" His mum flapped her hands, jingling her bracelets, wet eyes wide. "No!"

"Of course not!" Liam pushed back his chair, the wood legs scraping over the flagstone. He perched on the edge of the cushion, forcing himself to stay put instead of running. "Cody's twenty. He's younger, yes, but he's an adult. I'm not a child molester. I'm not—" He had to suck in a breath. "I'm not a pervert." Part of him still didn't quite believe that, but his submissive desires sure as hell had nothing to do with true perversion.

"No," Greg agreed. "God, no. We know you're not."

"And there's nothing wrong with being gay," Cora said, her voice shaking but defiant.

"You're no damn fag," Stu snarled.

Leanne gasped, her breathing ragged. "It's sick. Two men? My God. That's wrong." Her voice rose. "That's disgusting!"

"*Mum,*" Greg said with wide eyes. "It's our Liam. *Don't.*"

"And I love him," she insisted, her manicured nails digging

into Liam's forearm as she stretched toward him. "But darling, this isn't right. We raised you boys to have proper values. Good Christian values."

Cora scoffed. "Like homophobia and racism? And when was the last time you or Stu set foot in a church? Jamie's christening?" She sat taller, shoulders back. "You've taken Greg for granted for years while putting Liam up on a pedestal. Now that Liam's finally being truthful with you, this is your response?"

"It can't be true!" Leanne insisted.

"No son of mine is a faggot!" Stu's face was red as a tomato, spittle flying from his mouth. Beside him, Leanne clasped her hands and went silent. Like usual.

And there it was, an echo of the words that had haunted Liam for decades. It was a gut punch. Part of him still couldn't believe that this was real. Part of him wanted to weep and beg for forgiveness, shame rising up.

But the biggest part of him stood his ground on shaky legs, the phantom ache in his knee flaring as he pushed to his feet. His ears buzzed, his own voice distant. "This is who I am. That's not me in the shrine in there. I wanted it to be, but it never really was. I've hated myself for almost as long as I can remember. I can't be ashamed anymore. I didn't want to lose you, but I already did by hiding away."

"I won't have this talk under my roof!" Stu thundered, shoving unsteadily to his feet, his fists clenched. Liam towered over both his parents, but his father had never seemed quite so small, frothing with impotent fury.

Liam wanted to beg him to understand, to *try*, to still love him. But he was out of words. His feet somehow followed his brain's instructions to move, and he opened the sliding door to the kitchen with its familiar brown cupboards and the old rotary phone still on the wall. Past the dining room.

The shrine.

He stopped, itching to tear it apart, to rip that massive picture off the wall and shatter it, to hurl the meaningless trophies and awards. A scream clawed at his throat. He stared at the ghost of himself, muscles straining, so young and focused on winning. He'd been hiding in front of millions. He'd never been real.

Liam's thongs slapped down the driveway, and he climbed into the passenger side of his SUV, Cody reaching for him, ready to hold him together at the seams. Liam clutched at him and croaked, "Drive. Please."

But then Greg was at the passenger window. Liam fumbled for the button and lowered the glass. Greg glanced at Cody behind the wheel and extended his hand past Liam. "Cody, right? I'm Greg. Good to meet you."

Cody shook his hand with a tentative smile. "You too."

Cora appeared beside Greg, slightly out of breath and flushed even though it wasn't far from the house to the street. She blurted, "I just screamed at your parents. And it felt bloody good." She looked at Cody and went up on her toes, squeezing her arm through the window, nudging Greg over. "I'm Cora."

Cody took her hand. "Cody. Really good to meet you."

"Do you guys want to have lunch?" she asked. "And drinks? I could really use a drink. I'll ring Jill, and we can pick up food and a carton and meet at their place. I'm sure she and Teddy will be happy to have us all. We can talk more—or not. But we'll be together. From now on, no matter what."

"And Jamie'll be beside himself to see Uncle Liam," Greg said.

Liam's mind spun with the mix of emotions. "You really still want me to see the kids?"

"Of course!" Cora exclaimed.

Greg dropped his head for a moment. When he raised it, tears filled his eyes. Liam gaped, and he realized he hadn't seen him cry since they were kids. Greg said, "I want my brother back."

Liam's own tears fell, a sob choking him as Greg took his

shoulder through the window. Cora burst into tears, and then the three of them were somehow laughing, and Liam could actually breathe again.

Cody joked, "Jesus, you're going to make me cry too. Let's—" He looked beyond them, and they turned.

Leanne stood in the doorway of the house like one of the statues in her rock garden. For an endless moment, Liam prayed for her to step toward him. *Please, Mum. Please love me still.*

She shut the door, the thud echoing dully.

Cody had hold of Liam's hand and said, "We'll meet you at Teddy's."

Greg and Cora nodded, and Cody drove down the street that was so familiar Liam could close his eyes and still see every detail. He did, tears flowing from between his eyelids. He felt the vehicle slow and eventually stop, the engine going quiet. He didn't look to see where they were as he folded against Cody and wept, safe in his arms.

PEELING OFF A magnet from a snake removal company, Liam used it to stick up Jamie's newly scrawled artwork on the fridge. It depicted the two of them in Teddy's pool that afternoon, when Jamie had indeed been beside himself to see his uncle.

Arms wrapping around Liam's waist from behind, Cody said, "This was a good day. I mean, also a bad one. But good. If that makes any sense." He chuckled, resting his head against Liam's shoulder blade. "I haven't even taken pain meds today, so no excuse."

"No, I know what you mean." Liam admired the drawing, which he'd stuck up above the old one. "Good and bad. It was...necessary. I finally did it. And I survived." He caressed Cody's forearms, loving that solid grip around him. "It doesn't quite seem real. I feel like I should be more upset. Not that I'm not, but... Probably doesn't make any sense."

"No, it does. Grief isn't linear, baby." Cody murmured against Liam's back, "I'm so proud of you. Was it as bad as you always thought it would be?"

"In some ways. Yes." He wasn't sure he'd ever erase the image of his parents' horror from his memory. But he was going to try. "Better in other ways, though. Much better." He turned and leaned down to nuzzle the freckles over Cody's cheek, then frowned. "You didn't take any pain pills? How're you going?"

"Okay." Cody hesitated. "I can probably go back to my place soon. I'm healed enough to get around on my own—cook and all that. Well, pour my own cereal and pick up my own takeaway."

"Right." Liam knew it made sense, and maybe Cody wanted his own space again. They'd only known each other a couple of months—that was too soon to really live together, right? He nodded and was about to say that he'd drive Cody home whenever he liked, but instead blurted, "I don't want you to go."

Cody blinked, his eyebrows up. "You don't?"

Liam could feel his face going bright red, heat all the way to the tips of his ears. "No. I've been alone for so long, and I don't want to be alone anymore." He quickly added, "Not that I want just anyone—I want *you*. I want this. You and me together, all the time."

A grin lit up Cody's eyes, his cheeks dimpling as he did a little bounce on his toes. He winced, but his smile returned a moment later as he asked, "You want to wake up with me?"

"Yes." Excitement zipped through him, hope for a life of love and belonging that was suddenly in his grasp. He wasn't going to let go. No matter what his parents or anyone thought, he had happiness right here in his hands.

Liam took hold of Cody's face, thumbs pressing on his dimples. "Yes," he repeated. "I love you."

"I love you too." Cody went up on his toes and kissed him, his fingers tight on Liam's arms. "I'd suggest you sweep me off my feet and take me to bed so I can fuck your brains out, but maybe we can walk there, and I'll get settled with my pillows, and you can ride me gently."

Kissing through their laughter, they did just that.

Epilogue

"**M**MM." CODY MUMBLED something, stretching and bumping Liam in the nose. Cody's eyes flew open. "Shit!"

It didn't hurt, but Liam touched his nose dramatically. "Oh God, I think it's broken. Good morning to you too." He nodded to the closed bedroom door, where the scratching and yipping had just started. "Wanna get that? I'm mortally wounded."

Chuckling, Cody rolled off the bed and crossed naked to the door, his tight arse on fine display. He admitted Charlene, who thundered inside, her fluffy tail wagging almost violently as she rubbed up against Cody, then leapt onto the mattress, pink tongue out and delight on her shaggy face as Liam scratched behind her ears.

Cody flopped back down on the left side, Charlene squeezing between them, her tail whapping their shins. Cody yawned and said, "We should probably stop letting her up. Establish a rule early if we don't want her in the bed." He smiled at her as he pet her flank. "Although it might be too late."

Liam frowned. "You don't like having her in here in the mornings?"

"No, I do. Just wasn't sure if you'd get sick of it?"

"Not at all." He stopped scratching Charlene, and she nudged his hand with her head. He scratched again for a few seconds, then stopped. She nudged again. He laughed and scratched before stopping. *Nudge.* She would do that all day if he let her, and sometimes he did. "I don't really want her *in* bed with us at night, but in the mornings, yes."

"That sounds good to me too. I'm going to take her to see Mrs. Delfino at the hospice today." Cody groaned. "And I need to declutter the guest room. Mom and Gwen'll be here before we know it." He watched Liam silently for a few moments, rolling toward him and reaching around Charlene to stroke Liam's collarbones. "You seem pretty zen this morning. Or 'centered,' as Dr. Lincoln says."

His belly flipped, but Liam smiled. "Well, all that therapy has helped. Plus I had a great fuck last night."

"Oh yeah?" Cody teased, caressing Liam's face and giving his hair a sharp tug before smoothing his palm over Liam's head.

"Mmm." His morning erection had flagged, but Liam's balls tingled at the remembered pleasure of submitting on his hands and knees, Cody holding his head up with demanding fingers in his hair, pounding him. Owning him. Loving him. "Just what I needed."

"Sore?"

"Perfectly so, or I'd beg you to fuck me again." He'd stopped scratching Charlene without realizing, and she squirmed up higher, wedging herself between their faces, panting happily. Liam and Cody both groaned and turned their heads.

"Jesus, Char, your breath reeks!" Cody pushed her back down. "Not so close."

"My breath is probably just as bad." Liam laughed.

"I'll take my chances." He drew Liam near for a long, slow kiss. When they parted, Cody traced Liam's lips with his thumb. "Have you looked at your phone?"

"Uh-uh. Not going to. Not yet. Just going to go to work like any other day."

"You're starting at eight? We'll walk over with you. Have a swim at the dog beach."

Charlene's tail thumped rhythmically, and she excitedly watched them, her golden curls getting a bit too long over her eyes. No matter the day, she greeted it with the same enthusiasm and optimism, and Liam leaned down to nuzzle her, stinky breath and all.

The walk to Barking only took minutes. It would be a hot spring day, this October getting busy already, beachgoers arriving early. Charlene trotted ahead of them on her leash eagerly.

Wordlessly, Cody threaded their fingers together as they crossed the park. Liam realized it was the first time they'd actually held hands in public. They'd met a year ago on this beach, and it seemed like a lifetime.

Sweat beaded on his forehead, and he imagined the prickle of hundreds of eyes on them. He kept his gaze locked on the endless blue of the horizon. Were people watching? Maybe they didn't notice at all. But if they did, what were they thinking? Were they pointing? Filming with their phones? Laughing? Judging? His pulse raced.

But Liam didn't let go of Cody's hand.

Charlene tugged at the leash, eager to get in the water, whining as they reached the tower. All three of them climbed the stairs, Liam clinging to Cody's hand, and at the top, he felt like he'd scaled a skyscraper, his heart hammering.

Cody squeezed his fingers, then let go, murmuring, "You've got this."

Inside, Damo spun around in his chair at the front of the tower with a grin, his hair whipping. "Look, it's the big TV star!"

Teddy was there by the windows with Ronnie, Baz, and Bickie. They all greeted Liam like some kind of hero, with handshakes and back slaps as Liam, Cody, and an overstimulated Charlene joined them. Then Chalkers, Hazza, Mark, Mia, Ryan, Nicky, and a few others piled out of the locker room.

The season had just started, everyone back after the skeleton crew of the winter, but there were never this many guards on, even at Christmas. As they squeezed up by the windows, Liam realized they were there for him.

Teddy said, "Everyone wanted to tell you how brilliant you were last night. You nailed it."

"You're a legend," Baz said. "A bloody legend."

Chalkers said, "There were a few times you looked like you were going to spew, but you pushed through it." He slapped Liam's shoulder. "Good job."

Liam shifted from foot-to-foot, wishing everyone would stop looking at him even though they were being so nice. He tried to laugh. "Still might spew now."

Mia said, "I think it was really smart to come out publicly on your own terms. My feeds were full of supportive messages this morning. I think it's probably good you don't have social media since there are a lot of trolls out there, but so many people think you're really brave."

Liam scoffed. "If they only knew." He paused. "Trolls? Are there lots of negative comments?" The hair on the back of his neck stood up.

Everyone insisted a little too hard that there weren't. Mia added, "Look, on any news story online there will be ignorant arseholes spouting off from the safety of the anonymous internet. I can screen-cap the awesome messages for you. Ignore the rest."

Chalkers said, "Maz is right. And mate, you're brave *as*. End of story."

Bickie whistled softly. "That reporter lady didn't go easy, hey? Did you know what she was going to ask?"

"Yeah, I approved the questions. Glad I did okay. I don't know if I can watch it." He'd recorded it, but... Not yet.

They reassured him in a chorus that he'd been brilliant. Ronnie said, "Tazzie, you did a great job too."

"Yeah?" Cody asked, taking Charlene off her leash so she could nose around and get pats.

"Oh yeah," Damo said. "Super confident like usual. And I think I saw my head in one of those beach shots."

Cody had sat with Liam to answer a few questions, and the *60 Minutes* crew had shot what they called "B roll" of Liam and Cody at work. It had been winter, but they'd picked a sunny day with a few rescues.

"That was definitely my elbow in the tower shot," Mark deadpanned. "No doubt."

"All right, those of you rostered on, get back to work," Teddy said. "Hungover backpackers are starting to rock up from the new hostel. Rest of you, clear off." They did with waves and farewells, giving Charlene more pats. Dogs may have been officially forbidden on Barking, but they all bent the rules sometimes.

To Liam, Teddy said quietly, "Have you talked to anyone? Greg said he rang this morning but hasn't been able to get through to you. Jill and I watched it with him and Cors. We're all damn proud. I want you to know that."

Without warning, Liam's eyes burned. "Thanks," he managed gruffly. His phone felt heavy in his pocket, and he took it out. Holding his breath, he pressed the power button.

Messages crowded the home screen—supportive texts from the lifeguards, Cora, Jill, Greg, and Cora's lesbian cousin, who'd gone out of her way with her wife to be supportive the past year.

Liam opened his phone and realized there were *dozens* of texts, including from old teammates he hadn't spoken to in over a decade. "How did they get my number?" he muttered.

Cody appeared at his side. "What is it? Something nasty? Maybe you should let me read them first."

Teddy nodded. "Not a bad idea."

Liam scrolled with his finger, skimming. "No, I think it's okay. Just surprised to hear from so many people."

"Anything from Stu and Leanne?" Teddy asked.

They wouldn't text, so Liam tapped on the phone icon. There had been calls and new messages, but most of the numbers on the list were unfamiliar. No Mum or Dad. He shook his head. Cody squeezed Liam's elbow, keeping his hand there, warm and strong.

"Give them time," Teddy said, sighing. "Greg and Cora are working on them."

Anger and hurt surged, and Liam almost snapped that his parents shouldn't need time or cajoling to love him the way he was. To accept the son they had instead of the one they'd wanted. But in the ten months since he'd come out to them, he'd only gotten one call.

It had been a month ago, when Liam had emailed his mum to let them know about the upcoming interview. She'd rang within the hour, her voice tight and high, begging him not to humiliate his father. Not to humiliate the family.

"Don't you see? If you do this, you can't take it back!"

It had knocked the wind out of him to realize his parents were still hoping after almost a year that somehow he would "take it back." Marry a nice girl from the neighborhood and be the son they'd idolized who'd never bloody existed.

He'd had to hang up so he didn't scream.

Liam swiped through a few screens, going one too far, the news feed appearing. And there were the headlines.

Ex-AFL Star: "I'm Gay and Not Ashamed Anymore"
Liam Fox Comes Out as Gay in Shock Interview
Former Eagles Megastar Comes Out
Gay Footy Star Says He Won't Hide Again
AFL Players Praise Liam Fox After Shock Gay Reveal

For so many years, the idea of these headlines made him sick to his stomach. Now here they were, for better or worse. *Better*, he thought, even though he wasn't ready to read the articles, or answer any messages, or watch himself laid bare on TV.

"I should grab my gear and get out there," Liam said. "Those hungover backpackers won't tell themselves to stay close to shore if they can't bloody swim."

Cody followed him down, Charlene back on her leash. The sand was warming, and Liam dug in, slipping on his sunnies and hat, tightening his bum bag and making sure his radio was on.

"Ready?" Cody asked.

His mouth was dry, and he felt lightheaded. "Can I say no?"

"Absolutely. Teddy'll call in a sub, or I'll stay. You take Char home." He squeezed Liam's hand, grounding him.

Liam took a deep breath, shifting the sand with his toes. "I can do it. The world knows, and my parents won't talk to me, but... I can do this."

"Damn right you can." Cody leaned in, going up on tiptoes, his voice barely a whisper. "And tonight, your *aaass* is mine."

Arse, heart, soul. "Damn right." Liam took a deep breath and pressed his lips to Cody's. Because he wasn't gutless anymore. He was going to kiss his boyfriend at the beach no matter who was watching.

And one day, he'd make Cody his husband. Maybe one day soon.

Cody gave him a dimpled smile before he and Charlene jogged off toward the dog beach. Liam drove an ATV up to the north end, eyes on the water, the crowds already growing. He stopped to get on the mega and shout a warning to a group of fully dressed teenagers who were probably tourists, telling them to stick close to shore.

He stood with hands on hips near the buggy, watching the kids ignore him. They likely couldn't swim and could get in a panic meters from shore if the sandbank dropped. He'd seen it too many times to continue his patrol and radioed the tower to let them know he might be going in.

The kids were still obliviously splashing around when a man approached. Liam tensed, realizing he'd been concentrating so hard he'd actually forgotten for a few minutes about the interview and that he was officially out.

The man was middle-aged and portly, wearing saggy boardies. He said, "G'day."

Liam nodded. "Hiya." It was incredibly bizarre to think this man probably knew Liam was gay. That Australia knew.

"You're Liam Fox? From the Eagles?"

He supposed he always would be, and he'd have to make peace with that. "Uh-huh." He kept his sunnies on, watching the water. Bracing.

"That was a brave interview last night. Good on ya, mate."

Liam's breath *whooshed* out, and he grinned and stuck out his hand. "Thanks…?"

The man told him his name, and they chatted until Liam had to rip off his shirt and grab the rescue board, panicking teenagers flailing and close to drowning one another. He paddled them in, Damo lending a hand, and they rolled their eyes at each other as they toweled off.

Before continuing his patrol, Liam spotted Cody and Charlene running back toward the park, soaking and smiling, Charlene bounding across the sand like a giant, delighted muppet with paws too big and ears flopping.

My family.

Liam Fox from the Eagles was out, and for the first time, he was truly proud.

THE END

Afterword

Thank you so much for reading *Flash Rip*, and I hope you enjoyed it. I'd be grateful if you could take a few minutes to leave a review on Amazon, Goodreads, your preferred bookseller, or social media. Just a couple of sentences can really help other readers discover the book. Thank you again.

Wishing you many shirtless lifeguards and happily ever afters!

Keira
<3

p.s. Keep reading for an excerpt from Ethan and Clay's romance *Honeymoon for One*! Discover how they met and ended up together before they visited Barking Beach.

Honeymoon for One

Before Ethan and Clay visited Barking Beach and left an impression on Liam, they had their own journey of discovery, acceptance, and love. And also some scorching first-time m/m sex. :D

Keep reading for excerpt from *Honeymoon for One*!

AS ETHAN WALKED through the resort on Fraser Island the next afternoon after a tour to gorgeous Lake McKenzie, he finally admitted to himself that he was looking for Clay.

Because he's nice! He's fun to talk to. Besides, my harmless crush on the tour driver is just that. Harmless. Why shouldn't I enjoy it? Nothing's going to happen. He's apparently straight, and I'm on the rebound. But we can be friendly. I like his accent, and he's a nice guy.

Of course, Clay wasn't just nice. He was *sexy*. His accent? *Sexy.* The Australian slang he used that made him sound like Crocodile Dundee sometimes? *Sexy.* His broad shoulders and solid build? *Sexy.* That he didn't have chiseled abs and was a little soft around the middle? *Sexy.* Those blue eyes, and how the auburn in his hair gleamed in the sun, especially in his beard and the hair on his arms, and how he had freckles…

Sexy, sexy, sexy.

But the sexiest thing of all was how thoughtful he was. How he made such an effort to make sure Ethan could hear him when he spoke. How he'd told him the secret of the Mission Bay sunrise. How he'd copied the tour guide notes for him. Even back in Cairns, how he'd held Ethan's backpack while Ethan was snorkeling and watched over him, then later took him to buy a hat.

Ethan was wearing the hat now, and it gave him a giddy little thrill.

Is he straight though?

The question had been niggling at him. Clay had been married to a woman for years and had kids, but of course that didn't mean he was straight. He could be bi or pan. Although he'd mentioned the right woman coming along.

Still, when Ethan had touched his arm that morning on Mission Beach and looked into Clay's eyes, he swore there had been a flicker between them. That unnamed frisson of *knowing.*

Wishful thinking. Don't be an idiot.

There were four pools at the resort, and Ethan strolled around the first two. It was sunny, and through his polarized sunglasses, the water, surrounding palm trees, and forest beyond were vibrant. He waved hello to Shiv—who was reading on a lounger since there was nothing planned for the day after that morning's trip to the lake in four-by-four jeeps—and continued on to a smaller, kidney-shaped pool that was more tucked away, and—

Fuck. Clay.

There he was, stretched out on a chaise lounge under the shade of an umbrella and surrounding trees on the deck at the far end of the pool. There were a few adults in the water paddling

318

lazily, others on the more exposed side of the concrete deck sunbathing. Kids seemed to be in the bigger pools, their splashing and shrieks distant noises now.

Oh so casually, Ethan ambled around the pool, stealing glances at Clay from the corner of his eye. The chaises on either side of him were vacant. In fact, that whole shady side of the pool was empty and quiet. There was no music piped in, just the rustle of leaves in the breeze. It was perfect.

Clay wore his sexy-AF aviator sunglasses, navy bathing trunks, and nothing else but his gold-colored watch. It was kind of old-fashioned to wear a watch, and it was *sexy*. He'd apparently taken a dip, since his hair was wet and darker, and drops of water dried on his skin.

His long, muscular legs were crossed at the ankle. There was a newspaper folded over his stomach, his fingers laced on top of it. His nipples were pink amid the reddish hair on his chest, and as Ethan got closer, he imagined licking those nipples.

Heat roaring through him, he swallowed thickly. This was a bad idea, and he should turn back the way he came. But now he was close enough that if Clay saw him, it might seem rude, like Ethan had turned around and left because he was avoiding Clay. So he kept walking slowly around the curve of the shaded deep end, where one woman in a bikini swam a slow side stroke.

Clay's chaise was partly reclined, and it was entirely possible he was napping and didn't have any idea Ethan was even there. Ethan slowed even more so his flip-flops didn't flap on the concrete.

Okay, if I walk by and he doesn't notice me, that's a sign. I'll keep going and stop being ridiculous.

He was still at least ten feet away when Clay called, "Ethan!" and lifted a hand in a wave.

"Oh, hey!" Ethan replied too loudly. *Calm the fuck down.* He smiled as he approached. "You found a good shady spot."

319

"Yep. Got skin cancer once when I was younger, so I reckoned me and the sun aren't mates."

Ethan gaped. "Oh my God. I'm sorry. You said before that you had to be careful, but I didn't realize."

"Nah, nah. Don't be sorry." He casually motioned to the chaise on his left in invitation. Ethan spread out his striped resort towel and settled in, his heart beating too fast as he took off his hat since they were in the shade. Clay added, "I shouldn't be so dramatic—it wasn't melanoma. Basal cell carcinoma. Quite common in Australia. It can't spread, so it's not dangerous like other cancers. Still, I had to have surgery to remove it, so it's not nothing."

"Wow. I'm glad it wasn't melanoma. Obviously. Where was it?" he asked before realizing how intrusive that was. Even though Clay really felt like a friend now, Ethan had to remember it was probably mostly in his head. "I'm sorry, I'm being totally nosy! You don't have to tell me."

See? This was a bad idea. I'm going to make a fool of myself with this crush. Maybe it's not so harmless after all.

"No worries. It was on the back of my left shoulder." Clay leaned forward, angling so Ethan could see. He reached over that shoulder with his right hand, his fingers finding a pale circle of a scar. Just below it was a tattoo, a green sort of shield with a yellow sun rising over a green horizon and five stars dotting the shield. It was a few inches wide and several inches long.

"Cool tattoo." Ethan had never been compelled to get one, but he enjoyed looking at other people's. Before he could stop himself, he traced it with his fingertip. Clay's back was freckled as well, and *goddamn*, why was that so sexy? The seconds ticked by as he touched Clay, neither of them saying anything.

Finally, Ethan asked, "Does it mean something?" He was still touching, and Clay shivered. Ethan dropped his hand, his mouth dry.

Clay cleared his throat as he sat back. "It's part of the Cricket Australia logo. On their uniforms there's a roo on the left and an emu on the right, and 'Australia' written underneath." He laughed and muttered something Ethan missed.

"What was the last part? Sorry."

"I thought having the full logo was overkill for a tattoo. Didn't want it too big, but I like having a little something."

"You really love cricket, huh?"

Clay laughed. "What gave me away?"

Ethan chuckled. "Oh, you were going to tell me about that thing. The..." He racked his brain for the right word. "Ashes?"

"Ah, yes." Clay tipped his head forward and peered at Ethan over the rims of his aviators with his intensely blue eyes. A thrill of desire shot through Ethan's veins. Clay asked, "Are you sure you really want to know? No need to humor me, mate."

"No, I really do!" He laughed, and it came out shaky, so he faked a cough. "I always loved sports when I was younger, and I want to get back into them. Although the Mets were epically bad last season, so I wasn't very inspired to hop back on the bandwagon."

"What happened to make you lose your interest? I can't imagine."

"Oh. It was..." Ethan motioned to his ears. "I lost interest in basically everything. I was really depressed for, like, four years. But the last year's been a lot better. I've come to terms with it, I guess. But I'm still not the way I was before."

"Ah." Clay nodded sympathetically. "I understand. Still finding your footing. It can take a while. When I first moved down to Sydney, it was quite a culture shock. My entire life was upended. Home, work—the whole bit."

"Yeah." Ethan hesitated, but the way Clay watched him so patiently and without judgment gave him the confidence to say, "And now, being single again, it's just so...weird. Like, who am I

321

if… If I'm not with Michael?" Saying his name aloud was painful, but felt good at the same time, to release some of the pressure inside him.

Clay nodded again. "I was half of Mr. and Mrs. Kelly for so long. It hurt to lose that, no mistake." He smiled sadly. "Hell, I still feel like I'm finding my footing. Thought I should have figured it all out by now, but that's life for ya, I reckon."

Warmth filled Ethan's chest, affection and understanding flowing. "Always full of surprises, right?" *And some that were actually good surprises. Like meeting a sexy older man who somehow likes me. Somehow* gets *me.*

"Indeed." Clay looked at him for a moment. Then he said, "You know, it's nice to chat about it with someone on the same page. Haven't really made many mates since I moved, and aside from Facebook, I don't see the blokes from the Curry. Not that we'd talk much about this sort of thing."

It made Ethan feel so damn *good* to be in Clay's confidence. He had to stop himself from grinning delightedly. Instead, he joked, "Strong silent types in the outback, huh?"

Clay chuckled. "Something like that." He sipped from a bottle of water. "Glad to have met you." Then he jolted and looked horrified. "Not saying I'm glad at the trauma you've had. It's awful that your wedding was called off." He grimaced. "Maybe it's best for me not to talk about all this after all."

"No, no. It's okay. I know what you meant. No offense taken." He smiled genuinely, relieved when Clay visibly relaxed. But maybe it was time to lighten the subject. Sitting back on his chaise, Ethan said, "All right, tell me all about the mysterious Ashes. Maybe cricket can be my new sport." And since it was something important to Clay, he really did want to know about it.

Clay grinned. "If you insist." He sat back and re-crossed his ankles. "What do you know about cricket?"

"Um…nothing? It's kind of like baseball and takes forever to play?"

Throwing his head back, Clay laughed, exposing his neck. Ethan watched his Adam's apple. Clay said, "I'll start at the beginning."

Ethan nodded and uh-huhed as Clay outlined the basics. Stumps, bats, a wicket, a pitch, creases, bowling—Ethan wasn't sure he really understood all the info, but he kept nodding, loving the rumble of Clay's voice.

"Is this making sense?" Clay asked.

"Yes! I mean, it's a lot to try and take in, but I think I get it."

"We should watch a match. It's really the best way to learn."

Belly somersaulting, Ethan tried to keep his voice casual. "That would be cool, yeah. So what's the thing about ashes?"

"The Ashes is a test series between England and Australia. Test matches can go five days, as opposed to an ODI—" He cut off. "You're going to be bored shitless if I go into the overs and innings and all that. In a nutshell, England and Australia play a series every year or so of five matches. It's very competitive. Lots of patriotic pride tied up in it. The name comes from the late 1800s, when we beat England for the first time over there. Being beaten by the colonies on English soil was quite a shock for the poor pommies, bless their hearts. Our bowler went fourteen wickets for ninety."

"I have no idea what that means, but it sounds good?" Ethan laughed. Clay laughed as well, and God, he was so hot.

"It was very good. So one of the London papers published a mock obit for English cricket after we won. At the end it said, 'The body will be cremated and the ashes taken to Australia.' The Brits were determined to get the ashes back, and over the years, *mumble mumble*."

A chattering couple walking by made the last part impossible to hear, but Ethan guessed, "Over the years that became the name of the tournament?"

Clay frowned after the couple, who thankfully kept walking. "You've got it. Legend goes that when England came back to Australia to play, a lady gave the captain an urn with the ashes of a burnt cricket bail inside. That urn's in a museum at the MCC in England, but now the winning team gets a crystal version of it to keep until the next series."

"Are you serious?"

"Mate, I never joke about cricket. Ever."

Ethan grinned. "I love that the trophy is an urn. That's awesome. Thanks for explaining all that."

"I'd give you an ear-bashing all day about cricket if you let me."

I'd let you do so many things to me.

Before Ethan's mind could veer too far down the path of wondering what Clay's beard would feel like against his face if they kissed, Clay said, "Tell me about baseball. Your Mets aren't doing so well?"

"Not last season. But there was one year when I was a kid? We didn't make the World Series, but it was still amazing. You know, when everything seems to go right during the season, and the players are all awesome guys and you feel like you *know* them, and you're rooting so hard for them. And when they win, it's just the best feeling in the world."

Clay grinned. "Nothing like it, mate." Then he laughed, his shoulders shaking.

"What?" Ethan laughed too. "You get it, right?"

"Absolutely." Clay looked like he was trying to stop laughing but couldn't manage it.

"*What?*" Ethan nudged Clay's bare arm with his fist, resisting the urge to flatten his palm over the firm, hair-dusted muscles. He groaned as he thought back over what he'd said. "Oh, I see. 'Rooting so hard.' You know I didn't mean it like that. 'Root' doesn't mean sex in the US." He giggled, because he and Clay were apparently twelve.

As they laughed together over the silly joke, Ethan's hearing aid battery beeped in his left ear. That meant the right likely would go soon too. Grimacing at the loud beep, he said, "Sorry, I need to go change my hearing aid batteries. They beep to let me know."

"No worries. I'll try to compose myself. Of course now my mind's full of stupid jokes."

Ethan grinned. "Tell me one before I go."

"Well, did you know Australians don't have sex?"

Hearing the word "sex" come out of Clay's mouth had Ethan's balls tingling and his head going light. His voice sounded too high as he said, "No? What do they do?"

"They mate."

Ethan burst out laughing, and Clay joined in. Sure, it was childish. But he didn't give a shit. It was *fun*. Michael would have rolled his eyes because he was always too snobby for puns. And wow, Ethan realized he and Michael hadn't had goofy fun in a long, long time.

He'd missed feeling so relaxed. Like, he didn't have to worry about what Clay would think if he made a dumb joke or announced, "that's what she said" after a double entendre. Because Clay would laugh along with him.

Because Clay was *awesome*.

Ethan gave him a wave and circled the pool, walking on air. He imagined he could feel the heat of Clay's gaze on his body. *I might have to go jerk off if I don't get my shit together. He's only being friendly. Stop imagining things!*

The eco resort had raised, wooden, covered boardwalks with guest rooms along them and lots of foliage around. He was smiling to himself—okay, grinning—and waved as he passed Stan and Violet. Inside his room, Ethan kept his suitcases neatly packed and closed since he'd read to never put a suitcase on a bed due to the threat of bedbugs.

A few minutes later, Ethan's belongings were strewn across the spare bed, his heart racing and mouth dry. His hearing aid batteries weren't there. "Fuck, fuck, FUCK!"

He pawed through his clothes again. Nothing. Telling himself they had to be somewhere, he tried to be methodical as he searched. Nothing. He ran into the bathroom and looked there again. Nothing. The reminder beeps from his hearing aids as the clock wound down did not freaking help, the right one chiming in now, as he'd expected.

Ethan opened drawers even though he hadn't put anything away. He dug through the trash bins, which hadn't been emptied yet by housekeeping. Finally, after searching three more times, he had to declare defeat. His batteries were not there. Trying to catch a ragged breath, he stood in the middle of his room, which looked like a hurricane had passed through.

Then he remembered the little balcony with a forest view. He unlocked the door and slid it open with a bang, his heart pounding. Nothing. He tried to think of when he'd last seen the pack of little round batteries and came up blank. Had he left them in the Whitsundays? He couldn't imagine doing that, but he'd taken everything out of his big suitcase to reorganize.

And of course he usually kept a couple batteries in his little hearing aid case, but hadn't replaced them since he'd been on one of the flights when his batteries had gone.

"Fuck!"

If he was on the mainland, it would be easy enough to buy more at a drugstore. Heart in his throat, he rushed out of his room and down the walkway back toward reception. Maybe they had a store. He hadn't noticed anything—maybe a gift shop wasn't eco-friendly?—but there had to be somewhere to buy stuff on the island. Right?

Wrong.

The young guy behind the front desk shook his head apologetically. "We only have a few essentials available." He added something else that was lost in the four ominous beeps in Ethan's left ear, signaling that battery would die momentarily. Sure enough, after a few heartbeats, it went quiet. The guy was saying something else, and Ethan strained to understand with only his right hearing aid, turning his head and leaning in.

The guy looked at him like he was waiting for a response, and Ethan said, "I'm sorry?"

He waved a hand dismissively, and Ethan easily read his lips since he was used to these words: "Never mind."

"Can you not fucking—" He caught himself and breathed deeply to choke down the frustration. He lowered his voice, or at least he hoped he did. "Can you please write down what you said?"

Glancing at him warily as if Ethan was a lunatic, the guy scrawled on a piece of hotel notepaper:

I'll ask housekeeping to go through the towels and make sure nothing was accidentally picked up.

Still breathing hard, Ethan nodded. "Thank you." He turned and walked away from the desk, his lungs tight. As he descended the wide stairs leading down to a restaurant on one side and the pool area beyond glass doors, he spotted Stan and Violet sitting in the shade outside in an area with padded wicker furniture and tables. He approached them to ask what kind of batteries Stan used.

Of course not the same kind—Stan's were smaller. He and his wife were very kind and sympathetic, and Ethan was going to fucking *cry* like the loser he was, so he quickly thanked them and escaped back into the lobby. Where he stood as the minutes ticked by, trying not to completely lose his shit. His right aid was going to go soon, the reminder beep making him wince.

Then Clay was there, his face pinched in concern as he said

something Ethan didn't hear in the murmur of noise from the restaurant nearby and people through the lobby. Ethan told him about the missing batteries and added, "I guess I left them at the last place? I don't know. Doesn't matter now. They're not here." Clay said something that was probably sympathetic, and Ethan shook his head. "Sorry, it's hard with only one now. And the right one won't last much longer."

Clay nodded and glanced around, then guided Ethan to a little tucked-away corner, his big hand warm and comforting on Ethan's shoulder before dropping away. Ethan blew out a long breath. "Anyway, I asked Stan, but his hearing aids are different and the batteries won't fit mine."

"Damn it." Clay was clearly trying to speak even more carefully. His sunglasses were perched on his head, and he leaned in, looking at Ethan intently. "Where do you get more batteries? Does it have to be a specialty-type place?"

"No, just a drugstore. But they don't have one here."

"I'll ask the desk when the next boat to the mainland is. If you tell me which batteries, I can fetch them from the chemist and come back as soon as I can."

Clay's kindness made Ethan's eyes burn again with the threat of tears. His right hearing aid beeped, but with Clay's steady presence, he was able to take a deep breath and calm his spiky pulse. "That's really cool of you to offer. But no, it's your day off. I'll be fine."

"It's no bother. I always enjoy a boat ride."

Clay was amazing. It was *entirely* a freaking bother, but he was so comforting and unruffled. *So sexy.* No, no, this wasn't the time to be thinking about *that*, but it loosened the massive knot of tension in Ethan's chest. "I'll be okay." He blew out a long breath, glancing around the high-ceilinged lobby. No one seemed to be watching his meltdown, at least. "I'm okay. I can get batteries in the morning. I'm sorry. Sometimes my anxiety just…" He made an exploding motion with his hands.

Clay smiled, and Ethan really, *really* wanted to kiss him. "No worries. We all have our moments. I can imagine it's a frightening thing, not being able to hear. Would make a bloke feel awfully...bare. If you know what I mean."

Do not think about Clay naked. "Yeah, that's it exactly. Vulnerable, I guess. But it helps—" He broke off. Would it be weird to say it? What the hell. Before he could lose his nerve, he said, "It helps having you here. Thank you."

Of course now he was a hundred percent thinking about Clay naked, and when Clay slung an arm around Ethan's shoulders and gave him a manly half-hug squeezy thing, that did not help.

He spoke quietly and steadily near Ethan's right ear, not shouting like a lot of well-meaning people would. "How about I buy us a couple of tinnies of Four X—they'll allow those by the pool, but no glass. There's a bar over by the main deck, and we can take 'em back to the shade."

Ethan was pressed against the side of Clay's big, strong body, a situation his dick was very interested in pursuing further. Afraid of how high-pitched his voice might come out, he simply nodded. Clay clapped his back and let go, and they made their way outside. Ethan tried to get the beer charged to his room, but of course Clay waved him off, not accepting any arguments.

"This shout's on me."

Ethan's brows drew together. "This what?"

"Shout." He motioned to the cans of beer the bartender put on the counter.

"I thought that's what you said. A shout's like a round of drinks?" At Clay's nod, Ethan grinned. "Cool. Thanks. Then I'll get the one after." His smile faded. "I mean, unless you have other stuff to do. You don't have to hang out with me all day."

Clay shrugged. "Nowhere else to be, mate."

Ethan tried to contain himself, but he knew he was grinning at

Clay. Probably mooning at him, but he was grateful, the feeling of safety flowing through him reassuringly.

Back at their loungers with their sunglasses on, Ethan drank the wonderfully cold beer, the can housed in a foamy insulator with the resort logo on the side. Breathing easily again, he said, "Thank you. This is perfect." And despite the impending loss of his hearing aid, he meant it. "We should go swimming. I can hear better under water."

"Yeah?" He said something else that was a mumble.

Ethan guessed that he'd been asking why. "I think because any sound is conducted through the bones in my skull, not the air."

"Huh." Clay sipped his beer, his throat working. There were a few freckles across the hollow of his throat that Ethan wanted to lean over and kiss softly. "Is it like that for all deaf people?"

"I don't know. I think it depends on the degree of hearing loss, and what kind you have." He paused. "Am I talking too loudly?"

"Nope," Clay said. "There's no one nearby anyway."

So he probably was talking too loudly, but Clay was being kind, like always because he was *awesome*. Ethan tried to modulate his volume.

"There are two basic kinds, but lots of variety within those two categories. I think I told you mine's sensorineural? Basically the nerves and sensors in the inner ear are damaged, and it can be caused by lots of different things. Conductive hearing loss is more mechanical. Like a punctured eardrum or build-up of wax or water. Something blocking the sound. Some people have a bit of both. It all depends." His right hearing aid gave the more urgent, faster beep, alerting him that the batteries were about to give out. "Well, these are toast until tomorrow. Going off the air." He winced as he eased out his hearing aids, rubbing at his sore ears.

Then he realized Clay was wincing too, and quickly switched the right one off. He tried not to shout. "Sorry, guess the batteries still had another minute." He couldn't hear it, but if he took out his hearing aids while they were on, or if the ear mold came loose, there was a high-pitched squealing whine that Michael told him was like torture.

A vindictive thought came when he thought of all the times Michael had complained: *Good.* But Ethan was by a pool with Clay, and he didn't want to think about Michael, or Todd, or any of it. New York was the other side of the world, and Ethan was going to be in the now. He was going to be with Clay.

After they finished their beer, they went for a swim, Clay trying to talk under the water and not doing a very good job. They surfaced and laughed, then played a little game, sort of like Marco Polo, with Clay closing his eyes in their empty end of the pool and trying to catch Ethan. When Ethan stood, the water was up to his chest, the perfect height for goofing around.

Ethan tried not to laugh and cry out as he bobbed and dodged Clay's outstretched hands. And maybe after a few minutes, he totally let himself be caught, Clay's big hands wrapping around his arms. Clay's eyes popped open, and water dripped from the end of his nose. They grinned at each other, standing so close that Ethan would only have to move a few inches before their lips met and…

Laughing, he pulled away and made a rolling motion with his hand. "Let's play again!"

They did, and Ethan managed not to kiss Clay and ruin it all.

Read the rest of Ethan and Clay's tale of discovery and romance!

The wedding is off, but the love story is just beginning.

Betrayed the night before his wedding by the supposed boy of his dreams, Ethan Robinson escapes the devastating fallout by going on his honeymoon alone to the other side of the world. Hard of hearing and still struggling with the repercussions of being late-deafened, traveling by himself leaves him feeling painfully isolated with his raw, broken heart.

Clay Kelly never expected to be starting life over in his forties. He got hitched young, but now his wife has divorced him and remarried, his kids are grown, and he's left his rural Outback town. In a new career driving a tour bus on Australia's East Coast, Clay reckons he's happy enough. He enjoys his cricket, a few beers, and a quiet life. If he's a bit lonely, it's not the end of the world.

Clay befriends Ethan, hoping he can cheer up the sad-eyed young man, and a crush on an unattainable straight guy is exactly the safe distraction Ethan needs. Yet as the days pass and their connection grows, long-repressed desires surface in Clay, and they are shocked to discover romance sparking. Clay is the sexy, rugged *man* of Ethan's dreams, and as the clock counts down on their time together, neither wants this honeymoon to end.

Honeymoon for One is a gay romance by Keira Andrews featuring a May-December age difference, a slow burn of newfound friends to lovers, first-time m/m sex, and of course a happy ending.

Read now!

Discover more age-difference romance from Keira Andrews!

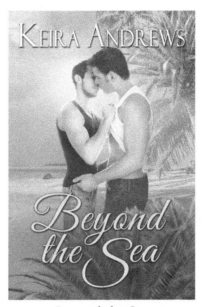

Beyond the Sea

Two straight guys. One desert island.

Even if it means quitting their boy band mid-tour, Troy Tanner isn't going to watch his little brother snort his future away after addiction destroyed their father. On a private jet taking him home from Australia, he and pilot Brian Sinclair soar above the vast South Pacific. Brian lost his passion for flying—and joy in life—after a traumatic crash, but now he and Troy must fight to survive when a cyclone strikes without warning.

Marooned a thousand miles from civilization, the turquoise water and white sand beach look like paradise. But although they can fish and make fire, the smallest infection or bacteria could be deadly. When the days turn into weeks with no sign of rescue, Troy and Brian grow closer, and friendship deepens into desire.

As they learn sexuality is about more than straight or gay and discover their true selves, the world they've built together is thrown into chaos. If Troy and Brian make it off the island, can their love endure?

This LGBT romance from Keira Andrews features bisexuality, finding love where you least expect it, eating way too many coconuts, and of course a happy ending.

Valor on the Move

He'd give his life to protect the president's son. But he never expected to risk his heart.

Growing up gay in the White House hasn't been easy for Rafael Castillo. Codenamed "Valor" by the Secret Service, Rafa feels anything but brave as he hides in the closet and tries to stay below the radar in his last year of college. His father's presidency is almost over, and he just needs to stick to his carefully crafted plan. Once his family's out of the spotlight, he can be honest with his conservative parents about his sexuality and his dream of being a chef.

It's definitely not part of Rafa's plan to get a new Secret Service agent who's a walking wet dream, but he's made it this long keeping his desires to himself. Besides, it's not like Shane Kendrick would even look at him twice if it wasn't his job.

Shane's worked his way up through the Secret Service ranks, and while protecting the president's shy, boring son isn't his dream

White House assignment, it's an easy enough task since no one pays Rafa much attention. He discovers there's a vibrant young man beneath the timid public shell, and while he knows Rafa has a crush on him, he assures himself it's harmless. Shane's never had room for romance in his life, and he'd certainly never cross that line with a protectee. Keeping Rafa safe at any cost is Shane's mission.

But as Rafa gets under his skin, will they both put their hearts on the line?

This gay romance from Keira Andrews is the first part of the *Valor* duology. It features an age difference, Jane Austen levels of pining, forbidden love against the odds, and of course a happy ending.

Join the free gay romance newsletter!

My (mostly) monthly newsletter will keep you up to date on my latest releases and news from the world of LGBTQ romance. You'll also get access to exclusive giveaways, free reads, and much more. Join the mailing list today and you're automatically entered into my monthly giveaway.

subscribepage.com/KAnewsletter

Here's where you can find me online:
Website
www.keiraandrews.com
Facebook
facebook.com/keira.andrews.author
Facebook Reader Group
bit.ly/2gpTQpc
Instagram
instagram.com/keiraandrewsauthor
Goodreads
bit.ly/2k7kMj0
Amazon Author Page
amzn.to/2jWUfCL
Twitter
twitter.com/keiraandrews
BookBub
bookbub.com/authors/keira-andrews

About the Author

After writing for years yet never really finding the right inspiration, Keira discovered her voice in gay romance, which has become a passion. She writes contemporary, historical, paranormal, and fantasy fiction, and—although she loves delicious angst along the way—Keira firmly believes in happy endings. For as Oscar Wilde once said, "The good ended happily, and the bad unhappily. That is what fiction means."